INSIDE JOB

SILICON BILLIONAIRES

ALEXIS KNIGHTLY

Inside Job

Editor: Mackenzie at Nice Girl, Naughty Edits

Proofreader: Samantha W.

Cover Designer: Ashley at Book Cover Couture

Photographer: Wander Aguiar

Model: Chase R.

To my parents,

This book wouldn't have been possible without your endless support and encouragement.

That being said…

Mom and Dad, if you're reading this, turn back this instant. The following scenes are not suitable for Thanksgiving dinner discussion!

CONTENT WARNINGS

This book contains a very possessive hero, sexually explicit content, profanity, and topics that may be sensitive to some readers. For a list of content warnings, please visit:

alexisknightly.com / content-warnings

The Playlist

Don't Call Me Up - Mabel

Dangerous Woman - Ariana Grande

Crazy in Love - Sofia Karlberg

Collide - Justine Skye, Tyga

Karma - Taylor Swift

L*** is a Bad Word - Kiiara

How Deep Is Your Love - Calvin Harris

Powerful - Major Lazer, Ellie Goulding

Same Ol' Mistakes - Rihanna

The Only Exception - Paramore

Whatever You Like - T.I.

Dirty Mind - Boy Epic

Swim - Chase Atlantic

Butterfly - Crazy Town

Smoke - Bobi Andonov, Son Lux

Come a Little Closer - Cage The Elephant

Apartment - Bobi Andonov

Who Do You Want - Ex Habit

Do It For Me - Rosenfeld

Something to Believe In - Young the Giant

ONE
HANNAH

"WE'RE GOING TO ENIGMA TONIGHT."

Sofia twists the cap off the bottle of tequila, before grabbing two shot glasses from our cupboard. With chipped paint and aged wood, our tiny apartment's kitchen has seen better days, none of which we were here for.

"Ha." I pale at my roommate. "You are, like always. But I'm not."

Enigma is a new club in New York, with lines that usually wrap around the building. This is my roommate's third attempt at convincing me to go, and she makes a tempting case—It's Sunday, masquerade night.

Salting the rims, she tops both off with a lime wedge. She pours the liquor to the brim, before sliding one my way. The glass sings across the countertop, landing perfectly in my hand.

No shock there, coming from an ex-bartender.

"Yes, we are," she says simply, bobbling her head. Gold hoops swaying on her earlobes, her dark brown hair and olive skin are flawless.

"Why?" I challenge. "I'm perfectly comfortable in our apartment."

"Oh, I know you are." She raises her eyebrows, lips pursing. "You've cooped yourself up in it for three whole days, wearing those pjs like a second skin."

"I have *not.*" I gasp, glancing down at my red-and-white polka dot set. They offer me not an ounce of sex appeal and only help me wallow in my newfound self-pity.

"I know what Sterling did was terrible, but it's time to replace eating half a tub of ice cream a night with sweaty dancing and hot men."

I stew on it, appraising the clear shot between my fingers. I *do* rather like tequila. And I *should* dance my sorrows away... "It just makes the breakup ten times worse when it costed me my job too."

He was my boss, and I was his personal assistant.

Rookie mistake, Hannah. Don't mix business and pleasure.

She gives me a pitiful look. "I know, Han. But you know that jackass never deserved you."

I try to banish the memory of how I found him, but fail anyway. He sits on the edge of his desk, the city skyline his background as a woman bats her eyelashes at him. On her knees. *Unbuckling his belt.*

"You're right," I croak out, my throat feeling raw from the tears I don't let surface.

Lifting my shot, Sofia does the same before we clink glasses. I mimic her movements, licking the salted rim, throwing it back in one go and mercilessly sucking on the lime edge. The burn travels down my throat, pooling at the base of my stomach.

Sofia motions to the speaker by our coffeemaker. "It's your night. You play DJ. What do you want?"

An involuntary giggle bursts from me, and I quickly bat it down, meeting her wide grin.

Get it together, lightweight.

"You already know."

"I do." She winks at me as *"Yeah!"* by Usher plays about five notches past our apartment's agreed-upon limit.

After another shot for me and two for Sofia, we grab the speaker and race to her room, our laughs echoing inside the narrow hallway.

Tiny like mine, her room has a modern flare, with black-and-gold wallpaper she placed herself. I remember watching her slap on the gesso, one foot balancing atop a ladder and the other on a dresser. It was when we first moved in after college, right around the time she started her job as an engineer at Innovex Microchips—

Oh, no.

"Shit!" The music nearly drowns out my voice. "I forgot about my interview in the morning."

"Is that tomorrow? Well, we're already drunk..." She slides her closet door open and starts sifting through dresses. "What time is it at?"

"Eleven."

She retrieves a hanger, dangling a short red dress out in front of her. Fuzziness slinks around its hemline, sparkling against the light of a nearby desk lamp. "That's not early at all. Don't worry, we won't be out late."

Lies. Lies. Lies.

"Okay." I smile, snatching the dress she offers me.

"Plus, I already got us a table booked."

Nervous jitters flutter inside me, thinking of the club. It's often so packed, they rope off tables to offer at a steep price. Sofia once told me they're five thousand dollars. *Minimum.*

"Shocking," I tease, shooting her a glance. "Which handsome divorcée paid this time? John, Patrick—oh, maybe Marco?"

Her mouth hangs low, morphing into a wide smile. "Hey! I can't help it that the silver foxes can't get enough of me."

I remove my comfortable pajamas and slip into the dress, appraising myself in front of a thin mirror as I run my hands across the smooth fabric. It's so tight, my thong's outline is slightly visible.

"Wow. You're definitely wearing that. Try this on." She offers me a red mask. Intricate patterns of rhinestones shine along its perimeter, feathers sprawling upwards above its nose.

I lie the piece against my skin, tying a knot with the ribbon behind my head. Pushing my honey-brown hair past my shoulders, a pit of nerves swirl in my stomach before they're quickly tamed by the alcohol.

I look at Sofia, my peripheral vision partly limited through the eyeholes. "You're right. Tonight is going to be my night."

～

OUR TAXI FLIES DOWN 5th street.

We're a few blocks from the club, and rain pelts the car as the windshield wipers zoom from side to side. I sit in the middle of the backseat, squished between Sofia and Jenna, who we picked up on the way.

We met Jenna a few months back, after we moved out of our dorm room into our apartment. She works at our favorite pizzeria, Matteo's, as a waitress.

"—and he doesn't even realize how understaffed we are."

Jenna squints through a tiny makeup mirror as we hit a considerable bump.

"Mmm," Sofia sounds to my right, texting someone named *Daddy 2*.

I roll my eyes.

The girl is so shameless... I love it.

"Like today—he expects me to handle ten tables. *Ten.*" She pumps her mascara in and out of the tube violently, huffing an exaggerated breath. "And then he gets mad that customers are complaining about the food coming out too slow. I swear, I'm so close to quitting."

Sofia pinches the bridge of her nose. "Please, please. You're killing my buzz. Did you even pregame?"

She scoffs. "Like I had time to. I barely got my dress and mask on by the time you picked me up."

We stop before an intersection, a streetlight casting the car with a red glow, giving me a better look at them. Jenna wears all black with a plunging neckline, contrasting her bleach-blond hair, and her mask sits on her lap, attached to a stick. Sofia's dress is of a similar cut but shimmers a bright pink, her mask wrapping around her head like mine.

They look hot as fuck. There's no other way to put it. Honestly, we all do. It helps that I'm wearing red, because it appears I'm the only one not wearing sky-high heels.

"My god, what are *those?*" I point down to Sofia's feet. Her shoes sparkle silver and have to be at least six inches tall.

"These are my *fuck-me* heels."

We all laugh in unison, right as the driver announces our arrival. He pulls up to the curb in front of the club, and I lean across Sofia's lap to peer out the window.

Holy... It's slammed.

People in masquerade attire spiral along the building wall

in a colorful splash of fabric, feathers and suited men. The line offers no inch to breathe as they shuffle their way towards a red rope accompanied by a scary-looking bouncer. The last thing I see before I lean back is the electric blue light glaring through its double doors and the fog settling on the ground.

"I should've had another shot," I mumble.

Sofia whips her head to me, her door swinging open. "You'll be fine. You look hot. Stop acting like Bambi and come on."

After thanking the driver, I immediately hear the music thumping from inside the building. We walk up to the bouncer, shielded from the rain underneath a cover.

Looking over, a girl in an orange getup crosses her arms, raising her eyebrows. I bite my lower lip when I catch Jenna *winking* at her with a grin.

I lean into her. "Don't we need to wait in line?"

Jenna just smiles at me.

A small man dressed in all black approaches through the haze. He appears to be some sort of host, judging by the clipboard in his hand. "Hi, ladies." His voice is hardly audible over the nearby chatter and clattering of thick rain. "Are you on the list?"

"Yes. We're with Marco." Sofia twists a strand of hair between her fingers, confidence radiating off her in ripples.

The man runs his finger down the page, stopping midway. "Ah, yes. Marco. He hasn't arrived yet, but I can show you to your table." He nods to the bouncer, who then stamps the backs of each of our hands. I inspect my skin, lifting a brow when I find nothing there.

He unhooks the red rope. "Right this way, ladies."

We follow the host man into the smoke, the music getting

louder as we cross a narrow hallway. When we ascend a flight of stairs, I stop dead in my tracks.

The club is a massive open space, with a circular bar positioned in the center. Lasers fly across the room, and people in masks writhe to the beat of the music, jam-packed in front of a DJ on stage. Within the crowd, two iron cages suspend in the air by chains with scantily dressed women inside, dancing in unison to each other.

A tug on my arm breaks me from my trance. "Keep up," Sofia says, before I follow her, my eyes still scouring. Her laugh barks in my ear. "I had the same look when I first came here."

The man takes us to an alcove blocked off by another red rope. Inside, there's a leather couch that curves its way around a table. Similar alcoves seem to be scattered around the space. After he unclips the rope, we each sit, Sofia hoisting herself on the back of the couch, her stiletto nearly puncturing the leather.

He clips the rope shut and neatly gathers his hands behind his back. "Shots will be brought to you upon request. If you'd like a mixed drink, please head to the bar. The rest of your party should arrive soon. Have fun." He turns, disappearing in the direction we came.

"Wow," I say, in a state of awe. "This place is... a lot to take in."

Sofia plays with her hair. "Just wait. Marco usually comes with a big group, and I can guarantee there'll be a hottie wanting to dance with you. You'll forget about *you-know-who* in no time."

I laugh. "I'm just trying to enjoy myself tonight. Nothing crazy."

"Mhmm," Jenna hums to my left. "Sure, girl. Whatever you

say." She waves to a redheaded server carrying a tray stacked with bottles. "Three tequila shots, please."

"—And some waters!" I add.

She nods, continuing on her way.

Sofia grabs my shoulder. "Smart idea. Don't want to be hung over for your job interview tomorrow."

"Exactly. I'm going to take it slow and pace myself."

EMPTY SHOT GLASSES litter our table.

I feel alive. *Revived.*

Music pounds through my body, each pulse sending a much-needed shot of electricity through my veins.

I don't know why I moped around over Sterling for three days. It's much more fun being sad here.

I can't remember when I took my shoes off or when I started dancing on the leather couch, but it feels so *right*. Sofia is on the other side, matching my movements, and Jenna is nowhere to be found.

"You should've taken me here *months* ago!"

"I tried!" She laughs, full of energy.

Swinging my head back and forth, I grab hold of my mask, the feathers tickling the pads of my fingers, and push it higher on my face to keep it from slipping.

Raising my gaze, I notice a group unclipping our rope. The strobes illuminate them, and their bodies seem to blur together. I gauge there must be at least six of them, the women in bright cocktail dresses and men in form-fitting suits.

One man pats his blond friend on the shoulder, motioning his head towards me, prompting him my way. It's hard to tell what he really looks like in the concealed mask he wears, only the tip of his strong jaw poking underneath. Shock pulses through me as he looks me up and down, but I don't stop dancing, the alcohol making me bold as I smile at him.

He comes near, at the foot of the couch I'm standing on, and holds his hand out to me. When I accept it, he pulls me down to the floor. With his chest standing at the height of my head, his eyes crane down to meet mine. His stare is hard, and the darkness from the alcove makes it difficult to decipher the color of his eyes.

I open my mouth to ask him a question, but he springs his finger to my lips. He presses it firmly, dragging down until my bottom lip pops back out. Goosebumps line my arms from the intimate touch, before he sits down below me, lounging on the couch.

As I'm standing between his parted knees, I peer over my shoulder and see the rest of the group taking shots and dancing. Sofia has her hands delving deep in the hair of an aged gentleman, who I presume to be Marco. She's in a similar predicament, with him sitting and her body cascading into him.

My mysterious man leans back with his arms sprawling along the back of the couch. The song changes to a slower beat, playing something oddly *sensual.* He tilts his head at me, seeming to expect something.

I roll my hips to the beat, staring right through him. His lips part, eyes raking over my body, causing heat to pool in my center and a flood of arousal to burn between my legs.

Wordlessly, he twirls his finger at me. I obey, turning around to continue my serenading dance. Leaning forward, his hands grip my hips hard, pulling me down to his lap. I turn into him, my legs falling over his thigh and mouth inches from his gold mask.

Grabbing the corner of my jaw, he angles it to the side, exposing my neck. A pressure on the small of my back forces me into him, before his lips press against the column of my throat.

I gasp, grabbing hold of his shoulders. He hums darkly at that, his hold tightening as he feasts on my neck. He trails his tongue higher, to the sensitive spot behind my ear. A moan escapes my lips, and I tilt my head back to give him better access.

When I lower myself to grind my clit on his leg, he groans. "Mmm, babe. I much prefer you this way for me."

I freeze. That voice...

Sterling.

TWO
HANNAH

"DON'T GIVE ME THAT FACE." Sterling runs a finger down my arm.

I jerk away, feeling as if a bucket of ice water dumps over my head. "I'm not *giving* you anything."

The music blares, and our table is busier than ever. No one pays us any attention. Each person is drunker or higher than the next, dancing or fondling one another in the dimly lit alcove.

"But you are," he coos, removing his mask and revealing the strong, porcelain features beneath. Amusement dances in his eyes. "I think I'm feeling some moisture on my knees."

"You're disgusting." I shoot to my feet, looking around for my shoes. "You think this is some kind of game? It's not. We're done."

I snatch my short heels before I plot my behind on the cushioned seat, avoiding his gaze.

"Stop being so overdramatic. What you saw—you know I can explain if you'd actually let me."

Anger pumps through me, and I shove my foot into my

shoe roughly. "I'm overdramatic? Okay. Well, you're delusional. Delusional that you think there's any explanation at all that would fix the fact that you *cheated. on. me.*"

When I burst back to my feet, so does he.

I make to storm off, but he grabs my arm and squeezes hard. "You're the one playing games, babe. Don't pretend you didn't take what you saw as an opportunity to make me chase after you. It's what all girls like you do."

What?

He's so twisted, so fucked up in the head. As if I'm some mastermind after his money. I couldn't care less about his money or his company. I don't want *anything* to do with him or his family, not that he cared enough to introduce us or tell me anything about them.

I hate the tears that well up in my eyes as a month-old memory floods into my mind.

He sits at my apartment's dining room table, his blond hair slicked straight back, wearing sporty shorts and a T-shirt.

I told him earlier at the office that we should go to dinner tonight. He had nodded like always, nose deep in his phone, looking at something I couldn't see as he informed me his dry cleaning was ready for pickup.

Sometimes being my boyfriend's personal assistant leaves a sour taste in my mouth, especially when his tasks feel so demeaning.

Dry cleaning. Tidying up his apartment. I know it comes with the job title, but I've never once sat in on his meetings, which is the only reason I took this job before we started dating—to learn how a large-scale business is run, from close up.

I sigh.

We're clearly not going out together. Nothing new there. I don't know why I got my hopes up. We'll stay here, pretend to watch some movie and then fuck. It wouldn't be all bad if our sex wasn't so one-sided.

I lean against the kitchen counter. "So, are we not going out to dinner?" I'm wearing my most form-fitting dress, and he's not even looking at me.

He finishes sending whatever text he's working on. "Oh." His eyes meet mine. "I didn't know we had plans."

My heart sinks.

When did he stop noticing me in the office? When did I become so *invisible* to him?

"I asked you today. You agreed." My voice is nearly a whisper. I turn away, fighting back the tears threatening to surface. "Are we not... serious?"

"Of course, we're serious, babe." His body presses against me from behind, his arms looping around my center. "I'm under so much stress at work right now. I get little free time, and when I do, I just want to relax."

I sniffle, some of the ache in my chest lifting. "And your friends? Your family? Don't you think it's time I meet them?"

He frees a substantial breath. "My family's so busy running the conglomerate right now. You know I don't want to bother them. The timing isn't right."

The club's music blasts me back into focus.

He's a liar—a liar *and* a cheat.

I'm a fool for putting up with him for so many months, letting him string me along, waiting for affection he's incapable of giving. I'm tired of the explanations. The diplomatic answers. And being the idiot who believes them.

Trying to love Sterling Bass is like trudging down a one-way street, with one step deep in hope and the other in disappointment.

I resist, yanking hard and breaking free from his grasp.

I'm over the bickering, the need to please him or best him in a battle of wits that will resolve nothing. I'm done. We were already done, but somehow when I look him dead in the eyes, it feels like I'm breaking up with him all over again.

"Goodbye, Sterling."

I turn before I see his expression, slipping underneath the rope and letting the crowd swallow me. Faintly, I hear him shouting my name, anger edging his words. He must be hot on my trail, so I push further, shouldering people, my adrenaline too high to offer apologies.

Bursting through a swarm of people, I crash straight into a hard object. *"Oof."* I grasp against it, steadying myself on what feels like solid muscle underneath silky fabric.

I come to my senses, realizing I've pummeled into the back of a poor stranger seated on a barstool.

"Sorry! I'm so sorry." The apology flies from my lips, my heart racing.

Get it together.

He turns to face me, and I'm met with warm green eyes that are somehow calming in such a climactic place. A black mask covers the upper third of his face, but there's no mistake. *He's gorgeous.* With tousled brown hair and a strong frame, his jawline could cut through glass.

A second passes.

And another.

"Easy there." His deep tenor breaks our silence. "Wouldn't want a little thing like you getting tossed around in that crowd."

My heart contracts, and I wobble, the alcohol going straight to my head. He grabs my arm gently, his hand warm and calloused.

"Let's get you some water," he says, motioning to the empty stool beside him, before waving to the bartender. "Sit."

It's a command, not a question.

I listen, trying to tame my hair as I'm suddenly conscious of my appearance. I can't imagine what I must look like after dancing for who knows how long and booking it through a crowd of sweaty bodies.

We're so near, my shoulder grazes the sleeve of his navy suit, and an unexpected wave of comfort washes over me. A complete stranger has decided I need watching over.

I smile.

"Something funny?" Amusement laces his words. He takes a sip of what appears to be straight bourbon, a large, spherical cube of ice clinking against the glass.

"No—nothing."

"Are you sure?" His eyes bore into mine.

Heat rushes to my face, and I wonder if he can spot the redness underneath my mask. "It's just that... You found a way to be caring in a place like *this.*" I wave my hand, particularly at the stage and dancers.

A gloom casts over his features before he looks away. Tipping his glass skyward, he finishes the remainder of his drink. "I'm not the kind of guy you think I am."

"Maybe not. We *did* just meet." I nurse my water, my head beginning to clear. "But you're better than who I was running from." I'm unable to stop the wobble in my voice.

He sits straighter, wearing an alarmingly serious expression as he reaches for my arm. "What do you mean? Did someone hurt you?"

"No!" I lurch back. "It's not like that. My ex-boyfriend just can't take a—"

"There you are, babe!" A cackling voice like razor blades

sounds behind us, eliciting goosebumps to scatter up my spine. My body goes cold, completely numb. "You think you could hide from me?" His mask is off, his blue eyes wild.

I peer back at my new companion to offer an apology, not wanting to bring him any problems. But I find him giving Sterling a calculated, murderous look.

"Maybe she prefers my company over yours."

My lips part—the man who speaks is *different*. The tenderness and concern in his voice are gone, replaced with a dark authority that has my heart thumping.

Sterling freezes, a frown forming on his face. "This doesn't concern you, Damien."

Shock courses through me. *They know each other?*

Damien... I don't recognize the name.

"Please." When my voice comes out small, I cringe. "I said it's over. I don't want to be around you."

"You don't..." He sways, knocking against someone next to him, before he stabilizes himself against my chair. "You don't know what you're doing." He points at me. "No one in my world would ever associate with a girl so *common.*"

"That's enough." Damien clenches his jaw.

"You're lucky, and you know it. I could have ten girls just like you." Smiling, he grips my bare thigh, the alcohol on his breath blasting through my senses. "So, tonight, you're going to quit being such a *brat* and apologize." His hand travels higher, the tips of his fingers sliding underneath my dress, making my stomach lurch with nausea. "By opening up that mouth of yours that's only good for catching my cu—"

Glass crashes against his skull, shattering on impact. Sterling's eyes roll back before he slumps over, colliding with strangers until he hits the ground *hard*.

Gasps spark around us, and my breathing stalls. Patrons

sitting at the bar turn their heads and stare at the man appearing lifeless on the dirty floor. Others pay him no mind, stepping over him while they dance.

Damien retrieves a towel from over the bar top and holds it in his hand, blood bleaching through the white cloth.

I stand on shaky legs.

But his free hand reaches out in front of me. "Don't go. Sit and look at him." Venom spews from his lips. "It's important that you know. That's how a man who disrespects you should look. On the ground, unconscious."

I whip my head, searching the unwavering gaze of the man I just met.

He's serious.

Returning to my seat, my mind runs empty on an explanation. No one's ever spoken to Sterling like that before, let alone laid a hand on him. That doesn't happen to a man with that kind of power. But there he is, sprawled out like a bag of sand with his mouth drooping downward.

Harsh flashes of light shine our way and drag down to Sterling's body, before two security guards approach us. One grabs Damien by the arm.

"Oh." Startled, he releases his grasp, looking him in the eye. "Sorry, sir."

What the fuck? Did I hear him apologize?

The man faces me, and I straighten in anticipation.

"She's with me."

When the guard snaps his attention away, no questions asked, my shoulders slouch as a surprising sense of security envelops me.

With a single command, I'm off limits.

"Understood." The guard nods, glancing down at Sterling. "What should we do with him?"

"Get him out of my sight."

The two men hoist Sterling's body between them, carrying him away through the crowd. Then it's like nothing happened, as if he's just another club rat kid causing trouble.

The bartender comes over with another glass of bourbon, setting it on the counter in front of Damien.

What is going on...? Who is this guy?

On the one hand, I'm filled with shock and hesitation that I should be around this man. But on the other... I'm drawn to him by such a visceral force that it's impossible to ignore.

Waving down the bartender, I remain in my seat. "A tequila sunrise, please."

Damien places the bloody rag back behind the bar.

"You should get that looked at."

He smirks. "Not my blood."

I bite the inside of my cheek, stifling a smug grin, right as the bartender returns with my drink, setting it on a square napkin. Unzipping my purse, I—

"It's on the house."

"Oh..." I say, unable to finish my sentence before he's whisking along to the next customer. "Okay."

This night keeps getting weirder and weirder...

My head has sobered up in record timing, and I don't know if it's because of the water or witnessing possibly the most satisfying thing I've ever seen—Sterling Bass being denied the final word.

Laughter bubbles deep in my gut, spilling outwards. I shouldn't feel so happy, but I do. Damien side-glances at me, taking a sip of his drink. A widening smirk lines his lips, too, and it only fuels my hysteria further.

I tilt my head back, tears brimming my eyes. "I guess I should thank you."

"No need. He's had it coming for a while."

"So, is he a friend of yours?"

He pauses, squinching his brow.

"Not quite, but you could say that." His smile fades. "We had a... falling out. You shouldn't give a guy like that a minute of your attention." He's closer now than ever, leaning towards me on the edge of his stool. "I take it you didn't know he was here?"

A whiff of his cologne dances its way into my nostrils. I breathe deep, basking in the allure of citrus and smoky undertones.

"No, I didn't. He wasn't a part of tonight's plans." I wet my lips, noticing the slow thrum beating between my legs. As his green eyes capture mine, I'm unable to look away.

"And how was tonight supposed to go?" His tone strains, eyes flickering to my lips.

Feeling like prey under the stare of an experienced predator, my voice shrinks to a near whisper. "I was supposed to forget it all. This one night, I didn't have to be me. I could slip on a mask and be someone else entirely."

He grabs underneath my knee, applying a subtle pressure. "And what would that someone do, coming to a place like this?" Grazing higher, his hand slips underneath the seam of my dress. And this time, with this man, the move washes arousal over me.

I'm liquid putty in his grasp.

I uncross my legs. "Sh-she would..."

"Tell me." His thumb runs across my inner thigh, prompting my legs to widen.

My breathing hitches as he explores further, an agonizing need building inside of me that forces me to confess. "She would fuck the pain away."

"Would she? Hmm." His finger reaches the corners of my panties, scarcely missing my most sensitive spot and causing torturous friction. "Ask me."

Shock reverberates through me. He wants me to cross the line. He wants me to offer myself to him... and I'm surprised that I want to. *Desperately* want to.

"Would you—"

"Say my name." He presses against my clit, hard.

I buckle in my chair. *"Damien."* His name leaves my lips on a breathless moan. "Would you fuck my pain away?" Mindlessly, I grind against his hand.

"Fuck. You don't know what you're asking." His voice is thick and dripping with desire. He leans in close, his lips grazing my ear. "For one night, you'd belong to me."

"I know my limits."

"Do you?" He hikes up my dress, uncaring of who may watch in the club's darkness. It only heightens my arousal, blood screaming in my ears. "I'll ruin you for all other nights. Are you sure you want that?"

He tugs harder, and my ass makes cold contact with my chair.

I haven't touched my drink. I'm dead sober at this point, yet keenly aware of the train we're on that's barreling ahead at full speed, threatening to run off the rails if we don't pull the brakes.

But desperation tugs at me. "I need it. Just this once."

Who are you convincing? Him or yourself?

Squeezing a fistful of my ass cheek, he reaches into his pocket. He dials someone named *John,* holding the phone to his ear as our eyes lock in a smoldering gaze.

"Enigma in five, and book me a suite... Yes, The Ritz."

THREE

HANNAH

AGREEING to hook up with a complete stranger from a club an hour after meeting isn't one of the smartest decisions I've ever made.

And neither is letting him book the hotel. *The Ritz*, I heard him say on the phone. Perhaps I heard him wrong. The club *was* deafening. But if I didn't... that's the most expensive hotel in the city. And he booked a suite.

For a one-night stand.

A privacy wall separates us from the driver as we sit in the backseat of a spacious vehicle. I take the middle, with my knee brushing against Damien's thigh.

What were you thinking, girl? Are you trying to end up on Dateline? I imagine Sofia lecturing me after she finds out I ditched the club without saying goodbye.

Who has their own personal driver, who shows up in five minutes to pick us up outside a club? Sterling didn't have a driver. Why am I only now asking myself these things?

More intelligent and sensible questions flood my brain,

but when a strong hand brushes against my knee, all the thoughts exit the same way they came in.

You're doomed. Might as well enjoy it.

A nervous air enters my space, and all my boldness from the club seems to fizzle out. I should say something. *Anything.* Because the way he's looking at me is making my heart beat faster by the second.

It then occurs to me that Damien hasn't asked me my name.

Maybe it doesn't matter to him.

A sinking feeling pools in my gut, one I shouldn't be feeling. We agreed this would be a one-time thing, so what does it matter if he knows anything about me?

But I cave, anyway.

"I'm Hannah, by the way." A nervous laugh passes through my lips.

"Mmm. Hannah." *Oh god.* The way he says my name causes heat to shoot right between my legs. "A beautiful name, but I thought you were being someone else tonight?"

"I am—Hannah's being different." I shrug, trying to appear nonchalant, but still feeling silly. He probably doesn't understand. I'm not trying to be someone else. I'm pretending *I'm* different, someone who isn't afraid of taking what they really want.

"Is she now? Be careful. Pretending is risky business. You might discover you like that version of yourself. Or, pretend too often, and you'll become the very thing you've been playing."

A lump forms in my throat, but I say nothing. I only stare at him, dumbfounded that a borderline stranger is speaking such words to me. He doesn't know the first thing about me.

Reaching a hand behind his head, my lips part when he

tugs at the string of his mask. Anticipation builds inside me, not because I'm wondering if he'll be attractive or not, but because *I know* he will be.

The mask passes from sight, unveiling him as more intense, with a hardened exterior. But it's worse than I thought. He's not just attractive—he's *devastating.*

"Your turn," he says with a cocky grin, seeming to read my reaction.

He leans into me, reaching around my head. I breathe in his musk, my eyes fluttering as my mask comes loose and falls to my lap.

Time seems to slow to a leisurely beat, and then all I can hear is the rain pattering against the roof of the car.

He cups my jaw, so near I can hear his jagged exhale. "Beautiful." His jaw tightens in awe, almost as if he's in pain, beholding some prized painting.

Before I can respond, he captures my lips between his, and my eyelids fall under their own accord. The kiss surprises me. His lips are soft and his touch tender, with a promise that I could end our night short if I wanted. That it could only be *this.*

Sweet. Flirtatious.

No regrets, the safe side of me warns.

But I don't pull away, melting into his touch and widening my mouth. He groans and tightens his hold on my jaw, his restraint withering as he bruises his tongue to my lips. Another hand sinks into my hair, before mine flies to his chest, deepening our kiss. When a small moan escapes me, it seems to be his undoing.

Skin barrels into mine, my back sinking into the leather seats with his waist pressing in between my legs. When the hard bulge in his pants rubs me right where I want it to, I moan again.

He lifts my chin, delving his lips to my neck as he grinds his erection into me. His teeth scrape against my delicate flesh, sparking a needy pain before he soothes it with his tongue. My body grows hot, and I try to nurse the throbbing sensation between my thighs by straddling my legs around his waist.

More friction. I need more...

Collecting both my wrists in his hand, he pins them above my head. I resist, but don't budge. A satisfied look blooms across his face, before he licks from the base of my throat to my jaw. I squirm, failing to stifle my desperate cries.

"Mmm," he murmurs in my ear. "So responsive."

He lowers himself, licking again, slower this time. I buckle hard, letting out a whimper, and his hold on my wrists tightens.

"Such a needy little thing, aren't you?"

Blood pulsates loudly in my ears, and I'm practically panting by the time a quiet knock sounds against the door.

His lips trail across the column of my neck once more. "Almost have you all to myself." Staring into my eyes, he sits back up and fixes his tie. Mirroring his actions, I bat my hair flat and adjust the bottom of my dress.

When Damien opens his door and exits, the grand hotel entrance comes into view, its lights shining bright in the darkness.

"The Ritz Carlton, miss." John holds the door, offering his palm to me.

"Thank you." I grab his hand, hardly able to look him in the eye. The lust coursing through my veins is a living, palpable thing, threatening to expose my dirty secrets to everyone around if they only look at me long enough.

Damien holds his arm out to me, which I take.

We stride to the front entrance, his steps long and powerful. The sidewalk is busy for a Sunday night, and several heads turn in our direction. He *is* quite important looking, with that suit of his practically molding to his skin.

Wearing such a provocative dress, they must think I'm his plaything. *But that's exactly what I am tonight.* The corners of my mouth lift as we depart the revolving doors, entering the hotel.

Holy. Shit.

All my conscious thoughts of becoming someone else tonight zip away, eddying from my mind as I stare in wonder.

The lobby is a masterpiece of white-and-black marble. Two-story, vaulted ceilings provide room for wrought-iron balconies and a gold chandelier. A group of men and women clothed in business attire pass us by without a glance, briefcases and purses in hand.

Damien motions to a collection of chairs. "Go look pretty for me. I'll get our key."

His warm body leaves mine, and I feel like my lifeline strips from me, never having been to such a place.

Steadily, I walk to a mass of gold-cushioned chairs surrounding a flower fixture, my heels clacking in my wake. Sinking into the plush padding, I stare at Damien's large frame facing the front desk, his hand burying into his pants pocket.

Just play it cool, Hannah. No need to get attached. He's just some rich guy. That doesn't mean he's good in bed.

$\sim$

MY BACK SLAMS against the glass wall, Damien's breath hot on my neck.

"Lift up your dress," he commands, his thigh pressing between my legs.

Floor 5.

My eyes glue to the elevator, watching in anxiety as we climb the floors. It only takes one click of that button on the other end, and we'll open on some random floor to a potentially happy voyeur.

He sucks against my soft flesh, and I grind against his leg, the slickness inside my panties heightening the sensation.

Floor 10.

"What if someone catches us?" I pant.

Floor 13.

"I don't care." He turns my face back to him, away from the numbers. "I'm not going to tell you again."

My heart lurches in excitement at his tone, and I snag the skirt of my dress, lifting it above my waist to reveal my lace panties.

Heat sizzles behind his eyes, and he hoists me up from behind my thighs, setting me onto the wide handlebars with my heels dangling in the air. The metal is shocking, shooting coldness through my bare ass. Through the mirrors lining the elevator, I watch him bend to his knees before me.

"Spread your legs," he growls, and I widen them, both hands gripping the golden bars. "Good girl."

My heart races, and I fight the urge to look at the elevator doors. His thumb brushes against my panty fabric, and my legs involuntarily jerk.

"So wet for me." He pushes it to the side, exposing my

flesh. "Now watch while I feast." His head delves between my legs, immediately suctioning my clit.

My back lifts off the mirror, and both my hands shoot into the depths of his dark hair. *"Oh my god."* Pleasure radiates through my entire body, each a pulse of heavenly euphoria.

His pace quickens, the butt of his tongue flicking my clit between his teeth in expert strokes. My moans fill the space, and my grip loosens on his hair. Lifting my head to the ceiling, I arch my back and grip the bars tighter. His sucking sounds echo against the walls, and he eats me like a starving, depraved man.

Strong hands clutch my thighs as he pins me in place, swirling his tongue again.

"Damien..." His teeth scrape against my clit. *"Oh!"*

Any shame and all anxiety fizzle to nothing as I grind against his mouth, each of my thrusts finishing on a sharp cry. He groans in response, the sound reverberating against my pussy. I grind harder, my muscles beginning to tighten, chasing the edge of pleasure I crave.

Someone could come in here. That door could open right now to a complete fucking stranger, and I wouldn't want him to stop.

His pace slows, the friction against my clit lessening. My pussy throbs with aching need at that, and I suck my bottom lip between my teeth.

"Not yet." He licks from the bottom to the apex of my sex, sending a shiver down my spine. "You'll have to earn that." I can't stop my legs from quivering in the air, and I let out a frustrated moan. He smirks knowingly before he licks once more.

Ding.

My heart plummets, betraying my newfound bravery.

Whipping my head to scour the numbers lining the wall, air whooshes from my lips when I see what floor we're on.

Floor 70. *We're at the top.*

I peer past the elevator doors, surprise tickling the back of my neck. A single black door.

Shouldn't there be a hallway to other rooms?

Damien rises to his feet, and so do I. He exits, pulling the key card from his wallet. I look to my left, then right. No hallway.

That can't be right. The whole floor can't be for a single roo—

The door *zings* open, Damien holding it for me, his eyes a smoldering flame. "After you."

My steps slow, scanning the room. With a modern design, the space is huge. I was expecting a bed, a bathroom and maybe a sitting area. But this room has that and then some.

A full, state-of-the-art kitchen lines the near wall, and a sitting area with a rounded green couch positions in the very center. Windows line the perimeter, giving a stunning, one-eighty view of Manhattan in the night. The clouds seem to have cleared, leaving the moon casting dark shadows against the furniture.

Damien's body presses up against mine, seeping heat into my back. Shifting my hair behind my shoulder, he runs his hands down the length of my arms.

"You said..." Anticipation makes my heart thump. He's so near it's hard to think. "I have to earn *it*. How do I do that?"

"Be specific, Hannah." His breath kisses my ear. "Earn what, exactly?"

His hands creep down my torso, the light touch meant to tease. My legs shoot together, loving the friction it provides me. He already made me so wet in the elevator, that I don't know how much more torture I can take.

"How do I earn my... *release?*"

He moves fast, lifting the rear of my dress, squeezing my ass cheek hard. "Try again."

A breath shoots out of me, followed by surprising lust.

Fingers tangling in the locks of my hair, he drags downward and lifts my chin high. "Try again." His voice is dark, laced with a promise of repercussions.

I hesitate before he squeezes again, so roughly this time there must be a mark.

"Orgasm!" I moan out, my hips rocking of their own accord. My pussy throbs so hard it's almost painful. "H-how do I earn my orgasm?"

"Such a filthy girl, asking a question like that." His free hand reaches over and palms my pussy roughly. I lurch back on a cry, the pressure too much. "And grinding those hips of yours?"

I fall back into him, bathing in his demanding aura. The sheer way he handles me is unlike anything I've experienced, and right now, I'm willing to do anything he tells me to.

He *tsks* with his tongue, wiggling his hand to separate my thighs. "That won't do."

With the friction lost, I nearly whine. *"Tell me.* I'll do anything."

Releasing his grip, he walks over to the couch and drops down, never breaking our stare. He leans back, propping his elbows on the back of the couch. "Show me why you deserve it."

A sudden shock jolts me. He's expecting something, and I think back to the way I danced at the club before Sterling. Before I knew who it was I was pleasing.

It's as if Sterling stole that fantasy from me, the heat of the moment I was feeling. And now I can take it back, but with the right man. The right *somebody*. No strings. One night, I can feel the power of truly seducing a man. A powerful man, it seems, maybe more powerful than Sterling.

Satisfaction burns its way through me and need dominates my thoughts as I slip my dress strap over my shoulder. Damien's eyes seep into mine, and I hold his gaze. The other glides over my skin before I peel the top of my dress down towards my bare breasts.

I slide it down an inch.

And then another, slower.

Shadows paint his face. Even in the darkness of the room, I can read the anticipation of his features. He removes his suit coat and unzips his pants, and I try my best not to halt my movements. With my nipples peaking hard against the silk, I stop just before releasing them.

"Show me," he growls, unbuttoning his white-collared shirt as the impressive bulge in his gray boxers seems to twitch. With his chest entirely exposed, his tie dangles low in front of abs so defined I can make them out in the darkness.

Holy—

Losing control, I shove my dress downward. The cloth drops, pooling at my feet when my breasts bounce with the motion. I stand breathless, in nothing but a black thong and stilettos.

Noticing his boxers, the tip of his cock peeks out the top before he slides them down, exposing his full length that has me swallowing roughly. "Come here," he grits out, on the edge of his restraint.

I meander his way, making to sit next to him, but he wraps a massive hand around his girth. He pumps down as his eyes snap from the front of my sex to my face. "No. On the coffee table."

I lower myself, my knees grating against the glass as I face him. His cock looks enormous at this angle, with a large vein running along the bottom.

"Touch yourself."

Yes.

My hand shoots between my thighs, my sex whimpering for pleasure. I graze my soaked panties, pleasure radiating through my legs—

"Not there," he growls. "Your nipples—pinch them."

I open my mouth, but then think better than to voice my protest. Snapping both nipples between my pointer fingers and thumbs, I squeeze. The sensation is powerful, sending sparks of lust throughout my whole body.

"Harder."

I do as he commands, my touch nearing pain as a moan flies from my mouth. My legs tighten, but then I recall earlier. I spread my knees wide, holding the position, not allowing my thighs to rub.

"Eyes on me," he says, watching the evidence of my arousal drip down my thighs. "Yes. Now *twist.*"

I rotate my fingers, soft whimpers falling from my lips as I now stare into his hungry eyes. Rotating the other way, I have to bite my lip to keep the sounds at bay.

Damien pumps slowly, his jaw locking in restraint. Pre-cum gathers on his tip, and I suddenly have the urge to have him in my mouth, to feel his head thrusted into the back of my throat.

"Fuck, Hannah. Your body is fucking incredible."

His words inject confidence in me as I stand. Turning from him and arching low, I clutch my panties and push them down. My ass in his face, I don't give him much longer to look as I whip around, facing him.

Standing tall on my heels, my pussy is slightly higher than his head. He sits up hastily, his mouth so close I can feel him exhale against my folds. When his tongue darts out in an abrupt swoop, I shiver, clutching his shoulders, as a violent shake ripples through me.

"Do you like that?" He peers up at me, lapping again.

I clutch my breasts, fingers squeezing firmly around my nipples. "Yes. *Yes.* Your tongue feels amazing." His licks grow more purposeful, and I'm lost in a blinding barrage of pleasure, grinding against his mouth. "So good... feels so good, so much better than—"

His fingers dig into my thighs, cutting my words short.

"Better than who?" His demeanor is so calm, it's alarming.

Oh, no. This is why you shouldn't blabber.

"Than..." My voice is almost a whisper, my pussy still throbbing. "Ster—"

In a flash, he forces me low, my knees colliding with the carpet as my heels come loose from my feet. Pinching my chin hard, he guides me to look up at the sheer sight of him. Shirtless, abs bulging underneath his loosened tie, and cock jutting upwards in front of his pants.

That's not going to fit. My mouth waters. *Not in my mouth or—*

His fingers knot through the tendrils of my hair, gripping harshly as he angles my head skyward, a single command on the tip of his tongue.

"Open."

FOUR
DAMIEN

HANNAH'S A MINX.

Forbidden fruit. A needy temptress under my touch. And as I drive her head down, the tip of my cock smacking the back of her throat, I force myself to remember why I can't have her.

She's my younger brother's ex-girlfriend, and she doesn't even know. I had multiple opportunities to tell her, but I didn't.

I yank her head up, relishing the way she gasps for air.

I did warn her I wasn't the kind of guy she thought I was.

But then my brother showed up at the club, all drunk and idiotic as usual. I remember how he touched her, his hand marking her leg. Anger swirls inside me.

The way he spoke to her...

My grip tightens on her hair. *"Apologize."*

"W-what?" Her voice wobbles in the most perfect way.

"For making me crazy. That a perfect little thing like you would ever be with a man like him."

She stares at me, shock laced with desire in her eyes.

"Sterling? I—"

Plunging her head down, her answer dies on a choked yelp. I hold her there, my cock buried in her throat. *"Don't say his name. Ever."* As I buck my hips back and forth, she makes the sweetest sounds.

Fuckkkk.

I pull my cock all the way out, before I end our night short and spill into her mouth.

Not yet.

Anger sparks in her eyes. "That's ridiculous—"

I force her down for another round. As I hold her longer this time, her moans turn desperate, pleading for me to relent.

I let up, and she nearly chokes, catching her breath. "I'm sorry!" Her black makeup smudges around her eyes.

"Are you?" I coo. "For what?"

"For ever being with him."

My gut clenches when her jaw slackens, sincerity emerging from behind her eyes. She's frozen for a moment, before her gaze falls with a keen hunger to my cock, saliva dripping down its length.

"Good girl." I pinch her chin with two fingers. "Now open that little mouth of yours."

She unclasps her lips wide.

"Stick your tongue out and look at me."

Her flat tongue darts out, her eyebrows scrunching together and eyelashes lifting.

My cock twitches.

I love seeing her this way, on her knees and needy for me. Leaning in close, I spit down her throat. She jerks back, her mouth clamping shut.

"Now thank me."

She hesitates, a glimpse of anger sparking behind her

eyes. But then she bats her eyelashes and bites her lower lip, her demeanor completely anew. "Thank you." Placing her hands on both knees, she opens her mouth again, squishing her tits between her elbows. "Can I have your cock again?" she asks sweetly.

She's asking me to continue face-fucking her... while looking like that.

"*FUCK,*" I growl. "So fucking perfect."

I resist the urge to flip her over to her stomach and fuck her right on the floor. My head spins, astounded before her words, making me question who's really the one in control here.

Standing, I thrust my cock to the back of her throat, both hands buried deep in her hair. "You're such a good girl when you listen."

I widen my stance and thrust harder, retracting all the way to the tip and crashing it back in with a punishing pace. Her tits bounce to my rhythm, rewarding me with a gasp each time I pull out, followed by a high-pitched moan when I slide it back through her tight lips.

"Get on the bed, on your hands and knees."

She scrapples to her feet, rushing to the bed. When she gets in position, I pause, my mouth falling open. Moonlight shines through the large windows, brightening the way her round ass points in the air.

Juices flow down the insides of her thighs, her pussy thoroughly soaked. And when she flicks her head over her shoulder to look at me, her curled hair draping downwards, I nearly weep at the sight.

Rushing over and dropping to the floor, my knees scrape the plush carpet. When I grab the front of her thighs and yank her back towards me, a gasp escapes her lips. Groaning, I plunge my tongue into her pussy.

"Oh!" she screams.

I spread her ass cheeks with both hands, working my head in quick motions. In and out. In and out, I fuck her with my tongue. She finds a rhythm herself and pushes back against my face as I lie my arm across her tailbone, driving her stomach into the mattress. She wiggles against my hold, but I tighten my grip in response.

Delving back in, my tongue dances between her folds, savoring her nectar, her essence. Her pussy mewls with slickness with every swipe of my tongue, making her taste even sweeter, like precious honey waiting to be devoured.

Her cries turn desperate, awakening something carnal within me as I lower my head, suctioning her clit. *"Yesss,"* she sighs, her knees sliding against the silk sheets. I suck harder, followed by the swirl of my tongue, before I pull my head away, leaving her panting in a wild craze.

Wetness spills from her entrance, trailing down her skin. Groaning again, I lower myself and collect it with my tongue, dragging all the way to her sex, stopping just before her puffy flesh. "Your taste is so... " I repeat the motion on the other thigh. *"Addictive."*

She shivers. "I need—"

"I know exactly what you need." I sink two fingers deep into her sopping cunt, and she lets out a high-pitched moan. "You need to open up before you take my cock."

Tilting my fingers downward, I let my thumb rub against her clit. Her walls grip against my digits as I withdraw to the tip.

So tight.

Increasing my pace, I angle towards her G-spot, clamping down hard against her clit with my thumb.

Her moans fill the room until they devolve into cries. "Please, don't stop!" She lifts onto her elbows, arching her ass to the sky. "Don't stop, don't stop!"

Pumping faster, my biceps bulge as I pull her head back by the strands of her hair. Her face contorts, mouth sprawling open in the exact way I want it to. I add another finger, and she takes it all the way, right to my knuckles.

"Come."

She shuts her eyes, her body tensing. I want—no, I *need*—to see her unravel. Be set ablaze. Succumb to an ecstasy so great that she'll come crawling back to me every night.

She sucks in a sharp inhale, holding it.

I growl. *"Look at me when you come."*

The whites of her eyes meet mine, her mouth stretching taut on a silent scream. Swaying her hips, she grinds her clit against my thumb desperately as her pussy contracts on my fingers at a delicious pace.

She slows her movements, chest heaving.

I expect her to topple over on the sheets, breathless. But instead, she rolls over on her back, looking me right in the eyes, a challenge brewing in hers.

She grabs me by my tie, leading me to a sage accent chair next to the window.

"Sit and watch," she purrs.

My heart somersaults with anticipation, before I sink into the seat.

Strutting to the windows, her bare ass is nothing short of hypnotizing. My eyes glue to her, flicking from her silky legs to her full breasts. With the city lights her background in the darkly lit room, she presses her peaked nipples to the glass.

Fuck...

She tilts her head up, her hair falling behind her. Bending her knees, she scrapes her nipples down the hard surface.

FUCK.

I jerk in my chair, ready to spring to my feet and fuck her against the window. But she flings her head in my direction, focusing her fiery attention on me. "I didn't say to move, Damien." Then she resumes to her full height, nipples dragging upwards with a torturous speed.

God, she's gorgeous.

I've never thought a woman was truly gorgeous before.

When I catch her eyes, there's a fierceness to them, something untamed I wouldn't have expected from the girl I met hours earlier. And I realize at this moment, I'll give her anything, buy her anything. All she would have to do is open that pretty mouth of hers and ask.

If I don't get a hold of this soon, she'll be the one ruining me.

But I don't move, continuing to worship each of her motions. She slaps her palms against the glass, high above her head, stretching her ass outwards.

"You don't know what you're doing."

"I'm not doing anything." Her undertone edge with innocence, in a way that tempts me to fuck her senseless, until the only name she can remember is mine.

She's really enjoying herself.

A subtle smile prints on her lips as she grabs both her ass cheeks and spreads them—*that's enough.*

I burst from my chair.

Her smile widens, and I grip a fistful of her hair. "You think it's funny teasing me?" Ramming my body against hers, I slam my cock inside her in one solid thrust.

"Ah!" she yelps, before I flatten her cheek against the glass.

I fuck her with a punishing pace, not waiting for her to compensate for my size. When her cries fill the room, I plunge two fingers into her mouth. Pleasured screams turn to muffled moans, mingled with loud slapping sounds as my hips pound against her ass.

I pin her tight against the glass. "You like making me crazy, don't you?" Her pussy squeezes on my length in response.

My lips brush her ear. "Whose cum are you catching tonight?" I tighten my grip on her hair, thinking about what Sterling said to her. My mind goes visceral, and the slapping sounds grow louder. *"Huh?"*

Our eyes connect, hers utterly glazed over. "Yours!" Her cry coats my fingers with saliva.

I remove them from her mouth, and she gasps. "Whose?" Pummeling into her, I sheath my cock deep inside her, as far as it will go.

"Yours!"

"That's right. Mine. Beg for it."

And then I witness the apex of her undoing.

"Please! Please, Damien, give me your cum. Please—"

Licking up her neck, I silence her, feeling her shiver beneath me.

Her body arches instantly, indicating her release. I grab hold of her tightly, continuing to thrust into her as she writhes against me, riding out each pleasurable wave.

When her pulsations ease, I pull out of her quickly, my hand wrapping around my cock. In a rush, she twists and drops to her knees, hunger flashing behind her eyes. When her tongue slides past her lips for me, my knees nearly wobble.

Fucking. Hell.

Pumping my hand across my length, I chase the need to mark her as mine. I press my palm to the glass, supporting my weight, until my tip becomes so tight it almost hurts as cum shoots out.

Angling down to her face, I watch as she eagerly catches the droplets. A white pool forms atop her tongue, some dripping off the sides, landing on her tits.

I've never come so hard in my life.

Air whooshes from my lips as I glance down, trying to fight the surprise that must be visible on my face. But she smirks knowingly, a dribble of cum visible on the corner of her mouth, before she swallows.

Yep. I'm ruined.

FIVE

HANNAH

HAVE you ever had such earth-shattering sex that you almost feel guilty over it? Like something that great couldn't just *happen*, not without losing something—dignity, innocence... something you haven't realized yet?

Maybe I should feel bad for everyone around me. They're missing out on something monumental, life-altering, and they don't even know it. And how could they? They didn't experience what I did last night.

I twirl a strand of hair between my fingers, bed sheets sprawling about my body like a sea of clouds. Did last night even happen, or was he some ghost figment of my imagination? But the lingering scent of him reminds me it was real.

All of it.

I noticed he was gone when I woke up five minutes ago, leaving me feeling disappointed but glad at the same time.

I chew on my bottom lip.

Would I have been able to look at him after that?

Do I know how I feel?

Do I regret it? No.

But what if nothing will ever compare to that? Possible—probable, even.

No, no, don't think like that. It's good we'll never see each other again. I'm better off this way. A clean cut, never given the opportunity to know each other.

I continue contemplating the consequences of the most delicious night of my existence, when the most terrifying, horrible thought blooms in my mind, arriving late on the caboose of the *you're-so-fucked* train.

MY. INTERVIEW.

I fly out of bed, standing naked and startled in the glorious hotel suite. Feeling like a fish in a glass bowl, with the daylight streaming in through the windows in every direction, I scramble for my phone.

Kitchen counter? *Nope.* Bathroom? *Nope.* Racing around, I search and snatch my littered clothes from off the floor.

I'm fucked. So, so fucked.

What was I thinking? Going out and hooking up with some devilishly handsome man the night before such an important interview. Stupid.

Sofia said we'd only be out for a little while, and I was downing tequila shots like they were Capri Sun. STUPID.

Hanging out of my purse on the sofa, I find my phone.

I had all this time to remember something so important. How did I not? Not once did I think of it—not at the club table, not during the car ride to the hotel and DEFINITELY not last night while—

Okay. It's fine. Stop spiraling. I probably have time.

I check the time on my phone. Ten-thirty. My interview is in thirty minutes.

Oh my god. There's no way. I have nothing to wear, and I still need to make it all the way to Silicon Avenue.

Sweat prickles the back of my neck as I scroll through a flood of messages, all from Sofia.

Sofia: *Come back to the table. We got more shots.*

Sofia: *Where are you?*

Sofia: *Jenna said she can't find you either.*

Sofia: *Oh my god. I didn't know Sterling came. What an ass. I'm so sorry, I don't know who invited him. Also... I swear I just saw Sterling get taken out of the club unconscious, but it was probably someone else.*

Sofia: *You probably went home. I'll see you there.*

Sofia: *Alright... not at home. I'm officially worried.*

Sofia: *Ohhhh, I see you're at The Ritz (fancy, get it, girl).*

How did she...? I shake my head, reminding myself I don't have time to ask such questions and continue to read.

Sofia: *I'm going out on a limb here and assuming you're too "preoccupied" to remember your interview tomorrow.*

A row of winky faces line the end of her text.

Heat rushes straight to my cheeks. *I'm never going to hear the end of this.*

Sofia: *Morning sunshine. I tried to call you, but no luck. I brought some clothes over. The stingy front desk guy wouldn't tell me your room number and I didn't have time to pry it out of him, so they said they'd bring them up to you. Also, don't worry about leaving the cocktail dress. I have a million of them.*

Sofia: *Knock 'em dead, Han. Innovex needs both of us under the same roof.*

My eyes nearly shoot from their sockets. *She brought me clothes?*

I glance around, but don't spot any. Maybe they're outside? I rush to the large front door, peeking through the peephole. Standing on my tippy toes, I can barely make out a blur of black and blue on the ground.

Cracking the door, I rummage my hand low to the floor through the small opening. Don't want to subject an unfortunate worker to a frazzled, butt-naked lady when they walk out of the elevator.

Once in the bathroom, I toss the clothes on the counter. There's no time to inspect them. Then a pouch spills open, mascara and other items scattering on the marble.

No way did she think of makeup. What an angel.

I wash up in record time, scrubbing my skin so hard it nearly falls off. Anything to keep my interviewer from getting a whiff of my poor decision-making skills.

Now clean, I shimmy into the clothes and finish getting ready. Sofia brought me a black pencil skirt that kisses my knees, a ruffled sleeveless blouse and nude heels. Hugged by the tight material, I examine my backside. The look is confident and sophisticated, yet sexy.

Damn. She might be an engineer, but she sure knows how to put an outfit together.

Inspecting the place once more, I check if I've left anything important. But when I'm sure I didn't, I sigh. It's as if I'm leaving some dream behind, and I'm worried that the more time goes by, the less I'll remember how it felt.

I turn to rush out, but then freeze. There's a note on the nightstand.

Hannah,

If you ever need to pretend again.

His pristine handwriting ends with a number at the bottom.

Standing with my legs straight like a pencil, I hold the note between my fingers.

Leave it.

The urgency of needing to go creeps up my back.

Just leave it.

Crinkling the paper, I shove it inside my purse.

MY HEAD CRANES BACK, staring up at the skyscraper shining beneath the sun's rays as business personnel pass me by on the street without notice.

Headquarters to Innovex Microchips, the building stands like a beacon in the heart of Silicon Avenue. The shorter, neighboring skyscrapers house other miscellaneous tech companies. From Sofia's explanation, Innovex is the top microchip company in the world, supplying the processing units for just about anything. Computers, cars, microwaves, hairdryers, gaming consoles, televisions, *everything*.

I recall Sofia's explanation last week, while cracking eggs into a frying pan with wonder on her face.

"If it needs computing power, it needs a central processing unit —a microchip. And chances are, it was designed and manufactured by Innovex." She smiled, like she was so excited about bringing me into her nerdy world. *"Maybe I even soldered its prototype."*

"Right... Like I know what that means."

She then gave me a long-winded explanation with a precursor of *"don't worry, it's not that complicated"* that went miles over my head.

I still can't reiterate why or how they work, but that's not my job. My interests are on the business side of things, management specifically, which is why I need to nail this interview to be their next client relations assistant manager.

My heart pumps, thinking of the vast number of clientele Innovex has. They cast such a wide, global net.

I breathe through my nose, giving myself a pep talk. *No need to overthink it, Hannah. It's just a building. Look around, there are plenty of them.*

Willing my legs into motion, my first steps are like trudging out of a cement mold. Every suit I pass, I keep a level head. It's unimaginable to me that all these people work for a single company.

You can fit in. You're qualified for this position. You graduated in business management with honors. Your outfit is great. And your resume is up to par.

Reaching the revolving doors, I slip into a crowded section.

And although you didn't have time to ask for a sparkling reference letter when you dumped Sterling the first or second time, you can make up for it by acting confident and professional.

I exit and check my phone. Ten-fifty-nine. One minute to spare. If it wasn't for Sofia's quick thinking, there's no way I would've made it on time.

Say it again. Act confident and professional, I repeat in my head. *The interviewer won't know what a slutty, dirty plaything you were last night for a man you just met.*

Slipping my phone back in my purse, the scrunched paper scrapes my fingertips. The thought of calling him and hearing his sultry voice crosses my mind. Heat squirms up my bare legs as I think of all the ways he ordered me around.

I bite the inside of my cheek.

Maybe it's best to refrain from any and all thoughts of last night. While I'm here, it never happened. That shouldn't be too difficult to manage.

∾

"AS I'VE SAID, we were most impressed by your previous employment." The lady in the plaid blazer holds up her clipboard.

We sit on opposite sides of a glossy mahogany desk in a room of enclosed glass. Outside, people bustle about and huddle around whiteboards or desks littered with computer monitors. Surprisingly, there's no cubicle in sight.

The interview is nearing an end, and I'd say it's gone well, having avoided some uncomfortable questions about what I specifically did at Sterling's company. I didn't *lie*. Call it stretching the truth. In short, faking it until you make it is a better option than explaining I was no more than a well-dressed errand girl.

All the initial promises Sterling made when I took the job as being his personal assistant went out the window the first day I started. No attending interviews. No listening in on important calls. Nothing substantial for me to grow and learn about how the business is run.

"We particularly think it advantageous to have you on our Bass Mobile team—still as an assistant manager, of course—to help continue our relationship with them."

I nearly choke on a piece of air when I hear Sterling's company name. "Continue?"

The auburn-haired woman gives me an odd look. "We've been supplying them with our G7 chip since its launch last year."

Of course, I don't know that. Of course, Sofia forgot to mention that, and my dumbass neglected to ask it. Maybe I was subconsciously refusing the possibility. My mind must've not been able to go there. That my non-public relationship with Sterling Bass might *still* affect my job search along Silicon Avenue.

Feigning my knowledge of something so obvious, I smile. "Yes, of course. I thought you were speaking of some new relationship with them. I've been to the Bass manufacturing center and seen the workers place the chip firsthand."

The lie twists my stomach. It seems my future in this field may be at risk, once again, by none other than Sterling Bass.

It's only an assistant manager job. And besides, Sterling would send one of his minions to meet with outside personnel. I might not even see him.

"Excellent." Her eyes brighten, and I loosen a breath. *She believes me.* "We have always worked closely with Bass Mobile, obviously because of the connection between—" She stops her sentence short, eyeing the door.

A cheery-looking man pops his head in. "Carol?" He smiles.

"Yes?"

"Pardon the interruption, but it seems our CEO has opened a new personal assistant position. Hannah's name was mentioned, given her previous job and her already being here."

I straighten in my chair. *They're requesting me for a different job on the spot?*

"Oh?" She gives the man a quizzical look.

Yep, this is definitely out of the ordinary.

"Well, we were just wrapping up here, anyway. Hannah, if you have no more questions for me, I'll hand you off to Angelo, if you'd be interested in the position."

I'm not... But I don't want to seem ungrateful.

"Sure." I nod. "That sounds great."

She stands. "That's good to hear. It's been a pleasure, Miss Lockwood. We'll be sure to give you a call if you're chosen for the position."

"Thank you." I stand as well, shaking her hand. "It was great to meet you, too."

Leaving the room, I trail Angelo's quick footsteps. He ushers me across the working floor, employees zooming by us.

"Sorry for such a short notice, but I thought I'd give you the chance to interview now while you're here."

We approach the lines of elevators, and he hits the up arrow with his knuckles. A pair of metal doors instantly swing open, and we enter.

Angelo swipes his card attached to his lanyard, and the top floor button lights up.

Floor 75.

My mind buzzes with questions as we ascend, all of them ones I shouldn't ask, because I'm really not interested in this personal assistant job.

"Are you taking me to meet with him now?"

Or her? Sofia's information didn't reach as far as who owns the company. And I don't do extensive research beforehand, as that often makes me too nervous for the interview.

"Hopefully, yes. His time is very limited, so we'll see if he can fit us in."

My toes curl in my shoes, nervousness and excitement nipping at me. If I had known I was meeting the CEO of Silicon Avenue's largest corporation, I *really* wouldn't have gone out last night.

The door opens to reveal a long corridor. A porcelain-white desk faces us, with an older woman behind it.

"Hi, Angelo." Her eyes glue to the computer screen in front of her, nails clacking against a keyboard hidden from our view. "His meeting with Mr. Langley finished a few minutes ago. You may see him now."

"Perfect." Angelo leads us down the corridor, his eyes flickering towards me. "Seems we lucked out. Getting time to meet with Mr. Bass is difficult"—my ankle wobbles, causing me to nearly tumble—"especially if..."

I don't hear the rest of his explanation, not when a boulder the size of the moon splashes down in the pit of my stomach.

Mr. Bass? I walk straight-backed, feeling lucky that Angelo is in front of me, or he would have seen my obvious reaction. *He did* not *say that, because if he did, that would mean...*

Anger flows through my veins.

Sterling asked for me.

No one else in his family knows about me. He said his family owned a conglomerate, but he never mentioned owning Innovex too. It doesn't have Bass in the name. He must want payback for what happened to him at the club last night.

My adrenaline hikes up. *Should I leave? Should I say something?*

A closed door comes into view at the end of the hall. Each step feels like ticking a bomb down to zero, counting the remaining seconds I have left to be taken seriously on Silicon Avenue.

With burning eyes, my throat tightens. His laughing words sing a vicious melody in my ear.

You—a manager? Be serious, baby.

Oh, Hannah. You and your little dreams.

You could only do that with my family name.

Can't you take a joke?

I never said that. You're crazy.

Everyone agrees with me.

NO! My heels stop hard in front of the door. *He won't take*

*this from me too. If he wants to try to fuck with my career, fine. I'm
game.*

Angelo holds the door open for me, my chest heaving in
fury. I exhale slowly, needing to face Sterling with a clear
head.

But the man in the navy suit typing on a laptop doesn't
look like Sterling. His hair is brown, not blond. His frame is
much too large. And when he lifts his head in a calm manner
to meet my fiery gaze, his eyes aren't the cold blue ocean I
expect. They're green, sultry and rake their way down my
body.

Damien?

Damien *Bass.*

SIX

DAMIEN

MY FATHER TAUGHT me many life lessons, one of them about taking what I want.

If I see something I want, I take it. No questions. I don't need a reason or a moral justification to lull me to sleep at night. All I need is the comforting fact that it's mine and no one else's.

Just like the brunette standing in my personal meeting room, staring at me with the most intriguing anger. She doesn't realize it yet, but she's mine. The moment I saw her up against that window in the hotel with hunger and determination flashing behind her eyes, I knew she was my next taking.

I want more than a one-night stand. I want her on her knees every night, batting her eyelashes and puckering her lips for me. I want to own all her moans, all her orgasms. And the thought of her under the touch of another man, *especially my brother's*, makes my skin boil.

Call me obsessive and controlling, but it's the reason I

started a multi-billion-dollar business using nothing but my brain and the power of negotiation.

I won't pretend my last name didn't help. It did. But my business doesn't wear the Bass name like the rest of the businesses in my family's tech conglomerate. Innovex Microchips is its own entity, founded on outside investors, I vetted myself and paid back in excess. I didn't take a single drop of my father's money.

I strategically hand-pick each of my employees, like my head of human resources, Angelo, who's been here since the beginning. Sitting in a leather chair in front of my desk, he wears a serious yet inviting expression. Hannah sits next to him, seeming to snap out of her daze before her angered aura dampens.

Offering her my hand, I fight my smug look that's threatening to surface. "Miss Lockwood, it's a pleasure to meet you."

Her hand fits perfectly in mine, soft and supple. "And you, *Mr. Bass.*" My name comes out on a clip.

We shake for a moment too long, staring into each other's eyes, hers swirling with a complicated concoction of anger, lust and confusion. The friction in the air is so thick I could reach out my hand and grab it.

My gaze falls, zeroing in on the way she's biting her lower lip, the same way she did last night. She must realize what she's doing, because her lip plops back out, before she lets go of my hand.

Then she sits, her heels making her knees slightly higher than her waist, accentuating her slender legs. I take a seat behind my desk, closing my laptop.

Angelo clears his throat. "I went ahead and skipped the vetting process, as she was already here for another interview.

I thought it best for you two to meet now and get any questions out of the way."

"I have a question." Hannah crosses her legs, craning her neck towards me. "A few, actually."

Excitement curls in my chest. *There's that look again.* My cock hardens against my pants. Luckily, my desk hides it from their viewing.

"I'm listening." My voice comes out silkier than intended.

When she came into my office, I expected her to be shocked, unable to speak. What a surprise it must be to find out that, not only am I her ex's brother, but also her future employer. But here she is, with fire in her eyes, ready to question me.

"When did this position open?"

"Today."

"Really?" Her tone is sweet, but there's no missing the hint of malice underlining her seemingly innocent words.

"Yes, really."

"And what would I be doing?"

She's testing me. Interesting.

From her records, she applied for a client relations assistant manager job, a far cry from being my brother's personal assistant. Such a waste of time it must've been, given he does short of nothing at Bass Mobile.

"Attend meetings, take notes, manage my calendar, that kind of stuff."

She sits up straighter with an intriguing seriousness.

That got her attention. What kind of bullshit did my brother have her doing? I won't lie to myself. I know what I really want from her. But I'm not about to damage her career and growth, not when her body tells me she's eager to learn.

And when I'm so willing to teach her...

"Would you like that?"

"Yes," she answers quickly.

A grin curves over my mouth. *It seems my relation to my brother isn't a problem.*

Wetting her lips, she uncrosses her legs, shooting heat straight to my groin. At this angle, I have an opportune view of her panties tucked inside her skirt. Red and lacy.

My grip on my armrest tightens, before Angelo chimes in, "The position is newly formed as well. I want to assure you no one was let go or left recently."

"Of course." Hannah nods. "Do you not have other assistants?"

"I do, but this job would be more... on-call."

"Does that include in-house assistance?"

Fuck... She gets it.

I imagine her in my apartment, desperate and needy for me. Her eyes plead for an answer, and my boxers suddenly feel suffocating around my hips.

"Yes," I say. *This was easier than I thought.* "I know you're qualified, given your recent employment. I'd hire you right now. Are you interested?"

She stands and smiles at me, the light hitting her figure in such a way it could bring me to my knees. I prepare to dismiss Angelo and cancel my next appointment the moment she accepts my offer, only so I can have my way with her, preferably ass-up on my—

"No," she says sweetly.

Wait, what? My hard-on vanishes. *Hold on—*

I open my mouth to protest, but she whips around and walks a tight line all the way across and out of the room. The last thing I see is the back of her tall heel *kicking* the door shut.

I blink.

The door rattles on its hinges, and Angelo's eyes are wide like saucers as his hand covers his mouth.

"Stay here," I growl, bursting from my chair. After discovering her half-way down the hall, I'm hot on her trail when she stops suddenly, whipping her head around.

"You like making a scene in front of my head of HR?" My voice is low and laced with annoyance.

"I'm not here to be your little errand girl who can get you off," she counters with ten times the wrath. "I've already tried that, you know, with *your brother?* Thanks for telling me, by the way. So mature. You're a lot alike."

"We're *nothing* alike." Hot rage bubbles in my gut. "So what? He's my brother. You wanted a night with a stranger, and that's what you got. I could've been anyone."

She doesn't respond.

"Don't act all innocent, Hannah. I know what last night was for you." Before I know it, her ear tickles my lips, a familiar lilac perfume sousing my senses. *"An awakening."*

Her face pales.

"For me too," I whisper. "We can help each other. I'm giving us the opportunity to experience it again... and again."

Doe eyes flutter to meet mine. *Yes, like that.* She glances at my lips. *Hand yourself over.* Leaning in, her lips are so close to mine I can feel the tickle of her breath. *Entangle yourself in my web.* My eyelids fall, preparing to taste her wet tongue—

"Fuck. You."

My eyes shoot open, only to watch her racing down the hall, her laughter echoing off the walls.

"Hannah!" I bark, chasing after her.

My next appointment swings his suit-clad body into my view, and I stop dead in my tracks. He gives her a confused look as she darts past him. Trying to appear natural, I wave an apology to him, as if I wasn't about to hunt down a girl in my hall, who's laughing like a maniac.

Fuck you—*Fuck you?* I can't believe she said that. Not only to my face, but *in* my face. Inches away. I don't know if I should be pissed or turned on.

While I contemplate my reaction and usher my bewildered appointment through my door, a single thought burns a hole through the back of my consciousness.

That won't be the last time I see Hannah Lockwood.

JOHN PULLS UP to the curb in front of my apartment building. I thank him before entering through the doors, my phone buzzing in my pocket.

Harrison: *I'm here. Same spot.*

Taking the elevator to the basement, I soon pass by empty cars. Automatic lights flicker on in response before a black Cadillac sedan comes into view, parked in the corner with no headlights.

I hop into the front seat, already knowing the man I'll see when I turn my head. A wise face with a receding hairline meets my sight. Harrison Thornton prefers to meet in private for such sensitive occasions.

"The board needs an answer." He skips the small talk, like always, which I respect. It's something we have in common when it comes to business. "Have you given any more thought to our proposition?"

The driver's side window cracks, the smoke of his lit cigar escaping out the slit. He hands me another, the smooth texture sliding between my two fingers.

"Yes, I have." I lean into his lighter, sucking in my first

puff. As I settle back into the leather seats, the tobacco floats straight to my brain, making me feel light. "And I agree it's the best course of action, if we are to expand further into the tech industry."

Harrison has been on my board of directors and a big investor since my company's infancy. In fact, he's a major investor in countless successful businesses scattered across New York. I've always admired him for his straightforward-ness, particularly his ruthless business maneuvers.

"Good. The board extends their gratitude." The motion lights in the garage go dark, the car's interior glow the only thing illuminating his coarse features. "There's no length you won't go, no line you haven't crossed, to see the furthering success of Innovex. I've been around long enough to know that's why you'll always stay on top. You're a rare breed."

My gut sings to his words, and a familiar, dark hunger nips at my insides. Ruthless as he may be, not Harrison nor my entire board could force my hand to do anything. I'm the majority shareholder.

I hold all the power.

He continues, "It's a significant but necessary sacrifice. But, as you know, this type of thing will only be temporary."

I take a long drag, letting the heat simmer deep in my chest. "Of course, as it should be." The smoke bellows from my lips. "What's our time frame?"

"Several promising companies are set to go to market in about two months. It would need to be before that."

"Soon, then." My mind races with urgency. "I'd wager it's not the first time you've been on a board that's requested such an arrangement?"

"Correct. I've recommended and orchestrated it myself multiple times."

"So, it can appear believable in such a short time?"

"Yes, if done correctly." His eyes bury themselves in mine, searching for information he won't find. "I'll have my guys on it tomorrow, unless you already have a candidate in mind?"

Stifling a smug smile, I adjust my cufflinks to appear disinterested. "I do, actually. She interviewed at Innovex today."

SEVEN

HANNAH

RAIN SPLATTERS AGAINST THE WINDOW.

I sit curled up on the couch in our living room, watching *Seinfeld*. I'm on season five, even though I've seen the show all the way through twice. It's my go-to comfort show that I turned on the instant I got home.

Sofia is still gone. She texted me saying she's staying late for work. I haven't seen her since the club on Sunday night. We agreed to a late lunch together after my interview, but I texted her it ran long and to go without me.

I'm still debating if I should tell her what happened today. I'm not sure how I feel. It's more complicated than when I dealt with the aftermath of Sterling. Then, I felt sad and stupid.

And now? I shove my spoon into my tub of chocolate chip ice cream. *Now I feel stupid and something else...*

Pissed. Yes, that's it.

For two reasons.

One, my chances of working on Silicon Avenue are approaching zero. The Bass family owns half of it, and their reach and influence must stretch down the entire street. My promising client relations interview practically went out the window the moment I stepped foot into his office.

And two, Damien knew I was his brother's ex when Sterling found me at the bar, and he said nothing. *The whole night*, he didn't tell me. I blow out a breath of annoyance. That arrogant billionaire thinks he can get whatever he wants, that he can conjure up some fake position at his company, and I'll drool all over it and his cock.

Images of us in the hotel room flash behind my eyes. The first is me on my knees, looking up at him and his impressive length inches from my mouth. The next is me dragging him by his tie to the window. *Sit and watch*, I tell him, feeling so confident in the moment.

I know what last night was for you—an awakening. Damien's words replay in my ear.

So what if he's right? It doesn't erase what he did.

Neglecting to tell the truth still counts as a lie.

I'M four episodes deep into my shameless Netflix binge, that has now migrated to my bedroom, when my phone lights up. It's face up on my old nightstand, and the number isn't in my contacts, but I recognize it immediately as the same one crinkled inside my purse.

I hit deny, for the third time in the past hour. I don't want to hear the sultry voice on the other end of the line, but there is another I'd prefer.

I sigh.

I don't want her to know anything's off, though. I can't bring myself to talk about what happened today. I want a normal, happy call from my ever-cheerful mom. Pulling up her contact, I plaster a fake smile on my face, hoping it'll resonate in my voice.

She picks up on the second ring. "Hi, sweetie."

"Hey," I say brightly.

"How's it going? How'd the interview go?"

I put her on speaker and pick at the sides of my nails, preparing myself for the lie.

Focus on the beginning, before everything took a turn for the worse.

"It went well. They seemed to be impressed with my previous employment."

My mom knows I worked for Sterling, not that I *dated* him. I strategically kept that information out of our conversations. I didn't want to worry her, with her knowing I'm dating someone from a completely different world than I grew up in. She would think I'd get taken advantage of...

Which I did.

From a trailer park to a run-down farm, my family never had it easy. But my parents remodeled the whole thing and started a small farm business, growing corn and potatoes. They opened the door to a whole new life for themselves. It's quite inspiring, actually. My mom's the one who pushed me to chase my big city dreams from an early age.

"That's great! I knew they would. You'll be a great fit."

"Hopefully they'll call back soon. If not, I'll interview at a few more places."

"They will. All the years helping with the farm made you a hard worker, and they'll pick up on that."

I smile. "Thanks, Mom. Speaking of the farm, how's it going? I bet the yield this year's big." I chuckle, remembering hours upon hours of harvesting corn by hand, piling them so high my wheelbarrow could barely roll on the dirt.

The line goes silent, and my face drops. "Mom?"

She clears her throat. "You should come by sometime, Hannah."

She never sounds like that.

My heart sinks at the thickness in her voice, and I dare to think of the worst. "... It's what happened last year, isn't it?"

"Yes," she whispers. "The soil hasn't quite recovered from the flood. Crops this year are producing next to nothing."

My eyes burn, reluctant to believe her words. She played it off so well, not wanting me to know how bad it must've ruined their chances for a high yield, for the farm's chances of survival.

"I can come help."

"No." Her tone is urgent. "No, sweetie. You stay there. It's where you're meant to be, you know that."

"I know... but I don't mind. It would only be for a while."

"It wouldn't do any good. The soil needs at least another year or two to fully recover. There isn't much we can do."

I swallow hard, stifling the sniffles sitting thick in my throat. I'm not particularly attached to the farm. Never have been, not like the rest of my family. But my younger brother grew up his entire life on it. He must be devastated.

"Your dad's looking for work in the town. It's going to be fine, Hannah."

"Are you sure?"

"Of course. We're a strong bunch."

Grinning, I roll my eyes, weathering the inspiring speech I've heard a gazillion times, all coated in optimism and the *resilient Lockwood spirit.*

"Oh my god, Mom. Stop. I believe you, everything's going to be fine."

"Good," she says, and we laugh, chatting a while longer before we say our goodbyes.

Shutting off the TV, I sink further down my squeaky mattress, tugging my comforter up to my chin.

In comparison, my boy problems are nothing.

"YOU WHAT?" Sofia's eyes shoot from her sockets.

A few days later, we're seated on the patio at Matteo's, sharing a pineapple and pepperoni pizza. Her slice drops from her hand, slapping face-down on her plate.

"*Shh!* Keep it down." Two tables over, a pair of heads turn. I give them a thin smile. "I didn't know it was him! He didn't tell me."

She rescues her pizza, flipping it over, and starts picking at the pineapple pieces like popcorn.

"So, let me get this straight. You slept with Damien Bass... *Damien Bass.*" I cringe. *Why does she have to say his name like that?* "Interviewed at his company without knowing it, and then he called you into his office to be his personal assistant?"

"... Yes."

"Wow."

"I know." I take an unnecessarily large bite, chewing at a rapid pace before swallowing. "You could've told me Sterling's brother owns Innovex."

"I'm sorry." Her expression softens. "It's such a large company, and I know how much you want to work on Silicon Avenue. I thought you'd never see him, let alone work with him."

"It's okay. If it wasn't for running into him at the club, there's no way I'd see him working there." I sigh. "I want to learn about business at work, not... *other things.*"

The corners of her mouth rise. "Why not learn both?"

"Sofia!"

"Woah, woah." She pumps her hands, palms facing me. "There's nothing wrong with mixing business and pleasure. I say go for it, if you like the sex, of course." She narrows her eyes, baiting me to give her more information. When I don't budge, she leans over, her eyebrows lifting. "So, anyway. How was he?"

I open my mouth, then shut it. I can't answer that, not without spilling each and every dirty detail from our night together. My cheeks burn.

"It was that good, then?" Her eyes light up.

"It doesn't matter how it was." I angle my head down to conceal my smile. "It's not happening again."

"Oh, it *so* is."

"It's not!"

"You poor, poor girl."

"No. He's just some pretty guy in a suit who's probably got nothing going on upstairs. I've tried that. Not interested. I bet his family gave him that company as some birthday present. Isn't that what high society does for their children?"

"Most of them, ya. But not Damien. He started his company on his own when he was twenty-three. He invented the new family of G-line chips himself. *Everything* that's high tech uses them, and no other company has successfully reverse-engineered them. And that's not from a lack of trying."

I should cover my ears, block out all this new information. I don't need to make this any more complicated for myself.

"And he double majored. In electrical engineering *and* applied physics. Nobody does that." She sighs, a twinkle dancing in her eye. "I'd hate you if I didn't already have my eyes set on Ross in the computer engineering department."

"Oh, really? No more club-hopping, silver foxes for you?"

"They're just for fun and can't catch my eye like a man who can solder a circuit board so cleanly it makes me wet." *Oh my god, am I listening to nerd porn?* "So, I'll take cutie Ross and you can have the king of Silicon Avenue."

Before I can start my deflective response that is sure to further my denial, Jenna stops in front of our table. She wears Matteo's signature black and red colors, with an apron wrapped around her waist.

She plops down in the seat next to me. "I'm *so* done with Aldo." *Oh, no. Here we go about her boss.* But I let out a sigh of relief, grateful for the change of topic. She swipes a piece from our tray. "I don't care if he sees. He can go ahead and fire me already."

Sofia quirks her brow. "What'd he do this time?"

"The usual. Apparently, I can't make friends with my co-workers." She purses her lips in a pouty fashion. "I was keeping up with my tables, I swear. I was only trying to get Gabe's number—he's the new cook, by the way. *So* much better than Leo."

Jenna has a habit of dating half of her staff, each one the next love of her life—for a month or two, until she's onto the next lucky boy. Sofia and I are often stuck listening, along for the ride, but I'd be lying if I said I don't get sucked into the drama more often than not.

"He makes a mean pineapple pepperoni," I say with my mouth full, grabbing my next slice. I don't know how many

I've had, and I'm not keeping count. "And they can't fire you. You bring in the most tips."

"Exactly! Thank you. They need me."

Sofia and Jenna keep chatting, and I lean back to soak in the sun. We haven't had a nice day in weeks, so it's nice to take it in while it lasts. A calm feeling washes over me, something I haven't felt in weeks.

Everything will be okay. I can always job hunt elsewhere. Some company on Silicon Avenue will be the right fit. Besides, maybe what Sofia said is right. There's nothing wrong with mixing business and pleasure, as long as I'm still furthering my career.

But not with someone who's my ex's brother.

Releasing a slow breath, I study those passing us by on the sidewalk, an iron railing separating them from the tables. Most wear sunglasses and loose-fitting clothing, all except a dark-haired man crossing the street. He's wearing a charcoal gray suit, holding a phone to his ear, and he's *looking right at me.*

I gasp, sitting up straight, prompting my friends to snap their heads at me.

Jenna follows the line of my gaze. "Who's *that?* Do you know him?"

I ignore her.

He lowers his phone and beelines it towards us, getting closer. I hear Sofia's quiet gasp, feeling like I can't breathe. Snatching a tall menu, I open it and stare a fiery hole right through the *Lunch Specials* section.

"Oh my god." Jenna's breath tickles my ear. *"Oh my god.* He's fucking hot!" She clutches my arm. "I think I've seen him on the cover of GQ."

"Stop staring!" I hiss, lowering my head. "He's no one."

"No one? Well, *no one* looks pissed, and he's heading straight for you."

Sofia stands with a grin, tugging Jenna's sleeve. "I'm going to the bar. Could you make me a drink?"

"W-what?" My eyes ping-pong between my two friends and Damien's long legs eating up the pavement. "Sofia, no. I know what you're doing. Don't go."

"It'll be quick." Teeth flashing in the sun, her smile is brazen. "I *really* want a drink. You understand, don't you?" She nudges Jenna, pulling her from a trance-like state.

"Oh—ya, sure. I'll make you one." She guides Sofia into the restaurant, stealing looks over her shoulder.

Shitshitshit.

I slide further down my chair, my menu swallowing my face. Be invisible. Blend in. And don't look.

It's not him, I tell myself. There are plenty of men in the city who have perfect hair, suits tailored to their body like silk gloves, and the bone structure of a Greek god. *Plenty.*

And besides, on the highly improbable chance it *is* him, it's not like the last interaction I had with him ended with *fuck you* and me scurrying off like a madwoman with her rear end in flames.

Because that would be bad.

Very bad.

Crunching footsteps atop gravel sound to my left, on the opposite side of the railing and my very interesting menu. I don't breathe. I don't make a sound.

"Hannah," a sultry voice, that does *not* belong to Damien, purrs.

Waves of shivers run up my spine, but I suffer through them.

Okay. Act natural.

I flip to the next page.

"Are you serious right now?"

I clear my throat and flip again. Pictures of chocolatey deserts cloud my vision, two inches from my face.

"You are *not* reading that."

I reach for the corner of my menu, but it's snatched away from my grasp. Damien's striking features come into view, before he clasps the menu shut with one hand.

I purse my lips. "You're no fun."

"Oh, I'm sorry. I thought I was the one who was immature."

I say nothing as he walks along the railing, then opens a latch to enter onto the patio. In a whirlwind of time, too soon ago, I was watching him cross the street, but now he's sitting across from me, with a no-bullshit look on his face.

He seems so out of place here underneath our red-and-yellow umbrella. The other guests steal glances his way, and for good reason, too. They're all *summer breezes* and *happy-go-lucky*, and he's just downright suit and tie and no smiles.

"Are you here to get the last word?"

"Maybe I wouldn't have to track you down if you'd pick up the phone sometime."

It's truc. He's called me at least fifteen times in the past three days. I should've blocked him by now, but a little part of me gloats every time I press deny.

"How'd you get my number? I know I didn't give it to you."

"You *did* interview at my company."

"Wow. That smells suspiciously like some sort of privacy violation." Appraising his frame that's much too large for that wrought-iron chair, I suppress my laughter.

His face scrunches, morphing into an expression of annoyance, like he's explaining times tables to a fifth grader. "No, you agreed to a background check the moment you stepped foot into my building. Your private information is mine."

Sucking in a breath, I push my thighs together, burning under his intense stare. *No, don't get turned on.* I shove the traitorous feeling back down. *That's wrong and an abuse of power.*

I cross my arms. "Is this going to be a thing—you, showing up out of nowhere? Nowhere for me to hide in all of Silicon Avenue to avoid the Bass family's tyranny?"

A grin dances across his lips. *Asshole.*

"We're not everywhere." He grips his chin. "But now that you say that. Yes, until you listen to what I have to say."

"Fine."

I wonder if he can spot the steam shooting from my ears as I keep my arms crossed, planting the soles of my feet to the ground. I'll hear him out. Listen to whatever nonsense he wants to spew at me about how I need his magical dick, only so I can be done with it and move on with my life and career.

He takes a considerable breath, the knuckles of his thumbs dancing around one another, and for the first time since meeting him, he lacks complete control. Is he... *nervous?* Whatever he has to say, he's working himself up over it.

Is it something bad?

Okay, Hannah. Don't get mad and storm off. Let him finish, so we can be completely done with each other.

He looks me dead in the eyes.

"We need to enter into a fake engagement."

EIGHT

DAMIEN

THAT DID *NOT* COME OUT RIGHT.

I've never done this before—how are you supposed to say that to someone? I sound like I've completely lost my mind.

Her chair bursts away from the table, her mouth open on a silent exasperation. She looks frozen, as if she's deciding between staying here with me—who says crazy shit like that —or to bolt and run.

My eyes travel downward, to the yellow sundress she's wearing, something so different from anything I've seen on her. It's no less distracting, with its cinched waist and floral design that brings out all her feminine features.

"Please, tell me I heard that wrong."

My collared shirt suddenly feels too tight at the neck. "Hannah, we can help each other."

She finally gets to her feet, grabbing her purse and rummaging through it, presumably for money to put on the table so she can ditch me.

Her laugh edges with anger. "I don't care about some awakening or your stupid money. You're bad news, and I don't want to hear your fake reason why we need to *pretend* to be together."

Annoyance pricks at my temple. She's not staying to hear my sugar-coated explanation. Fine. The same time she presses a twenty-dollar bill to the table, I slap down a piece of paper face up.

"It's not fake. See for yourself."

She slows, eyes focusing on it. When she grabs the paper, her shoulders instantly slump.

That's a curious reaction.

"You've seen that before, I take it?"

Harrison's crew works faster than I predicted, extracting sensitive information about a person. The paper is a list of her parents' debts, which is quickly approaching the two-million mark.

She sits back in her chair, wearing a defeated look as she nibbles on her bottom lip. "I heard they were having problems on the farm. But I didn't know repairing damaged land costed them *that* much. They're in deep... Too deep to come back from."

An unwelcome blend of sympathy and compassion resonates within me, one that urges me to give her a cushy job and wipe her parents' slates clean for nothing in return. Anything to erase that pitiful look on her face.

Quit it. This has to be black and white. Don't get attached.

I force myself to focus on the spark of satisfaction burning a bright fire in my gut. I want her to need me, to give herself up to me fully.

Her eyes flicker. "They don't find that kind of information during a background check."

"It doesn't matter how I got it. All that matters is it's true, and if we help each other, both our problems go away."

"Both?" She purses her lips, an annoyed look on her face. "If you're trying to buy my *apparently two-million-dollar* pussy, just say so. You don't need to come up with another reason."

We lock eyes. "If that's what it would take to have more nights with you, I'd write a check in full right now."

Her lips part, and she suddenly can't make eye contact with me. *God,* I love the way I get underneath her skin so easily. I'm tempted to push her further, to see her squirm in that chair of hers, but I stop myself.

"But don't worry, I have a legit use for you. My company is looking to expand in the tech industry, to buy out another company. My board advised me it would be best if I appear to be settling down. We have our eyes set on several promising companies, all of whom are looking for buyers in two months."

"Right, right." She messes with her hair. Our eyes lock once more, hers with a brewing challenge. "Like those companies wouldn't simply choose the highest bidder. Why would your image matter?" An eagerness she can't hide laces her voice, one I yearn to satisfy.

My father's lessons strike red-hot, once again.

"Because image is all that matters in business, my little protégée."

With a straightening posture, her pupils visibly dilate. Whether it's from my lesson or her newfound nickname, I don't care. I love the way she responds to me, and if I need to teach her a hundred more lessons to see more, I will.

I continue, "The companies who are selling need to know whoever they're passing their company onto won't let it crash and burn. Even though they'll no longer be the owners, they often still have smaller shares in the company. Shares they hope to receive dividends from."

She soaks in every word, nodding to herself. "So, you think if you are engaged, it'll make you look more focused?"

"Exactly."

"And if I do this, you'll pay off my parents' debts?"

"Yes, in full. If you agree, you'll be my personal assistant for at least two months, until the buyout finishes. So, along the way, I hope to give you a good opportunity to learn from me."

Her eyes narrow. "I'm going to need that in writing."

A surprising flicker of pride prods at me. "Of course, Miss Lockwood. We'll write up our own conditions and discuss them over a meeting tomorrow. How does that sound?"

Her nod is the only confirmation I need.

Come tomorrow, she'll belong to me.

I PAY THE TAB, leaving an adequate tip before we pass through the patio gate.

"Here." She offers me the white to-go box. "You paid, so you get the leftovers."

"I'm good, thanks."

She puts her hand on her hip in the most interesting way, like we're going to spar out here on the street over some measly scraps.

"I should've known. You don't think pineapple belongs on pizza?"

"No. I just don't like pizza."

She flinches, proceeding to stare at me like I told her the sky is red or the moon is made of Styrofoam. "Excuse me?"

"I don't like pizza."

"Who doesn't like pizza?" She whisks her freehand

through the air. "I don't know what's a bigger red flag—you proposing a fake engagement plan for us or not liking pizza."

"Goodbye, Hannah." I turn and walk in the opposite direction, wearing a smirk that she can't see.

Her bristled reaction sounds in the distance, and the most peculiar, warm feeling pools in the hollow of my chest.

NINE

HANNAH

WHEN DAMIEN TOLD me the conference room would be next to legal, I didn't realize legal made up an *entire floor*.

I meander across the tile flooring, passing by sophisticated men and women dressed in pantsuits, each radiating confidence and knowing exactly where they're going. Unlike me, who's checking each door marked with a number, trying to figure out which direction I'm supposed to go.

Room 2090, Private Accord Chamber A.

Bingo.

The glossy doorknob stares me down as I brush off my dress and nibble the inside of my cheek. I'm about to enter an unknown domain, where I suspect to be a minnow up against an experienced shark.

I wrote my conditions and sent them to Damien last night, but I don't know if they're final or need to be negotiated. He seems to hold all the power and expertise, so I dressed for compensation.

Pink pumps and a small, sophisticated black dress with a modest neckline. Sofia didn't pick it out for me this time, because then I'd have to tell her the insane arrangement I'm about to agree to.

Jitters spark through me when I press down on the handle.

The first thing I notice are the six sets of eyes darting to me. One is Damien's forest green, and the rest are on the heads of sharp-looking suits. All of them men, except one impeccably dressed woman.

"Glad you could make it, Miss Lockwood." Damien's voice is a smooth purr from the head of the long table.

With dim lighting, the room has a warm and intimate color palette. Where an impressive view of New York city should be, sandy blackout curtains stand tall. The only seat available is the head opposing Damien, so I motion over and sit.

"Of course," I reply.

Damien nods to the woman sitting adjacent to him, prompting her to stand, her dark curly hair bouncing as she walks to me. She switches seats with another, to sit directly to my right.

"I'm Tiana. It's a pleasure to meet you." She outstretches her hand, which I accept. She's surprisingly young compared to the other suits here, with knowing, alert eyes. "I'm the head of the in-house legal division here at Innovex, and our team of lawyers have been assigned to this agreement."

Heat threatens to shine on my skin. I didn't expect so many people to be here. I thought it would be Damien and maybe one other lawyer, not an army of them. But it's not surprising. Lawyers must surround a person with his kind of power, like ants to sugar.

Her voice softens, as if she reads my mind. "Damien has personally assigned me to guide you in this matter, meaning it's my fiduciary duty by law to aid you whenever you need help." She smiles at me. "In short, I'm on your side."

I can't help but return the smile. "I understand."

"Good." She slides a stapled pack of paper towards me, trailed by a black-ink pen. "We wrote up both of your conditions."

It dawns on me that the people in the room really know *everything*. The fake engagement. My family's debt... My face must *really* flush now. Some of the things I sent Damien—I didn't know there'd be other eyes on them.

If she thinks it's odd, she doesn't show it. Her words flow confidently. "We will leave you two to discuss your conditions. Make agreed-upon amendments or add clauses. When you're complete and both parties believe its state to be satisfactory, sign the bottom. Does that sound good to you, Miss Lockwood?"

I nod, stealing a glance at Damien. His shoulders are relaxed with his fingers interlaced neatly on the table. He stares at me with an unreadable expression.

"We'll be off, then." In unison, the other lawyers stand. "Let me know if you need any clarifications or assistance." She nods to me before following them and closing the door on their way out.

Then it's deathly quiet, and I'm afraid he can hear my erratic breathing. Inspecting the front page of the packet, through the dim lighting, I read the font printed in jet-black ink.

CONDITIONS OF CONSIDERATION BETWEEN DAMIEN BASS "THE PROMISOR" AND HANNAH LOCKWOOD "THE PROMISEE"

My eyes race down the page.

"Remember, at any time during this process, you may call Tiana for help." Damien's features glow when I glance up at him. Three chairs on either side separate us, but it might as well be fifty. He feels miles away.

"How do I know she's on my side? They were all here with you when I arrived."

"They were advising me to give anyone who was with you your first day here an NDA form to sign." His eyes bore into mine. "I assigned you Tiana because she's Innovex's top lawyer. But if you prefer, we can postpone this meeting, and I'll have any lawyer of your choosing flown out on a jet tonight."

My heart beats faster. I don't know if I can last through the whole negotiation, not with the way he's looking at me. I shift in my chair before he cocks his head at me.

"You like that, don't you? Possessing the ability to have anyone you want at your disposal."

"It must be nice to have enough money to snap your fingers and solve any problem."

A smug smile blooms across his face. He flips to the next page and presses the crease down. "Let's see your conditions, Hannah."

"Haven't you already read them?"

"No. That would give me an unfair advantage. We will learn each other's demands for the first time together."

I nod and flip my page, forcing myself to sit tall and square my shoulders. "I think it best we go down one by one. You read a condition of mine, we'll discuss it and come to an agreement, then I'll read yours."

I find it shocking he wouldn't seize the opportunity to read my conditions earlier than I could read his. It would give him an edge, more time to think of solid disputes and get his way.

He could be lying.

I swallow, my saliva thick in my throat.

Or he doesn't need the extra time.

My gut drops right as Damien clears his throat. "Condition one. The promisor will pay its dues in full immediately after the buyout deal finishes." He nods. "Agreed."

"A necessary precaution." My index finger scans down the document, stopping at his first condition, which I read aloud.

PROMISOR CONDITION 1: THE PROMISOR AND PROMISEE MUST BE SEEN IN PUBLIC (OUTSIDE OF WORK) TOGETHER ON A REGULAR BASIS.

I raise my head, and Damien's voice fills the room. "The public must believe this relationship to be real. Preferably, we'll end up in a tabloid or on some gossip site."

"Do you really think that'll happen?"

"Yes."

I bristle at his confidence. Sterling rarely took me out, let alone allowed people to take our picture. I lower my head to read further. The condition has a clause.

MUST APPEAR INTIMATE. INTIMACY INCLUDES BUT IS NOT LIMITED TO GAZING, KISSING, TOUCHING AND FONDLING.

My eyes widen, before I quickly conceal my reaction. I lift my head to find Damien studying me intently. "Any questions?"

"U-um. Because we'll be in public..." *Don't ask.* He doesn't break his gaze, and the room's temperature seems to climb. *But I need to know.* "It says fondling and touching, d-does that really mean—"

"Yes. It does. I'm sure a smart girl like you knows I mean

what I say. But I'll clarify for you, Hannah." My name on his tongue causes intense sensations to skate across my body. *Big mistake.* "It means in public, your body is *mine*. Mine to show off, mine to touch, mine to own. I'll make it weep for me, then everyone will know exactly who you belong to."

A rhythmic throb starts between my thighs, beating faster as I wet my lips and stare at him. I say nothing, because if I do, then he'll know exactly how much his words affect me, the way they coerce images of our night together into my head.

"Do you have an issue with that?"

I can't contend with him. I can't hear any more of his words, not with his eyes holding my willpower hostage.

"No." My voice comes out in a whisper.

"I couldn't quite catch that. Speak up."

"No." I hold his stare, knowing I'm sentencing myself to torture with a single word.

"Such a good girl," he praises.

God. I push my thighs together in a feeble attempt to douse the fire already raging beneath the table. His words are molten honey, and I'm losing control fast.

Like some glorious lifeline, the door swings open, allowing bright light to trickle in. A woman in a classy dress sets a tray of refreshments down on the table. My eyes never stray from Damien's. Not once, as she pours water out from the pitcher, then hands him a glass.

The crisp clacking of her heels ricochets off the walls as she approaches me in our silence. I can't form the words to thank her when she gives me mine. I merely snatch the water, letting the ice-cold liquid race down my throat. The door snatches shut at the same time I set it down, half its contents gone.

I breathe deep, and a calmness washes over me.

Damien smirks. "Condition two," he reads. "The promisor must provide the promisee with tasks that provide business education. This does not include washing dishes, ironing clothes, picking up dry cleaning..." His brow scrunches to form a tight line, and his voice turns skeptical as he reads the lengthy list. *"... general cleaning duties or similar activities?"*

He looks up at me. "Of course. This seems unnecessary. I'd never ask you to do anything like that."

"I've heard that before."

His jaw ticks, and he proceeds to the subclause. "The promisor will provide the promisee with a letter of recommendation after the two parties have split ways."

He doesn't add a comment, so I sit straight. "I need it to be taken seriously afterwards. Future employers on Silicon Avenue can't assume hiring me would damage their relationship with Innovex."

"It will sparkle then, Miss Lockwood." He smiles.

I nearly giggle, bubbles of amusement dancing in my stomach. The feeling oozes away when I glance at Damien's next condition.

"The promisee will not get intoxicated beyond her limit." I purse my lips, crossing my arms. "I'm not an alcoholic or some club rat, for the record."

"I recall meeting at Enigma. A club. *On a Sunday.*"

Raising my eyebrows, I fuel my verbal arsenal. "For your information—" I stop, catching the blatant amusement marking his features. *"Fine.* No going out or getting drunk."

"Excellent."

I tap my feet in annoyance, but they slow once I realize he's reached my final condition.

"The promisor and promisee will not engage in sexual activity." His lips thin, giving me a flatlined look.

"An explanation isn't needed," I add quickly.

"I require one."

I shimmy in my chair. "You're my soon-to-be boss. You're my *ex's brother.* And..." I trail my fingernails through my hair, determined to come up with a third. "I looked you up—you're old."

The words fly past my lips before I can stop them. *That's a low blow, Hannah.*

"I'm thirty-three." He scowls.

"Case in point. I'm twenty-three. You have a decade on me." I bite my lip, pushing my case. "You could take advantage of me."

His low chuckle bounces off my skin, leaving it hot. "There are many reasons I could take advantage of you, Miss Lockwood, but my age should be the least of your concerns. So, I'll uphold your condition, but I'll add a clause."

"A clause?"

His eyes lock onto mine, and I grip my pen too tightly. *How could he add a clause to no sex?*

"We won't have sex, Hannah. Not unless you *beg.*"

A shiver splinters across the back of my neck. "I would never—"

"You will," he challenges, the confidence in his voice unmistakable. "But if that's true, then there should be no problem adding in the clause. Hmm?"

"You can add it, but you'll be left disappointed, Mr. Bass." I collect myself, squaring my shoulders. "This will be a professional arrangement."

"You must understand. This clause isn't for me. It's for you." His expression lights a fire in my gut.

Arrogant ass.

"Whatever. I'll keep a distance between us, anyway." I glance down to move on, but what I see causes my brain to hit a snag.

His final condition.

THE PROMISEE WILL LIVE IN PERMANENT RESI-DENCE WITH THE PROMISOR UNTIL THE ARRANGE-MENT COMMENCES. A SINGLE BED WILL BE SHARED BETWEEN THEM.

My jaw swoops down, nearly touching the table.

"What was that about *distance?*"

"You can't do that." I can't come up with a solid argument, let alone breathe. I *cannot* share a bed with Damien Bass. That's... unthinkable. A death sentence.

A sweet, delicious death sentence. My mind wanders, somewhere between the realms of silk sheets and steel, washboard abs.

Stop that.

"I'm sorry to say my final condition is non-negotiable." His face is smug. "I can't have my housing staff thinking our relationship is anything but genuine. Gossip regarding my family spreads quickly, and secrets are worth more than gold in my industry."

Oh, god. I believe him. He's making sense, and I'm doomed. "I never lived with Sterling when I was his personal assistant." *Or saw his apartment,* I neglect to add. The embarrassment is too much to handle.

His jaw clenches, the brightness of his pupils dying out. "That's another thing. Never say my brother's name."

"Ya, ya." I flick my wrist in the air. "I know it's off the contract, but I understand. Our relationship wasn't public. So, around other people, I'll never mention us having been together."

"No. You don't understand." He leans in, his voice turning to gravel as he strains to hold back his temper. "I don't want to hear his name fall from your lips *ever again.*"

TEN

DAMIEN

TONIGHT'S the worst night of every month.

My car creeps by the pristinely shaved hedges and rose bushes that line the perimeter of my family's estate. Rounding a central water feature, I parallel park my McLaren between a shimmering Rolls-Royce and an Aston Martin.

It appears most guests have arrived already for our family's monthly dinner. But I don't spot my brother's sports car.

He's late, as always.

Stepping out, I stare up at the building. I know those excluded from the highest echelons of society would be in awe of such a work of architecture, with its cobbled walls and tall pillars. But all I see are harrowing reminders of a past I shove deep inside myself.

Taking a deep breath, I ascend the long row of steps, passing through the front door.

Instantly, I recognize the foyer is different as I shrug off my long coat, studying the space. What was once gold with green accents, is now black-and-white checkered tiles and crystal chandeliers. When I dispose of my coat in a nearby closet, I hear my mother's call.

"Damien." She saunters across the long corridor, her modest silver dress swaying.

I smile, motioning around the room. "You've really outdone yourself this time." She hugs me, her frail arms wrapping around my middle.

"Nonsense," she says, her subtle French accent peeking through as she gives me a familiar look. Cheery, with a promise of light that doesn't quite reach her eyes. "Wait until you see the new ballroom. I flew in a crew from Italy to paint the ceiling murals."

My mother is constantly adding to the house, or remodeling portions merely two years old. There's nothing her creative eye hasn't changed since I was young, and the estate is twenty-five thousand square feet.

It keeps her busy. She needs that.

We all need that.

"Did you now?" She takes my arm, and I guide her through the hallway, sounds of distant chatter growing louder.

I may be a grown man now with a successful company, but I still can't quiet the hammering in my chest. The anticipation of seeing the face that still haunts my dreams is hard to bear every month, each day an agonizing countdown to our next encounter. I wish I could skip these gatherings altogether. But I don't, for my mother.

We leave the foyer, turning towards the dining room. Our estate has three dining halls, one of which is only used for intimate family gatherings like today. I spot its double French doors, held open by two doormen who dress in black tuxes. There's no doubt my mother assigned them there. She prefers the house to be crowded, with assistants or guests bustling around.

The dining table dominates the space, with familiar faces seated around its marble top, conversing and helping themselves to appetizers. I chauffeur us inside, the smell of smoked salmon caviar and cologne piquing my senses.

"Damien." A firm hand pats my shoulder before I'm met with wild red hair and emerald eyes.

Felix. I grin at him. I haven't seen him in almost a year, since he took off traveling in Europe.

My cousin never fails to have the most eccentric fashion. While the rest of the men in the room wear black and rustic gray, Felix boasts a silk green polo with plaid slacks, somehow blending in with the extravagant taste of the estate.

It's no wonder my mother and he have always seen eye-to-eye.

He takes a drag of his champagne glass, his eyes traveling down the length of my mother's silver gown. "Stunning as always, Camille."

"Oh, stop. You always know how to charm a lady." The subtle wrinkles around her eyes lift, a genuine glow lighting up her face that causes a warmth to well up inside me.

Unclasping from my arm, she surveys the room. "Help yourself to a beverage, Damien. Additional appetizers should be on their way. I'll go check on the first course." She whisks away. The bottom of her dress grazes the floor, the doormen at attention as she passes.

"I've been away too long." Felix's eyebrows raise. "I forgot your mom really *is* superwoman."

"I know." I snag a glass from a server holding a stacked tray of assorted mixed drinks. "Bring Bourbon next, please."

Purple and bubbly, the flute with a cherry sunken

comfortably at the bottom isn't really my drink of choice, but I'll take anything for tonight.

"So..." I take a gulp of the champagne concoction, finding it perfectly chilled when it hits my tongue. "How'd they take it?"

My eyes dart across the room, noting which guests mingle with each other. The majority are relatives, aside from the two aged gentlemen talking with my father near a large French window. Scotches in hand, their lips sputter in a drowned-out discussion I can't hear.

Revealing his full head of gray hair, I recognize my father's back as it faces me. And my gut drops all the same.

"Take what? *Oh.*" Felix lowers his voice. "You heard. Who am I kidding? The moment ByteBuzz makes you their headliner, I'm sure everyone knows your business... About how you'd expect. My father says I'm distracted from my future, and my mom thinks it's *just another traveling phase.*"

He breaks our stare, the emotions thick on his tongue. "I knew they wouldn't approve. I expected them to shout or cry or threaten to pull my trust fund—show *any* kind of emotion. But somehow, this is so much worse."

Felix has been on the cover of several gossip magazines as of late, hands intertwined with a young man, presumed to be a famous Greek model or influencer of a name I can't remember. Not that I keep up on that kind of stuff like my mother, but even *I* can't escape the reach of ByteBuzz.

The popular tech gossip blog has mentioned me several times, spouting rumors of me dating certain actresses or threatening to buy out particular companies. Their identity has remained a secret, and whether it's some syndicate or a single person acting alone is unknown. Either way, it's no doubt they have an influential sway of the public's opinion of companies and key players on Silicon Avenue.

My mother showed me Felix's headline last month. *Felix Astor, heir to Silicon Avenue's top security company, caught romancing Greek mystery man.*

The Astors are my in-laws. My aunt on my father's side married Nicholas Astor, both of whom have said short of *nothing* to anyone about their eldest son being involved with a man. Maybe they could start with the fact that he looks happier than ever in each picture the paparazzi releases. But no. Silence is their way of handling it.

Needless to say, Felix has my mother's unwavering support and mine—not that it does him any good, though.

"That's awful," I grunt, feeling my sympathy stretch out to him like a physical touch. "Maybe this is their weird way of processing... They'll come around."

But I know it's a lie the moment it leaves my lips, and he knows it too. Not because he understands me so well, having grown up side by side our whole lives. But because the people in our world, with pockets so deep they themselves don't know their depths, stay stuck in their self-assured ways, forever resistant to change.

We're all guilty of it.

Even myself.

"Right." His lips form a tight line, uttering impossibly quiet words. "Mommy and Daddy Astor will approve of my gay lover right around the same time Oscar Bass stops being an abusive tyrant."

No one is near us, but I can't stop the way my eyes cautiously sweep across the room. My father has no power over me anymore, but that doesn't mean my mother isn't at his will.

Felix is right. He'll never change, and I accepted that fact a long time ago.

"What about you?" He speaks up with impeccable timing, the server returning with my Bourbon as I swap out drinks. Felix gives me a devilish grin. "I heard you've been named New York's most eligible bachelor. Ladies must be flinging themselves on you like rabid animals for a chance at the Bass name."

My thoughts instantly draw to Hannah, and I'm overtaken by a smirking hunger. But I bat it down before he can read the obvious lust clouding my eyes.

"Not exa—"

"We know who the *real* bachelor of the Bass family is." Sterling's voice rakes up my back. "Don't we, brother?"

He steps beside me, with a tall and slim brunette I've never seen holding his arm. Her perfume is harsh and violates my nostrils, making my drink taste sour.

When I meet Sterling's eyes, they couldn't possibly shoot more hatred. A white bandage wraps around his temple, but I don't hide my stare.

"Always the last to arrive, aren't you?" I ignore his pathetic jab, my lips curling. "Some of us have actual obligations to attend to, and we still show up on time."

His date's giggles ring in my ears. To her, it must appear like ordinary, combative brotherly love, not the sincerely complicated mess that it is.

Sterling leans into her, mimicking her amusement with a smile. "Grab us some drinks, babe." She beams at him, and the instant she disappears, his façade fades into disdain.

"Such a bachelor, you are," Felix scoffs. "Not even introducing your date. Damien needs to give you some pointers."

His eyes darken, further highlighting the miserable state

he's in. "And what could he possibly help me with? Damien prefers my *leftovers.*"

A glaring silence spreads between the three of us, and a fire flickers deep inside me. The room itself seems to quiet for a moment, and it's short of a miracle my feet stay where they are with the blood pounding in my ears.

"What happened to your face, Sterling?" I ask beneath the chatter of the room.

My cousin's wary eyes flick to mine, but I hold Sterling's stare that drifts down to my drink. The same drink I used to smash glass against his skull. Fear splinters across his features before the calm, uninterested mask he loves to wear replaces it.

His blue eyes narrow. "Whatever little moment you and Hannah had at the club, that's all it was. She'll come back to me like she always does."

He's so fucking slimy. My jaw clenches so hard my teeth threaten to shatter.

"I'll let you in on a secret." He shoves his hand into his pants pocket, resting on the backs of his heels. "I know her—*the real her.* She may act all innocent, but she loves to play cat-and-mouse. So, if she messes around with you, it's only to get my attention."

A sliver of doubt creeps up my shoulders, but it's quickly overshadowed by simmering annoyance. He's so confident I'll keep my temper in check, here surrounded by family.

"As if you were serious enough to know her." I tilt back my drink, hoping the cool liquid dampens my mood. I glance at Felix, who shoots daggers at Sterling, eating up the conversation. "You never brought her here. And you bring a new girl each month."

"Please," Sterling scoffs. "She doesn't belong in our world,

couldn't survive it. She told me she was born in a *trailer park."*
He nudges Felix, a laugh blooming on his lips. "Come on.
There's only one thing you'd want from her."

Hot rage pumps through my veins. Rage that's untamed.
Palpable. And... *unexplainable?* Because that *is* all I want from
her, all my common sense *should* want from her.

Then why am I getting so worked up?

Thoughts barrage my conflicted conscience. I could pick
another girl, *any girl*, for a fake engagement. Hell, my name
alone could land me ten fiancées. But I'm selfishly choosing
her, knowing in doing so, I'll make her mine and ruin her for
all others.

Before I comprehend my movements, I'm inches from
Sterling's face. His smile is still smug, assured I won't take
this any further. I move another inch, and his tilted lips fall.

"Boys, boys." My mom's light tone douses water on my
anger. "Not an opportune time to make a scene." She hooks
her arm around Sterling, sweeping him away as she offers me
a smile.

"Jesus." Felix's eyebrows upturn. "He can't possibly
remind me enough of how I *really* lucked out with my
sibling."

"Yep."

I overhear my mother's cheery tone inform the room that
the first course is to be served.

"Anyhow, let's smoke later." He pats me on the chest. "You
can puff on one of those cigars you're obsessed with, and I'll
opt for something... actually enjoyable."

I chuckle as he departs, aiming for a seat next to his
younger sister. Her fiery hair matches his, and she flashes him
a smile.

As my gaze roves across the room, I watch as patrons take

their seats. I always sit by my mother, so I wait for her to choose hers.

My father's group breaks, a sea of gray hair and cocky grins departing from the window.

We lock eyes, and I hate the way my stomach churns. But I keep a hardened exterior, one I've learned to fall back on when I'm near him. I coolly break our connection, not because I want to seem unfazed. But because I truly can't hold it for long.

I've never been able to.

Not without scarred memories invading my mind.

ELEVEN

DAMIEN

IT'S AMAZING, really, how it takes a single man to ruin a family, leaving the rest obsessive, irreparable fragments of their former selves. My mother and brother bury their heads in their own unique addictions, while I strive for a revenge fantasy that might leave me more broken than before.

I can never dethrone my father. I abandoned that notion years ago. His portfolio is too strong and too expansive in the tech industry. But Bass Mobile is his crown jewel, the highest grossing asset he has, and I have them in my back pocket.

During the growth of my business, it was essential that they were my client. It sickened me to admit it, but I needed Oscar for the revenue, and he needed me for microchips no other company could outperform. They still can't, and now I no longer need him. Companies around the world line up to be in business with me, and Oscar knows it.

He knows his time using Innovex's technology is ticking, and there's nothing he can bribe me with before I cut him off completely.

I plan to do it. *Soon.*

I stumble down the hallway, grabbing at a stone column for stability. Moonlight streams into my eyes through nearby windows.

The guests left a time ago. And although every so often I pass house servants, they pay me no mind. I'm not about to get behind the wheel in my drunken state. So, I continue to pace the halls, not wanting to see a familiar face.

I turn left at a marble centerpiece with no destination in sight. It's not the first time in my life I've been thankful for the vastness of the house.

It makes it easier to hide.

I don't know when the constant renovations started with my mother, or the playboy lifestyle of my brother. But both are on destructive courses, whether they'll admit it or not.

Sterling's an idiot. A swirl of envy churns inside me. *A complete fool. He's not the one dad fucked up. He's not the one lucky enough to receive dad's lessons.*

All he has to do is stay out of trouble, but instead he wastes away his excuse of a life using women who don't deserve his treatment and being a sharp thorn in my ass. It couldn't be simpler for him to live a healthy life, with kids and a loving wife and whatever else unscarred *normal* people do.

So why doesn't he grow the fuck up and do it already?

I stop before a cherry-oak door that clashes with the surrounding decor. I don't need to enter to know it leads to the only portion of the house left untouched.

I haven't opened it in over a decade.

Staring at the silver knob, my blurry vision splits in two, and I sway before I grasp it. Coldness seeps into my palm, sweat prickling the back of my neck. I force myself to hold it.

But before I can muster the courage to turn it, I scurry away, my breaths coming out in struggling, uneven heaves.

Continuing my wandering, I think of my mother.

Camille Bass.

Her light died out long ago and molded into something fake and unrecognizable. Perhaps everyone but me believes her façade. As if she couldn't be anything other than the ex-world-renowned ballerina from France turned hostess with perfect style, smiles and class.

If putting up a front is her way of coping, then power is mine.

My colleagues and competitors openly refer to me as ruth-less and heartless, and I bask under their words. It's praise to my ears, really. Because with it, it's the only time I feel like the time lost in obsession and expansion is worth it.

As if there's some foreseeable future where I'll expand my empire *even more* and feel fulfillment. Because I can't accept the real truth—how is someone to fix themself when they have all the money in the world and are *still* ruined?

Maybe we'll never change. We'll go about our lives talking and smiling. But really, we're stuck here in this very house.

I pick up my pace, a destination in mind, one I should avoid but can't escape. For years, I've thought of the room, of the beauty and the horrors that occurred within it.

As I approach the oak door, the knob glares at me once more. I don't think. I only rip it open.

There.

I stop, stuck frozen in the doorway. Across a long corridor lined with windows lies the object of my dreams—and my nightmares.

A white grand piano.

My heart shoots to my throat, pounding so violently it's hard to breathe. I will my body into motion, taking a step on the marble flooring. And another. My legs scream at me to turn back, but I can't. Not with the voices streaming into my head.

The voice of my instructor.

The boy's a prodigy. The best I've seen of his age.

A gift to the artist world, like his mother.

The voice of my mother.

Heaven sent me my own personal angel. Of course, he'd be talented.

But, Oscar, the instructor says it's helping with his condition.

I step faster, harder, until I'm barreling down the corridor, windows and statues soaring by the corners of my strained vision.

And the voice of my father.

You said that the old man was only here to teach him French, not piano too.

Stupid woman, what use is that?

No Bass boy of mine will touch those keys, or any instrument, for that matter. Especially not one with a stutter.

I'll make sure of it.

My adrenaline kicks in, and I pump my arms to drown out the memory burning its way through my consciousness. But it only proves futile.

"Please, Damieennnn." The shrill whine slices through the silence in my room. "Play for me. One more time, please. Then I won't ask ever again, I swear."

I roll over on my side. My cousin sits criss cross on the opposite twin bed, my night light casting shadows on his soft features. He's not sleeping like we're supposed to be. Mom said even though he's sleeping over, I still have a bedtime.

I sit up to get a better look at him, my comforter sliding down my chest. Red pajamas that match his red locks hug his small frame. And in the darkness, I can make out his impeccable pouty face.

"D-dad said I c-can't play anymore."

"Why not?" His eyes go wide.

I flop back down, my face to the ceiling as I heave a sigh. "H-he s-s-sa—" Frustration burns my cheeks. I take three deep breaths, like my piano instructor taught me, concentrating on the words. "He thinks it's a waste of time."

"That's not true!" The box spring squeaks, before his chubby cheeks fly an inch from my nose. "You play the most beautiful sounds in the whole world! How could that be a waste of time?"

"Y-you really think s-so?"

"Really."

I nibble on my lower lip. "I-I don't know..."

"Oh, please." He tugs on my pajama sleeve, his eyes shutting. "Please, please, please, please—"

"Okay!" I push off the corner of my bed, the coldness of the hardwood floor seeping through the bottoms of my feet. "But we have to be q-quiet."

His pupils line with white and eyebrows shoot to his hairline.

"P-promise?"

"Promise." His head bobbles up and down violently. "I promise."

Our feet scurry across the room. Creaking open the door, I pop my head out, surveying the hallway as I listen for any noises. Everyone in the house should be asleep, but I don't want to risk waking someone, especially not my nanny, whose room is next to mine.

I take the lead, tiptoeing down the hall. After scouting the next corridor, I wave Felix along. We hurry through the kitchen, the tops of our heads as tall as the countertops. Next is the ballroom, then a flight of stairs before we arrive at a tight hallway lined with windows.

Felix and I grin at each other.

Confident the coast is clear, we race down the hall until we're standing in the middle of a tall, cylindrical room with a vaulted ceiling. A staircase winds up its walls and disappears into another wing of the house.

Felix nudges me, his voice a whisper. "Go!"

I step onto the round platform the piano stands on and pull out the stool to sit. Stretching out my arms, I readjust the distance between the stool and the keys. Once satisfied, I peer over my shoulder.

Felix sits criss cross on the floor, his back straight and mouth parted on a silent word.

"I-I'm going to p-play softly." My voice seems to come out louder than intended, the sound echoing in the barren room.

I cringe. Maybe this is a bad idea... But we're already here. And everyone's asleep.

Staring at the large instrument, a bubbly lightness surges excitement and anticipation through my body, all the way to my toes.

I glide my hands across the keys like I always do before I play, not making a sound. I've always loved their smoothness and the sheer number of them.

Taking a calming breath, I press the A-minor key as lightly as I can, testing the sound. When I let up, I listen intently. No echo. I smile, moving into an F-sharp, then following with a combination.

I don't have music sheets with me. Dad took them all away, including my instructor. But I don't mind having no notes to guide me. I prefer the freedom.

My eyelids fall like stone, and my hands move candidly across the keys, darting left and then right. Humming along to its sound, I stretch down to the lower notes, sliding across the stool to compensate for my short arms. My touch hops between the keys, producing a flurry of staccato melodies.

I don't know how long it's been. Time seems to stretch with a sigh and stop completely when I play, but I slow once my fingers tire.

They knot into a complicated combination as I scoot to the edge of my chair, my tippy toes weighing down on the rightmost pedal. The note elongates with pride until it dies out on a gentle breath.

"Wow!"

I whip my head back, and Felix's hands shoot to his mouth. "Wow," he repeats quietly.

Our eyes lock, his wide saucers and mine confident slits. When I let my grin surface, he combusts in a fit of giggles, scrambling towards me.

"Did you really like it?"

Shock radiates through me. No stutter.

He sits on the stool beside me, nodding his head. "Play another, play another."

"Yes." A dark rumble sounds above our heads. "Play another."

Dad.

Felix's quiet gasp sounds in my ear, and it's as if razor blades scrape up my middle. I crane my neck to see him descending the steps. The sounds of his footfalls are achingly slow, counting down the seconds to my damnation.

"I said play." Metal scrapes on metal as he drags his hand on the railing.

My eyes burn, unable to catch my breath. I turn to Felix. "G-g-g-o now."

He hesitates, but I nudge him harshly. Tears well up in his eyes before he takes off in a dash, retracing our steps from which we came.

With wobbling hands, I force myself to press the keys. The sounds they make don't spark a beautiful fire inside me like they always do. They don't echo off the walls and manipulate time the way they should.

They sound wrong.

When his steps halt, I feel his presence behind me, as a hawk would circle its prey.

"I said there'd be consequences, boy."

"I-I'm s-s-sorry." A hot tear races down my cheek, and I blink in rapid motions. *"F-Felix—"*

"Your mother will be so disappointed." He tsks. *"She knew you couldn't handle this. It's already got you bending the rules."*

Lies, lies, lies, lies. *The next note comes out harsh. She would never want me to stop practicing music.* You're a liar! *I want to scream at him.*

He steps into my view. "She doesn't run this household. I do."

Rage bends my fingers to its will, contorting them into tiny fists that I wish were strong enough to send right through his lying teeth. "F-Felix—"

"I SAID PLAY." *Icy threads of hair shoot across his forehead above feral blue eyes.*

What feels like my soul leaving my body compels me into action, slamming my fingers on the keys right as the butt of his belt smashes against my knuckles.

With a broken screech, I tuck my hands into my chest. And I stare in horror. Scarlet dots litter the white keys, like the flick of a paint brush kept coated in blood.

"Again," he says calmly.

It's the first word in his string of commands that would prove very long to me. A first taste of what he called "teachings" for me that would not only extend over the piano, and not only on this night...

But years.

I lift my shaky hands back into position.

FOOTSTEPS ECHO BEHIND ME.

Staring at the piano with my back facing the corridor, I plant my feet. I don't turn around. I don't need to. The sounds of his stride tell me it's him.

I remind myself I'm not a boy anymore, but it does little to calm the angry concoction of nerves simmering inside me.

The steps halt.

"I had a feeling I'd find you here." An unwelcome shiver trails down my spine. The softness in his voice is unsettling.

Raising my head, I make out his distorted figure in the reflection of a window, the chandelier illuminating his form. He's clad in a full suit, shoving his hand in his pants pocket.

He's come to grovel.

His speech tonight at dinner about family unity and fatherly pride told me so. The following applause still rings in my ear.

He knows Bass Mobile is at my mercy.

I stare down at the keys, the glossy ivories inches from my fingers. But I can't bring myself to touch them. I can't bear the sounds they'd make. I haven't touched this piano—or any piano—since that night.

"You never speak to me during these gatherings, so I don't expect you to start now. But I need you to listen—"

"Why didn't you take it away?" I turn around, facing his aged figure. "The idea didn't occur to me until I got older. If you didn't want me to play, why not make the piano disappear?"

He steps onto the platform, eating up the distance between us. Even on equal grounds, I have half a foot on him and at least fifty pounds.

He's so... frail.

"Always the victim, Damien." *There he is.* Like the flip of a switch, his posture changes and an assured coldness replaces his light tone. "I knew your potential, your *real* potential. You were destined for this industry. I won't apologize for creating you, the king of Silicon Avenue."

A fragmented part of my heart lifts to the praise. A part of me that will always crave a father who is proud of me.

King.

He's the king. Or was. Now it's my name written on the headlines of news articles and the titles of tech radio shows. And it's my company whose stock they value highest in all the tech world. So, it may be true that I'm the one on top now, surpassing even him. But for him to actually admit it...

He must be truly desperate.

Gratifying darkness clouds my heart, fueling power into my veins.

I cross my arms. "What do you want, Oscar?"

"I know you're working on a new line of chips."

"And? That's no secret. We're showcasing it at the Summit this year."

The Nano-X chip is leagues above our previous models, and is set to go to market by the end of this year. I don't know how much he knows. Oscar Bass has the uncanny habit of knowing things before anyone else in the tech world.

Slipping his hand into his suit jacket, he retrieves a tan folder and offers it to me.

I tighten my knotted arms, a smile I conceal tugging at my lips.

"If you only inclined yourself to read it, you'd—"

"I'd what? Add you back on my list for the new chip?" I chuckle darkly. "Tough luck. I've scraped all child-abusers from my clientele."

I burst past him, heading for the corridor.

"Damien, wait."

I whirl on my heels at the tone laced with desperation I've never heard from him. Such a beautiful song in my ears. "There's nothing you can say to change my mind."

I should make him beg. On his knees, preferably. Only to turn him down. It's not enough for him to admit defeat, for my company to surpass his in every way. I want him to witness the slow encroachment of his competitors with no way to stop them. I want him to reduce to *nothing*.

"This isn't about exclusion. It's about exclusivity. I want to be your new chip's *only* client—for a short time."

I nearly laugh. "You're crazier than I thought. Gone completely mad. You have nothing I want."

"Yes, I do."

He sounds so confident... I should walk away, but intrigue gets the best of me.

"And what's that?"

The folder in his hand trembles, and his eyes morph into heartless voids.

"Your brother's shares of Bass Mobile."

TWELVE
HANNAH

IF WORKING for Sterling is swimming in the shallow end of the pool, then being Damien Bass's personal assistant is getting thrown out to the mercy of the sea with no life jacket.

"Keep up, Miss Lockwood."

I'm going to drown.

Trailing his long steps, clipboard in hand, my heels dig into the thin carpet. I don't know what time it is, and I sure as hell don't know where we're going. He gave me access to his online schedule—which I'm apparently supposed to run now—but it's not much help.

This man is *in demand.* So much so, that I wonder if Sterling did any work at all. I barely saw the inside of Bass Mobile, but when I did, he was never in meetings, never on phone calls. In fact, his office was notoriously empty. I never thought it odd, but I do now.

Does he slow down? Eat? Take potty breaks? I huff a breath. *And does he really need to walk so fast?*

"Where to next?" I pump my legs harder, finally catching up to him at the rows of elevators.

This morning, when I got ready for the final time in our apartment before moving out, I opted for a low bun. But that doesn't seem to have worked how I wanted. I brush my frazzled bangs to the side.

"You should know the answer to that question." He looks down at me with not a hair out of place on his perfect head, amusement twinkling in his eyes. "Check the schedule. It should be easy."

I flip through my stack of papers. I thought I'd appear on top of things by printing out his schedule today, but I now realize my mistake.

How does one man's schedule change so frequently?

I stare at the chaotic ink.

Meetings crossed out. Appointments rescheduled. Phone calls cut into half the time so others can fit. Arrows going from here to there in a jumbled mess. My handwriting looks less like diligent notes and more like chicken scratch.

I didn't know someone's time could be so valuable.

We enter the elevator, and he chuckles.

I narrow my eyes at him. "You know, this wouldn't be so difficult if you didn't change who you're meeting with ten times, *Damien.*" My meltdown clips right as a group of employees round the door, cramming into the space with us.

Heat rushes to my cheeks. The thought of them overhearing me berate the owner of the company they work for is mortifying. The chatty one in their group sneaks a peek at Damien, halting her sentence midway.

When the metallic doors seal, the area grows silent.

"What did you say, Miss Lockwood?" The backs of those standing in front of us straighten. With a single question, he seems to suck all the oxygen from the space. "I didn't quite catch that."

My bottom lip falls on a protest. But when he lifts his eyebrows at me, I shut my mouth, lest I say something that will land me in even more trouble.

He wants me to apologize in front of them? He can't be serious.

He's so near I can feel the heat radiating off his body. The smell of his cologne plunges into my senses, threatening to weaken my knees.

I meet his unblinking gaze.

Oh, he's serious.

"I-I said..." Biting my lower lip, I shuffle in my heels. His green eyes dominate mine, demanding me to submit to him. "I need to be more prepared for your very busy schedule, *Mr. Bass.*"

"That's better." His voice sends heat straight below my waistline. "There are many things I've still yet to teach you."

I grit my teeth, trying to ignore the slow throb growing in between my thighs. He gives me a knowing look, a smirk lining his lips.

Why does he have to look like that?

A head taller than everyone in the elevator, he gives me an impeccable view of his muscled neck as he nonchalantly adjusts the cufflinks of his steel-blue suit.

God, help me.

The doors open and the other group darts out, murmuring amongst themselves. When the doors close and we're left alone, I add more distance between us, only to allow myself to breathe again.

I whip my head, but he beats me to the first word. "You said you wanted to learn, Hannah."

I roll my lips between my teeth, not responding. That *is* a major part of my terms of our agreement.

"Now, what's next on the agenda?" he presses.

Annoyance pricks at my temple, but it's quickly overshad-owed by the need to improve, to show him I'm qualified for this job.

I study my clipboard again.

Appointment with Mr. Rodgers swapped with supply chain management meeting, and the call with the aluminum vendor bumped to twelve-thirty. That would mean...

My head pops up. "Nano-X chip progress report."

"Excellent," he praises, and I feel it in my gut.

The elevator dings, lighting up the bottommost floor number. We're three levels below the lobby.

I didn't know it went underground.

The doors fly open, and I'm met with a room so drastically different from the others, I question whether we're still in the same building.

Brightness shines into my eyes, and I survey the white room with no windows and a single, heavy-duty door. Personal protective equipment lines the walls. Gloves, hard helmets, lab coats and glasses all dangle from hangers.

My forehead scrunches as Damien guides me inside. "I thought the chips were only designed here and manufactured in outside warehouses."

"They are." He grabs a pair of wide-brimmed glasses and comes right next to me. With a delicate finger, he guides a loose bang behind my ear, causing my heart to flutter. Time seems to slow, and I'm stuck staring into his smoldering gaze as he slides the glasses across my eyes. "But designing chips is a very hands-on process."

He breaks away, leaving my heart thumping loudly in my ribcage as he retrieves his own pair.

After slipping on blue latex gloves, he hits a panel on the wall and punches in a long digit code. The door zooms open, and a new world unlike the rest of the building reveals on the other side.

The room is enormous. Fans and pipes run along the ceiling that must be three stories high. Metal tables scatter the area with computer monitors and colorful wires lying everywhere. Scientists in white lab coats march around, carrying equipment and paying us no attention.

A man wearing a long lab coat approaches us, trailed by two younger men. Instead of a clipboard, he holds a smart tablet.

"Mr. Bass." He nods, causing the additional pair of reading glasses he wears to clink underneath his protective ones.

"This is my new personal assistant, Hannah Lockwood." Damien skips the small talk, motioning his hand between us. "Hannah, this is Ross, the head of our computer engineering department at Innovex."

Ross. I keep my face straight, batting down the grin wanting to surface. *That's who Sofia told me about at lunch. Her crush.*

I inspect him. He's short and thin, not at all Sofia's normal type. But as he stretches his hand to me, there's an unmistakable confidence about him.

"Miss Lockwood, it's a pleasure." I take his hand, quick with the formalities. "Right this way."

Stepping carefully on the concrete floor, I follow and scan the rows of metal tables and scientists clad in protective equipment. They discuss around whiteboards and sit in chairs with arched backs, consumed by their work.

We reach the final row and see a group huddling around a single chair.

"Our most recent chip mockup is being soldered as we speak." Ross shoos the gawkers, to reveal a woman with dark hair flowing from a high ponytail. Her lab coat kisses the floor, right next to her pink heels. "The changes you requested will soon be in place."

Pride wells up in my chest. *Sofia.*

Her head is low, peering through a thick microscope that's inches from her protective glasses. All her focus is on a rectangular, green slice of silicon about the size of a quarter. Sparks and smoke bellow from the tip of the metallic, pencil-like instrument she's using to mark indiscernible changes on the chip.

She raises her head confidently. "Done." She smiles, her eyes connecting with mine for a brief moment. Grasping the chip between a two-pronged tool, she gently places it on a transparent tray before handing it off to Ross.

"Excellent work, Sofia."

"Thank you." She beams, her feet crossing at the ankles. "You taught me well."

Did I just catch her blushing?

He hands Damien a microscope, who leans in to inspect the chip. In the matter of five seconds, he simply nods.

"What's our next step?" Ross asks.

"Testing. I want full reports on throttling, core capability and frequency thresholds. Hannah will be my liaison on this matter." I poke my head up at the mention of my name, catching Damien glancing my way. "She will come down here weekly so she can update me on your progress."

He's testing me, seeing if I'll crumble under the pressure.

I can rise to his challenges and survive here, I tell myself. *Even if our soon-to-be relationship is fake, I can still learn from this bizarre experience.*

Straightening, I face Ross, locking my hands behind my waist. "I look forward to your report."

Damien's eyes sparkle with approval, a look that sends butterflies dancing in my stomach. Sofia winks at me, and a much-welcome air of confidence floats about me.

It's just day one. I'll take it day by day. Everything's going to be fine.

"When she's down here, demonstrate the tests to Hannah." Damien's tone is authoritative.

I'll play this little charade he wants from me. We'll both get what we need, and I'll learn along the way.

"I want her to get a close look at all their results and intricacies."

I'm not even worried anymore. I got this.

"Because she's presenting the Nano-X chip with me at this year's Silicon Summit."

I choke on my saliva.

THIRTEEN

DAMIEN

THE WAY HANNAH paces in my office gives me the best view of her ass.

"I *cannot* present with you, Damien. I'm serious." She whirls around, heading in the opposite direction, giving me another angle to admire. "How could you expect me to talk in front of all those people?"

She might think she's being modest in her turtleneck top, but her skirt screams otherwise. It's the same one she wore during her interview, black and tight in all the right places.

She must know what it does to me.

"Because you can." I recline comfortably in my chair, stifling a groan. She doesn't have to work. I'd pay her to simply be in here. "It's not bad. There won't be *that* many people."

She flicks her head at me, her pupils glaring.

I'm lucky we're in my main office that has no glass for workers to see through. Otherwise, my employees might think my new personal assistant has lost her mind.

"I know what the Silicon Summit is." She pops her hip out,

her hand snapping to rest on it. "There will be *thousands* in the audience and who knows how many watching live."

God, I love pushing her to the limit, seeing her all flustered. The way her eyes shoot daggers at me reminds me of how she *really* is. Each time she flings fire at me, I'm taken back to our night in the hotel, where she wears the same gaze, her nipples dragging down the window.

My length strains against my belt, and I hunger for the sweetest words to leave her mouth, the ones that beg me to take her again. Even though it's only been a week, it might as well be months since I've tasted her.

"Exactly. Only a couple thousand." I grab hold of my arousal before it gets out of control and I nullify our contract.

"This wasn't a part of our contract. A normal personal assistant wouldn't give a speech."

"You said you wanted to learn as much as possible. This will give you the best opportunity. Thousands will see you and want to hire you after our agreement ends. It's only a speech. Nothing to work yourself up over."

Flipping open my laptop, I try to focus on work. Although my schedule is busy, I purposely spread out my meetings today to make sure we really got around the office. Having her shadow me, showing off to everyone who works for me, lets them know she's off limits. And that's truly necessary. A hot thing like her, with *that* body, would have men flocking on her first day here.

And I can't bear to watch that, not without going on some rampant firing spree.

"Right. It's *so* easy." She sighs heavily, plopping down on a chair in front of my table. "Because public speaking isn't your number one biggest fear."

Gazing over my laptop, I recognize the genuine trepidation of her features. A sinking feeling pools in my gut, and for a moment I feel like I gave her too big of a task.

But I didn't. I saw her rise to the occasion today in the engineering department. This is no different.

I try to ignore her, burying my head in my work, but all I can see is that pitiful look on her face. I sigh, rising from my chair before I round my desk to sit on the chair opposing hers.

She raises her head, waves of unease clouding her eyes.

"I wouldn't give you something you couldn't handle, Hannah."

It's true. If I thought she couldn't, I wouldn't have assigned it to her. I'm not an idiot. I know it's unheard-of to ask a new hire to perform on a stage graced by senior business owners on Silicon Avenue and the occasional post-doctoral graduate.

But it's important. Not only for her and her future career, but for our agreement. Having us up on stage together shows the world—and company owners who'd like to sell—how serious we are. How serious *I* am.

"And how could you know what I can handle?" She folds her arms, worry dripping from her teeth. "Don't act like you care. You hardly know me. I'm only a means to an end for you and your precious board."

"Fine. Maybe you are. But don't forget this is a two-way street. I need you as much as you need me." I lean in closer to her, needing to change the pitiful look in her eyes.

"But this particular fear you have... it's no different from any other. I'll be there the whole time if you fumble, but you won't. Because we'll practice, and I'll give you every resource to succeed."

Her shoulders are still tense, her voice a whisper. "Even

with all the help... I don't know if I can *get there*. Have that sort of confidence."

A part of me yearns to open up with her, to share each detail of my broken past. If only I could tell her what it was like being looked down upon by my peers, for a stutter hardly in my control. The way they'd whisper and snicker around me, creating for me a cold, lonely childhood. But I don't, because I shouldn't. Not when our paths don't meet at the end. Not when our fake connection has an expiration date.

"Fear is just another obstacle, Hannah. One that you can *choose* to conquer." Grasping her knee under my palm, I capture her eyes in mine. For a heartbeat, I decide whether to ingrain in her the wisdom my mother taught me, when she realized I was different. Then, I deem it necessary.

"Don't water seeds of doubt others plant in your head, even the ones you plant yourself. Because that's all they are until you give them too much attention: *seeds.*"

Shoulders drooping, her eyes speak more than her silence. The shadowy storm clears in them, and it's enough to calm the ache inside of me.

Her attention flickers to my hand. I let it stay there for a moment too long, loving the way her warm skin feels under my touch. When I release my hold, I try in vain to ignore the coldness seeping into my palm.

I sit up straight, needing a distraction. "What's next on the schedule, Miss Lockwood?"

She seems grateful for the change of subject and saunters over to her desk that stands near the window. Her hips sway a bit too much to be natural, and my eyes zero in on them. When she motions to sit, time seems to slow to a measly pace until she's leaning over, her elbow propping on the desk.

I clench my jaw. Maybe stationing her desk in my office was a bad idea. It's going to make me want to cancel every single one of my meetings.

Her nails dance atop the keyboard as she crosses her ankles together, pointing the tip of her heel towards me. She flings her head around.

"You have a meeting in five minutes," she says sweetly.

Hunger pools in my stomach at her tone, because I've heard it once before.

"Good girl." I don't register my words until they're halfway out of my mouth.

Her expression wavers slightly before she returns to her professional mask, eyes locking on mine for too long. When she wets her lips, a satisfaction burns brightly along my skin, tempting me to push her further.

"Now stay there and look pretty for me while they're here."

FOURTEEN
HANNAH

MY SUITCASE COULDN'T LOOK MORE WORN out. I heave my body on top of it, forcing the clothes further down. I try the zipper, but it gets stuck.

Sofia sits criss cross on my bed, watching me with an amusing look on her face.

She knows everything. I thought I'd keep my arrangement with Damien a secret from her, but I caved. We tell each other everything. It's been that way since we shared a dorm room in college.

I'd feel bad for leaving, even if it's only for two months, if it weren't for Jenna moving into our spare bedroom next week.

I glance up to find her sipping her blended beverage.

"It's not even Tuesday," I say.

She raises her eyebrows. *"Any* day is a good day for a margarita. Not just Tuesdays." Her blended strawberry concoction chills her glass cloudy. A tiny umbrella and a straw point out of the top. "You're still coming, though, right?"

Practically belly flopping on top of the fabric, the zipper finally seals shut. God, it's going to be humiliating dragging this raggedy old thing into whatever mansion Damien lives in.

My tailbone crashes against the carpet, before I heave a sigh. "I wouldn't miss margarita Tuesdays for anything." I smile at her.

"Good." She grins at me, her straw bending between her front teeth. Gurgling noises fill the space as she finishes her drink. "We'll have plenty to talk about. Specifically, all the filthy, hot sex you'll be having."

"We are *not* having sex. It's all fake."

Heat rushes to my cheeks when I think of how he spoke to me in his office earlier. I shouldn't have provoked him like I did, but it was like my body was out of my control.

Traitorous uterus.

"Right." She gives me a look that says I'm full of shit. "You'll only be *sharing a bed* every night with the most eligible bachelor in New York."

THE DIMLY LIT lobby of Damien's apartment is so porcelain, I bet there isn't a speck of dust anywhere.

Besides myself and the two employees standing behind the main desk, who focus on the computer screens in front of them, there's no one else. Which doesn't come as a surprise, given the late hour.

I take a deep breath, my heart pounding. Even though Damien gave me a key to his penthouse during work today, it still doesn't feel like I belong here.

Remember what he said about fear?

Lifting my head up, I wheel my suitcase behind me. The desk seems miles away, and the sounds of my heels mingle with a quiet melody playing on hidden speakers.

It's so peaceful. I smile to myself. *No suspicious characters moseying about like at my apartment.*

My steps grow stronger, my chin points higher and—

EEEEE—

Stopping suddenly, I lock eyes with an employee behind the desk. Her auburn ponytail bobbles in shock.

I take another step.

EEEEE—

My feet grind to a halt.

Oh my god...

Whipping my head around, I focus on the culprit of the ear-jarring sound. A hole I haven't seen before juts out the side of my suitcase, allowing the ruffles of a pink blouse to poke out.

I drop to my knees in embarrassment. I'm in the direct center of the lobby, with not a chair or pillar to hide behind. I might as well be on a stage with a spotlight pointing at me.

Come on, girl. I say a silent prayer in my head, shoving the fabric back inside. *You've been with me through a lot. Please, please, please don't pick right now to die on me.*

I straighten my legs. Collecting myself and plastering a cool smile on my lips, my eyes cross paths with the girl *again*. Her gaze darts back to her screen, a smirk lining her lips.

Annoyance crawls up my shoulders, and I resume my trek across the lobby. Ignoring the awful sound, I pump my legs harder, refusing to look at her. I don't need to. I know her smile is growing larger by the second.

Passing the white desk, I aim for the row of elevators in the corner, thankful to be nearly out of the open space.

A snickering sound ricochets off the walls behind me. "Maybe with your new maid salary, you can do us a favor and buy yourself something less *distracting.*"

I stop, shock pulsing through me.

Did she really say that? She's assuming I'm a maid?

With my mind racing, I decide whether to reply, as hot, angry tears well in my eyes. But I blink them away.

Cool it. This arrangement won't work if I get banned from the building.

I don't look at them and press on until the screeching ends inside of a clean-smelling elevator. Swiping the key Damien gave me, I take deep breaths on the ride up, forcing her out of my mind. I won't allow her to psych me out before such a big moment.

It feels like I'm in the elevator for eternity, not once stopping on its ascension to the very top floor. The door slides open, and I'm met with a similar scene from our night at the hotel. No hallway. Just a single, black door. Study the keycard, I hold it to the lock.

Its red light switches to green, followed by a clicking sound. Hesitantly, I try the door handle, finding it very heavy, before I enter and it whooshes back closed. I expect it to make a loud slamming noise, but it seals shut with a whisper.

I *hmph* before turning around, glad to no longer cause *distractions* to others—

Oh my...

All my annoyance flows straight out of my mind. If I thought the hotel was impressive... nothing compares to the vastness of Damien's penthouse. I take slow, cautious steps forward, my sad suitcase still crying in my wake.

The space is incredible and enormous, not something I

could imagine possible in an apartment. With a ceiling two stories high, balconies from the top floor jut outwards.

The floor-to-ceiling windows throughout the space are just as high, and I head straight for them. Passing a stately kitchen and a couch rounding a flatscreen, I'm more and more sure of what I'm about to see. I pump my legs harder until I stop dead in my tracks.

Covering my mouth, I gape in awe at the most picturesque nighttime view of Central Park. Not a single skyscraper disrupts the view. Rectangular and green, the way the park contrasts against the enclosing buildings is... is...

"Breathtaking, isn't it?" an unfamiliar voice answers my thought. Released from my trance, I watch a stout man dressed in a black suit approach me.

"Miss Lockwood"—he outstretches his white-gloved hand, and I take it—"it's a pleasure to meet you."

He knew I was coming?

"You too." I pale in surprise. I didn't expect Damien to announce me so soon to his staff.

"I handle all affairs regarding the household of Mr. Bass." With straight posture, he clasps his hands behind his back. "You may call me Arthur."

"So... does that mean you're a butler?"

"Precisely." He smiles, the warmth reaching his chocolate eyes. "I arrange gatherings if Mr. Bass so requires, book appointments, manage the housing staff, among other things."

"Wow, umm." I look out the window, not knowing how to respond, before I settle on honesty. "I've never had a butler."

"I understand. I'm the only live-in staff member. But I have my own quarters, separate and on opposite ends from

Mr. Bass's—and now your—residence. It'll be like I'm not even here."

That's unlikely...

I fight to keep my face neutral. Damien *did* inform his staff of me. They must think we've been together for quite some time. I gulp, remembering what he said during our nego- tiation.

I can't have my housing staff thinking our relationship is anything but genuine. Gossip regarding my family spreads quickly, and secrets are worth more than gold in my industry.

"Let me take that for you," he continues, his eyes trailing down to my suitcase.

My neck snaps downward, spotting another indiscernible garment poking out the hole. "Sorry." I chuckle nervously, shoving it back in. "It's been rather... faulty. And it has a terrible squeak." I feel silly, explaining its state in a place like this, to someone who must only deal with the extraordinarily rich.

"Not a worry, Miss Lockwood." He pushes down its handle and hoists it from the top-grip. "I'll arrange for its replacement. A new one will arrive on the morrow."

"Oh," I stammer. *Did I hear him correctly?* "You don't need to do that."

"Nonsense." His wrist flicks in the air. "It's my job to satisfy the needs of all guests. And as a new resident, you are of my top priorities."

"Oh—okay." I pick at the side of my thumb.

This treatment is otherworldly.

"Make yourself comfortable, and I'll sort out your clothing items." He motions to the white sofa. "Mr. Bass should accom- pany you soon. He wishes to show you the residence person- ally." And with that, he turns and walks off, lugging my suitcase until he disappears through one of the many doorways.

The tension in my shoulders droops as I approach the couch. Appraising it, I run my hands across its plush back. Happy to relax with no one around, I stretch out my arms and make to sit.

But before my ass touches the fabric, the most delicious, most mouth-watering sight I've ever witnessed crosses my vision.

Damp hair that falls effortlessly. Bulging pecs that *shouldn't* belong to someone so successful. All topped off with a low-riding white towel, knotted neatly beneath rock-hard abs.

Damien's grin is cocky, and his eyes flash with hunger as he saunters towards me. My knees go weak before I feel my tailbone sink into the cushion.

He rounds the coffee table in seconds, before forcing his legs between mine. My protest catches deep in my throat as he lowers himself, his heavy weight against my center sinking me further.

His lips bruise against mine in a blinding kiss. I make to turn my head, but I find myself with a lack of restraint and a moan threatening to surface. His tongue laps my bottom lip in a slow swoop, and when he realizes I won't fight him, he delves in further, invading my mouth.

Then he pulls away, our lips resounding with a clasp. I stare at him in shock, my heart beating wildly.

What did I sign up for?

I squirm, trying to relieve the hot, needy sensation building in my core, but I don't budge beneath his weight. He bucks his waist hard and pleasure spikes between my legs, causing me to lose a lustful breath as I clutch his biceps. His mouth tilts in a satisfied grin.

I'm way beyond saving.

When his eyes flicker to my lips, they stay there for a short time before his elbow drops beside my head. Lowering himself further to leave no air between us, his soft lips graze my ear.

His chuckle is a dark whisper that causes a violent shiver to race up my spine.

"Ready to play house, baby?"

FIFTEEN
DAMIEN

I RELEASE her from my weight, my feet landing on the floor. Her hair sprawls out on the white cushion and her cheeks flush a bright crimson.

She's dressed much more casually than when she left the office. Instead of a blouse and skirt, she wears tight jeans and a sweater. Even in less revealing clothing, she's still sexy as sin. Seeing her dress in something normal for a change gives me a glimpse at the true side of her, and it seems to awaken something carnal within me.

She bristles and stands to her feet, frantically smoothing out her hair and struggling to look me in the eye. Actually, she's avoiding looking at my half-naked body altogether.

"I didn't expect such a *warm welcome,*" she hisses, staring out the window with her chest heaving up and down.

A dark contentment burns in my middle.

I already informed my housing staff of her arrival, but they still need to see us together. I need them to believe we've been together for some time, and soon the world will think so too.

A smug feeling nips at me. The thought of my brother seeing us on a news headline... He sure as hell didn't care for her or deserve her. I don't pretend to either, knowing a portion of me—and I don't know how large of a portion that is—wants Hannah for sex.

Because the night in the hotel burns a hole so deep into my memories, there's no amount of booze or women or sex in this world that will allow me to forget it.

I study her. My new little obsession. The top of her head barely reaches my lips. Pinching her chin between my thumb and forefinger, I lift her head to me.

"How else would I greet my girlfriend?"

Her eyes widen slightly, and her lips curl in a retort. But she freezes when quiet footsteps sound across the area. A lady carrying a mop and a yellow bucket makes for the front door without looking in our direction and exits.

I grin, releasing her from my hold. "She was finishing up."

"How much housing staff does one man need?"

"Not much. Only Arthur, maids and personal shoppers." I run my fingers across my jawline. "Oh, and a chef."

"A chef? You can't be serious," she drawls, whirling her head. "You mean, you don't use *that?"*

She motions her hand towards my kitchen. Even *I* know it's quite impressive, with its top-of-the-line appliances, marbled countertops and enough room for an army of cooks.

Now that I think of it...

My chef meal preps each Sunday for me. I've instructed him to provide me with a high-protein diet, usually consisting of salmon, chicken and generous amounts of greens and healthy fats. I hired him the day I moved in here years ago, so...

No. I don't think I've ever cooked a meal here.

I shake my head, finding her eyes like saucers.

"Ever?"

"Nope."

"Well"—her hand flies to her hips, wearing the most insulted look on her face—"that has to be the most cliché, rich-guy thing I've ever heard."

"Mmm, funny." Feeling my towel loosen, I readjust its knot before I take a step, lessening the distance between us. "Is that all you see me as—some rich guy?"

"Y-yes." Her eyes wander downward, then quickly shoot back to mine. "I mean, *no*. I'm only saying that the kitchen is the best part of any house. And I know you're"—another step—"b-busy running Innovex and all, but cooking is such a basic life skill anyone would need to practice and especially baking is so—"

"Are you always so chatty when you're nervous?"

She blinks, holding our eye contact like her life depends on it. "I am *not* ner—"

"It's cute and all," I tease, "but time is money, Hannah."

She folds her arms. "Fine. You can show me around, but don't you have something less..." Her eyes peruse down the length of my chest to my lower abdomen.

"I'm sure I can figure something out for you."

THROUGHOUT THE TOUR of the penthouse, Hannah keeps a neutral expression, but she can't hide the wonder sparkling in her eyes. Every room I show her, each with its own unique interior design, makes her face brighten further and fuels my ego.

Not that it needs any further pumping.

Even though I changed into more appropriate attire—sweatpants and a T-shirt—it doesn't change the way she blushes and stumbles over her words when I get near.

What is it with women and gray sweatpants?

I hide my grin before we walk into my bedroom. It's the last on our tour and it's no less impressive than any of the previous rooms.

Her lips part with shock.

With the lights off, the nighttime glow through the windows is the only thing shining against her skin as she slowly assesses the space. She runs her hands across velvety curtains and the back of an accent chair positioned in the corner.

"No couch?" She looks to the bed.

There's no doubt the room is large enough for a couch, and there was one, a few days ago. But I had it removed, knowing she would try to sleep on it instead of with me.

Not that I'm going to tell her that.

"No couch." My voice comes out thicker than intended.

It feels like I'm moments away from a prize I've been craving for days. Finally, I have her where I want her, with doe eyes and apprehension, as she realizes she'll be sleeping with me every night.

She motions towards the bed, tossing many throw pillows and ripping back the sheets. My cock strains against my sweatpants when she bends down low, giving me a mouth-watering view of her backside. The tip of my length grows sensitive, brushing against the soft fabric and further heightening my urge to take her.

She has no protest.

I loosen the strings of my pants, taking another step. She

must be giving in, admitting we're better off succumbing to our carnal urges rather than lying to ourselv—

She pops back up, smacking a throw pillow on the bed. *What?* Long and yellow, it divides the bed perfectly in half.

"There. That should do the trick. My side." She waves her hand across the space. "Your side."

Dumbfounded, I stare at her. "You're assigning us *sides?*"

"Oh, my bad." She walks around the California king, breezing past me to the opposing side. "Do you want the other side by the window? You can have it. I don't mind."

I blink, my jaw hanging on its hinges. *Who is this woman? Who does she think she is?*

Any woman—literally, pick *any* woman at random in all of New York City—would jump my bones right now. In fact, I think this is the only time in my entire life I've ever brought a woman to my bed, and her intentions are solely to sleep.

What am I, some one-stop shop for her?

"Okay…" She wears a puzzling look. "So you'll take that side, then?"

The gears in my brain turn so fast they must be close to melting into putty. "You can't be serious."

"I am very serious." She flips on the nightstand lamp and sits on the edge of the bed, peeling her socks off before she discards them to the floor. "I'm drawing a line. Literally."

"Whatever you say, Hannah." A challenge brews in my chest, a feeling I'm growing to love around her. I bring both hands over my shoulders, consciously bulging my biceps as I peel the shirt from off my back.

Sucking in her bottom lip, her cool persona falters. But she bursts to her feet, averting my gaze the whole way to the bathroom.

"I'm going to take a shower"—she flings her head around, stealing one final glance at my abs—*"with the door locked."*

THE DOOR CRAWLS OPEN, steam filling the room behind her. I don't hide my surprised stare. She's wearing red-and-white polka dot pajamas with a white towel wrapped neatly atop her head.

I move to enter the bathroom, passing her by. When she pays me no attention, I turn and watch her.

She snuggles underneath the covers on her assigned side of the bed with a book in her hand. Nestling further into the sheets and letting her head fall back on the pillow, she removes a glittery bookmark and flops the book open, holding it between two delicate fingers.

The book cover is sweet, with an animated couple entangled in each other's arms. A hockey stick logo stands out in gold on the top corner.

I can't hide my snicker.

Her eyes dart to me, narrowing. "Something funny?"

"Nothing, nothing." Trying to keep a straight face, I bite my lower lip. "Enjoy your cute little read."

"I will." Her tone comes out innocent, but when her eyes return to the pages, she grins like there's something I don't know.

Another first for me.

Once in the bathroom, I shove a toothbrush between my teeth.

A woman is in my bed, not trying to take my clothes off and reading a romance book, presumably about some fictitious boyfriend. What's going on?

Chuckling to myself, I wander around the large space, brushing small circles with the white paste.

I didn't arrange the decor in here—or anywhere in my house, but the designer did an impeccable job. Twin sinks curve into the dark granite and LED lights line the rim of the mirror, giving the room a moody glow. I glance down at the other sink. A freshly pressed hand towel hangs near another I've never seen before, with the word *makeup* threaded into the material.

Arthur forgets nothing. I smirk, disposing of the paste in my sink before rinsing out my mouth. *I saw him in here earlier. He must've hung her clothes.*

I enter the primary closet, intending to snoop. Immediately, I cock my head. The rows of shelves opposite of mine that I had cleared for Hannah are nearly barren.

I offered to hire movers for her, to bring all of her clothes, but she denied the help.

My palm runs across the silky material of the blue blouse she wore when she interviewed with me. And another that she wore today. Other than that, there's only two other shirts and two skirts.

I furrow my brow. *If that's all she can move in one day, then she'll be back and forth from her apartment dozens of times.*

Flipping off the lights, I head back to the bedroom. Hannah is in the same spot, eyes glued to the page of her book. I take a step towards her... and another... But her gaze doesn't budge.

Does she see me? I clear my throat, but her focus stays the same. I clear it *again*, and her eyes fly to meet mine.

"Yes?" she grits out.

"My apologies. I know your hockey boyfriend must be *really* captivating."

"He is, thank you." The spine slaps against her stomach, irritation digging lines into her forehead.

"What's his name—this man I must compete with for your attention? Brad? Andrew?" With each name, her brow lowers further in disgust. "Oh, no. I got it. *Harry.*"

"It's Cole, if you really must know. Cole Huntington." She huffs a sharp breath, her cheeks turning red when our eyes connect. "Now, do you need something, or are you just going to stand there and sour my book?"

Her blatant sass simmers down my body, leaving it hot. I suck my bottom lip between my teeth, repressing the retort that so desperately wants to surface as I round to my side of the bed.

"You should accept my help when I offer it."

"What're you spatting off about now?" She rolls her eyes in a way that begs for reprimanding.

"Your business clothes." Amusement bubbles inside of me, imagining Hannah lugging up suitcase after suitcase to my apartment. "If that's all you can muster to bring in one trip, it's best to leave it to the professionals."

"Oh." Her eyebrows tick up before she buries her eyes back into her book. "I got it. Don't worry."

Why does she have to be so proud?

"Seriously, Hannah." I pull back the covers, my lips flattening. "No need to prove anything."

Let me take care of you, I almost say, but the realistic side of me kills the words in their tracks. Surprise radiates through me as I slip off my sweatpants, leaving me standing in nothing but my boxers.

She doesn't look my way, her face remaining perfectly neutral. That's odd. She usually heats up the moment my clothes hit the floor. I grab the hem of my boxers to get a reaction out of her. But before I do, her soft voice mumbles between the pages.

"There's nothing else." I can barely hear her, can barely get a read on her eyes.

"What did you say?" Leaning onto the bed, I get closer to her, the weight of my knee dropping into the mattress.

"There isn't anything else to get." Her voice is shockingly calm.

A sinking feeling overtakes me, replacing all the playfulness and tension in the room with dread. Silence practically drips from the walls, and seconds feel like hours as I contemplate how there could be nothing else to get from her apartment. Dread morphs into confusion... and then resolve... and finally splintering anger.

"Didn't my brother pay you?" I spit out, teetering dangerously close on the edge of combustion.

How could someone only have five clothing items to go to work in? How come she never mentioned it?

She nods.

She's hoping I drop the subject.

I don't. "How much?"

She sounds tiny and unfamiliar. "It doesn't matt—"

"It. Does. To. Me."

Her hands reveal a slight tremble when she sets the book down and finally faces me. She balls her fingers into tight fists, banishing the tremor. The look she gives me is potent with embarrassment and might as well drag a shard of ice down my heart.

"Fifteen an hour."

Minimum wage. That's hardly livable in New York City. I can hear the air pushing through my nostrils growing more powerful, more ragged. *That fucking asshole paid her minimum wage to put up with his bullshit.*

"Please, drop it." Her eyes soften. "It's not a big deal."

Not a big deal...

I pull the comforter over me, hoping in vain that it might douse the burning ball of fire inside my rib cage.

"Okay," I say, harsher than necessary.

Her concerned voice comes from over the pillow wall. "You're not going to drop this, are you?" I can't see her, but I hear her book snap shut again. Her night lamp switches off, forcing the room into darkness.

No is my final word between us, before I send off three texts.

One to my head of HR, tripling Hannah's hourly pay.

One to Arthur, telling him to make new arrangements for tomorrow.

And another to my father.

SIXTEEN

HANNAH

I'M DREAMING.

I've never been a lucid dreamer who's acutely aware of the distinction between dreamland and reality. Every night, if I dream at all, I go about them blissfully unaware that my actions are anything but real.

Except for one dream.

One I wish would stop coming. I've learned to recognize its signs. An uneasy feeling prickling at the back of my neck, followed by loud blood pumping in my ears, until—

The shed.

I freeze in place, staring at the surrounding sunflowers and its rusted white paint.

That's how it is. Average, pleasant dream, followed by a shed in the most peculiar of places. Sometimes it reveals itself while I'm walking the dreamlands of Central Park, or outside the office I work at, or in my very own living room, balancing atop the couch and coffee table.

But tonight... tonight it seems to be where it truly lives, where it's always been.

My family's farm.

I approach it with caution, the backyard's overgrown grass brushing up against my shins. Over my shoulder, I glance at my family's house, looking a far cry from how it should. It's even worse off than the shed. Yellow paint chips its sidings and the windows smash through, curtains blowing into the holes.

I trudge on, seeming to be at complete mercy to my legs, that won't stop even though my mind is screaming at them to. Stretching out my arms to the double doors, I make to grasp their iron handles, but before I can make contact, they blow open by some unforeseen wind inside the structure.

By now, my heart has fully escaped my ribcage and thumps powerfully inside my throat. Because it knows what's inside, knows what's lying on the workbench that locks up hidden secrets inside a manilla folder labeled with blood-red ink.

Project Cache.

The name is nonsensical. It means nothing to me and never has. It's why each time I see it, including now, I flip through its pages at a blaring speed, hoping if I reach the end, I'll see something different. Something that'll tell me why, with each new page, I'm met with a new photograph. A new face, always focused on something other than the lens.

They're eating dinner at restaurants, they're walking down the city streets, they're sitting in their cars, they're talking with each other. And worst of all, they're completely unknown to me. And while their faces *shouldn't* disturb me now and *shouldn't have* disturbed me the moment I first laid eyes upon them at the age of seven, then why is my conscious screaming *wrong wrong wrong* all the same?!

But I never reach the end.

"Hannah, Hannah." My mom's soft touch grazes my shoulder like always, just as I feel I'm nearing the final photograph, nearing *an answer*. "You shouldn't be in here." She nudges my hands away, collecting the papers before shoving them into a nearby drawer. "Come on, sweetheart."

Except... *She's not here*, I realize. *This time is different.*

A different voice.

A different hand.

A calloused one that seeps comforting heat into my shoulder, whose voice calls my name with care and lulls me back to safety, the walls of the shed *poofing* into misty dust. They collide and dance and reform into the grains of a sandy beach and the soothing waves of the ocean.

I sigh with relief, resting my head back to find it connecting with a plush pillow while my legs stretch out along a white outdoor bed. I'm alone on the beach under the shade of a canopy.

Rolling onto my side, I discover a man lying beside me with a perfectly chiseled chest and a face that could make any woman weep. He wears tight swim trunks with palm trees imprinted on them, and he holds a fruity drink with an umbrella sticking out the top.

"Thanks for saving me."

His eyebrows raise as the straw plops out of his mouth, setting the beverage on the table beside him. His smile is warm and bright, such an unfamiliar sight on him.

"No, Hannah." Pleasure radiates through my body when I hear Damien's deep tenor. He hooks his hand underneath my knee, positioning me on top of him. "It's you who saved me."

I'm overcome by the butterflies buzzing in my stomach, and when he grabs the back of my neck and pulls me down for a kiss, they take flight. His lips are supple and gently ease into our connection as his tongue prods my lips. When I part them to allow its entrance, a moan escapes from the back of my throat.

The sound seems to be his undoing. He growls hungrily and flips me over, my back sinking into the bed. Gathering both of my wrists in one hand, he pins them above my head before pressing his body weight against mine, gaining complete control over me.

He threads his fingers deep into my hair with his free hand, gripping tightly, before his lips crash against mine. Positioning his knee between my legs, his thigh connects with the apex of my sex, and I writhe with the intense contact. When the sharp sensation subsides, I rock my hips against his skin.

Slowly... Up... Down... Up... And then down, I ride the delicious waves of pleasure. With each motion, the friction lessens as wetness seeps through the thin film of my bikini.

"You're making a mess, baby," he scolds in a soft voice, eyes glazed over with lust. "Such a greedy little thing, aren't you?"

I squirm underneath his strength, grappling for any sense of control. Chuckling darkly, he tightens his grip on my wrists and hair, angling my head to the side, exposing the column of my throat. He latches on instantly, suctioning and scraping his teeth against my delicate flesh, and every sensible thought eddies from my mind. I whimper when the wetness of his tongue follows up to soothe the burn.

"What a sweet, sweet sound. Sing for me, baby. Louder." His teeth graze up my throat to below my ear, and I can't contain the cry that follows as a shiver explodes through my body. "Yes, just like that. Such a good girl." He flips my head, feasting on the opposite side of my throat.

A torturous burn rages inside me as I soak his thigh with my need. I'm shameless as I grind desperately against him, craving the friction, craving the release, craving *more*. And when my body tightens up, teetering on the edge of climax, Damien hooks his finger around the bottoms of my bathing suit, exposing my flesh, before he hurries down between my legs. Hunger flashes in his eyes as he watches me, swooping his tongue through my folds.

"Come, baby." He swipes again, and my body convulses. His arms clutch around my thighs. "I want to taste you on my tongue."

Suctioning my clit into his mouth, his tongue toys with it like prey caught in its web, and I feel myself falling off the cliff and—

And my eyes flutter open.

Confusion surrounds me as I blink, my vision taking time to adjust to the light streaming in through the crack in the curtains. Scrunching my brow, I study them. Except... they aren't the familiar deep blue I'm used to. They're beige and much taller.

I go deathly still when I take in my body's senses. My head rests on what feels like warm rock, my leg cascades over a much stronger one and sheets entangle between limbs.

"Good morning, sunshine."

I gasp, my head snapping upwards. Damien's mouth is inches from mine, his arms rest comfortably behind his head, and his biceps buldge as he wears a cocky smirk.

"No, please. Go on. It sounds like you were having a wonderful time."

I shoot to my elbows, looking around, soon spotting my precious divider pillow lying on the foot of the bed. I'm lost for words, utterly speechless, and I feel the heat creeping to my cheeks.

"D-did you—"

"Tell me," he says playfully, "what *exactly* are authors putting in those cute books of yours?"

My eyes crawl across his body, lower, past his rock-hard abs, and even lower, to the impressive bulge pressing against his boxers. And when they finally land on his thigh, I gasp.

Oh... My...

A slick of wetness shines there, right on his skin. My eyes flicker down to the coarseness rubbing against my leg, to the waist of my pajama bottoms hanging around my knees, to the soaked panties sticking to my pussy.

The most intense, mortifying and unescapable embarrassment consumes me. *Oh my FUCKING god. I ground on him—I ground on him in my sleep.* My chest heaves up and down, and my jaw drops low on a response I haven't even come up with yet.

"No need to explain yourself, baby." He beats me to it with a blatant, wicked grin on his lips. "We can pick up where you left off."

I dart away from him, jumbling sheets between my fingers to hide my sex. When his grin widens, I scrapple and pull up my pants, the movement tightening the panties against my clit, rubbing in just the right way to remind me of my unfinished need.

"I-I—"

His eyes gleam with satisfaction.

Shutting my mouth, I rush out of bed, my bottoms probably giving him the best view of an obvious wedgie all the way to the bathroom. I slam the door shut, trying to ignore my thoughts that swim with stone muscles and wet tongues and pure heaven.

∿

MY SHOWER TOOK LONGER than expected. And it may or may not have been due to the retractable shower head and amazing water pressure.

A girl's gotta do what a girl's gotta do. There's no shame in that.

When *that* didn't completely erase him from my mind, I turned the handle completely to the right, basking in the ice-cold water. Then, and only then, did I feel in control enough to go to work today.

I stand in the closet with a towel wrapped tightly around my chest, staring at my clothes. There really aren't many, but with the right combinations, there are enough outfits for me to be presentable, even at a place like Innovex.

"I'll be working from my study today." Damien strides in, heading for his side of the closet.

"Why's that?"

I try to ignore the way his eyes travel down the length of my body, of what he must be thinking at the first time seeing me in nothing but a towel.

Keep it together, Hannah. Don't acknowledge what happened this morning, and we'll all silently agree to forget about it.

He slides a white-collared shirt over his broad shoulders. "I have a contract to go over." Starting at the bottom, he pushes the buttons through their holes at an achingly slow speed. "One of a more personal manner."

My eyes narrow in suspicion.

"Not our contract," he clarifies, coming up next to me.

"Oh, okay." I nod and pick a skirt from off a hanger, breathing in the scent of his alluring cologne. "Is there anything you need help with?"

He intercepts my hand, pushing it down. "Actually, you won't be needing those today. I have work for you here."

"You're working from home, too. And you're allowed to get all fancied up." I press my knuckles to my hips, furrowing my brow. "What'll I be doing?"

"You're meeting with Cyna."

SEVENTEEN

HANNAH

I'VE BEEN in the same room with her for all of five minutes, and I already know Cyna is one of those types who thrives in madness.

She doesn't have one assistant. Or two. She has *five*.

They wrap yellow measurement ribbon around my waist, hem pantsuits and skirts on the spot here in the apartment, and refuse to slow down. No, anything below a brisk walk is positively unacceptable, like Cyna herself might pull out a ruler and smack them for slacking off.

I hold my arms out as a tape circles around my breasts. I'm wearing nothing but a bra and underwear, staring into the keen pair of eyes behind round black spectacles. We're in the middle of Damien's penthouse in the living room, clean windows surrounding us on a beautiful sunny day.

Anyone in Central Park or the neighboring buildings with a set of binoculars could see me right now. I chew on my bottom lip, trying to avoid the intense gaze Cyna's been giving me for the past ten minutes.

She puffs on a thin cigarette held between her two fingers.

Smoke bellows above her shortly cut, fiery bob. "You seem nervous." Cyna cocks her head, appraising my body up and down through her thick glasses. "Is this the first time your boyfriend has requested such a service?"

Alarm bells ring in my ears, reminding me to play the part. With the type of apparel she's showing me, I assumed she thought of me only as his personal assistant... Apparently, Damien told her more than that.

"Yes." I swallow, beads of sweat threatening to form on my armpits as I watch the assistants pull clothes from the rows of racks lining the windows. "I've never been measured before like this... I don't own many clothes."

Heat creeps up my neck. Even though Damien never said I needed to act rich, I shouldn't have admitted that. The ultra-rich are surely her only clientele. She probably sees me as some charity case.

But maybe that's how Damien sees me. I wonder if he brought over Cyna because he feels bad for me or because he can't bear to be seen with an assistant who wears five outfits. I haven't been able to ask him since he disappeared into his office. Maybe this really is only for our deal...

For me to look appropriate as his soon-to-be fiancée.

Crunching the butt of her cigarette into an ashtray, she flicks her head to the sea of racks. "Less black, Andrea. More vibrant colors," she barks, her eyes narrowing. "The girl needs to be seen."

"Darling, please." She scoffs, refocusing her attention on me. "Rich or poor, money is of little guarantee of taste. Many of the rich stuff their closets full of unwearable apparel."

Weight floats off my shoulders, and a part of me forgets I'm standing half-naked and talking to a complete stranger on the edge of a New York high-rise. I offer her a thankful smile before glancing at my curves in a tall mirror.

My bra is nude and provides little-to-no lift for my modest breasts. Trailing my eyes downwards to my panties, my lips thin... They've held up fine over the years, but I can't quite remember how old they are. It seems lingerie is yet another department I'm lacking in, one I'm sure as hell Damien *won't* discover.

Cyna shoots to her feet, which does little for her petite height, and claps her hands in short repetitions. "Present."

I arch my brow, watching her assistants fall in line with their arms full of clothing. *If her career as a designer ever falls short, maybe she should look into being a drill sergeant.*

Assistant one doesn't say a word. She precisely lays the pile of clothes on the dining table and picks an outfit. Her arm juts in front of me, the two-piece suit cascading down my figure.

"No." Cyna paces around me, smoke trailing in her wake. Her serious expression is of deep concentration, like she's deciphering the meaning of some abstract painting.

Another look is offered, this time a cheery yellow dress. "No." Another. "No." And another—the bottoms of her loafers screech. She cocks her head, and the tip of her cigarette blazes a soft fire between her lips, a pebble of ash free-falling to the mahogany floor. "Yes." The smoke vents from her mouth.

The remaining assistants present their pieces, all under the same scrutiny as the first before setting their approvals on a new rack. By the end, the rack of *yeses* overflows with a large assortment of colors.

"Wow," I breathe, running my hand along their sleeves, wondering if it's time to wake up from this dreamland. "They're beautiful. Thank you."

"We're nowhere near finished, darling. You have the final say. But there's no way to know how each one will make you feel until you try them on."

"All of them?" *That'll take some time.*

"Yes, you must try each one."

I'll go from left to right then.

I hook the first hanger atop my fingers, holding the outfit in front of me. I glance around. The assistants seem busy doing various tasks like ironing clothes and organizing.

An uncomfortable spark slithers up my spine. But when I look down at myself, I nearly giggle. They've been staring at me in my underwear this whole time. I shouldn't think twice about using the common space as my dressing room.

I slip my legs through two pant holes and shimmy my head through the shirt.

The first thing that shocks me is the material. It glides against my skin, clearly of higher quality than anything I'm used to wearing. The second is when I look into the mirror.

I stop my movements, allowing my eyes to travel down the length of my body. A brown sleeveless blouse. It's a shade darker than my hair and brings out the color of my eyes. And the plaid pants... they remind me of the ones the female lawyers wore at Innovex, something I wouldn't dare pick out for myself. I usually opt for things more soft and safe, like skirts.

"Do you like it?"

"Yes," I breathe. My eyes glue to the mirror, and a confidence settles in me as I sway to the side.

Could I really be that girl? a voice chimes in my head. *The one with a strong presence, the one who delegates the meeting?*

"Excellent. While you try on the next, Cameron will hem those pants to your appropriate height."

A curly-haired assistant approaches me, and I quickly slip them off, passing them to him.

Feeling naked again, I snatch the next hanger from the rack, seeing only a deep red color before I step into the outfit. After I shove my arms through the holes and brush my hair over my shoulders, Cyna's delicate fingers zip up my back.

I smirk to myself in the mirror, loving how the dress hugs my breasts with a sweetheart neckline, giving me unmatched sex appeal. Another wave of confidence soars through me as I touch the material.

"—tell him that's too bad," Damien's voice booms from afar, echoing in the large space.

My back instantly straightens. Nerves and excitement pump through my veins at the thought of him seeing me wearing this. Cyna seems alert, too, watching him appear through the corridor with a cellphone pressed against his ear.

She clasps her hands behind her back, a self-assured aura radiating off her. "Impeccable timing, Mr. Bass. Would you care to look—"

"I don't care if he gets the chip for one fiscal year." His legs bound across the hallway, eyes focusing ahead of him. "His shares will be in my name permanently. That's the deal. He can take it or leave it."

Both our faces fall as he disappears through a different archway.

He didn't even look. Disappointment creeps into me. *What did I think, that he'd stop in his tracks when he saw me?*

Don't be stupid. I shouldn't need approval from him. None of this is real.

Cyna must notice my appearance, because she shoves a different dress into my hand. "Put that one on."

I smirk at her, quickly unchanging. A sliver of hope trickles into me as I appraise the new dress. It would be daring of me to wear something like this at Innovex. It hugs my curves like the last one, but it's shorter and has a plunging neckline.

Damien's footfalls sound again, and I can't help the way my head arches to see him. His face scrunches, still talking on the phone. But, again, he walks by without so much as a glance my way or acknowledging Cyna's call.

My shoulders slouch the same moment our eyes lock, hers with caution that shows she sees the gleam of disappointment in mine.

Damien is reducing me to some schoolgirl with a crush, needing approval to feel good about herself.

I shrug the skinny strap off my shoulder, averting my gaze. The material is halfway down my body, pooling at my waistline, when my breath hitches in my throat. Through the standing mirror, I meet Arthur's white-brimmed eyes.

"Oh!" He nearly drops the tray balancing on his white-gloved fingers as he twirls around. "M-miss Lockwood, my *most sincere* apologies."

A smile shines through my glum mood. "It's okay, Arthur."

The sounds of scissors snipping and the hum of sewing machines break through the silence.

"Turn around," Cyna barks at him. "There's nothing to fuss yourself with."

His shoulders tense, but he obeys, gently placing the tray of assorted fruits and ice waters on the dining table, unable to meet my stare.

"And bring the girl another glass. Champagne. Wine. Anything with alcohol." She snaps her fingers at him, much like she does with her assistants. His steps hurry toward the kitchen, glad to be dismissed.

Lowering her spectacles, she appraises me. "Darling," she says in a soft voice that sounds unbefitting to her, "the only thing worse than a rich woman with no taste is a beautiful muse who mewls."

I shimmy off the rest of the dress, and then get comfortable back in my pajamas. Biting my bottom lip hard, I refuse to succumb to its tremor.

Blinking furiously, I feel foolish as Arthur returns with some drink bubbling in a flute, white foam peeking over its rim. The moment he whisks away, I take a long sip. "I shouldn't get so upset. He's busy working, and I should accept that men like him are always on the go."

"Men like him? Hmm," she mulls with a hum. "They are often distracted, yes. With strings pulling them in many directions, but they come back."

Eyes burning at her words, my voice grows coarse. "No, they don't. They forget who they once needed."

I finish the rest of my glass in our silence, but the alcohol only seems to fuel my misery.

"I tell you how to get that man to notice you. I tell you how to get anything you want in life." Her accent thickens as our eyes lock, hers eddying with an intense seriousness that causes my gut to drop. "Dress for it. Dress for it, and most importantly, act like you deserve it. Like it's already predetermined to be yours."

"So..." I laugh, cringing when it surfaces as a bitter noise. "You're saying I should wear these clothes to get his attention?"

"No, darling—" She snaps her fingers and crosses her

arms, wearing a dubious smirk. Moments later, a smaller rack wheels around the corner.

She didn't…

My palm shoots at my tugging lips, eyes darting between the delicate lace and straps, all flowing from their individual hangers.

"—you wear *these* underneath."

"Did..." I shuffle myself towards the lingerie, my mind racing at record speeds. "Did Damien request these?"

"Of course not." She scrunches her brow, like I have the audacity to question the *bustiers and thongs* here to dress *me—his personal assistant.*

"Be serious."

"I am. I dress actresses, business tycoons and design for the catwalks of Milan and Paris. I do it all, darling, because I'm the best. And the best must always be serious."

"Well... aren't you supposed to be dressing me for *my job?"*

"Yes." She blinks.

I blink even faster. *Is she for real right now???*

Sighing, she flicks her wrist towards the lace. *"And* the best knows a woman's sexuality is a powerful gateway to her confidence—in or out of the bedroom."

I nod slowly, finding myself agreeing with her. I think back to what Sofia said that day at Matteo's—*There's nothing wrong with mixing business with pleasure.* Maybe what she said is right... but in a different way?

There's nothing wrong with wanting to look sexy, even if it's just for me.

"Should I try one on?"

"Not yet, darling." A smile tugs at her lips. "Not without a second opinion."

EIGHTEEN

DAMIEN

I PINCH the bridge of my nose, my elbows jamming on top of my desk.

I should've seen it coming. Typical of my father to propose one thing, and then ask for three times as much. The deal is simple, or *should be* simple—Bass Mobile gets exclusive rights to the Nano-X chip for one fiscal year, and I get Sterling's shares indefinitely. Not for an allotted time.

Forever.

The back-and-forth with their lawyer has been exhausting. Not that I don't have my team of lawyers scouring through their proposal. In the end, we'll settle on the version we originally agreed to, because my father's desperate. His company is in need of my company's chips for their cellphones, and they're in no position to negotiate.

My father is only trying to drag this out, clinging to what little dignity he has left.

A smile creeps along my lips, right as a knock sounds at my door. "Mr. Bass." Arthur pops his head in. "I hope I'm not intruding."

My shoulders relax, happy to see a familiar face.

Arthur is the epitome of professionalism, and he's been a part of my life since the age of twelve. My brother and I both have our own butler, gifted to us by our mother, who will accompany us wherever we decide to go in our lives. He has been a great source of stress relief, wisdom and has even shown me fatherly love at times growing up.

"Of course not. What is it?"

"The lady Cyna is..." He clears his throat, and an uncomfortable look blooms across his face. "Asking for your assistance."

Why would she need my help? I scrunch my brow. My request for her was short and sweet—*My girlfriend needs a completely new wardrobe, with a business focus in mind.* Nothing someone of her experience couldn't handle.

"Alright then." I push off my desk, my chair wheeling in the opposite direction. "Tell her I'll be out in a moment."

I'VE WATCHED companies fall at my hand. I've negotiated multi-billion-dollar deals. And I've stared down my competitors with a face as hard as stone. But *nothing* in my years dominating Silicon Avenue could've prepared me for the sheer torture that is watching Hannah Lockwood prance around in lingerie without being able to touch her.

"Show him the back," Cyna commands.

I should've known the instant I came into the room and all her assistants filed out of my apartment one-by-one, that Cyna had devised for me her own personal brand of sick and twisted torture.

I sink further down my chair, my back slipping against the

wood, trying to think of *anything* else, anything at all, to contain my restraint.

Waking up to Hannah grinding her pussy on my leg could've been one of the hottest things I've had to endure. She was *so* wet. And her moans were sweet music to my ears, and it took all of my self-control to not wake her up. To not take her for myself.

Which is why I chose today of all days to handle something so distracting, but that contract's far from my attention now.

Hannah's wearing a one-piece with intricate lacing that travels down her breasts all the way to the apex of her legs. She smirks at me before turning a one-eighty, giving me a full view of the G-string thong riding between her ass cheeks.

Fucking Christ. She looks devastating.

I don't notice my knuckle in-between my teeth until sizable divots engrave into my skin.

"What about this one?" Cyna props her chin on her palm, cocking her head to the side as she looks at me.

"Yes, it's great." I clear my throat, my voice sounding like under-watered gravel. "Is this really necessary?"

"Of course, it is."

Hannah turns around, her hair falling to graze her nipples. They're hard, peaking against the dainty fabric, and I can physically feel the moisture in my mouth, salivating as I stare at them.

Cyna flicks her chin at her, and she leaves to the direction of the restroom to try on the next piece.

"I told you she needed *business* clothes," I hiss.

"You said Miss Lockwood needed a completely new wardrobe. Is this not a part of the modern woman's wardrobe?"

I don't respond, thankful when my heart rate slows and cock loosens against my pants underneath the table.

"And besides," she continues. "I need to know what styles please you—what looks good on your girlfriend. Everything *is* being charged to your card, like you requested."

The bathroom door clicks shut in the distance, and my body's temperature prematurely rises again. When Hannah saunters across the hall, the light trickling in from the windows shining against her skin, I nearly fall off my chair.

Bright red molds to her body in a two-piece leather set. Straps line the material, and strings hook from the garter belt that kisses her belly button down to thigh-high stockings.

She prances around the coffee table like a mouse taunting a bobcat, and time seems to stop. She could've been showing off for five minutes or five hours, because I don't have a fucking clue. All the while, she wears a dubious grin, with mischief gleaming behind her eyes.

"And this one, Mr. Bass?"

I say nothing, barely registering her words. I can only stare, dumbfounded, at the goddess in my living room.

"I think he needs a closer look, darling."

Hannah prowls to me like a tantalizing panther, the leather shifting with her movements, and every bone in my entire fucking body screams at me to claim her. To fuck her raw against the dining table until she cries so loud there'd be no doubt to any of my staff, or to this whole building, that she belongs to me.

Coming to a stop a breath away from my chair, her lilac scent dances around my head, lulling me into an enchanting trance. She walks around to my other side, and my head snaps to her. My hand peels from my leg, closing the distance to her supple skin—

"No touching." Hannah's seductive tone scolds me, batting my hand away.

My gut swirls with lust at the way her eyes demand my compliance and steal my attention. I sit up straight, my teeth grating against themselves as she *bends over* the dining table. Her ass cheeks spread to reveal the leather string hidden between them, and it's all I can bear.

"Every. Single. One," I grind out, before I shoot from my chair and stride away in hopes they don't peek my raging hard-on underneath my pants.

"Buy them all."

NINETEEN

HANNAH

BAD DECISIONS, bad decisions, *bad decisions.*

I tap my heel in quick repetitions, sitting quietly at my desk.

You taunted him. You taunted him, and now you'll have to endure sitting through a date with him... with him touching *you in public.*

Burying my head low, I try to read the notes the engineers gave me today during their progress report. Even though Sofia was there to explain half of what they showed me, I'm still having a difficult time deciphering their jumbled-up, scribbled mess.

Seriously, do any of them have handwriting that's half-legible?

I exhale sharply, translating the notes to a pristinely organized report. Damien told me it's due within the hour, and it's proving *very* difficult to finish, given the flurry of thoughts arguing inside my consciousness.

So, what, you have one little wet dream, and you go along and decide to try on lingerie *in front of your boss? Seriously, who does that?*

It wasn't my idea, I counter, knowing this internal feud is pointless, and I'm screwed all the same. It was Cyna's idea— *that I went along with*, I conveniently forget to add.

I was so distraught from the way he didn't even look at me yesterday that I stooped to desperate measures to get his attention... And his attention I've surely gotten in full.

"Clock's ticking, Hannah." His voice is a velvet purr across the room.

I lower my head further, ignoring his taunt. I chose the most modest thing in my new wardrobe today, a charcoal pantsuit with a matching blazer. I hoped it would let Damien forget all about me. But it seems my assumption was wrong.

"Ignoring me now, hmm? Tick. Tock." I hear him get up from his chair behind me. His steps grow near, and annoyance spreads through my chest like wildfire. "Tick. To—"

"Do you have something you want to say, Damien?" I whip my head around, craning my neck to see him.

"I'm only looking out for you."

"And how's that?"

"I'm saying you better hurry." He shoves his hands into his pants pockets, trickery gleaming in his eye. "The longer you take, the less time you'll have to practice your presentation to the board."

"What?!" I burst to my feet, my mouth falling open. "W-when? I didn't know—"

"Today."

"Today? I-I can't be ready for that by *today."*

He's punishing me. He's obviously punishing me for what I did to him yesterday. I'm practically hyperventilating now, staring at him with the whites shining around my eyes, fumbling for any ounce of leverage.

"You—you can't—"

"Can't what?" He cocks his head, his perfect features showing how much he's enjoying my frantic outburst. "Expect *my assistant* to do her job—which is to listen and do as I say."

"Damien, *please.*" I devolve into a nervous wreck. My hand flies atop my head, my fingers intertwining with my hair as I pace around the room. "I know we agreed I'd practice for the Summit, but I shouldn't be practicing in front of *the board.* And I won't have anyone else with me, you know, who *actually* knows all the tech jargon I'll be saying, and—"

"There is *one* thing you could do to change my mind."

I stop in my tracks at the sheer mischief in his voice. He clearly baited me into whatever he has planned, but my nerves are so intense, I lick my lips and bite his hook.

"What's that?"

He swaggers over to me, his eyes never leaving mine until he's a hair away from me. "Tonight, when we go to dinner"— he pinches my chin between his thumb and forefinger, lifting it higher—"the dinner our contract dictates I can touch you, tease you and show you off to the world"—a shiver runs down my spine at the hunger in his eyes—"you'll wear *exactly* what I want."

My heart somersaults in my chest, knowing he's winning. Because if he chooses what I wear, that could mean...

"And that includes what you wear *underneath.*"

Lingerie.

I remember the ones I tried on, each more revealing and seductive than the last. He bought all of them, all *fifty* of the scanty fabrics, including the ones he didn't see. The price tag must be upwards of some number I can't fathom, given they were all surely designer. I looked at the ones I hadn't tried on, and some of them weren't very... *restrictive.*

"At least let me choose which lingerie..." I don't finish my sentence, because the laugh he lets out is low and savage.

"Oh, you're in no position to negotiate, baby." His thumb trails across my jaw in a possessive swoop, coming back to press against my bottom lip, surely smudging my gloss. "What'll it be? Shall I alert the board you'll be giving the report, or will you be my good girl and try on *one more* set for me?"

THE LINES ARE BLURRED. The lines are *so* blurred that the hand Damien wraps around my middle as we exit the elevator, *that should be fake*, feels as real as the hunger in his eyes.

Moonlight shines onto the rooftop restaurant, the one I've heard Sofia talk about in the past. She said an older gentleman she had been dating at the time had to book the reservation six months out—*after bribing the hostess.*

John drove us, and Damien called on the car ride over. And, somehow, here we are, following a hostess across white tablecloths and dim lighting. The tables lining the perimeter have an impeccable view of the city and are surprisingly private, with tall, rounded booths facing outwards.

His arm tightens around me as his lips brush against my ear. "You look ravishing." Eyes seem to flicker towards us, towards *him*. I notice a woman pull out her phone, angling the lens towards us.

Nerves prickle at my arms. *Damien wasn't kidding. Maybe we really will end up on some gossip site.*

Even though this is all play and we're not really together, a blush still creeps up my neck as we round a corner. We find a single table vacant, and not just any table. It's pushed up right against a corner facing the Empire State building. Small and square, it seems to be the only perimeter table in the whole restaurant that's not a booth.

A slight breeze hits us, reminding me of what I'm wearing underneath my fiery red dress. Or should I say, what I *don't* wear. The lingerie set Damien picked out for me is special... Its strappy fabric lacks in the panty-department, as in the panties *are* two elastic straps running tightly between inner thigh and labia, leaving my pussy completely exposed.

Each step I take squishes my sensitive flesh against my clit, sending pleasurable electricity racing through my body. I bite my lip, savoring the friction as we arrive before our table.

The hostess waves her hand. "Mr. Bass and Miss Lockwood." My head shoots back in shock that she knows me by name. "It's our honor to dine you this evening. Let us know if there is *anything* we can provide to make your night more special."

Damien pulls out my chair, and I sit as the hostess places our menus flat across the table. "Your server will be with you shortly." After pouring us waters, she whisks away.

Sitting to my immediate right, Damien outstretches his arm to grip my knee. He keeps it there, a comforting warmth sinking into my skin.

I appraise the menu, trying to ignore the candlelight flicking against his handsome features, and nearly gag on my water when I see the prices.

"Fifty dollars for a salad?" I suck in a breath before gently setting my glass back down. Damien raises his eyebrows, and I lower my voice. "I mean... what do you think you'll be having? The seasoned duck or the... *lobster frittata?"*

What on earth is a frittata?

Turning my back, I study the other guests. Some type of

food art appears to decorate their plates. Fish tails stick upwards. Sauces draw intricate designs over the porcelain. And thin noodles wind in tight knots, all with shockingly small portion sizes.

"For my main course, I'll order what I always get." Damien gives me a funny look when I face him again. "Something that's off the menu."

Main course? Oh no.

My eyes flicker downward to the unnecessary amount of gold silverware lined up next to my plate. *What're all those for...?* I pick up an obnoxiously tiny spoon. There are *three* forks.

"Don't fret." His hand tightens on my knee, causing me to stiffen. "You work from the outside in. It's really quite easy."

"Right," I chuckle nervously, peeling my eyes away from the intimidating silverware. "How'd you get us a table, anyway?" *Especially this one,* I don't add. "Sofia says it's impossible to come by one here."

"Oh, they're willing to do favors for me." He unfolds his napkin, laying it neatly across his lap. "I come here frequently."

An uneasy feeling creeps up my back. Judging by the others here, it's definitely a date hot spot. Maybe he's taken actresses here or models or...

Damien's thumb drags across my skin in an almost comforting way, reading my mind. "I own the place," he says nonchalantly.

"You *own* this restaurant?" Okay, now he's just making up stuff to make me feel better.

"My family owns plenty of investments. And this is one of mine, outside of tech. All great places to let your money sit and accrue passively. Apartment buildings, oil, gold, hedge funds, and smaller businesses, like this restaurant."

I shouldn't lift my brows the way I do. Damien and his family have an unfathomable amount of money. It's not a shock they spread it out.

"Have you taken me anywhere else you've *happened* to own?"

"Well..." He rubs his fingers along his jaw. "The apartment complex I live in, for starters. And I'm considering being part owners of Enigma. My uncle owns the place, and he's trying to convince me to go in with him for an expansion. That's why I was there when we met."

Enigma. I chew on the thought, and it starts to make sense why he was there. At the time, I wouldn't have thought anything of it. But now that I know him better, it really doesn't seem like his type of scene.

"Wow." I twiddle my thumbs together, feeling like I have nothing impressive to add to the conversation as the server comes, jots down our orders and leaves. "Don't you ever want to do something… normal?"

"Normal?"

"You know, live a little." I don't know why the words are coming out, why I'd ask such a question, but they are anyway. "Not having to worry about your business. Taking a vacation. A *weekend* off..." The more I explain, the further his head cocks to the side. "No calls. No meetings. It must be stressful for you."

To my shock, he is quiet for a moment, as if he's unsure of how to answer. *Has no one asked him that before?*

"I don't think that's how I function."

"Everyone needs a break sometimes."

"I take breaks." He scoffs, and I lean forward. "I lift weights and go for runs."

My shoulders droop. "That's *not* taking time off, Damien."

"Yes, it is. And it's necessary. I need to stay in tip-top condition, in order to maximize my energy."

Oh, this poor man. I shake my head, pitying him and the pressure he seems to put on himself. Even for all the money in the world, what's it worth if you never have time for yourself? *Well, he's definitely not poor, but... sad, in a way.*

"Your first course," a light voice announces behind us and sets our plates in front of us, as well as our drinks. Thankful for the alcohol, I grab my cocktail by the stem and bring it to my lips as I glance at Damien's dish.

Steamed oysters. I raise my brow. *There are only five of them.* My eyes travel to my lobster risotto, discovering a similar quantity of food. *Rich people are ridiculous. Pay an arm and a leg for what, two bites?*

"It's only the first round, baby." His cocky persona takes over, going straight to his eyes that dance with amusement. "I'll make sure you get your fill." My mouth drops at the innuendo, but before I retort, he challenges me with a raised brow. "Take a bite."

Narrowing my gaze, not believing this will be worth anything close to its price tag, I collect my first spoonful. Lifting it to my mouth, I stare him in the eyes as I chomp down on a slice of lobster.

Oh... I chew. *Oh my.* I chew some more. *HOLY SHIT.* I try to contain my reaction, but it's futile, revealing itself in the form of widened eyes and raised cheeks. *THAT'S INCREDIBLE.*

"Mmm," Damien drawls, an unmistakable tease in his voice, "it's up to your standards? Oh, good."

The corner of my lips lift, before I set my fork back down, forcing my face to relax. "It's... good.*"*

"Right." Using his fork, he skewers an oyster out of its shell. "So, tell me. What would a normal person do to *live a little.*"

He's really going to have me spell it out for him.

"I don't know, plenty of things. Go see a movie, try painting, bake a cake, go grocery shopping ..." His lips line with disgust.

"That all sounds like a waste of time."

"Exactly." *Well, grocery shopping isn't... But surely for him to do it himself, it is.* "It's supposed to be unnecessary."

"Hmph."

"Maybe you're right." I shrug my shoulders. Now it's my turn to use a teasing tone. "You probably couldn't handle a bit of normal."

"Oh, no." He slaps his drink down on the table, trying to seem serious, but I read the smile tugging at his lips. "I know what you're doing. That doesn't work on me."

"Mhmm." I offer him a sweet smile as I chew, the complicated mixture of flavors sending sparks to my tongue. "I dare you."

"You dare me?" He crosses his arms. "What're we, on the playground? To do what?"

"To let me decide our next date." *Fake date,* I remind myself. "To spend the day with me, being *normal.*"

"No way." He shakes his head.

I'm nearing the bottom of my tequila sour, and I'm already drunk enough to do what *always* made my little brother crack when I dared him to do something.

"Ohhh," I tease, swigging back the rest of my drink. "It sounds like someone's being… chicken."

Silence.

He's speechless. Pure. Speechlessness. But I hold his stare, long enough for him to roll his eyes and smile... And for that smile to disappear slowly, realizing I'm dead serious. "You did *not* just say that."

My eyes turn to slits. *I did.*

"That would be ridiculous." His teeth shine before his cheeks peek over the napkin he presses to his mouth. "Pointless."

I purse my lips hard, fighting the laugh bubbling up my stomach and the drunken urge that's telling me to *do it.*

No, don't do it. Don't. Do. It. I warn my intrusive thoughts, glancing at my jaw-dropping date and the impeccable view. *Not here. That would be embarrassing, that would be...*

I swirl my spoon, focusing on my risotto. *"Bock,"* I whisper underneath my breath.

Silverware clinking against a plate rings in our space, but I don't look at him. "What did you—"

"Bock," I say again, this time louder.

"Are you—"

"Bock."

"Oh my god."

I meet his wide eyes, teeth visibly biting his lower lip, trying not to laugh.

"Bock, bock, bock ..."

"Hannah Lockwood," he gasps, peering over his shoulder.

"... bock, bock, bock ..."

"Our second course is coming," he hisses in an unusual tone, dripping with desperation. But I don't relent. "Stop it. Stop it, right now." His hands fly to the sides of his face, his composure blown to bits.

I look too, watching a stout man balancing a black tray

approaching us, passing by diners wearing glittering dresses and suits.

"Hannah." He rounds the corner. "Stop." His steps are long as he eats up the distance between us. "Please." Closer. *"I'm serious."* Even closer now, seconds from us.

"Okay!" He tugs on my arm, and I instantly stop.

Whew.

I nearly double over with laughter, the alcohol bubbling in my brain. When our server arrives, setting down our next course, I'm nearing hysteria until he's bounding away from our table, probably thinking I've gone mad—or that I'm heavily intoxicated.

When I compose myself, tears brimming my eyes, I look at Damien, only to find his face lit up with a smile I've never seen before.

TWENTY

HANNAH

TONIGHT WENT SHOCKINGLY WELL.

It felt almost... *real.* Like we aren't playing a game, acting as a serious and happy couple, ready for photos to be taken of us at any second.

As we're walking by the tables, that sensation creeps back in, one caused by the intense friction from the lingerie I'm wearing. Each step is torturous, lulling me into a submission in Damien's arm that loops around my middle.

Maybe that was his plan all along. I manage to think through the clouds of euphoria, my sensitive flesh pinching between the two elastic straps. *Flirt, don't touch me, but the moment I get up to leave, he knows I'll walk myself into liquid putty for him.*

Damien's arm tightens around the small of my back, his thumb sweeping in a slow rhythm, tempting me to give in to him. He wants me to be easy for him. He wants—

"Well, well, look who it is," a drunken voice slurs to our immediate right, followed by a high-pitched cackle.

Oh, no.

Damien and I both stop in our tracks at the same instant,

because I know that voice. We *both* know that slimy, knife-slicing-up-your-back voice anywhere.

"Well, isn't that so sweet?" He's seated at a rounded booth near the edge of the restaurant with three others. "My *beloved* brother and his *date.* Won't you two care to share a drink with us?"

We pause, standing pencil-straight with what feels like hundreds of eyes around the room on us.

"Let's go," Damien whispers in my ear, his voice full of treacherous promises that I know aren't for me. "Don't let him spoil our night."

Anger seethes within me.

What're the chances he's here? In all of New York City, this one night, he is *here.* I scan his group, each dripping more money from their sleeves than the next, hiding smiles behind their palms. All except one, whose body brushes up against Sterling's with wide eyes darting back and forth between me and Damien.

Do I know her? I cock my head. Auburn hair, high pony-tail—*looking an awful lot like the girl from the lobby.* The one who sneered at me, at my poor appearance and crying suitcase.

I remember what she had said to me with her laughing friend very well—*Maybe with your new maid salary, you can do us a favor and buy yourself something less distracting.*

I don't know the reason. Maybe it's the alcohol. Maybe it's the coaxing straps between my legs. Or maybe it's the bitch across the table that causes me to run my hand down Damien's long coat, feeling the smooth fabric kiss my fingertips.

I bat my eyelashes, craning my neck up at him. "There's no harm in one drink, sweetheart." Whipping my head to her, I spot her brows furrowing with anger, and my gut pools with satisfaction.

Guess I'm not looking quite like a maid anymore, am I?

Damien's eyes widen but quickly fill over with lust, as if he's reading my mind and agreeing with me about how to handle this situation.

By rubbing their noses in it.

I'VE LEARNED HER NAME. Priscella.

Yes, *Priscella*.

For the past ten minutes, she has seemed less interested in her date—my cheating, lying, man-whore of an ex—and more interested in *mine*, who indulges me by turning down each of her advances.

"So, Damien," she purrs like a hungry cat as she picks the olive from her martini glass. "I've never seen the Penthouse at Acacia Heights. The view must be *amazing.*"

His fingertips trail up my thigh, goosebumps following in their wake as his eyes never leave me. "It is."

"You should show me sometime." Her glossy lips wrap around the green skin before she slides it off its skewer.

My eyebrows raise. She's not even trying to hide it anymore. She might as well take off her clothes right here in front of him.

"And why would I do that?" he asks flatly. His thumb sneaks underneath my skirt, invading its boundaries and making tight circles across my skin.

Sterling is so drunk, so oblivious to his date, who's clearly trying to jump ships to the other brother right in front of him. His empty glass clasps against the table before he waves his hand to a server, requesting another. The other couple isn't as drunk, but is definitely heading down the same road, I decide, watching them clink their tall shot glasses together.

"Because"—her fingers intertwine in her pony, twirling the long locks—"I work at Acacia. Not that I need to, of course, with my daddy's trust, but for people—the party connections."

"That's right," Sterling chimes in. "My Priscella is quite the socialite."

"Is she now?" His fingers dip further, brushing against the fabric of my crotchless panties, causing my skirt to brush up higher. "I've never seen you there."

She bristles right when Damien's free hand grazes my shoulder, trailing a possessive, searing touch all the way down to my ass.

"I work at the front desk."

"Really?" He couldn't possibly sound more preoccupied. The rest of the group, chatting amongst themselves, seems unaware of what's going on underneath the table. "I guess you're not that memorable."

Her face morphs into hot rage, and her jealous eyes lock in on mine. "Do tell me." I'm taken aback by the change in her voice, from sultry to sweet in the matter of seconds. "Have we met? Do I know your family?"

Sterling's cackle rings across the table, quieting the other couple. "No, sweetheart." He pats non-existent tears underneath his eyes. "No one knows Hannah's family."

"Oh, stop it, babe." A smirk lines over Priscella's mouth. "That can't be true."

I feel Damien tense beside me, his hand retreating from me. But I clutch his wrist, keeping it there.

"It's true." His eyes don't leave mine. "Hannah's life has

been very... *simple*. Nothing that someone like you should bore yourself with."

"Ahh, yes." Irritation races down my middle in a flurry of sparks, but I will my face to remain neutral, unfazed. "The story of my family dragging themselves out of a rundown trailer park to a farm is *so* boring." My eyes don't break from my ex's, not once, as I drag the hand of New York City's most eligible bachelor straight to my clit.

Sterling's back straightens. He's not used to me talking back—*and neither am I.*

Damien's hum of approval resounds in my ear as he rubs his fingers up my middle. I grind in response, needing more friction, already feeling my slickness. His touch fuels me to continue, while I, too, keep my voice and smile just as sweet. "And harvesting crops and tilling soil for hours on end beginning at age five? Simple, really. The only way I could've had it simpler was if I partied and fucked my way across New York with daddy's trust."

A choking sound shoots out from the other girl at our table. She sets down her glass a little too roughly, before she appraises Sterling with an appalling expression. For good reason, too. Because Sterling and Priscella both look like their heads might spring from their necks, faces shining bright red.

Guess no one's ever spoken to them like that.

"*Farm work*, huh? Wow... That's nothing to be proud of." Sterling ignores my insult, trying his best to appear unbothered as the flush creeps further up his neck. "Must be why you're so good at mindless tasks. Hopefully, you've been putting that to good use, Damien."

Damien sighs, keeping a steady rhythm between my legs. "Whatever do you mean?"

"Don't play dumb. I know she's your new personal assistant. Word travels fast, remember?"

Embarrassment *should* eat at me right now, especially with the way Priscella's eyes line with glee. Surely, she's reassessing her jealousy of me. She must believe I'm not really his date, just his lowly assistant, probably expected to serve him all night long.

But it doesn't. I don't feel one ounce of embarrassment, not with the blazing fire shooting through my torso as Damien's fingers pick up the pace. I bite the inside of my lip, containing my reaction.

"Don't tell me you haven't used her greatest skills." His teeth flash against the moonlight. "What she's really best at—the dishes, laundry and other *special services.*"

Heat radiates off Damien's body as his fingers come to an abrupt stop. When they crawl up my skin and sneak underneath the top of my panties, I nearly whimper when a sudden cool night breeze invades the bareness.

"You seem to have left out the part where she's *my girlfriend.*" He shoots a finger underneath the two bands that push my labia together before he *pulls* tightly. I let out a gasp, my hands flying to the edge of the table.

His fingers return to their spot, pressing into my now puffed-up flesh. *It's almost too much, too painful*, I think, watching as Priscella eyes me with suspicion. But when his skillful touch twists in a slow rhythm, I can't stop the way my body curls inward, my grip tightening against the table.

"Hannah doesn't lift a single finger in my household." The scotch rushes to his lips, a large ice cube clinking inside his glass right as Priscella's jaw drops open. "I would never allow that."

She's catching onto what's happening underneath the

table. But she says nothing. Not a word. She only stares at me, her brows furrowing in a frozen expression. It's amusing, really, possibly the most satisfying thing I've experienced—her, the only one sober enough to read my facial expressions.

I hold her gaze with fire behind my eyes, making a show of it, twisting my eyebrows upwards as I grind my pussy against his palm.

"Whatever." Sterling scoffs. "I know your real type. The type that keeps you interested—actresses, models..."

Sterling's voice fades into the distance as Damien's fingers dip past my entrance, causing more juices to spill onto the leather beneath us.

"... dancers. Someone with connections and a reputation." His nostrils flare, the liquid sloshing from the rim of his glass as intoxicated clouds swim in his eyes. "Someone you could bring around the family."

I can barely hear his poisonous words, *can barely decipher where I am.* All I focus on are the fingers thrusting past my folds and the palm smacking against my clit upon his entrances. His lips brush against my ear, completely ignoring his brother and causing a shiver to race up my body. "You're making a mess, baby."

I stifle a mewl as I feel my ass cheeks get wet. He dives again, invading the slickness that's pooling beneath my opening, with no fabric to stop it, before plunging back into me.

He does all this underneath the judging eyes of Priscella, who steals a glance at Sterling. Her angry expression deepens when she realizes he's completely oblivious, as are the rest at the table, all too drunk to function.

"What am I to do with you?" Damien cocks his head, eyes roaming down my body. At his angle, I'm completely exposed, my dress bunching at my waist and the bareness of my panties leaving my sensitive flesh on full display. "Shall I make you clean it up?"

Haughty need nips at me when Sterling calls for another round. Priscella wraps her arm around his, wearing a look of desperation. "Shouldn't we retire? It's getting late." But Sterling shrugs her off.

I grin at her before I snap my head to Damien, keeping my voice low. "N-no."

"No? Well, luckily for you, I'm feeling generous. I'll give you three options." He hooks his free hand around the lingerie straps again. "Option one. You can keep your tight mouth shut and come for me in front of your ex, and I'll forget all about your needy cunt ruining these leather seats."

"Two. I can force you underneath this table and watch as your little tongue licks the leather clean." He tugs the fabric, cinching my lips even tighter. "Or three. I'll kick everyone out of *my* restaurant and mop the booth with your perfect tits as I fuck you from behind."

Blood pumps wildly between my legs, having never felt such a sensation. A fiery, needy pleasure mixed with pain shoots up my insides as I helplessly take the thrashing he inflicts upon me.

"Which will it be?" he coos.

The server hands off Sterling's next glass, and I fight so hard not to reveal anything from my face, but it's nearly impossible. He takes a sip, his glass rocking in his grip as I mouth the answer to Damien, unable to get the word out.

"One? Oh, you poor thing, you need to come?" His pace turns punishing, driving himself all the way to the knuckles.

Grasping the edge of my seat, I climb the wave of euphoria. And right as the wave threatens to crash, Sterling's glass slips from his grip, crashing against the floor.

"Shit," he curses, lifting the tablecloth before lowering his head—

Underneath the table.

I gasp, moving to cover myself up, but Damien's hand clutches my thigh, pinning me in place with my legs spread wide. Sterling doesn't return, which could only mean one thing.

He's watching.

"Such a good girl. Show him who you belong to." A hungry growl sounds in my ear. "Make my brother watch my touch do what his couldn't."

I try to stop the inevitable, but his fingers pound me into submission until I'm free-falling off the ledge with my head tilting backwards, an orgasm ricocheting throughout my entire body. Then I'm completely at his mercy as he widens my legs further, putting me on full display.

My inner walls pulsate tightly around him, desperate for every ounce of pleasure. When I slow, I'm met with Priscella's gawking face, her jaw in danger of smacking the table. Next, it's Sterling's eyes who cross my vision before they crawl to Damien.

And they're of pure jealousy.

A moan breezes past my lips when his fingers pull from my entrance, leaving me with a dull throb. I melt into the back of my seat, unashamed and overtaken by the sheer force of my orgasm.

With heavy lids, I watch Damien reveal two glistening fingers above the tablecloth, shooting a smug yet lethal stare towards Sterling. His gaze never wavers, not for a second, as he does something my eyes can hardly believe, something that whirls my head in circles like a spinning top.

He sinks both fingers into his mouth.

Sterling's expression unfolds past jealousy, his jaw hardening with potent wrath and hatred I can practically feel across the table. A popping sound rings out from Damien's lips, followed by a low groan that causes my legs to clench together.

"What was that, brother?" Damien's smile is brazen before he wraps a napkin around his wet digits. "It appears I got carried away with my dessert."

TWENTY-ONE

DAMIEN

EVEN THOUGH IT'S been a week since our date, I can still see the look my brother gave me at dinner when I close my eyes. The copious amounts of alcohol he ingested that night couldn't hide the rage on his face. Couldn't conceal the jealousy in its purest form when he realized what I'd done, how I'd corrupted Hannah.

But although I can't stop replaying the night in my head—the way she offered herself up to me, melted in my hands like chocolate—one nagging thought refuses to leave my brain.

Did she do it because she wanted it? Because she wanted me?

Sterling's words slither about in my brain, the ones he threw at me during our family gathering. *If she's messing around with you, it's only to get my attention.*

Maybe he was right. Maybe the notorious playboy broke her heart, and I'm a stepping-stone to get back to who she really wants.

John appraises me through the rearview mirror of the car, clearly reading my torment. I avoid his eyes, trying not to think about how good Hannah looks sitting beside me in her dress. And I *especially* don't think about how good she smells. Lilac blossoms dance their way up my nostrils as I stare out the window.

I shouldn't care if it was for me or him. All I should care about is that night was confirmation I'm getting one step closer to what I want. My eyes wander, trailing up her crossed legs.

And what I want is Hannah Lockwood spread wide for me in my bed, I remind myself.

I'm not a man who entertains relationships or the idea of them. I don't have the time. I've had them, sure, but they were never as serious as the tabloids made them out to be, and that's because I kept them that way, never allowing myself to get too close.

That's the way I prefer. I've never seen the merit in having a close partner. They're a distraction that never lands me any closer to what I truly want—the revenge fantasy that clouds my waking eyes and judgment since that night...

Piano keys and splattered blood shine behind my vision. I shut my eyes, hoping to disperse the awful memory. When it proves futile, I look at her instead, and the memory zips away.

Hannah...

She hasn't fully opened herself up for me, and many parts of her remain a mystery. How can a girl remain so cheerful and grounded, given the rough childhood she seems to have had?

She never talks about it, but somehow... she mentioned it to Sterling, with that familiar molten fire in her eyes I've grown to crave. I see it *often.* In my dreams, where I want that fire directed at me instead, but I can't realize my dreams into a reality.

Which is why today we're not working at Innovex headquarters. Because if I have to endure her tempting sass and perfect figure one more day in my office, then I really won't be able to hold myself back any longer.

"Won't you at least tell me where we're going?" Hannah whines.

"It's best kept a surprise."

"Hmph." She crosses her arms with a look on her face that almost makes me smile... *almost.*

"Patience, my little protégée," I tease, her lips tugging at her nickname. "Patience."

I don't know how her nickname came to be, but it just seemed fitting. She really has more power than she realizes, but she lacks the confidence to put herself out of her comfort zone. And that's where I plan to swoop in.

I hide my smirk, knowing damn well where we're headed to.

"Maybe you could tell me what we'll be *doing?"* She swipes through various emails on her work tablet.

"No can do. Focus on your slides. You *did* finish them, right?"

"Work, work, work." She eyes me. "That's all you think about. You *breathe* work... And, duh, of course, I finished my slides."

She's not wrong...

I *do* breathe work, which is why yesterday I assigned her slides to create. She thinks they're to be sent to me, and I'll read them later. They're to inform me of which companies my board members are interested in buying out.

I am due to meet with potential owners in nearly a month, and we hope to select a match before our Nano-X chip goes live. So, before then, Hannah and I will need to appear to be a happy, newly engaged couple. One who can gracefully handle the opening of a new product line together, in front of an audience of thousands, giving Innovex the shining image it needs during our buying market.

My father's teachings replay in my ear. *An owner needs to know they're handing off their baby to trusting hands that won't ruin their image.* While he may be abusive and self-righteous and a million other things, he is as wise in business as he is ruthless, a trait I seem to have inherited.

Hannah shoots me a curious smirk laced with her alluring charm I've grown accustomed to. I fold my hands into my lap, a little *too* tightly. Because I can't stop the aching feeling that crawls across my skin and into my next thought.

My allotted time with Hannah is closing out fast.

"WHEN YOU SAID I needed to finish my slides..." Hannah's steps are meticulous, her tall heels echoing in the open space. "This isn't what I expected at all."

I shuffle in the fold-up chair I'm much too large for, trying to get comfortable. My long legs jut out from the metal, spreading too wide to appear normal. I'm sitting in the front row of a sea of chairs, in the very center, with the best view of Hannah standing on stage.

"I said you needed to practice."

She picks at her nails, eyes squinting at the spotlight pointing at her.

"I know. But this is.... extreme—even for you. I could just practice to the board, or to you or... even better, all alone in my apartment. Maybe Sofia could watch."

"That won't do." My voice booms, echoing across the open

space. "You need to get a feel for your surroundings, the *exact* stage we'll present on during the Silicon Summit."

"O-okay." She shields her eyes from the bright lighting, and an aching feeling ripples across my gut. I crush it back down, knowing she's strong enough to handle this.

Even though no one's here but us in the enormous auditorium, I still remember practicing on the stage a day before my first Summit. I was a little younger than her, presenting research with my fellow university group members. You never know how it feels, how intimidating the rows of chairs look in their hooded darkness—even empty—until you're up there.

And I was just a nerdy kid then, enthralled with physics and science and the fastest-growing field in the world.

"You don't have to say anything yet. Just walk around."

She nods.

Luckily for her, she looks divine. Ravishing. There's no doubt, even standing next to me, all eyes will be on her that day.

Her heels clack as she walks, her modest dress clutching her knees. The smoky dress hugs her curves in just the right way, in all the right places. As tiny as she is, the stage doesn't seem to eat her away like it does with many people. No, her hair stands out beneath the spotlights and her heels give her a confident ray, even if her expression doesn't.

How could you not *look at her?* My eyes track her every movement, soaking her in like she might disappear and never return.

The bottom of her shoe scrapes against the wooden floor, stopping in center stage. "What now?" Her hand skates along her arm.

"Now, you get mic'd up." I hook my ankle on top of my

knee. Resting my elbow on a nearby chair, I pull out my phone. "She's ready."

No more than ten seconds pass before a skinny man walks onto the stage. His steps hurry, cords dangling from his arms with a tape roll hung around his wrist.

After a flurry of tape dispensing and looping cords discreetly under her clothes, Hannah looks seamless. Not a cord is visible on her, except the thin mic that runs along her jawline. A puffy ball settles on the end, inches from her red lips.

The man nods to her, urging her to speak.

"H-hello?" Her voice is meek, but it doesn't stop the way she booms across the walls, causing her to jump back.

A sheepish smile creeps across her lips, and the technician retrieves a remote from his pocket before twisting a knob. Again, she speaks, and this time the volume lowers, but it's still powerful enough to be heard anywhere in the room.

The technician gives her a thumbs up and glances my way. "The slides will be visible to her momentarily."

I nod to him, and he darts backstage again.

She eyes me nervously, but I refuse to go easy on her. She needs this. I know how big that night will be for her. It's *only* going to be her most important moment for her future career on Silicon Avenue. So, she needs to be prepared.

"Alright, Hannah. Let's see what you got."

"MR. LEE of Innovex's board has suggested buying out Lumen Link, owned by Jay Nielson, for two years." She clicks the remote in her hand, and the projector behind her switches slides. Keeping her head facing forward, she occasionally glances downward at a prompter kept hidden from the audience. "He states that while the company may be relatively new, it has promising projections and—"

I hold up my hand, and her sentence abruptly halts. "Move around a bit. It's a large stage. Slow, confident steps... Good."

She speaks, continuing about the company.

I've heard of it before, having done my own research. And while they *are* a quite promising company on Silicon Avenue, what Mr. Lee doesn't know is that I know his angle. He has substantial shares invested in Lumen Link, and if Innovex buys it out, their share prices will sky-rocket.

In fact, recently, any company I merely take on as a client has had the same effect. So, while it *is* a company worth considering, I won't take his interests into account.

"Try holding your hands at your middle when you don't know where to place them. No, not quite like that, like—" I stand to my feet before I round the stage and bound up the side steps.

The spotlights blare into my eyes, taking me a moment to adjust. The closer I get to her, the more regal she looks. She looks *made* for the spotlight, and when I'm inches from her, I decide to show her *physically*. Coming from behind, I wrap my arms around her tiny frame. Her gasp echoes through the speakers—not that I nor the thousands of non-existent audience members mind.

"Like this." Her hair tickles my lips as I run my fingertips along her arms. I clasp her hands in mine, gently placing her hands together, resting them comfortably at her middle with her palms facing upwards.

"Does that feel better?" I breathe deep, the scent of her hair dousing my senses.

"Yes," she whispers.

Her breathing is shallow and doesn't pick up on the mic. But a part of me wants it to, wants it to be apparent to the missing cameras and guests of how I affect her.

Her skin is soft in my calloused hands, and I'm keenly aware of my desire to intertwine our fingers together, to stay here as she continues her speech to no one. I could close my eyes and listen to her eloquently spoken words right behind her...

But I force myself to move, unclasping myself from her warm aura before returning to my seat.

"MR. THORNTON HAS RECOMMENDED BUYING out ShutterLux, owned by Mr. Victor Strauss. The camera company has been in business for over fifteen years, and has a market value of twenty-five billion."

She paces across the stage, her legs steady and confident.

"And, finally, Arison Hosting Services, owned by the Gonzales family, has a market share of fifteen billion with a stock value that has risen over twenty percent the previous fiscal year. Their company stands as the top hosting provider for over twenty-five years and is recommended by several board members, including Mrs. Carter, Mr. Garrison, and..."

In the short time I've been coaching her, Hannah is doing remarkably well, better than many who I've seen on stage. And I know they've had much more practice. Her back is straight. Head level. Shoulders back. Her speech is clear—

"... a-and..."

Oh, no.

Her eyes squint as she tries to read the next name on the

slide. "*And...*" She releases a substantial breath, her eyes growing wide before they find mine.

She's freaking out. It's normal, really. I did it once, years ago, but instead there were thousands of eyes and uncomfortable expressions staring at me blankly. *Everyone does it at some point, but she doesn't understand that.*

She makes to speak to me, but she stops, eyes glancing down at her mic.

"Move the mic up." I offer her a soft smile.

"H-hello?" No echo, only her sweet voice suddenly sounding close to me.

"The mic is very insensitive," I explain. "It needs to be right at your mouth when you speak or else it won't pick up anything."

"Good to know." She chuckles nervously, coming closer to the edge of the stage.

"Look..." Worry clouds her eyes as I crane my neck to gaze at her in all her lit-up glory. "I'm not cut out for this. I know it's important for our deal, but I don't want to damage your company's reputation."

She huffs a sad breath, and I let her continue, thinking if she does, it'll make her feel better. She settles down low, sitting with her legs dangling over the edge of the stage. "This is way out of my wheelhouse. I have a hard time talking in front of *any* crowd."

"And why's that?" I stand, my head coming to the same height as hers. "Because you've never practiced. No one who will be on this stage that night will have been comfortable their first time."

"Even then." Her head hangs low, avoiding my stare. "I don't even know the first thing about tech. I have a *business management* degree, not a doctorate in some science path from a fancy school like everyone else who'll be here."

"It's a speech. A pre-planned presentation. There'll be no test or unexpected topic you won't be prepared for. At the end, if there are questions, I'll answer them for you."

"People will see right through me and wonder why I'm there. You don't need me."

"No, Hannah." Clasping her chin between my thumb and forefinger, I lift until her soft brown eyes meet mine. My heart thunders in my chest, knotting in anticipation of what could come out of my mouth.

I can't breathe without you.

I can't think around you.

I need to be beside you.

But I don't utter the words, don't allow them to seep into our air. Because they're better left in the darkness that eats away the inside of me. Because I need revenge more than her light. Because I'm a coward, unable to admit the thoughts. Not to her. Not even to myself.

So I stay in the cold, and say what's easier.

"I need you by my side that night."

TWENTY-TWO
HANNAH

I'VE ALWAYS LOVED THUNDERSTORMS. But I've never seen one from this high up.

Sitting criss cross on the couch in fascination, my eyes glue to the white light rippling across the clouds, shining above central park. I shovel the next handful of popcorn in my mouth, the buttery goodness sparking my tastebuds.

The city is still as busy as ever, the color of grid-locked cars on the streets smearing through the wet windows. People who move along sidewalks look like little dots from up here.

I have all the lights off to get the best possible view of the storm. When the next strike flashes, I whip my head around, scanning the dark room.

No one.

Arthur already went to bed, seeing as it's nearing midnight, but it would be nice to watch it with *someone.* That doesn't seem to be the case, though. Just me in a multi-million-dollar penthouse in pajamas with my popcorn to watch the storm.

Couldn't he at least get a cat?

A knot twists inside me, thinking of how Sofia would kill to be here right now. Maybe I should've invited her—if Damien would even allow that. We always watch storms together, our necks craning out of our tiny apartment windows to look up at the sky, laughing as our faces get drenched.

Maybe she's watching with Jenna. The guilty feeling lifts a little. *She must've moved into the spare bedroom fully by now.*

Another flash... Still no one.

Where's Damien?

I stand, leaving my popcorn on the cushion and tightly wrapping a blanket around my shoulders. I creep around in the darkness, at first feeling my way about until my eyes adjust to the light.

I've never felt uneasy during a storm. Quite the opposite actually, but there's something eerie about checking dozens of rooms, flipping their lights on and discovering them, not only empty but shockingly *bare*.

What does a single man do with all this space? I discover a laundry room, next to a fully equipped workout room. *Who needs so many spare bedrooms, with no one else to live with?*

Reaching the end of the hall, I come face-to-face with the final door. No light seeps through the crack at the bottom, and no sounds either. So when I open the door, I expect to find a room similar to the others. But I don't.

I jerk back, my soul nearly leaving my body.

A laptop shines against Damien's face, glowing eerily in the room's darkness. With the curtains drawn shut, the crashing of thunder rumbles in the distance. Behind his enormous mahogany desk, he leans into the screen, his loose tie hanging around his neck.

I keep watching, stuck frozen in the doorway. He doesn't notice me at all, completely consumed by whatever he's looking at as his fingers swipe the trackpad. There's something... uneasy about him, like he's been looking for a long time. Hours, maybe.

"Damien?"

His bloodshot eyes snap up, but he doesn't quite look *at* me, only in my general direction. It takes a moment before he responds. "Oh, Hannah... I'll be out soon."

His eyes finally meet mine, red veins lining his irises.

"Do you want to watch the thunderstorm together, or have me open the curtains for you?"

His brows wrinkle, and it's then I wonder if he knows there's a storm. A muffled boom sounds in the distance, and his back straightens, confirming my suspicion. "That's alright. I need to finish up."

I feel a sudden urge to convince him to leave his work, as if it's some disease eating away at his life source. I don't know what he's working on, or if he'd care if I saw, but before I ask permission, my feet are already in motion.

His hand wraps around the top of the screen, but I snatch his wrist, lowering it back to the table. "Let me see. Maybe I can help."

The bright light blasts through my vision, but I force myself to peruse the black text on the screen. My brows furrow, confusion wrapping tighter around my middle the more I read.

Thud. Thud. Thud. My heart pounds at its ribcage, because the words make little sense. They shouldn't be there.

Why would Innovex give Bass Mobile the new Nano-X chip? Even for a year?

"Why..." I don't finish my question, scrolling further down

the document, until I discover the truth laid bare in all its twisted glory.

He's taking Sterling's shares of Bass Mobile.

All of them.

I think back to every insult he threw my way, about my family, about my capabilities, and the way he acted the other night at dinner. I *should* want him crushed. I *should* want him to face the merciless tendrils of karma. And, even better, at the hands of his brother I seem to be in a relationship with. There couldn't be a better scenario for me to gloat.

But the satisfaction that courses through my veins encounters something unexpected...

Pity. Only a sliver, but it's still there.

"Damien." I meet his eyes, to find not an ounce of shame in them. "That will ruin him. You're not really going to—"

His fingers slide along the trackpad, zooming through the endless ocean of legal jargon before hitting the bottom. A single dotted line lies there.

With his signature on it.

"Don't worry, he's needed a wake-up call for quite some time. And this way, he'll never be able to speak down to you again."

"But..." My gut drops at the thought of him doing this for me, for destroying Sterling out of jealousy. "Why would your father do that to him?"

"Maybe because he's dead weight at Bass Mobile."

An unmistakable guard shields his eyes as he looks away, and it's obvious he's not telling me something, keeping me in the dark from the whole truth. But I don't push, only place my hand on his shoulder, hoping to draw him away from his work.

What's done is done. Maybe Sterling really *does* need an

intervention, to be thrown to rock-bottom. I can't pretend to know him half as well as Damien, who's known him his entire life.

Maybe Damien really is *trying to help him.*

Or... that's what I'm telling myself.

My touch seems to draw him back to me, and when his eyes return to mine, I go still. I can hardly breathe looking into their depths. An unseen hollowness lies there, and the ire in his voice is unmistakable, sending shivers up my spine.

He shuts his laptop, plunging us into total darkness.

"Sterling's fate pales in comparison to what I have planned for my father."

TWENTY-THREE
DAMIEN

I TAP MY FOOT IMPATIENTLY, pressing my phone to my ear. "And *why* couldn't we let John drive us to this secretive date of yours again?"

A full duffle bag sits on the ground by my feet as I wait in the apartment's parking garage. She said we would be gone the entire weekend and hasn't given me a single hint about where we're going or what we're doing.

It's not that I hate surprises, it's just... *that I do.* They're uncontrollable. And that sentiment alone goes against my very nature.

"Where's the fun in that?" Hannah's voice spews from the phone, and I jerk my head away before bringing it back to hear the familiar honking of the New York streets coming from her end. "And besides, you offered me your company card for the rental, so I couldn't resist."

I sigh, staring at the rows of luxury cars, many of them mine. "Do you know how many cars I own?"

Twenty-two of them, I don't tell her, each one a different supercar imported from around the world, several a slim few of their kind. Admittedly, I need to take them out more. I've grown accustomed to John driving me everywhere, as it's easier to work on the way to and from the office.

"No... But I know none of them were quite the right fit for this weekend."

"I find that hard to believe." I pinch the bridge of my nose. "Well, you at least rented a nice car, yes?"

"Of course. She's a beauty."

"Good. And a nice hotel?"

"Mhmm. I know a pampered royal like yourself couldn't handle anything less."

I roll my eyes, not questioning her suspicious tone. "Are you almost back? I've been standing here for thirty minutes."

Thirty minutes I could've spent sleeping, I think, resisting a yawn.

She demanded we leave early, and it's now the crack of dawn, almost six-thirty in the morning. She must've scheduled my jet for takeoff like I suggested, and we probably have an early flight.

At least we'll beat the traffic to the airport.

"Yep!" she squeals, alarmingly cheerful.

The line dies without a goodbye, and I stare down at my phone, confused, right when a terrible groan booms throughout the garage. It collides and bounces against the walls, invading every corner and hurting my ears. What sounds like a mechanical beast wheezing and gasping for breath follows.

I lift my head, and I immediately wish I hadn't. Because what I see burns a clean hole straight through my eyes.

The most rusted, old, excuse-of-a-truck I've ever seen pulls through the entrance, making its way towards me. I glance around, hoping to see someone else waiting beside me, because *that* cannot be for me.

But no. There's no one. No one but me and the trash on wheels passing by rows and rows of shiny cars. It couldn't look more out of place with its offensive orange coloring that I can't tear my eyes from, almost as if I'm watching a tsunami on the shorelines of a beach, knowing there's no escaping its impending doom.

As it nears, I spot Hannah sitting in the driver's seat, wearing a sparkling grin that shines through the windshield.

Oh, no. What've I gotten myself into?

She pulls up to the curb, yanking the stick shift that causes the car to whine to a stop, before she beams at me through the window. When I don't move, her smile droops. She leans over the center console, working a mysterious lever I can't see from where I'm standing. With each circular sway of her forearm, the window lowers an inch, revealing her gleaming, chocolate eyes.

"Get in, loser."

Mean Girls…? Really?

"You're not Regina George. Not driving that dinosaur."

Her eyebrows tick upwards with a grin. "Who would've guessed? The heir to the Bass' conglomerate watches chick-flicks."

"Not me." I clutch my bag, sludging my feet from their invisible cement prison. "My mother is very fond of rom-coms."

"Suurree. However you like to justify it to yourself." She flicks her wrist, pointing her thumb outward. "Throw your bag in the bed and let's get on the road."

In the bed? I peer over its railing, spotting a purple suitcase lying flat on its back, appearing brand new.

Eyeing mine cautiously, I hold back a grumble. *This is ridiculous.* What's stopping someone from reaching in and stealing my stuff when we're at a red light? I packed valuables—watches, suit jackets, sunglasses.

After a deep sigh, I lug it over the ledge, admitting there's no better option. With only two doors, the truck doesn't have a backseat.

I tug on the passenger side handle, cringing as it creaks. The weight of the door is shocking. When it's open, I catch a view of what Hannah's wearing. Words catch in my throat and my heart beats fast in my rib cage as I try to not stare.

A red-and-white checkered blouse wraps at her middle with frilly sleeves hanging off her shoulders. Several buttons loosen at the top, revealing rings of gold necklaces. My eyes trail downward to the ripped blue jean shorts snagging at her legs, making her thighs look down-right delectable.

Suddenly, my mouth feels dry as I hop up onto my seat, getting an even closer look at her.

She's fucking divine.

"You're wearing that?" Hannah quirks her brow at my loose-fitting long-sleeve and white trousers.

"You said dress casual. I did. Is there something wrong with what I'm wearing?"

"Nope." She bites her lip, like she's holding back a laugh. "Nothing at all."

Ignoring the irritation pricking at my temple, I cross my arms as I try to get comfortable in the tight space, my knees cramming up against the glove compartment.

I don't know where we're going, but with the way she looks, I'll follow her anywhere. Hell, she could drive straight for a cliff, and I won't complain. I may not even notice it.

I CLUTCH onto the grip above my door, what I like to call the *oh-shit handle.*

"Quit being such a baby." Hannah rolls her eyes, wrapping her hand around the shifter, her glittery pink nails a glaring contrast from the metallic stick. She rams it into the next gear, trying to get up to speed. "Listen to it purr."

"Purr?!"

I whip my head, a bead of sweat forming on my hairline as cars zoom past us on the on-ramp.

We're not making it at this speed. We're going to get run off the highway into a ditch by some semi-truck. My breaths come out in choppy bursts. *We can't merge on the highway, not going...* I steal a glance at the speedometer—*FORTY?*

Fuck, FUCK. My grip tightens, bleaching my knuckles white.

"That's no purr. That's a hunk of metal on its last life, crying out for mercy. No, you'd know what a real purr sounded like if you'd *listened to me* and taken one of my cars to the airport."

This is exactly why I don't like surprises, why I feel the need to micromanage everything in my life. *Because I do.* And when I don't, I end up in situations that could've been avoided. Like this one—crawling down the highway with a questionable driver behind the wheel of *hardly-more-than-four-wheels-and-an-engine.*

"Airport?" Rummaging through the center console, she fishes out a piece of gum. While using both hands to unwrap the foil, she balances the wheel between her elbows.

We're going to die.

I blink. "Yes. The airport."

By some miracle, we seem at equal speeds with the other vehicles, and we begin to merge. Hannah jerks the wheel, prompting all my hairs to stick on their ends. She doesn't use her blinker. She doesn't look at her mirrors. And not a lick of sweat shines on her forehead as we sandwich ourselves between two tightly packed cars.

I release a breath, my fluttering heart rate calming.

"Why would we be going there?"

I flick my eyes to her, finding her containing a smirk. *Oh, she better be joking.*

"You said we'd be gone for the weekend."

"Yes... And that somehow involves a plane?"

"Of course, it does. *My plane.*"

"Pfft." She scrunches her brow at me. "We don't need your fancy jet to get to where we're going."

"I thought you said I needed to take my mind off work. Well, there's only so many places to do that—Mexico, Bora Bora, the Maldives, Hawaii. See what they all have in common? White, sandy beaches. And I surely know we aren't finding those on the shores of New York."

"No, no, no. You got me all wrong. I said you needed to *live a little.*"

"Okay, great. Let's fly to Vegas, then."

She rolls her eyes *again,* and I stifle the spark in my core that urges me to reprimand her. Instead, I sit back with my arms crossed and watch as she yanks the stick into another gear.

God, why is she so aggressive with that thing?

"Easy there, speed racer. This old hunk of junk might prefer a gentle touch. Who knows how much longer it has left?"

I shouldn't doom the vehicle we're currently driving. Talk

about bad karma, but I love the way Hannah scowls, shooting me a scolding look.

"This Chevy's a good year, with minimal mileage. It's got plenty of life left to live."

"Does it now?" I tease. "The sudden car expert, now, are you?"

"I..." Her expression falters before it's quickly replaced with confidence. "I just know good American muscle when I see it. That's all."

"Hate to break it to you, baby. But I think your American muscle is nothing but dry bones now."

Her laugh that follows shines bright in her eyes and sends a bundle of warmth darting across my skin.

IT'S BEEN SIX HOURS.

Six hours on the road. I don't know if I can take it for much longer. I don't remember how long it's been since I've been in a car half that time. Under any other scenario, I would've either taken my jet or Innovex's company helicopter.

Not only have I had to endure Hannah's sketchy driving and poor singing skills, I had to pee. *Off the side of the road* like some animal, because there hasn't been a rest-stop or anything remotely close to civilization in miles.

I bristle, thinking about the grimy feeling between my fingers. My hands need to be sanitized. Maybe my whole body.

Hannah, though? Hannah is *free*. In a way that's captivating and mysterious, with the radio blaring and hair flowing out the side of the window.

"Are we almost there yet?" I shift in my chair.

"Almost," she hollers over the speakers.

"You said that the last three times."

She whips her head at me, tendrils of her hair sliding off her shoulder. "Patience."

I groan, feeling like a child. Who am I kidding? How could she possibly know where we're going? We're in the middle of nowhere on a two-lane road, winding through a forest of trees so thick, I can hardly see through them. And twenty minutes have passed since we've seen another car—*at least.*

"Won't you finally tell me where we're going so—"

"There!" she exclaims, causing me to jolt back. Her arm juts out in front of her, a proud smile lining her lips. "I told you I knew where I was going."

Confusion wraps around me as I dart my head back and forth, feeling like some aimless windshield wiper. No buildings. No sparkling ocean breaking through the tree lines. Nothing. Only a blue, two-posted sign.

WELCOME TO MYRTLE LAKE

Population: 2700

TWENTY-FOUR
HANNAH

"WHEN YOU SAID I needed to live a little, this is *not* what I thought you had in mind."

Damien wears a scowl as he dips his gloved hand into his bucket once more, before tossing the next round of chicken feed. His back slouches, preventing his head from hitting the short ceiling of the chicken coop.

I mirror his movements but without gloves, the dry feed of grain and canola bundling in my palms. "A relaxing day at Lockwood Farms could lift anyone's spirits."

During our first date, when he agreed I could plan the next one, I truly thought he needed a change of pace in his life. But it wasn't until I saw the horrors in his eyes the night of the thunderstorm that I realized he was *desperate* for it. Fake relationship or not, from then on, I was determined to take his mind off work.

And when my mom called a few nights ago about needing someone to watch the farm for the weekend while they took my younger brother off to college, I thought it was a perfect opportunity to distract him.

"You call *this* relaxing?" He carefully steps over a pile of poop, scrunching his nose. I bite my lip, holding back a laugh. He really couldn't look more disgusted if he tried. "How about a massage? Or a day at the spa? We could've flown off to some European country or the Bahamas. But no. Instead, you decided I needed to pick up feces and tend to livestock."

"Hey, you're lucky, you know."

"And how's that?"

My eyes flicker up the length of his body, past the cowboy boots and overalls protecting his fancy clothes. "That my brother is remotely your same size. How many people do you know have size fourteen feet? Your pretty loafers would've been a goner."

He huffs a sigh. "Why are we even spreading food in here? The chickens obviously don't like to hang out in their coop."

He's not wrong. There's only a single hen nuzzled in her nest in the entire coop. The rest are outside, basking in the sunny rays. It's the last days of summer, and it's nice to let the chickens roam free when it's not raining.

"Because they come in here at night. We'll need to collect their eggs outside and usher them in here before it gets dark."

"What? We have to chase after them?" He stops in his tracks, and the hen—Bella, is her name, with the splattered feathers of orange and black—rustles. Damien jumps back, startled.

This time, my laugh breaks through. "Yes, they can't run around at night."

"Why not? I saw you guys have a fence."

"Well, they can hop the fence, and it's not safe outside at night with the coyotes and raccoons."

An uncomfortable look spreads across his face, but he quickly masks it. "Why don't they stay in here, then?"

Why is he arguing with me? This is simple stuff.

My hand flies to my hip, my red pail dangling in my other. "They're *free-range*. We aren't cruel here, like many other farms."

He cocks his head with a quizzical look.

"Never mind," I mumble. "Let's go. It's time for the fun part—collecting eggs."

"Thank god." His steps rush as his eyes scan for poop to miss, stomping all the way down the ramp until he's out of the coop.

Shaking my head, I follow his lead.

Once outside, the sun shines right above the tops of the trees, hitting my eyes. My shoulders relax, feeling its calming rays warm my spine.

Changing scenery from the big city to where I grew up is quite the shell shock. It's so... *slow* here. Even when the fields weren't damaged and farm hands bustled about our land, it still doesn't compare to the chaos of New York City. No wailing sirens or honking car horns along the cityscape. Only the subtle singing of birds and the distant cows mooing.

If I'm honest with myself, I can admit there are certain parts of the farm life I miss. The structure, the community. But deep down, I knew from an early age that I didn't belong in such a small town. That I *needed* to experience more. To see what else life has to offer. And now that I uprooted myself to a place vastly different, I know there's no going back.

The aspirations I have don't fit in a town the size of Myrtle Lake, no matter its charm and memories it holds.

I pick up another wide pail, handing it to Damien.

"This one's for the eggs," I say, feeling my phone buzz in my pocket.

He takes it, quirking his brow. I twist on my heels to avoid his prying eyes, but I can feel him over my shoulder in an instant.

I check the caller ID.

Jacob.

Why would he be calling? Worry swims through me. *Shouldn't they be on the plane by now?*

I whirl around, jerking my head to the side. "Go on—go pick some eggs."

His eyes darken, practically demanding an answer from me. But I'm not giving him one. We may have an agreement, but that doesn't require me to reveal each and every person I talk to.

What is with this possessive man?

He leaves and I press the phone to my ear before the final ring. "Jacob? Is everything okay?"

"Relax, *Mom.*" His snicker bounces through the line. "Everything's fine."

"Ha. Ha." All the concern fizzles from me. "I may have deserved that. But shouldn't you guys be on the plane?"

"Delayed. Guess the previous flight is late. Typical," he spats between his obvious munching.

Does he ever stop eating?

"That sucks. Well, don't worry. You'll be in Seattle in no time."

I make my way through the yard, scanning for eggs to gather and hens to miss. Their coats are fluffy with a vast array of colors, and their heads bob to and from the ground, nibbling on feed hidden between blades of grass.

"Ya... Well, I was just calling to see if you made it... And because I'm bored sitting here in the café. Mom and Dad went to get sandwiches."

Even though we've always been close, Jacob still won't admit it because he's too proud. But I can hear the worry in his voice, oozing out the other line like thick paint. Moving across the country for college to play hockey is a huge decision for him, especially because the farm life *does* suit him, unlike me.

He's a country boy, through and through, who'll need to adapt to fraternities and the big ice. So, as his older sister, even though I know he called for reassurance, I won't call out his bait.

"Ya, w—" I bite my tongue, feeling stupid. I almost blew my cover—it's only supposed to be me here. I definitely *do not* need my family knowing what kind of situation I got myself into for their sake. *"I* got here an hour or two ago. Going to herd the chickens in the coop soon."

His tone has an unmistakable glee to it. "Good luck getting Reggie in there."

"Oh my god." I pinch the bridge of my nose, bending down to gather my first egg. "Don't tell me—"

"Yep. He still does."

"Crap."

Reggie's our rooster, our *only* rooster, who has the annoying habit of hiding on tree branches to avoid being kenneled. When I still lived here, it was only him doing it. But ever since, I've heard he has set a bad example, and now the hens are doing it too...

The only way to get them down is with a broom.

A grin forms on my lips. *I know who'll be perfect for that job.*

"Have you thought more about whether you'll rush the fraternities there?" I gather another egg, gently placing it beside the first one in my pail.

"One hundred percent, I'm rushing."

There's the fiery Jacob I know. But my big-sister protective-ness still seeps in. "Don't do anything I wouldn't do."

"Oh, so I'm allowed to date a blond, rich douchebag, then?"

"Hey, keep it down. Mom and Dad aren't supposed to know about him." My face reddens at the mention of Sterling, making me instantly think of the last time I saw him. And the last thing *he* saw—Damien, with his fingers pumping in and out of... I shake my head, banishing the memory. "Besides, we aren't together anym—"

"Get off, get off!" Damien shrieks across the yard. I try to cover the mic, but it's too late. "Crazy fucking animal!"

I whip my head, only to discover him in a one-on-one match against Reggie, who's positioned himself between Damien and a flock of hens. His red comb atop his head flares in anger.

"Who's that?" Jacob spews from the speaker.

"Oh, uh..."

Reggie darts out, flanking Damien from the side, success-fully ushering him further from the flock.

"No one."

"No one?" He sounds pleased, as if he struck gold on future blackmail material to use against me later. "Okay, sis. Whatever you say."

I chuckle. "Well, I should let you go."

"Wait. There's one more thing."

My heart drops at the seriousness in his voice.

"What is it?" I look away from the chaotic scene, giving Jacob my full attention, Damien's hectic cries fading away in the distance.

"Mom and Dad won't ask, but they've been having problems with the tractor for weeks..."

A knot the size of a baseball twists in my gut, because I
know where this is going, what he's going to ask me to do.

"Dad obviously can't figure out what's wrong with it. It's
not really his area of expertise, like... You know what I'm
saying? A-and they'd never ask it of you, Hannah, never ask
you to go *in there* to take a look at it, but, but..." Wind crushes
against his mic in nervous breaths. "They were going to take
it to the repair shop, but things are rough financially right
now for them and—"

"I know," I whisper, and we share a silence through the
line for a few heartbeats. "I know it's bad."

I've neglected to look towards the fields the entire time
we've been here. Couldn't stand the thought of the way they
might—*will*—look so different. As if I keep it from my sight,
maybe it won't really be true and my family will hold on to
what they've built. They'll hold on *with their own hands,* not by
an unforeseen donation by some anonymous billionaire.

But that's not how the world works, not for us...

Turning my head, I cast my gaze upon the fields, past our
yellow house and its vaulted peaks. To the aftermath left
behind from the raging elements, from an unfortunate flood
no one could see coming. And the sight is *appalling.*

Pure devastation.

Erosion eats the ground, through and through. No proud
cornstalks shoot tall for as far as the eye can see. No neatly
packed rows of green. No farm hands tilling the soil and
gathering the yield. Just... *dirt* and weak leaves withering out
the sides of short shoots.

I whip back around, unable to look anymore, unable to

bear the reality. I swallow harshly, only to find my throat void of saliva. "I'll go into the shop. It's not a big deal."

"Okay..." His voice lacks conviction. And for good reason. Because I've hardly convinced myself to go back there.

Back to all the unsolved questions.

To the unfinished memories.

TWENTY-FIVE
DAMIEN

HANNAH POPS THE HOOD, lifting the green metal high above her head. The tractor she works on is a mechanical beast, with wheels the height of her chest and stairs leading up to the driver's seat.

I bury my hands in my pockets, balancing on the balls of my heels. I'll admit it. This place is impressive, a true man-cave that must be the dream of most middle-aged men. Metal signs hang high on the walls of the garage, spouting recogniz-able names like Ford, Coca-Cola and Shell. They appear to be retro, much like a truck in the corner, with its rounded edges and small wheels.

Through the windshield, glossy seats stand out in the inte-rior that was clearly refurbished by someone who knew what they were doing. Another car sits beside the truck, cloaked in mystery by a protective sheet draping over it, offering a vague outline of its exterior. The only other clue given is the shiny red paint left uncovered in one spot near a tire.

Hannah... *the mechanic?* I quirk my brow, a smile creeping

on my lips as I watch her size up the tractor. *She can't really think she's going to figure out whatever's wrong with it.*

My cocky grin disappears the instant she hoists herself up by the soles of her feet, balancing atop the wheels' axles like a gymnast on a trapeze. My lips part, as I can only stare when she cranes her body over the lip, shoving her bare hands deep inside the engine.

She's positively sinful, the bottoms of her ass cheeks peeking under her denim shorts and hair flowing down her back in pretty curls.

A flirty comment dances on the tip of my tongue that's sure to get her riled up, but I think better than to voice it, given her deafening silence. She hasn't said a single word since coming in here. I can sense the uneasiness and complicated anger coming from her, radiating off her body in unnerving waves.

"Do you need any help?" I ask quietly.

She takes a moment to reply, like she forgot I'm here. "Sure. Could you grab that flashlight?" She points. "It should be inside one of the drawers."

Rounding the tractor, I discover a shiny workbench pushed against the wall. Red drawers glide open, one after the other until a black flashlight reveals itself. I snatch it, but before I close the drawer, a dusty photograph steals my attention.

I tilt my head, studying the young girl in the photo on the shoulder of a large man wearing a mechanic's jumpsuit. Instantly, I know it's Hannah with two pigtails poking out the sides of her head, wearing a familiar smile. Behind them lies a proud Mustang convertible, its red paint glistening in the sunlight of their driveway. My eyes dart to the covered car, to the dust gathering on its sheet in thick clumps.

Guilt sweeps over me, because I've stumbled upon some-thing not meant for my eyes. I close the drawer and turn, only to find Hannah glaring down at me from her tall angle.

"I didn't mean to..." My head slumps to the ground, unable to hold her stare that clouds with somber mist.

"It's fine."

"Here." I offer her the flashlight.

But she doesn't take it, instead jerking her head. "Shine it in for me. Climb up the outside of the wheel."

I nod, stepping onto the rim. Once lifted, with my head returning to its comfortable height above hers, I shine the light into the engine.

A series of colorful wires weave between metal bolts and boxes, creating a daunting mess. While some components look vaguely familiar to the ones inside of a computer, I know when I'm outmatched.

This is completely out of my wheelhouse.

"Thank you." Her voice comes out small.

Curiosity nips at my heels like a rabid dog when our eyes connect. For a moment, I can see the need in them, the need to talk about it.

"Who is that with you in the photo?" I ask, my tone a gentle offering. "Your uncle?" She shakes her head, not meeting my eyes. "Your dad?" She says nothing, burying her hand between a jumble of wires.

"Was."

Was. I swallow.

"I'm sorry. I shouldn't have asked. I didn't know he—"

"Died?" Her laugh is hollow, eliciting goosebumps along my arms. "Oh, he didn't die. He just *left.*"

My light wobbles in my tightening grip, the grooves of metal burying themselves into my fingers. I shouldn't press, shouldn't ask such personal questions of her. But they're bubbling out of my mouth and burning a bright fire through my middle, needing to discover the deepest parts of her.

"Left? What do you mean—when?"

"When I was seven, and when my little brother, Jacob, was a baby," she explains, her voice void of a single emotion. Yanking what appears to be some belt out of the engine, she flings it over her shoulder before it clanks loudly against the floor. "He didn't say he was. He said he'd be back within a week, gone for *business*—quite odd, right? Coming from a mechanic who worked out of this shop. But then a week turned to a month, and then years."

My heart twists like a rope, and I have enough sense to remain silent.

"I guess he didn't have the gall to tell me the truth. To say it to my face. Instead, he left me here, waiting, wondering why all the other kids at school had dads who watched their sports games from the sidelines and laughed during the father-daughter dances and I didn't."

Her hands emerge covered in dust and blackness, the lights hanging high from the ceiling casting harsh shadows across her features.

"Have you had any contact with him since?"

"Nope. I found no trace of him online. It's like he disappeared from the face of the Earth. No explanation, no phone calls, no letters. Only me, my mom, and the two-year-old in her arms tending to a two-hundred-acre farm—until she met Marcus, of course. And soon, they married, and we all took his last name. Randall Farms became Lockwood Farms, and it's like he never existed. At least, that's how they tried to make it seem."

She hops down from her height, crossing the space before

returning with a long track dangling from her hand and a wrench in the other. "He could be dead for all I know."

"And your mom never told you why?"

"No." She hoists herself back onto the wheel, her brows scrunching in seriousness. "She knows more than she lets on, and even after years of pestering her, she still wouldn't tell me all she knows. She only said he wasn't worth finding and that he's bad for the family."

Sinking the track into the mess of bolts and wires, she loops it through a metallic ring attached to a square box.

A chill invades my gut at the thought of Hannah and I sharing a similar predicament. A man who's broken a family. I bite my tongue, my insides urging me to open up to her.

She's so full of light... I would've never guessed.

Is it possible someone like her handled it better than me? That she had the strength to move on with her life, not focusing on it and letting it destroy her?

"Unfortunately..." I swallow, heat crawling up my cheeks. "It seems we share that in common."

Her head whips to me. "What? Yours left too?"

"No." My eyes trail to her lips. The way they part screams at me to pick them as a distraction, to not go down this road with her. "But I wish he had."

"No, you don't." She feeds the track further in, the sounds of metal grinding against metal bouncing off my ears. "At least you have someone to hate. To potentially mend your relationship with. You have answers. You're not stuck chasing a *ghost*... But truthfully, I stopped chasing him years ago, and simply accepted that he either doesn't want to be found or he's dead."

Pain shuts my throat tight, my eyes burning with tears I don't allow to fall. If only I could tell her all that he's done to me, to my family, particularly my mother. How it consumes me, body and mind and soul, even after he loosened his grip on me. I need him to succumb to my wrath. I need to watch the empire he spent his entire life building crumble around him.

But I can't tell her—can't face the uncontrollable pity that would shine in her eyes if I did. She can't know about the monster who walks my nightly dreams, haunting me with the belt he wields as a makeshift whip.

"I don't know why I'm telling you all this." The way her voice cracks has me visceral. Panic and desperation claw at my insides when a single tear slides down her cheek. She jerks her head from me, running her forearm along her face. "Maybe it's easier, given that in two months' time we'll never see each other again."

I think hard about my next words. Because I'm vulnerable right now. I border on the slippery edge of saying anything she needs to hear, or giving her all that's at my disposal to find the man who left a ripple in her life.

"It doesn't have to be such a clean cut. If you ever need anything, any help... you can always call on me, and I'll come."

Our eyes connect, hers still damp but with a new defensive ice shining in them as she hardens her exterior from me. "You don't need to say that. I know what our situation is, and it's just that."

"Is it?" I dare to ask.

The air grows thin, a silence wrapping around us like a taut cord.

"*Yes,*" she clips out, her fingers clutching around the wrench. "We can't be more. Read our contract."

"What if I don't give a fuck about our contract?" I lean

closer to her, the mesmerizing scent of her hair invading my senses. "What if the very thought of setting it aflame pleases me?"

"Well, it shouldn't. Maybe we signed it more for you and not for me." Her words cut me like ice, cold and vicious. "I saw you, Damien, the other night—the darkness inside of you. Your priorities are... *elsewhere.* Condemning your brother wasn't for me. It was for *you.*"

My heart hammers in my chest, gnawing at me to tell her she's wrong, to explain what she really saw, to confess that from the very moment I saw his hands touch her leg at the club, I wanted them *removed* from his body. But there's no lying; the hate for my brother, for my father, was written clearly across my face that night. I'm sure she can't unsee the dark pit of nothingness clouding my judgment and fueling my need for revenge in my very soul.

I close my eyes when she continues.

"You're over *there,* in your world. Running your business, basking in the glamour. Everyone knows you. Hell, the entire city knows your name. And I'm just..." She looks around the shop, avoiding my gaze. "Hannah. Sterling knew it— *knows it.*"

"My brother made the mistake of his lifetime mistreating you, and especially by letting you slip through his fingers." I snatch her chin between my fingers, angling her to look at me. "His words are poison."

A sad chuckle escapes her lips. "Poisonous but true. In the light of you and your family, I really *am* common."

"Hannah Lockwood." Her name on my tongue tastes like royalty, like precious stone carved from peaks so high they grace the heavens. I sweep my thumb across her jaw, the soft skin that caresses my pad sending shivers through my body. "You're *anything* but common."

Her lips part invitingly, and I inch myself closer. Everything in my body, *in my very being,* burns for her, for her touch, for my lips to smash against hers and claim them as mine. But I lean back, for only one sick realization.

That she may be right.

That she's too good for me.

She must realize it too, because when she hikes down off the platform, I'm left standing in silence. I follow her lead, watching her close the hood, walk a trail around the front of the tractor, and climb up the ladder into the driver's seat. She turns the key, and the engine roars proudly.

But not loud enough to drown out the thoughts circling my conflicted consciousness, arguing I could really be there for her, be *right* for her. But I don't listen. Because the twisted truth is... I'll take down my father, using everything I have, even if that means I go down with him.

And if that were to happen, Hannah would be left alone all over again.

TWENTY-SIX

HANNAH

"I AM NOT DOING THAT."

Damien's face is so red it might shoot off his neck like a rocket, which would be amusing if I hadn't just dumped all my childhood trauma on him.

"It's not as bad as it seems." I snap the blue latex gloves against my wrists. "And besides, this is the last thing on our list, *and* you have Bessie, who's the easiest to milk."

I drag my stool across the dry hay, positioning it beside the dairy cow's feet. Before I sit, I run my hands along the side of my cow, its brown fur tickling my fingers through my gloves.

"Hannah, I'm drawing a line." His hand waves around, scrunching the gloves he holds between his fingers. "I'll pick up chicken crap and eggs and get dirty with a tractor, but this... this is too far."

"I've been going easy on you." My eyebrows lift to my hairline. "It's either this or the pigs."

"Pigs?" He whirls, appearing awkward in his boots as he clomps around the stall. "Oh, no."

"Oh, *yes*. Now—pig or cow? Choose wisely."

He huffs a sigh, sliding on his gloves and mumbling curses under his breath. "At least let me have the other cow."

"You want *Daisy?*"

"Of course. Look at mine. She's a beast."

It's true. His cow, Bessie, *is* a beast. A fifteen-hundred pound, black-and-white spotted Holstein. Daisy can't compete, seeming half her size. But what Damien doesn't know is Bessie is much older, gentler, and more experienced when it comes to being milked.

But I'm not letting him in on that little secret.

"No switching cows. Daisy is mine and Bessie is yours." I smile sweetly at him. "Now pet her. Let her know you're friendly."

He shoots me a look.

"I'm serious."

When he realizes I won't budge, his fingers hesitantly sweep down her back, sloping upwards along her tailbone. He keeps his face far from her like she's some horse that'll buck at any moment. But when she dips her snout further into the trough of hay in front of her, paying him no attention, his shoulders relax.

"Good. See? Nothing to be afraid of." I sit on my stool, coming face-to-face with Daisy's dangling pink udders. "Follow my lead."

Damien does the same, his knees sticking out high above his waistline on the short stool.

"Okay. Grab two teats, one in each hand, like this." I wrap my hands around them, careful not to squeeze yet.

Both cows separate us with their udders partially blocking my view of Damien, but I can still see the way his nose scrunches up as he outstretches his hands. I hold back my laugh. "Squeeze one and gently pull down at the same time."

I demonstrate, and a line of milk darts from the udder before clinking against the pan positioned underneath.

Ducking my head to the side to get a better angle on Damien, I find his face to be of pure, unmistakable revulsion. The corners of his lips curl downwards as his fingers squeeze, and when the milk comes flying out, he jerks backwards.

When his miserable eyes find mine, I flick my chin, commanding him to try again. His brows tighten in frustration as he sits back up, this time with a more confident grip before the milk sings into the pan.

"Now alternate. Like this." Switching my hands back and forth, I squeeze and pull, then repeat the same action with the other.

Damien mimics my motions, slowly at first, before continuing with more assertion. A subtle smirk tugs on the corners of his lips as milk shoots down in staccato bursts. When he catches me looking, he bats his smile back down.

"Are we done yet?" he whines. "Ol' Bessie here must be getting full by now."

"Is she now?" Our eyes lock between veiny pinkness and strong cow legs. Narrowing mine, I increase my pace. "Well, then you better hurry up and fill your pale, slowpoke."

His brows raise, lips stuck on a silent retort. He snaps them back together, before his fingers work in quicker motions. I increase my speed, the milk splattering into my pale. He does the same, filling the space with sounds of sloshing and ringing as the rim of the milk grows taller in our buckets.

His eyes widen, a challenge brewing inside them. "Am I besting you, Hannah? Already, on my first day?"

A smile tugs at my lips, and I bite it down as I study his movements, admittedly impressed by his speed. With hands as fast as darts, I swap for the other two teats.

He notices my change, and makes to switch himself. But as he does, his finger slips down the pink flesh, wrapping too tightly. Bessie's deep *moo* booms inside her trough as she sways, knocking against Damien, causing his other hand to rotate, angling in all the wrong directions before—

Milk shoots directly into his face.

I gasp. My hands fly to my lips, but I stop before they make contact, careful not to touch myself.

Silence encroaches the space between us, and we stare into each other's eyes as the milk dribbles, forming river-like patterns all the way down his porcelain features, exiting off his chin.

My heart pounds, preparing itself for the impending roar that's sure to explode from his lips. But what comes out of them is unexpected, and has a sweet, tangy taste to it, softening the hardest parts of myself. Because what comes darting out the two rows of his perfect teeth is...

Laughter.

I blink, staring in awe while the beautiful tenor has goosebumps racing across my entire body, sending warmth to the very tips of my toes. With each wave of the joyous bellow that escapes his lips, the green in his irises shines brighter with a light—*a freeness*—I've never seen in them before.

When it dies down, he stares at me. Not a single harsh wrinkle lines his face. The serious expression I've grown so accustomed to vanishes, replaced with a light, airy aura.

His eyes track my movements as I bound across the space to grab him a towel. Not once do they part ways with me, even when he stands tall as I approach him. My heart pounds as he accepts the towel, his hand brushing mine.

A heat forms between us, growing ever so hotter as he swipes the towel across the center of his face. He skims across his jawline, *slowly*, never averting my gaze. He finishes the rest of his face, lips and hair, until he discards the rag to the ground.

We stand, not sharing a word between us.

A war of conflicted emotions wages inside his head. He's holding himself back from a monumental decision, considering the consequences of crossing a line that can't be uncrossed.

You should move, the defensive part of my brain, that's used to calling the shots, nags me. *Don't let this get too far, not when it's temporary.*

But what if it's not?

Chewing on the inside of my lip, a flicker of hope sparks in my veins as I think of the way I opened up to him in the shop, and how *good* it felt to discover someone with similar pain. It's comforting... But also scary to know there's someone who understands it, and could make me vulnerable through such an understanding.

Because the idea that someone could know me so deeply...

"Damien, I—"

His hands fly towards me, cupping my jaw before his lips crash into mine.

At first, I freeze. *This is downright filthy. Disgusting. It's completely the wrong time in the wrong place with the wrong man...*

His finger trails a possessive touch along my jawline, practically branding me and melting me ever-so slightly.

Tightening the grip on the back of my neck, he angles my head upwards, giving him better access.

"Do you want me?" His whisper is strained, brushing against my teeth as he holds himself back.

... But it's also right in a million other ways.

"Yes," I breathe.

His hum of approval that sounds in my ear is dark, causing my toes to curl in my boots. My mouth slackens, a moan slipping free when his tongue darts between my lips and strong hands thread through the tendrils of my hair.

His body rustles between the tango of our tongues. Sliding one eye open, I spot him slipping an arm underneath the straps of his overalls.

I press my palm to his muscled chest. "Not here."

OUR FEET CRAWL up the stairs in a jumbled mess of tongues and hands and groans, careful not to trip on our way up.

My back slams against the porch siding wall, hitting with a bang before Damien angles my chin upwards. His mouth suctions to my neck as his hand fumbles for the doorknob.

I gasp between my breathless moans. "Our boots."

Kicking at my heels, I wiggle my ankles until the muddy soles soar across the wood. Damien does the same without so much as an acknowledgement, his oversized boots clanging against the ground before we burst through the door with his hands on my waist.

Although he's in complete control, I do my best to steer our direction towards the bathroom, well aware of our muddied state. We hit the door frame hard, Damien's moans hot in my mouth. The sound vibrates to the apex of my thighs that cries for attention, needy for his touch it's grown so accustomed to.

Our lips unclasp. His mouth is a hair's breadth from mine as his eyes flicker past my shoulder.

Remodeled within the past two years, the bathroom really is quite cute. A free-standing tub stands on four legs in the corner with a tall shower head peeking out over its beige curtains.

Damien's eyes slide back to mine, an obvious question burning behind them.

"I don't mind waiting—"

His finger finds my lips, sealing them shut with a confident touch. "I'm not waiting for you any longer, Hannah."

He grabs my wrist, and I have zero protest as he tugs me into the bathroom. Quickly, he shrugs out of his overalls. A satisfied grin marks his lips when they pool around his feet, glad to be rid of them. His shirt follows next, peeling from off his back until I'm left trying not to stare at his impressive pecs and washboard abs.

Nerves prick at me beneath his intense stare traveling down the length of my body, silently commanding me to unclothe myself. He turns on the water, the rippling patterns thundering against the tub.

My heart thumps louder with each item that sinks to the floor. When my shirt, underwear and ripped jeans lie in a loose pile around my ankles, his eyes flash with a deep hunger. Somehow, it feels as if it's our first time seeing each other in the nude.

Steam rises above the curtains, clouding at the ceiling and turning the air thicker than the anticipation that bounces between us.

"After you." He holds back the curtain, his voice growing strained.

As I step in, the hot water collides with my shins, making me gasp. I nearly withdraw, but I push through, allowing the heat to engulf me completely. The curtains rustle, zipping on their track and trapping me between the water cascading down my chest and the strong presence looming behind my back.

Instinctually, I grab the loofah dangling from the iron rod, applying soap between its crevices. But before I can rub the suds over my arm, Damien snatches it from my hand, turning me around to face him. He runs the material along my shoulder, then down the length of my arm, and I shiver despite being surrounded by warmth.

Biting my lip, I acknowledge the way my nipples peak under his touch, his attention. He notices them too, his gaze darkening as he trails a soapy line straight down my middle, past the twin ridges of my breasts, belly button and the apex of my sex. Stopping, his free hand travels lower to grip my thigh.

A silent command.

I widen my stance, intensely aware of the soap drizzling down between my legs. Need explodes within me, the water a tantalizing whisper, tempting me to touch myself. The pressure pounds against my back when my fingers find my clit, causing pleasure to bloom across my legs on contact.

"Did I say you could touch yourself?" The pleasure dies out on a cry when he snatches my wrist, tugging me closer until his breath is hot on my lips.

I whine, wiggling in his grasp, as the water returns to tickle my clit. He cocks his head, soap oozing down his veiny forearm before he releases my wrist. "Spread your lips. Show me where you want it."

Holding back a protest, I return my hands to my pussy, the flesh slippery beneath my fingers as I spread my skin.

"Wider." His voice is an intoxicating growl, luring me to obey. "Good girl. Hold it there for me... Yes, just like that. You're so puffy, so needy for me, aren't you?"

From his stare alone, a whimper flutters up my throat as the water cascades down my clit in torturous waves. His hand clutches the back of my neck, angling me to look up at him. With his chin standing taller than the top of my head, his eyes crane downward to look at me, dots of water highlighting his devastatingly handsome features. "Where do you masturbate, Hannah?"

Where. Not *if.*

"I-I don't—"

"Yes. You do. Tell me. In bed at night?" His grip pulls my skin taut, and I try to shake my head. "No?"

My eyes dart across the shower curtains. I bite my lip, thinking of the special way I use the retractable shower head at his penthouse, positioning the powerful blast between my legs as I ride out the delicious pressure until I come with muffled moans.

"Mmm," he muses, reading my gaze. "In *my* shower too?"

I don't answer, but the way his eyes glisten with satisfaction tells me he knows the truth.

"How often?"

"Every night." My whisper is barely audible over the thrashing of water.

"Every night?" He *tsks*, his thumb skimming across my jawline in one swoop. He jerks me away from him by my

neck, watching me still hold my pussy lips open. "Dirty girl, what are we going to do about that?"

I whimper again in response, and my hips buck towards the empty air in desperation to relieve the need winding tightly inside of me. He merely cocks his head, a shadowy possession emerging from behind his hungry eyes as he stares at the state of my sex.

Throbbing.

Waiting to be touched...

His for the taking.

His fingers curl through the tendrils of my hair. "Your pretty cunt is *mine,* to touch, to *use* whenever pleases me. And you?" When he grips tighter, the strands tug at my scalp. "From now on, you'll ask *permission* to touch yourself. Do you understand?"

"Y-yes," I breathe, without hesitation.

"Every orgasm, every dirty thought that crosses your mind—it'll be because... what, exactly?"

I feel like I'm signing away my rights, my very soul, but I don't care. I look him dead in the eyes. "Because you'll allow it."

He plunges the loofah straight down my middle, scraping my sensitive sex on a harsh descent. Air streams past my lips on a cry, and I grapple for his biceps to remain upright.

"Let's see if we can clean this dirty cunt of yours, shall we?" Yanking the opposite direction, he angles my head upwards and scrapes the sponge deeply between my folds. I cry out again, right as his mouth latches onto the column of my throat.

He works his forearm in a quick, brutal percussion, my sex shaking with each powerful thrust. His teeth shoot outwards, scraping against my delicate skin, causing me to mewl in relief when his tongue darts out after, lapping up and soothing the burn.

With each swipe, my aching fire grows slicker, more pleasurable, until I'm rocking my hips desperately in response, climbing the mountain of my release with his name on the tip of my tongue—

He withdraws his hand, leaving me bare and wide open and throbbing wildly. With a whine, I grab his wrist that holds the sponge, willing to force him back to the spot now dripping hot water and soap.

But he holds his stance firm, eyes pinning me in place. "I didn't say you could come, either."

TWENTY-SEVEN

DAMIEN

THE GUESTHOUSE IS QUAINT, with a partial kitchen connecting to a modest living room. A couch and two recliners surround a grizzly bear rug and a fireplace that even *I* admit is nice.

Why? Let's see... Wooden logs crackle from its cage, smoke funnels out of its long-tubed top, and its flames keep the place perfectly cozy. *Oh, and Hannah's in front of it —*

On her knees.

Naked.

The evidence of her arousal slides down the inside of her thighs, glistening against the flicker of the flames.

"Touch yourself."

I lean back on the couch, watching her listen to my command from across the room. When her petite hand dips between her folds, I grip my cock. I'm completely free of the clothes I decided not to wear after our shower.

Her eyes dance back and forth between mine and my proud erection, lying flat across my lower abdomen, nearly reaching my belly button.

"Good girl." The praise is thick on my tongue as I stroke myself from base to tip.

I bite my lip—*hard*—watching her flick her clit with her pointer and middle fingers. *I could watch that all day.* Squeezing my cock in response, her eyes glue to my hand as it travels from my sensitive tip to my base. Face alighting with heat, her whimpers grow louder.

Fuck. I bite back a groan, forcing myself to stay on the couch. Every muscle in my body screams at me to take her right here, right now, with her ass up from behind.

"I need to come," she whines.

"Do you, now?" Satisfaction burns inside me at her asking for my permission to orgasm. "So quickly?"

"Yes." Her voice strains.

"Hmm. Not yet. I want you on your back, spread open for me."

Her cheeks stain a deep shade of red that even I can see from over here. But she doesn't protest, presumably at will to her need, as she lies flat on her back. Her wet hair sprawls across the rug, a similar color to its warm brown.

Her legs bend, with her knees high above her body and feet flat on the floor. I know she's waiting for instructions, and I'm more than happy to give them.

"Spread."

One word from my lips. That's all it takes, and she spreads them. Resting the sides of her knees on the rug, she reveals her mouthwatering center.

Her body is amazing. Fucking perfection. The fire glows across her skin, illuminating her modest breasts, casting shadows along her torso and stopping above the apex of her sex.

Fucking. Hell. I stop touching myself, or I'll come right now just by looking at her.

"Good girl." The thickness in my voice is clear as I praise her again. "Show me how you pleasure yourself."

Her precious mewls are audible the moment her fingers skim over her flesh. I watch for a moment, unable to move, unable to *breathe,* as she dips lower. She coats her fingers with her own need before motioning back to her clit, a shiny wetness trailing along her skin following behind.

She makes small, tight circles around her sensitive bud. And the way she reacts, the way she bites her lower lip and grinds her waist... *God,* it has me clutching the edge of the couch so hard my nails leave indents.

"*Slower,*" I growl, watching her hips respond by bucking in the air.

Yes, just like that.

Squeezing my calloused hand down my shaft, I match her agonizingly slow speed. Her other hand slithers down her body, across her torso and hipbone until her glittery finger-nails stop at her entrance.

She's waiting. I smirk to myself.

Her eyes catch mine, and I leave them there for a minute, loving the way they plead. When I flick my head, she sinks a single finger into herself. She moans on its entrance, arching her back in the most delicious way, giving me a perfect view of her pumping in and out of herself.

"Add another finger."

Again, she whimpers softly as she stretches herself around an additional finger. They're so small, so slender. Even at three, it wouldn't be enough to compensate for my size. But I don't want her to add another. I want her to stretch open— around *me* as I fill her to the max.

Her legs wobble, lifting off the floor.

"Keep them down," I command, before she presses both knees back to the ground. "You're so perfect. Fuck yourself harder. Show me how you want it."

Just then, she cries louder, pummeling in and out of herself and speeding the circles around her clit. Her toes curl in seconds, revealing how close she is.

"C-can I—"

"No."

She gasps, keeping pace as her legs shake profusely.

"Do. Not. Come."

She lets out a frustrated moan, tilting her head back against the rug, clearly fighting from teetering off an explosive edge. *"Damien, please—"*

"Yes," I say, and her head flies back up. Our eyes connect, hers wild and raw with the whiteness lining her irises. "But only if you wrap yourself around my cock."

She doesn't whine. She doesn't protest. She only rolls off her back in a rush, a hungry gleam shining behind her eyes—

"I didn't say like that."

"Huh?" She stops.

"I don't want you on your feet. I want you on your hands and knees."

Her mouth falls open as she stares at me, knowing damn well what I mean, but she asks anyway. "What do you mean?"

"Did I stutter, baby?" I lean up, widening my stance so she gets an impeccable view of her reward. Her eyes laser in on my cock, and she bites her lip before my command...

"Crawl to me."

"What? That's—that's..." Her jaw slacks downwards, a challenge ready to spring from her eyes. "Why would I do that?"

I look down at her, at the way her perfect mask fleets the moment the words leave my lips.

"Because, my little protégée. I have your name in writing preventing me from fucking you... *unless you beg me to.*"

TWENTY-EIGHT
HANNAH

THIS IS HUMILIATING.

Twisted, *delicious* humiliation.

I slide my leg another inch, the movement rubbing intense friction against my clit. I hold back a whimper, knowing it would only satisfy him further.

He wants me to beg. For him to fuck me.

It was—*is*—in our contract, and I even signed it. Because it seemed harmless, at the time. Surely, I wouldn't sleep with this man again, after knowing him to be my ex's brother. Better yet, I wouldn't think I'd sleep with him, knowing all our interactions and flirting in public are *fake.*

But now the lines smear beyond recognition, unable to be redrawn. I don't even know what's fake or real anymore. Except the way he smiled, laughed and allowed me to open up to him today in the barn... *That* was real and nearly lifted my heart from my ribcage. I'd never seen him so free. A rare glimpse into such a complicated man.

The living room seems so small. I bite my lip as I take another step and avoid his intense gaze, looking down at the ground. *Until you're on your knees crawling on the edge of an orgasm.*

His invisible rein of control wraps tightly around my neck. Every command from his mouth is dark, velvety and practically yanks on the leash.

"Eyes on me," he says.

And I'm helpless but to lift my lashes.

Craning my neck to his high position perched on the couch, I discover his smug smirk growing larger along his lips. He knows he can ask anything of me, and I'll give it to him, because I need the release so badly. He has a way of *owning* me I've never experienced before.

Not with Sterling. Not with anyone.

The next step is brutal, cramming the lips of my sex against my clit, finally forcing a whimper to escape my mouth. Not even halfway there, I'm not sure I can make it without coming.

"I didn't say to stop." He leans back, resting his elbows on the back of the couch.

Breathing slowly out of my nose, I press on, holding eye-contact with him. The closer I get, the more enormous his cock looks, bulging straight upwards along his strong core.

When I arrive, I can feel the wetness dribbling down my thigh, a clear sign of my arousal—and he's yet to touch me.

He catches my chin between his fingers. The pad of his thumb sweeps across my lips slowly, and my eyes flicker down to his impressive length. Going the opposite direction, he swipes again, this time the tip of his thumb delving past my lips, hitting my teeth.

"Open."

I unlock my teeth, and his thumb slips into my mouth.

With his saltiness on my tongue, I bat my eyelashes at him some more. He presses down against my tongue in response, and I have to stifle the moan that begs to sound.

"You want me in your mouth?"

With the heat of the flame roaring against my back, I nod vigorously.

"Very interesting... " He pushes his thumb further inside my mouth, rubbing along my tongue. "I don't know if you deserve it."

Scrunching my eyebrows at him, it only seems to brighten the intense look in his eyes. "You want to know why?" He presses down harder, threatening to make me gag.

"Because you're going against your word, aren't you? You said we wouldn't sleep together. You were so sure, you wrote your pretty name along a dashed line. You said you'd keep your distance from me, but you know what you did today?" He leans into me, his voice low and in complete control. "You wore those tight little shorts that showed off your ass, didn't you?"

His free hand shoots between my legs, scraping along my folds. My cry muffles around his thumb as he flicks my clit between his fingers. His eyes darken, satisfied with my reaction. "Didn't you, Hannah?"

"Mhm!" I arch into him before he lessens his pressure, keeping slow circles that pin me on the edge of release.

"And what's even worse—here you are, on your knees, with a sopping cunt before I even touched you. But, you know what? I don't hear you begging, as per our subclause."

He wraps his fingers around my jaw, shaking my head. "And you must know how much I hate a violated contract. So, this time, you only have one option, Hannah, if you want your precious release, *beg for it.* If you want to be fucked so hard you forget your own name, show me why you *deserve* it."

I glance down at his cock in all its glory, raging hard and huge, with a vein trailing up its base. My mouth waters, needing it on my tongue. I'm beyond humiliation, beyond *thinking,* with a single goal in mind.

To find release while wrapped around Damien.

When he removes his fingers from my mouth, I lurch forward, eyes fixating on his length. But I'm met halfway with two fingers in front of my face, pads facing upwards, my slickness coating them thoroughly as it shines against the flicker of the fireplace.

He wants me to taste myself. He told me to show him why...

I slide my tongue out, offering him an opening. The growl that comes out of his mouth sends powerful shivers down my spine, and I can *feel* the look he gives in my very bones as he slides his fingers into my mouth.

The taste of salt is shocking at first, but I weather it, driving my head deeper, never leaving his eyes.

"*Christ,*" he curses.

I jerk back, sucking hard while hollowing out my cheeks. He doesn't move, appearing to be in some trance as he watches me with an incredulous expression, mouth parted on a silent oval.

Confidence barrels through me, and I push myself down again, faster this time. His other hand reaches for my hair, but I snatch it out of the air. I shove it back down to the couch, pinning it there as I pump my head across his fingers, my tongue lapping up his skin.

Right before he says some command I'll never know, I

plop him out of my mouth. Then I drive my head down, shoving the length of his cock to the back of my throat, pinning his other hand against the couch.

"*Fuck!*" His curse rings out as he makes to move, but I dig my nails harder, stopping him.

I bob my head up and down in expert motions, intentionally hitting the back of my throat so more saliva coats his cock. Whipping up, I look him in the eyes.

"Please, will you fuck me?" I ask sweetly, watching his expression morph into shock, before I smash my head back down. Taking him into my mouth again, his nails scrape against the couch as he clutches, visibly making indents into the leather.

Up, down, up, down, up...

I slide his tip out from my lips slowly, saliva dribbling down my chin as I curl my eyebrows upwards. "Please, *please,* Damien, will you fuck—"

His hands escape my grip. In a blur, he has me lifting off the ground and lying across his shoulder like a bag of sand as he bounds across the room. Twisting me, he practically tosses me on the rug, positioning my ass in the air before he slams into me.

I cry out, the force of his length stretching me so wide it brings tears along my eyes.

"You enjoy teasing me, getting me riled up, don't you?" He shoves my head down into the rug, the coarse fur burning as it scrapes my cheek.

His pace is punishing, shooting pain mixed with an overwhelming pleasure across my entire body. He reaches an arm around my middle before a *smack* sounds against my clit.

"Don't you?"

"Ah!" I wail, jerking back, but he shoves me down harder, nowhere for me to cover up the humiliating yet satisfying evidence that reddens my face.

Another round clips my skin, and a pleasure so powerful, so *foreign*, overtakes me.

"Yes!" I scream, before the next brutal whip. *"YES!"*

His thighs pound against my ass, sending sharp claps bouncing off the walls and echoing in the tight space. My interior walls clench around him, harder with each spanking upon my clit, until I'm shaking profusely underneath his weight.

"Yes, baby," he growls, releasing the pressure on my cheek before he grapples my hair in his fist. Then I feel his mouth hot on my ear. "Give yourself over to me."

I shake harder beneath his gaze, uncaring of how I may look. I reduce myself to a single feeling, a single need, realizing this is what it's like to be ruined for all others.

It'll never be this good with another man.

With anyone.

He jerks me backwards, craning my head all the way back to look at the ceiling as he bucks into me, completely to the hilt. My cries fill the space, unashamed of their loudness. Anyone outside this house could hear them, could recognize the severity with which he's taking me.

I feel his hand again, forceful against my clit. This time it's with a fast back-and-forth motion that has waves of pleasure crashing into me at full speed. His skill—the exhilarating power he exerts through me—is inescapable. And when my body tightens up in submission, unmoving and soaking up every thrust, he growls in my ear.

"Finish. I want to feel you pulsate around my cock, baby."

Gripping the backs of my arms, he yanks them behind me, until I'm suspended. I lean across the air with only his hands to support me as he drills into me.

My screams are raw in my throat as I find release, grinding desperately, panting like I'm going to die as I writhe out each and every clench. When my orgasm subsides, I'm left breathless as he slowly pulls out.

But then he pounds into me once more, as far as he can go. It's quick and brutal, gliding intensely along my interior walls and is almost too much to bear. He retreats again, leaving me throbbing inside. Then he pounds once more, *again* lurching my body forward in the air but keeping me in place by his iron grip.

A frustrated moan leaves my lips, and his response is a dark chuckle coming from behind me. It's like he's marking me, reminding me he owns me. And I take it again, and again, before he pulls me up against his hard frame. His growl of satisfaction raises goosebumps on the back of my neck.

"You're going to ride me, and I'm going to watch you come again."

Again?

I've never come twice from sex, but I don't voice my disbelief. Instead, I follow him to the couch, where he leans back and spreads his knees, giving me a clear view of his enormous length. Biting my lip, I'm brazen as I stare.

With a flick of his head, his eyes point to his cock. I climb on top of him, hooking my feet on his thighs and pressing my knees into the leather. My hands clutch his shoulders before they flex in response. Once again, I'm reminded of the specimen of a man that sits beneath me.

He's perfectly tan, with muscles so defined they're more akin to stone than skin. His eyes are a raging thunderstorm, casting a gaze that eats me alive and reminds me of who's in complete control.

Even if I'm the one riding on top.

TWENTY-NINE

DAMIEN

HANNAH'S A FUCKING GODDESS.

And it's my only intention to worship her.

She eyes me softly, the glow of the fireplace shining an orange halo behind her head. Her hands whisper down my body, starting at my chest and working their way along the harsh ridges of my core. She doesn't say a single word, and I can hardly breathe as she studies me.

I wonder what she's thinking, what she thinks of *me*. I wish I could scoop deep inside her consciousness, only to pull out its mysteries.

Touching her palms to my chest, she pushes me back into the couch as she lowers herself over my cock. But she doesn't put me in. Her pussy lips wrap around the base, her wetness warm on my skin.

"Grind on me," I grit out between clenched teeth.

"Like this?" She leans forward, her slickness sliding along my shaft as her breasts sway a breath away from my face.

Fuck...

"Yes, like that."

She sways backwards, slipping along her way. I rest my head on the back of the couch, unable to watch her any longer. But her soft hand wraps around my ear, her fingernails grooving through my hair, pulling me forward to look at her.

When she dips again, this time I capture her nipple between my teeth, sucking hard before she pulls away with a moan on her lips. Whipping her hand behind her, her nails scrape along my shaft in a way that could make me howl.

She grips it tightly, angling it towards her entrance until I feel her hot wetness on my tip. And suddenly, she releases her strength, letting her body fall and crash onto my cock. A high-pitched cry of pleasure parts her lips, voiced from deep within her chest. She stares down at me, a determined look on her face as she rocks herself along my length.

I'm right there with her, gently thrusting upwards as she makes her descent. I say nothing, because the view is breathtaking. Fucking astonishing.

Her hips arch out, forming a crease between her lower abdomen and thighs that's hot as sin. And her tits... they soar downward before bouncing back up, an enchanting rhythm that has my mouth watering.

Unable to take the tease any longer, I lurch forward, capturing her nipple between my lips, sucking hard as it wiggles in its newfound cage. Pulling her towards me, I push out my ribcage so her clit grinds against my mound, and it's her undoing.

When her head tilts skyward, her moans echoing across the room, I plop her tit from my mouth and move to her neck. She cries in response, writhing as I feast upon her flesh, needing to mark her skin with the grooves of my teeth and the suction of my mouth.

I pound into her, driving home all the way to the base of my cock, and *God* does she eat it up.

"Yes, *yes!*" Her tits bounce against my chest as I bury my hands into her hair, bury *myself* into her. *"Fuck me, fuck me, Damien!"*

My name on her lips is the sweetest song there is and drives me wild, reducing me to a bare need. I fuck her so hard it's not even her lifting herself into the air anymore. She bounces, enjoying the rough ride with wide eyes, sweat slipping off her forehead and through her damp hair, until she's bucking back against me, harder than before.

"I'm going to—I'm going to—" The whites of her eyes shine bright, surprise riddling through them—

She topples into me, her pussy clenching with suffocating strength along my shaft as unbridled pleasure blooms across her beautiful features.

Come spews from my tip, an enormous release that soars through my veins. But I don't let up as I'm overcome with the need to shove my seed so far into her, it will drip from her pussy lips for days after. So she'll remember who it was who made her feel this way.

So she'll know exactly who she belongs to.

"I'VE NEVER SEEN stars so bright," I murmur, gazing up at the night sky in child-like wonder.

"Said like the typical city-boy." She chuckles, her body vibrating against my arm. "That's because cities, especially New York, block out all the natural beauty in the world. No matter how high you are in your apartment, it'll never compare to this view at night."

She's right. I trace the Big Dipper with my eyes, noting how its bowl points downward to the smaller of the two constellations.

"It seems I've found a single redeeming quality in *Ol' Dinosaur* here," I tease, patting the metallic side of the truck. We lie atop an air mattress in the truck's bed, with a home-made quilt, pillows and other blankets.

"*You* did?" She perches herself on her elbow to stare at me. A post-sex glow marks her face underneath the moonlight. "I'm the one who had to drag us out here."

My heart aches as her bangs fall across her temple, framing it in such a way to highlight the slope of her nose and her warm-colored eyes.

God... She's so beautiful, it hurts.

Noticing my stare and lack of reply, she opts to settle back down with a relaxed grin.

Aside from the occasional *mooing* of the dairy cows from inside the barn, it's so... quiet. I've never felt this calm, this comfortable since I can remember. Maybe since I'd last seen a genuine smile on my mother's face, or since I didn't look at Sterling with such contempt, or since I started my company, hellbent on a revenge that walks my every thought.

But it doesn't now. I breathe deep, basking in the night air and Hannah's lilac scent.

Now... my mind is at peace.

THIRTY

HANNAH

I CLUTCH DAMIEN'S ARM, nerves pricking at me.

It's been two weeks since our weekend getaway at my family's farm, and I've come to terms with the fact that what we did in that guesthouse was borderline unholy. And ever since, not only have we been doing *it,* we've been doing it *often,* with my wails growing louder in the penthouse each night.

But even more surprising than that is the way Damien has changed. His flirting has increased tenfold, but so have his smiles. It's almost like being with a newly reformed man, who doesn't have work and stress and duties crawling up his back like spiders.

"There's nothing to be nervous about," he purrs beside me. He's the calming presence between the two of us as we walk across the marble flooring. "You look stunning."

"I'm not nervous," I lie.

The Bass family estate is beyond immaculate.

The minute John dropped us off at the front porch, I

spotted more Rolls-Royces and other supercars than I could count. Nausea sweeps over me then, remembering how far out of the norm I am to be in such hallways and endless corridors. Sure, I can handle Damien's ridiculous apartment and his towering company, but this is on a whole other level of high society.

"I can feel you shaking on my arm."

We turn a corner, entering yet another hallway before the sounds of chatter and symphonic music grow louder.

"I don't know if I can do this—meeting investors, business owners *and* your parents, all in one night. I don't even know their names."

The long skirt of my dress brushes against my legs when Damien's firm hands grip me. We stop in the middle of a marbled archway, allowing other couples to pass us as he skims his palms down my shoulders.

"Yes, you *can* do this. Investors are just people with money who want to do business with Innovex, meaning they'll try to impress *us*, not the other way around. And business owners? You're with me, baby. Let me handle them."

My heart flutters at the endearment he's been showing more often for the past two weeks, even when we're alone. "As for my parents—my mother's name is Camille. She's very sweet and will love you. I can almost guarantee that. And my father..." His eyes cloud as he pauses, his teeth gritting. "It doesn't matter what he thinks."

His fleeting look fades before I can prod information from him, an inviting smile returning to his lips. A dose of comfort with a pinch of anxiety twirls inside of me as I take his arm again. He leads us towards the double doors propped open by two white-gloved, suited gentlemen.

"See? Nothing to worry about. It's all fun and games tonight. Only a ball."

The words *only a ball* take on an unexpected magnitude when we finally round the door, entering inside.

My lungs freeze, the air whooshing from them.

Inside the ballroom, everywhere I look is white marble. Countless pillars, a double staircase leading to higher balconies lining the perimeter, and the floor traveling through dozens of French doors. Lacy curtains swing in the outside breeze, giving the green garden through them a mysterious allure.

"It's a lot. I know." Damien tugs my arm, pulling me out of my hypnosis. "My mother works wonders. She designed the whole space."

"Wow."

I watch flocks of couples pass us with interlocking arms, each the epitome of the upper echelons of society. Men wear tuxedos and women flaunt long dresses with flaring hips and vibrant colors. A younger lady around my age passes by, her eyes subtle as they peruse down the length of my dress. Her eyebrows raise, confirming my suspicions.

Cyna handmade my dress herself last week, just for this occasion. And I must admit, she did *not* miss a thing. Shimmering in all its silver glory, my gown sweeps the floor and cinches at my waist like a latex glove. She mended the dress sleeveless, with delicate lace diverging down my backside.

Heat brushes against my body before Damien's mouth finds my ear. "Look," he whispers, pointing upwards.

I quirk my brow, craning my head back... and back... and back, until my eyes land on the ceiling. "Oh..."

Impossibly high with the shape of an oval dome, the

ceiling boasts a mural so enchanting it must rival the Sistine Chapel. In a flurry of baby blue and gold, intricate horses run on water and robed men sit in thrones of clouds. Hidden spotlights round the ceiling, shining a soft glow on the paint.

"Damien..." I'm truly breathless, with little to say. "It's *incredible.*"

"It is... My mom said there are balconies higher up. I'll show you sometime, so you can get a better look."

"I would love that."

His arm envelops the small of my back, steering us further into the ball. He aims for the generously spaced tables that surround a dance floor. Heat creeps up my back at his closeness, his obvious possessiveness. So many sets of eyes flicker our way that it's hard not to notice. Hushed chatter springs from their lips, kept secret by the music filling the room.

"Here." Damien hands me a flute off the top of a passing server's tray. I slip the stem between my fingers, judging the rising bubbles inside the glass.

"I know it's no tequila sunrise," he teases with a contagious smile on his lips. "But we can get you one of those at the bar later."

I smirk, a blush warming my cheeks. He remembers my drink of choice. Well, tequila *anything* is my choice, but slim to none beats Sofia's margaritas.

"No, this is perfect." I raise the glass, taking a generous sip, enjoying the way the bubbles race down my throat and warm my insides.

As we near the tables, my heart thumps in anticipation of who we might meet tonight and how grossly unprepared I am.

I study the surroundings, particularly the stage. Dimly lit

and seated with two rows of musicians, they prop violins on their shoulders, balance massive wooden stringed instruments over their knees, and an aged composer waves a stick in the air in beat to the music.

Despite the alluring symphonic melodies, no one seems to dance. Not yet, at least. Everyone mingles around white-clothed tables and walks the gardens outside. I enjoy dancing, don't get me wrong. But whatever fiddly diddly dancing they expect of us guests here is positively *not* for me.

Damien smiles at a couple who waves at us from afar, bending down to whisper in my ear. "The man I'm taking us to owns a mobile company overseas in Japan. We haven't spoken face-to-face in years, even though he is one of our major clients. But rumor has it, he's planning to retire soon and is possibly looking to sell his company."

Apprehension knots in my stomach as we approach a table in the very center of the ballroom. With every seat taken, each person engrosses in conversation, except the back of a man whose bald head shines our way.

Let me handle them. I recall Damien's words, and my shoulders release some tension.

"Mr. Tanaka, I'd like to introduce you to my girlfriend," Damien addresses him. He whirls around, revealing his deep wrinkles and salt-and-pepper flaked eyebrows.

"Damien." He stands, fingers wrapping around the tip of a gold cane. The two men shake hands, smiling as if they're well acquainted with each other. "It's Haru. No need for such formalities, you know that... And your name, young lady?" He gestures my way, revealing kind eyes.

I offer him my hand, heart hammering as he takes it. "I'm Hannah."

"It's a pleasure, Hannah. And how long have you two been together?"

"Two years today, actually," Damien answers for me.

My body quakes with shock at the blatant lie, how easily it passes through his lips.

Two years? Who would believe that?

Then again, this man doesn't strike me as a socialite who reads the daily gossip, particularly ByteBuzz, who would definitely report on Damien Bass' love life. Maybe it doesn't matter if he finds out we're lying later. Only if *later* is after the buyout is through.

The old man eats it up, a bright smile beaming from him. He cheers his glass with mine, drawing the attention of nearby onlookers. "How wonderful to hear! Does that mean you've been settling down, Damien?"

"Oh, yes. Hannah keeps me very focused." His arm squeezes around me, a silent reminder to play my part. "Don't you, baby?"

Get it together. Two-million dollars and your family's future are on the line. Be sad later.

I smile brightly, fearing the falseness might shatter my teeth as I run my hand down the length of his coat jacket. "I keep you in line," I tease, returning my attention back to Haru. "Innovex is his top priority, *our* top priority. It must be, to ensure its future in today's competitive markets. All it takes is one plausible deniability to break their NDA and leak engineering secrets to hurt our market value. We always stay alert to not let that happen, to keep our seat at the top of microchip manufacturers."

Damien's hum of approval is a deep tenor that vibrates against my body. I try to shut him out, but I can feel the praise deep in my bones.

My chin raises, a subtle smirk lining my lips. *Even I surprised myself.*

"Smart gal you have there." His eyebrows lift. "And where did you attend school?"

Fuck it, let's take this all the way home.

"Princeton."—*lie*—"I studied Business Management." *Not a lie.*

"Brilliant." His eyes brighten as he turns to Damien. "You two make a great team, I must say. I'd like to arrange a meeting with you soon, if you'll have me."

"Of course. I'd like nothing more." Damien's eyes burn with satisfaction, before he nods and departs from the gentleman. His arm pulls me along with him.

"It seems I send you down to the engineers a little *too* often." His whisper against my ear pries a giggle from me. "I need to be careful before I make a shark out of you."

BEING on the arm of Damien Bass is like turning a spotlight on max, flipping it and shining it right into my retinas.

Everyone in the room is watching me.

Watching me greet business mogul after business mogul, each suddenly very interested in talking with me. And with each guest we meet—whether it be the owner of a tech conglomerate, or an internet service provider or simply an heir or heiress who struck it big—the lies come easier. Smoother. More believable. And I understand that much more about selling yourself and the art of business.

It's bullshit.

Complete, unequivocal bullshitting lies.

Image is all that matters in business, my little protégée. I recall Damien's words as he whisks me across the garden grounds.

But under the falseness lies some truth—that Damien and I might actually be *good* together. His presence seeps calmness into me, assuring my actions in a place I wouldn't have dreamt of being months ago. Before him, the thought of me, Hannah Lockwood, and the upper echelons of Silicon Avenue couldn't possibly mix. Even if I was with Sterling, he never took me around such people.

We pass green hedges and well-dressed attendees, all of whom make considerable efforts to acknowledge us—a wave of their hand, a formal greeting or compliment on our dress. But Damien proves to be picky with who he engages in conversation, seeming to *truly* only be here for business. Every trust-fund-baby, drunk party-type eats our dust after no more than a brittle head nod.

As we make our way back towards the French doors, I catch a glimpse inside. Guest capacity seems to have doubled since we left the ballroom, and the dance floor is actually getting some use. Adrenaline fills up my veins, and I wonder if Damien would want me as his dance partner. But before we make it inside to find out, a hand darts in front of us.

"There you are," a raspy voice calls. "I've been looking all over for you."

Damien stops this time, in front of a man who pinches a cigar between his fingers. His broad shoulders and stocky frame seem to blot out the setting sun rays.

"Oh." Damien's arm slacks against me. "Hey, Mr. Thornton. It's good to see you. You're looking sharp."

Hey?

My eyebrows scrunch when I hear the pause in Damien's

voice. I didn't realize *hey* was in his vocabulary, especially at such an event.

I recognize the last name, *Thornton*, but where from? I nibble on my bottom lip, uncaring of how it may look as my mind churns in thought... *The board.* My lip pops back out. *That's where. He's on Innovex's board. That makes more sense—he must know him well.*

"Thank you." His voice is a brass tenor trailing on the end of his smoke plume. "I wanted to inform you that the photographers are in place."

The ire with which he speaks has my defenses shackling ten feet high. And when I feel Damien tense against me, allowing a silence to ensue, they raise even higher.

"Photographers?" My eyes bounce between them. "What photographers?"

"Oh, excuse me," Damien butts-in before he can answer. "Harrison, you know Hannah, right? My personal assistant. I guess I never introduced her to you officially as my girlfriend."

For a split second, not an ounce of shock reveals behind the man's eyes. Not until he feigns a pleasant smile, extending his arm to me. "How wonderful. It's great to meet you."

His dry, calloused hand conforms around mine as Damien explains, "Harrison was only referring to the photographers set for this evening's toasts."

I blink, studying the monster of a man in front of us who sports a glistening black tuxedo. *This* man, on his board of directors, is arranging photographers?

I don't think so.

Damien is lying. *But why?*

We part ways with Harrison before I build up the nerve to

confront Damien. And soon, my glaring suspicion fizzles out, distracted as we encircle one another on the dance floor and marvel at the mastery of the violinists. Damien's gaze pours over my body like scorching wildfire, sparking a desire in me that dampens the uneasiness I feel between us.

Leaving my questions cold and long forgotten.

THIRTY-ONE
HANNAH

I TURN the faucet handle to the very right, letting the cold water splash against my hands. I'd hoped it would ease my rattling mind that's working like a beehive in overdrive. Too many resurfaced questions. Too many *people* watching us with whispers under their breaths.

The ballroom bathroom looks about how I expected. Porcelain sinks curve around gold spouts, and tall marble stalls reflect at me through the mirrors with glittery heels poking underneath the doors.

I release a breath, rummaging through my clutch, right as two girls come stumbling into the bathroom, their hands bracing the walls.

"Come on," the one wearing a purple slip-dress says, tugging the other. "There's good lighting in here."

They giggle on by, nearly running into me, before they whip out their phones. Twisting the bottom of my lipstick tube to unveil a deep red shade, I can't help but sneak peeks at the photoshoot that follows.

With a flashing phone pointed her way, the one in purple

sits on the countertop, leaning over as her breasts nearly topple out of her dress. The camera woman shimmies across the floor, dropping to her knee as she angles the camera upwards.

She hops down from the counter, hair whirling as she faces the mirror and pulls out her own phone. The two interlock fingers, pushing their backsides further out than their lips.

My brows lift as I leave them to it, lining my lips with deadly precision. *They're having a great time.*

I'm about to head for the bar to find myself a drink that'll get me to their level, when a snicker sounds from their direction.

I don't leave yet, acting like I'm fixing my hair as I flick my eyes towards them again, only to find them looking right at me. Their phones snap back down as they look the other way, like some kids getting caught.

They must be embarrassed? Maybe they forgot I'm here... They're just drunk.

"Keep doing your thing. I don't mind if I'm accidentally in the background." I smile at them, turning to leave.

"But we do." The hiss that follows rakes up my back, causing me to turn on my heels to find them both wearing devilish grins.

What the hell?

"What's *that* supposed to mean?"

A stall door swings open with a *clang*, unveiling a dress almost too large for the space, worn by a woman with a mean expression... *and auburn hair.*

Priscella.

"It means you're bad social cred," she sings, shooting me a look that could positively kill me where I stand.

My eyes roll. "You again?"

"Didn't I tell you, girls?" She ignores me, purposely going to the sink right next to me. But I don't move an inch. "It's bad for your reputation to be spotted with a gold-digger."

W h a t ?

My mind goes blank for a moment, at the brashness of her words. No one's ever spoken to me in such a matter. Priscella takes the opportunity to further twist the knife into my dignity.

"Flinging yourself from one Bass brother to the next? How tasteless." Suds lather along her hands as the other girls' snickers continue to burn down my back.

"Like you're any different."

"I am, actually. You want to know why?" Her voice is sweet but laced with a toxic venom. "Because I'm of the same class as Sterling—and, yes, I *do* mean social class. I'm at least on the same playing field, the *same league.* But you and Damien?" She nearly chokes on her laugh, yanking the paper towel out of its holder. "Everyone here knows you're from a different world, no matter how much money *he* paid for your dress."

Flushing a bright crimson, my knuckles whiten around my purse. She seems to eye that, too, and her smile widens.

"You don't know a single thing about us."

"Oh, don't I?" Her heels clack against the ground as she circles me. "I know what I saw at dinner. A man serious about you wouldn't do *that.*" She leans in, her whisper a knife scraping along my eardrum. "Sorry to break it to you, sweetie, but this isn't a *Pretty Woman* charity-case tale. You're just his flavor of the month."

"And you're Sterling's," I spit back, our eyes a hair's

breadth away. "He's never been serious about anything, *especially* a woman, his whole life."

"And who says I care? He's not the true heir to the Bass fortune. He's not the firstborn." Blood roars in my ears, knowing the innuendo she's about to threaten me with before she says it. "And when Damien's done playing around— *playing with you*—I'll be right there, as his formidable match. Just you watch."

"That's enough." She jerks back from me, her smile slithering across her mouth as my chest heaves up and down.

Calm down. Don't give her another reaction. That's all she wants. I berate myself, feeling stupid to have given her one in the first place.

She twirls her hair between her fingers. "Besides, Sterling and I *are* getting along quite well. Whether you think he's serious with me or not doesn't matter. You're only projecting about how he felt about *you*, not me. And he's positively in love with me. So, I guess I'll ride his wave for a while until—"

"Priscella." A gasp shoots across the bathroom, and I find the girl in purple wearing a horrified expression. She stares down at her phone. "H-how... *W-why*—"

"Spit it out, number two." Annoyance spews from Priscella's mouth as she bounds across the bathroom. When she cranes her head over to see what's on her phone, her eyes bulge out of their sockets. "What the *FUCK?!*" Priscella's screech rattles in my ears as she fumbles to retrieve her own phone from her purse.

"Delete it, *delete it,*" the girl whines, her hand covering her mouth.

Priscella's dagger-like nails stab at her phone screen, deep lines forming on her face. "I can't! It won't let me. Why can't I—"

I jump as the next stall door flings open, and what I see stops my heart in its tracks.

Sofia saunters out in blood-red velvet with a plunging neckline curving half-way down her center. She wears a contagious, dubious grin as she eyes the girls like they're garbage, merely bugs to squish beneath her soaring heels.

But they don't notice her, don't notice a single thing as tears line Priscella's eyes. She scurries to exit the bathroom, but before she can, Sofia snatches her forearm. Air seeps from the room like a vacuum, all of us watching in anticipation as Sofia seethes pure wrath towards Priscella.

Her voice is low, with a mysteriously dark undertone. "Damien Bass would be *lucky* to call Hannah his *anything*. You got that?"

Words seem to catch in her mouth, a response shoving straight back down her throat as she nods. Sofia releases her hold before the three girls race out of the bathroom door.

Sofia saunters over to a sink, flipping on the faucet with a calm expression. The water clatters between her fingers, and I bite my lip, eyeing her through the mirror. Her lips tug, and so do mine. And soon, our laughs squeal so loudly they must echo all the way to the dance floor.

"WELL, THAT WAS A MESS." I exhale sharply, taking a seat at the bar as I study my surroundings.

With the sun fully set, music floats past the ballroom doors to the patio. A stream of lights dangles from the bar's roof, illuminating the area enough to see the surrounding garden grounds.

"It was..." Sofia twirls her hair, her eyes sweeping the area like she's looking for someone.

It really is a stunning outfit, I decide, studying her dress, with its revealing yet classy style. Not that I'm turning into some designer girl—because I'm *not*—but I'm curious where it's from. She pairs it with her notoriously tall heels I've seen her race from club to club in.

I smile as the bartender comes over and takes our drink orders.

"How'd you get invited here, anyways?" *That sounded a little harsh.* "No offense," I add.

"None taken. By the same guy who got us a table at Enigma a month back."

I hum, trying to recall his name. It's hard to keep up with the men around a girl like Sofia. She has lots of admirers, many of whom are nearly twice her age. *"Marco.* That's right."

Her face contorts at the sound of his name. "You know, he's not all that great, if I'm being honest. He's too handsy— even for my tastes—and his breath smells god-awful half the time. But there are so many people here to network with, so many intelligent minds."

"Ahh." My eyes narrow her way. "You're a networker now?"

"Hey, *Miss Business Queen.* I'm trying my best." She shrugs before a grin blossoms on her lips. "But I'm not really the one we should talk about right now."

Oh, no. Here come the questions.

I avoid her stare when our drinks come, hoping she might drop the subject. But of course, she's Sofia, so she doesn't.

"How is he? I saw him flaunting you around like his royal prize earlier. I think he's trying to make a point, making sure every guy here sees you. So"—she nudges my shoulder, her lips conforming around her straw—"have you two—"

"*Yes,*" I spit out, only to stop her prying questions short, hoping she'll leave it at that. Short and sweet. I sigh when the next wave comes shooting from her lips.

"I knew it," she nearly squeals. "I knew you couldn't hold out. I mean, why should you? He's divine and I'm positive all the single women here would like nothing more than to see you end up dead on the street somewhere and, besides, you really, *really* needed to stick it to Sterling. But tell me. *Where* did you? Or—wait, no. Obviously, it's been multiple times, so it *can't* be just one spot. *When* did it start? *How?* Did you guys—"

"*Sofia.*"

"What?" Her eyes widen, hands shooting up in front of her. "They're harmless questions, really."

"It just sort of... happened. And then we started talking and—"

"Oh my god." The bottom of her glass scrapes against the wooden bar top. "You guys aren't only hooking up? You have *feelings?*"

The word comes out of her mouth so foreign, like some unobtainable, unimaginable experience only a few can attest to. Immediately, my internal walls go up.

"I-I... I don't know what we are." I swirl my straw in my tequila sunrise, staring down at the orange foam that nearly spills off the glass's rim. "But we shouldn't be anything, Sofia... Priscella may be a bitch, but she's making quite a lot of sense."

It's true. I really *don't* know what we are anymore. I don't even know what I want out of our arrangement, aside from getting the help my family so desperately needs. But the more

I replay her words in my mind, the more I agree with Priscella. Maybe Damien really *is* going through some phase. A man like him, with so much money and power and responsibility, has to get easily distracted.

You're his flavor of the month.

Her words hit me like a freight train, blooming a sickening realization I can hardly bear to consider. What if Damien is more like his brother than I first thought? Maybe they're cut from the same cloth, but one is better at hiding it than the other. I swallow, trying to stop the bleakness spiraling down my brain.

A long-term relationship might never be in the cards for him.

"Please." Sofia's tone infuses me with some confidence. "Who does she think she is to know the first thing about you and Damien? Nothing that comes out of that bimbo's mouth is worth any merit."

She manages a laugh out of me before I whither back down to reality. "But, come on, how am I supposed to keep up with him, with girls like *her?* I need to face it earlier rather than later. She's right. We really are from two different worlds."

"And why would that matter?" a feminine voice not belonging to Sofia asks.

I swivel in my stool to find a girl sitting next to me with flaming hair that frames her face. Her emerald eyes bare into me, as if she can read my every thought. "What does it matter if you two are different? All that matters is you are happy and so is Damien. And believe me, with you, he is."

"Um..." I quirk my brows at this complete stranger, who flaunts red-tipped fingers and priceless jewels along her neckline. "I'm sorry. Who are you?"

"I'm Lauren. Lauren Astor."

The sound of Sofia choking splits right down the middle of our conversation.

But still... not a single bell rings for me. *Should I recognize the name? Sofia sure does.*

"I'm Damien's cousin."

"Oh." Embarrassment overtakes me at the thought of his family member overhearing our entire conversation. She must think we have poor manners, truly from a lower class. My heart hammers to rewrite my mistake. "Look... I didn't mean to call Priscilla a—"

"A bitch?" Her smile is brazen as a laugh bellows from her gut. "No, I think you meant a *raging bitch.*"

My lower lip flops open.

"We go way back, I hate to admit. We went to boarding school together growing up, but that doesn't mean we get along. Now, believe me. You don't need to worry about her. She's all talk, and her lifeblood is drama and causing headaches for those of her same sex. But, a little advice, if for some misfortunate reason you *do* need to engage in conversation with her"—she raises her martini that's so clear it could be mistaken for water—"you're going to need an even stiffer one of *these.*"

She pries laughs from both of us, and I'm surprised when the sky darkens further and we're still talking to Lauren. The conversation between the three of us is light and flows with ease, and only stops short when a man speaking into a microphone is heard from inside.

He announces the next dance, prompting Sofia and me to both stand. A sad inkling sweeps down my spine at our soon departure. But Lauren is the first to act, retrieving a card from her purse. She hands one to me and then to Sofia, whose eyes look like sparkling saucers.

"If you ever need me, for business or merely a friend, don't hesitate to call."

I raise my eyebrows when I read her laminated business card.

Lauren Astor, Astor Associates

Attorney at law

She turns to leave, but before she does, she pauses, whirling on her heels as she eyes those around us with caution. She leans into me, her voice soft and quick but with an edge of seriousness.

"I haven't seen Damien smile like he does standing next to you in... I don't know how long. Probably since we were kids. Whatever will transpire between the two of you, know his past is of great struggle and a hardship very few could understand, let alone recover from. Meaning, whoever he needs in his lifetime to make him whole again should care little of status or wealth."

She simply turns and leaves without another word, not waiting to see my reaction before she walks herself back into the ballroom.

ALL MY WORRIES wipe away with Damien's swift touch, sliding down the length of my back. I study him, the cautious hunger in his eyes.

"Is the stoic Mr. Bass *nervous?*" I tease, swaying with him on the polished dance floor, enjoying the orchestra's peaceful melody. We move in tangent to the crowd of couples surrounding us, a tame ocean of delicate lace and suits.

"Is it so obvious?"

"We *are* in the very center of the floor. Is it all the people watching us?" I breathe in his scent, swirling my fingertips along the back of his neck, careful not to disturb his hair's gelled perfection.

"No, it's not them." He clears his throat, sounding dry. "It's you, Hannah."

A thousand spotlights could shine on me, and they still wouldn't grab my attention more than the precious way Damien says my name.

"I thought—"

"I know... But I'm realizing you're *good* for me. And I know we've been intimate, and maybe that's the only way you feel for me, but I don't. I feel more—*we* could be more than what our contract defines us as."

"Damien, are you saying..." The question lodges deep in my throat.

Piece after piece, I feel the walls around my heart crumbling into a pile of rubble, and I dare myself to imagine a life with Damien Bass. I indulge in the fantasy and possibility of wanting more from him, to feel love and trust in a relationship where one isn't out to hurt the other or abandon them for their own gain.

Is that possible?

He cups my jaw gently, staring into me so deeply I can feel it in my soul. "Don't you feel it?"

The attraction.

"Yes."

His lips capture mine in the most tantalizing of ways, uncaring of how he may smudge my red lipstick. Widening his lips, his tongue passes through mine to sweep against the roof of my mouth. His groan that follows reduces everyone around us to a blur as the music enhances our connection.

He pulls away, and for a moment, I'm eerily aware of

nearly a hundred eyes stealing glances at us. Brushing his thumb along the edge of my mouth, he fixes my lipstick. "You know everyone is watching, right?"

"What's new?" He kisses my cheek, whispering into my ear. "You know every man in this whole ballroom has looked at you all night?"

I may have noticed, once or twice, but I don't tell him.

"Have they now? You're the one who ordered me to wear such a noticeable dress."

"You could wear a paper sack, and you'd still steal the show from every woman here." A shiver runs up my spine at the seriousness of his compliment. "Meaning, no. It's not the dress they're tempted by. *It's you.* And they should be careful. Looking at what's mine for too long is dangerous."

His nose brushes mine for a moment, so close I can smell the mintiness on his breath.

"So..." He sinks his hand into his pants pocket, dropping to one knee. "I'm going to give them something else to look at."

"HANNAH LOCKWOOD, would you do the remarkable honor of marrying me?"

My heart hammers in my chest like the crashing of symbols.

It's hard to tell if the shock lining Hannah's face is because of the timely proposal, as per written in our contract. Or because of the diamond sitting inside of the velvet black box, I hold in my clammy hands—I wouldn't blame her, as the jeweler appraised it for just over five million. *Or* because she shares the notion that some part of this fake proposal is real.

Whichever the case, the way her jaw hangs low and her hands flicker to the corners of her mouth makes for the perfect snapshot. Flashes shine bright against the darkness of the dance floor. The photographers acted quickly, precisely how Harrison said they would.

The bodies and eyes surrounding us illuminate, all waiting in anticipation for Hannah's decisive answer. Her attention draws to the crowd, and some of that sparkling joy dies out of her eyes before she returns them to me.

I wish I could speak to her in this moment, away from the spectators, to ask her if she's capable of sharing in the belief that some part of this is real. I need to know if she feels the same as when our lips were locking only moments ago.

"Yes," she breathes, barely audible over the music, as she plasters a thick smile on her lips.

Cheers crash around us, and the flashing triples in capacity when I stand. Taking her left hand in mine, I slide the heavy diamond onto her finger. I freeze for a moment, lost in her gaze. She raises her eyebrows, waiting for something, and then I'm pulled from my thoughts.

Right.

Taking her jaw in both my hands, I press my lips to hers, prompting *even more* camera shutters to sound over the symphony.

In a whirlwind of time, we're hand in hand, splitting the crowd in two. Congratulations are on the lips of every couple we pass, all except Sterling's and his red-headed date's, who eye us with thin slits. But we pay them no mind, finally breaking through the crowd.

Hannah leans into me. "You could've at least warned me."

"I wanted you to be surprised." I regret the words the instant they come out, knowing how she'll respond. But it's true. Those pictures are the most important proof we got. It's no doubt we'll be the head of tech news—hell, *all* gossip news.

"Ya, right—for the cameras," she spits through clenched teeth, happily waving at others.

"No." I squeeze her hand as we make it through the clutter of tables, hoping to rekindle our connection we had earlier. Steering us towards an exit door, I plan to take us somewhere more private. "Because—"

"That's no way to treat your bride-to-be, Damien. Stowing her away before this evening's fun has commenced." A smirk tugs at my lips before I swivel on my heel, our interlinked fingers dragging Hannah along with me to face my mother. "I raised you better than that, did I not?"

Not that she ever *doesn't* look impeccable, even just around the house. But tonight, my mother made quite the effort. Her dress's considerable train drags along the floor with intricate floral designs decorating her yellow silk.

"Yes, you did." I un-link our fingers, feeling the tension radiating off Hannah like electricity through a wire. "Mother, I'd like you to meet Hannah."

"Gosh, aren't you a beautiful thing?" She skips the hand-shake Hannah offers her, going straight in for a hug, squeezing her shoulders tightly.

"Oh." The nerves in Hannah's voice are palpable, floating between the three of us like we could prick the words from the air. "I know it must be odd meeting this way..."

"Nonsense, dear." My mother appraises the both of us, no doubt deciding she likes what she sees. We *do* make for a very attractive couple. "Damien has always been on the private side, so it comes as no shock he waited until he *proposes"*— she smacks her tiny purse against my shoulder with a smile —"to introduce us. We were beginning to think no one would ever be good enough for him."

"Is that so?" Hannah's narrowed eyes point my way, and I can feel the heat of her stare.

"I am quite picky."

My mother turns her head, quietly waving a goodbye to a group of departing guests before she refocuses her attention on Hannah. *She really is the most attentive hostess on Earth.*

"And I know my son. He doesn't make any decisions

lightly, and I'm positive that notion has extended to you, my dear."

"Wow." Hannah's smile is genuinely bright as she loops her arm around mine, the attention causing my heart to flutter. "That means a lot, Camille."

"I'd very much like to invite you over for tea sometime. Maybe brunch? We have plenty to catch each other up on. Maybe I'll even pull out the family photo album—"

"Mom."

"But you really were the cutest baby."

Hannah's laughter floats into my ear as she beams at my mother, continuing on with their chitchat. And for a brief moment in time, everything seems easy. I'm not balancing billions of dollars of assets and crippling trauma atop my ten fingertips, and Hannah and I are truly engaged. She's with me because she loves and trusts me and wants nothing more than to dine with my mother on the back porch as the groundskeepers snip the hedges before dawn.

I breathe deep, their conversation lulling me to bliss.

"You really remodeled this whole place?"

"Yes."

"You must really have an eye for such a thing. Everything's exquisite. The dance floor, the porch, the ceiling and *the orchestra.* I've heard nothing like it, especially live."

"Yes, well, hiring them took some convincing. With thirty in the ensemble, including the composer, they perform biweekly at the New York Regional—"

My mother's gasp tears me from my peace. I whip my head to hers, following the line of her stare all the way to the stage.

"Damien." I feel her gentle touch on my arm. "I didn't—I would *never...*"

Blood surges to my ears, plunging the rest of her muffled sentence into deep water. I don't think. I don't breathe.

I only watch the piano wheel out to center stage.

More sounds come through my raging ocean. "Damien, why don't you introduce me to your lovely fiancée?" a male's voice I know so well asks, drowning under the crashing waves.

Coming to a smooth stop to stand on three legs with its slanted lid peaking proudly in the air, a spotlight beams at the piano in all its glory.

"Damien?" a feminine voice calls for me through the water, jolting my arm to get me out. "Damien?" it calls again, tugging harder and finally surfacing me until I hear crystal clear again, dragging my gaze away from the glistening object.

I observe Hannah, and the thick concern that swirls through her features. Then I lock eyes with my father, unable to speak. And the way my mother looks at me... she looks like she's about to cry.

"What?" My father stares down at her. "Do you not like my present for the newly engaged, *wife?*"

The bite in his tone would normally rally me to her defense, to draw his brutal attention back to me, if it wasn't for the quicksand biting at my ankles, forcing me to return my gaze back to center stage.

"It's wonderful." I hear my mother's dry voice.

For all those years, that piano has never left that room, not once. It stayed there, like some twisted time capsule, concealing all the horrifying memories I have with my father. And all the disgraceful and unspeakable things he did to me while he forced me to play, forever etching the thought of becoming a pianist from my mind. Since those days, that piano's never been touched. And the thought of hearing its beautiful yet terrifying sounds might finally be enough to break me.

My eyes lock on the man—or, should I say, *boy?*—who bounds across the stage, head held high as all those in the room watch him. He appears to be about thirteen with dark brown hair...

Bile rises in my throat, steaming hot and thick.

He sits in the chair, adjusting its position until he's at a proper distance. Fingers run along the porcelain keys as he fiddles his toes, testing the pedals.

Tears prick at my eyes as the bile rises further, to the top of my throat now. I feel Hannah's light touch on my arm, trying but failing to pull me from the final blow. His keys slam down in a complex crescendo, and every hair on my entire body stands to attention before I bolt from the three of them.

At first, I don't know where I'm going. All I know is it's *away* from the stage. I zoom by happy onlookers and the congratulations that are quick on their lips, zipping by photographers and the bar, heading straight for an emergency exit, with Hannah calling my name behind me.

I barrel through the door, picking up speed through the porch, until I'm down a flight of stone stairs, through a tight alleyway with green hedges on both sides of me. I make it one more corner with no one inside, before I topple over, releasing all of tonight's contents into an unfortunate rosebush.

Feeling light-headed, I sway before sitting on the grass. I'm suddenly aware of how dark it is, but not dark enough to hide Hannah's glittery shoes in front of me. She drops to her knees in silence, wrapping her arms around me in a comforting embrace.

"You don't have to tell me." Her voice is achingly soft as her hands caress through my hair and down my back.

But I want to.

My father, my childhood, the twisted, fucked-up man he's made me into and the horrible things he's subjected my family to. I wish for her to know everything. I *need* her to know the deepest, ugliest parts of myself, so maybe one soul in this entire world might sow mine back whole again.

So, I do—tell her.

Everything.

MY HEART SUMMONS up an inkling of rage as the last person I want to see right now rounds into view.

Sterling.

His bowtie droops around his neck as he nearly topples over into a rosebush.

"Ohhhh, hey, you two." He smiles.

My shackles rise at the glee in his voice. He never sounds that happy towards me, which can only mean one thing. He's not simply drunk. He's borderline blacked-out. Hannah must realize it too, because she seals her lips shut, staring at him with caution swirling in her eyes.

"Hey, Sterling." I sigh, noting the annoyance creeping into me. I'm not about to berate him. But I surely don't want to engage in conversation with him, especially after the one I had with Hannah moments ago.

"Why... don't you guys look perfect together? Having the privacy of the gardens all to yourselves. How wonderful! Makes sense. Get away from the cameras and chatter. Every-one's talking about you, you must know, about your *propos-*

al." His hands fly to his knees before he leans over, bellowing out laugh after laugh.

"What's so funny?" I grit out.

He steadies himself again, his eyes wet as he calms himself down. "Are you serious—what's *not* funny? Hannah *Lockwood*"—his laughter picks up again—"marrying *you? One of us?* So... what? We're all going to just sit around at family gatherings with the fattest elephant dancing around in the room—that the most average girl on this entire planet fucked me, and then fucked her way up the ladder. I'd call her brilliant, but it doesn't take smarts to have *that* ass."

I shoot to my feet, my patience completely blown into pieces, but Hannah snatches my hand. "Don't, Damien. Don't let him ruin our beautiful moment. When we look back on this night, we don't want to be thinking of him."

After a slow, calming breath, I soak in my brother's dreary state—how miserable and bitter he truly looks.

"Sterling." It's nearly impossible to keep the bite out of my voice. "I'm only going to tell you this once. Keep *my fiancée's* name out of your mouth."

"Ah!" his laugh barks out, snorts ringing against my ears. "No way. You're serious? Come on, you can cut the act. I know you don't actually intend to marry her."

My gut drops for a moment, wondering how he knows of our arrangement, but hot fire replaces it the moment he explains.

"You're willing to pay—what, millions of dollars?—for a ring, so you can dangle my *leftovers* in front of my face?"

He thinks this is about him?

I break from Hannah's grasp. It's nearly impossible to control my breathing, to see anything but red as I bound across the grass, uncaring of how drunk he appears to be.

But instead of shrinking away or apologizing, Sterling's eyes turn *accepting,* with a deep, complicated coldness shining through them as I grab him by the collar.

"Go ahead, hit me." His tone is strikingly calm, stealing a breath from me. "Just like Dad."

With clenched teeth, my grip tightens. "What. Did. You. Say?"

He leans into me, his nose brushing against mine. "I said. Hit. Me. Just like—"

"I'm nothing like him. He hit an innocent child. Is that what you think you are, a child? Well, maybe you're right, because you surely act like one. Fucking around, partying, snorting cocaine like it's the air you breathe, no future in sight. When it could all be there for you. *Right there,* to start fresh and do something useful with your life. But will you? No, never."

"Guess my days of being a complete fuck-up are over, aren't they? Dad pulled my trust fund. Simple as that—*poof,* gone." A swirl of guilt nips at me, my signature marked in black ink flashing before my eyes. "So, I'll ask one more time. Are you sure you're not like him?"

"What's that supposed to mean?"

"Tell me you had nothing to do with it."

And for once in my life, I don't hear his familiar poison.

I hear truth.

I loosen my grip on him.

"That's what I thought," he says.

And the next words from his mouth are another first of their kind, addressing the topic we both bury so deeply inside ourselves that we forget it's there, rotting us from within...

The true rift that's always been between us.

"You might think the way I am is all my fault, but at least Dad gave a shit about you."

THIRTY-THREE

HANNAH

DID YOU HEAR?

New York's most eligible billionaire put a ring on it. But you'll never guess on who... No, really, you won't. Because even I've never heard of Hannah Lockwood.

Photographs of Damien down on one knee amidst tech royalty in the Bass' family ballroom are zipping across cyberspace faster than the speed of light. And yet, no one's sent me a single tip regarding his young personal assistant or the Lockwoods.

If you know of them, please, I want to chat (online, of course).

In later, more scandalous news, have you seen the new sex tape starring none other than Sterling Bass and Priscella Vuitton? Even if you won't admit it, bet you have, seeing as its views are skyrocketing on dozens of sites ending in "hub." The raunchy video set in a glitzy yacht cabin mysteriously posted to all of Priscella's socials the same night as the Bass' proposal.

Coincidence?

I'll let you decide.

Albeit behind the mask of a keyboard and an anonymous pseudonym that shall forever remain a mystery, I'll be real enough to admit that I have watched it. Once. And my unofficial-official review…? **Meh.** *Seen better. Seen* **much** *better. My advice to the two co-stars for their next film: don't. Keep it to the professionals.*

Since then, the youngest heir to the Vuitton tech fortune released a follow-up video—in clothes this time—apologizing, no doubt attempting to mend ties with the Bass family, whom the Vuittons invest heavily into.

Good luck with that.

In the video, she—or should I say **her** lawyer—*explains the dangerous prevalence of artificial intelligence and deepfakes, painting Priscella as an innocent victim of some extortionate hacker, who has yet to be unveiled.*

Let me be the first to say, no one's believing that, Miss Vuitton. Not me, not my readers and especially not tycoons on Silicon Avenue. All of us know the truth…

Those pixels were realer than every one of your "orgasms."

Signing off for now. But don't worry, your next dose of tech drama is only one byte away.

- ByteBuzz

I place my tablet on the kitchen counter, letting the information float through my brain. Priscella… exposed to be in a *sex tape* merely two days after telling me how serious she and Sterling are. Figures. And the way she threatened to steal Damien once he's *through with me?*

Sitting comfortably on a stool, my eyes flicker across the marble island, watching Damien's impressive back muscles flex. He grinds a tall shaker, twisting its bulbous head to rain pepper down into a pan atop the stove.

Chopped tomatoes, bell peppers and onions stack neatly in their own piles on a cutting board in front of me. The smell of fresh produce fills the air, making my mouth water, but not more than the sight of Damien in an apron.

Just an apron—and boxers.

With a grin marking his lips, he turns, waving a spatula with a yellow eggy tip. "Something got your attention?"

Heat rushes to my cheeks, realizing I'd been caught staring. "Umm... Ya, this ByteBuzz article. Have you read it?"

"Nope. And don't plan to." He snatches the cutting board and whirls around before toppling the items into the pan, sparking a satisfying sizzle. "Most of what he—or she or whoever they are—writes is complete rubbish. Half the stuff they say is for attention and clicks, not even true."

It's been two days since the ball, and there's already been dozens of articles written about us, several of them from ByteBuzz and others unrelated to tech news.

"Did you hear what they said about your brother?"

He quiets for a moment, working the spatula, no doubt thinking about their intense moment Sunday night. I'd never seen such hatred between two family members, and the things Sterling said, coupled with the new information I learned about their father from Damien that night...

I don't think I've ever met a truly evil person in my lifetime. Not before Oscar Bass.

"Yes. Sterling is a complete..." He sighs. "He's been going through a hard time."

I jerk back in surprise. He's never expressed a fraction of sympathy for his younger brother. And even though we dated, and yes, he was horrible, I now believe he has wounds that run deep, similar to Damien.

I let the conversation die, instead focusing on the beauty of today. Dawn peeks through the horizon, between the skyscrapers in its path and through the floor-to-ceiling windows, casting an orangish glow on the kitchen.

Normally, we wouldn't still be here around this time on a

weekday—and sometimes even on weekends. We'd be bustling through Innovex, inspecting quality controls, conducting meetings, among other things eating away at Damien's extremely valuable time.

But instead, today, Damien did the most *un-Damien-Bass-like* thing ever. He rescheduled his meetings, pushed them to tomorrow, and said we'd come into the office later this afternoon. For what, exactly? Well, it seems the billionaire preferred to get up early and work out at ungodly-like hours like normal, then *cook me breakfast* after ordering his housing staff to give us privacy.

Who thought Heaven could exist in a New York City skyrise?

My eyes wander from the spectacular view outside to the cleanliness of the windows. Seriously, there's not a single streak on them, and they wrap around half the penthouse. But my blissful fantasy cuts short by the sneaky waft of burnt food entering through my nostrils. I hear Damien's quiet curse before he flips on the over-head fan.

"Are you sure you don't need any help?"

"No," he grumbles. "They're only omelets. I can handle it."

"Can you now?" I tease.

Rounding the island, I take in the pan in all its scorched glory. Eggy goodness and chopped vegetables line half the steel. A flopped and burnt disaster lies on the other. He sighs, offering me a pathetic look before he seizes his phone from off the counter.

"What're you doing?"

"Calling the chef." He swipes the screen, an endless list of contact names soaring by. "I'm not feeding you *that* for breakfast."

"Oh, don't be such a baby." I lower his phone before he hits dial. "Just scrape off the burnt pieces."

He looks at me like I admitted to murder.

Who doesn't *scrape off the bad bits...? It's like it never happened.* I don't explain myself, pushing my case. "And don't forget you have a meeting in an hour. We don't have time to wait for him."

More grumbles foam out his mouth, something about *eating char* and *it must be a bad patch of eggs* and *I've cooked omelets plenty of times.* Which I know can't be true, given this is my first time seeing him use the stove or any appliance besides the fridge.

The majority of our nights, it's the private chef manning the kitchen solo, meal prepping for us and cooking a wide variety of fresh dinners—beef wellington, risotto, fish, Indian and Italian cuisine, and dishes I've never heard of. I've eaten like a true queen by the hands of an ex-Michelin Star chef for the past month and a half.

Stealing the spatula from him, I unfold the burnt side, unstick the eggs around the rim and fold the omelet correctly.

"Hmph." Damien watches over my shoulder, the heat of his bare body enveloping my backside. "I'll make it up to you later." He gives my cheek a quick kiss.

"Will you now?" With a blush staining my cheeks, I try to act smooth as I walk to the cupboard, avoiding his gaze when I return with a plate.

"Mhmm." His lips brush my ear, his voice taking on a gruff tone that has my thighs rubbing together. Wielding the hot pan, I twist it until the omelet glides over the edge, landing on the plate.

"And how's that?"

His hand brushes the back of my neck that's exposed from the messy bun I have atop my head. Goosebumps bloom on my arms as he trails all the way down my backside. I'm only wearing a shirt—*his shirt*—that I've grown accustomed to wearing, loving the smell of his cologne that seeps into its fibers.

I brace the countertop, feeling a need building inside me again, even after the sex we had early this morning. He lifts the hem of the shirt, past my thighs to expose my ass.

"Do you make it a habit to not wear panties around me, Miss Lockwood?"

Yes. "No."

"That's a lie." He *tsks*, grabbing a fistful of my ass cheek. His groan that follows has me nearly asking for round two. "And because of your little lie, you won't be wearing panties tonight either, when I take you out to dinner."

"Oh..." I deflate, my shoulders sagging. "But it's margarita Tuesday."

He whirls me around to face him, his hands gripping the edge of the countertop, pinning me between his arms. "Margarita what-now?"

"Margarita Tuesday." I offer him a confused look, swearing I've told him about our girls' ritual before. Granted, I haven't shown up to one since moving in here.

Terrible, I know.

"Okay." He chuckles warmly. "I'll make sure wherever I take you has margaritas."

He's dangerously close, his shirtless body hypnotizing me in a way that tempts me to call off girls' night. *But I can't.* I remind myself of how Sofia informed me at the ball if I skip again, she'll *personally chew Damien's ass out.*

"No, no. I mean, it's girls' night."

His face falls. "You're going out tonight?" His tone is that of a father reprimanding his teenage daughter or of an over-controlling husband, and it completely rubs me the wrong way.

Margarita Tuesdays are historically between Sofia and me, at our tiny dorm in college, to then graduating into our tiny apartment. We do not, in fact, go out on this special tradition. And why would we? Sofia's an ex-bartender who makes the meanest margarita in probably all of New York City.

But the way Damien's speaking to me and looking at me right now...? I break from his arms, returning to my stool. *He doesn't deserve to know that comforting fact. I don't owe him an explanation.*

"Am I not allowed to go out or something?"

"It's in our contract." He spits with quiet venom.

Contract, contract, contract. The word rings between my ears, further escalating my rapid heartbeat. "Is *this* in the contract, too?" I gesture my hand between us. "And what we did this morning?"

"No." His jaw ticks before he rounds the table in a mad dash. "But it *is* in it. No going out and getting drunk. We agreed on this. *You* signed it."

Unable to look at him, I cut my omelet in half. "I've been doing that quite a lot, you know. Drinking. The past few weeks? The ball, the dinner..."

"Yes, *with me,* you have."

I shake my head, something inside me on the verge of snapping. *The fucking audacity of this man.* "Oh, so I can only get drunk when I'm with you? Ya, okay. That makes sense."

"You're. My. Fiancée. Hannah." He enunciates each word with the clip of his fingers through the air, the veins on his arms flaring.

"Fake—"

"Don't," he growls, dark shadows forming along his face.

My fork clatters against my plate before we stare at each other for several breathless seconds. His eyes flick to my finger, to the ring I wear, even when no one else is around us in the penthouse. Today, I discreetly grabbed it from my nightstand and slipped it on before he fucked me.

Try to explain your way around that, Hannah.

I swallow, understanding the implications, but I don't allow myself to go there. Instead, in my annoyance, I chalk it up to some newfound habit or muscle memory or being thorough in the *role* I'm playing.

"You don't own me."

"Five million dollars wrapped around your finger says I do."

I nearly choke but stop myself, forcing the food to slide down my throat, refusing to give him the reaction he wants. *Five million dollars?* My hand seems to weigh down heavily.

"I can't have my prize going out like the night we met, dressed like—"

I burst to my feet, shooting him a look that could positively kill. Maybe I need a fight. Maybe it's easier than figuring out whatever-the-fuck we are. "Like what? Like some whore?"

"That's not what I sa—"

Whipping around, I aim for the bedroom, unable to listen to any more of the conversation.

"Hannah... *Hannah,*" he barks from across the room, my name echoing between the walls. But I don't look back, dashing through the doorway before slamming it on its hinges.

I DIDN'T SPEAK to Damien once for the rest of the day. Not when he somehow pried the door open and walked in while I was taking a shower. And not at the office when tension slithered between us during every meeting and phone call he took.

When we got back home after our quiet car ride, I managed a single *fine* after he again lectured me on the terms of our agreement. He thinks I'm not going out tonight, but I am—*to Sofia's apartment.* But I know exactly what he'll assume I'm doing. Clubbing, partying, dancing in the arms of some stranger, and I don't know how much more reprimanding I can take.

He'd know that's *not* what I'm doing if he saw what I'm wearing—yoga pants, a sweatshirt and fuzzy socks with cats printed on them. But he won't get that chance, because I plan on leaving before he gets out of the shower.

Rolling my eyes, I slip my fingers into the pants he left on our bed, too pissed off in my brewing silence to debate the morality of what I'm doing. Not even understanding *why* I'm doing it, with little to no plans. Maybe I want him to freak when he finds out. I don't know. And I don't care.

Flipping open his wallet, I discover a plethora of debit and credit cards, some personal and others for his business. I scan through them all until I find what I'm looking for.

Damien Bass
Black Amex

THIRTY-FOUR
HANNAH

"HOLY. *Shit.* That's one hell of a rock, Hannah." Sofia eyes my finger as she pops off the top of the blender, exposing the strawberry goodness inside.

She's right. So big I can't blame it on forgetfulness that I'm still wearing it.

I should've left the engagement ring on the kitchen counter if I was aiming for maximum effectiveness and drama, but... here I am, wearing a ring that costs more than this apartment, probably more than the entire building.

The wealth disparity between the two apartments is quite appalling, but I can still find a lot of appreciation for this one. It's filled with so many memories of Sofia and I and has that homey-cozy vibe that makes you want to wrap yourself with a blanket and watch movies all day... which is what we're planning on doing tonight, anyway.

"I know. It's kind of ridiculous, really."

As the alcohol I've already consumed fogs my brain, she pours my next round to the brim of my wide cup. "Sofia, how many shots are you putting in these?"

She pours hers, then fills a sidecar with the leftovers. *She better not expect me to drink that.* I stare at my glass, with its intimidating volume. *Because I'm not.* And Jenna's not, because she bailed on girls' night to be with some new boy... But I'm in no position to judge.

"Not many. Each margarita should come out to about three shots."

My eyes bulge, the end of my straw popping from my lips. *Three? Is she trying to put me face down before we even start a movie?*

"I got work tomorrow morning, you know."

"So do I." She whips her hand in the air, a smug smile on her lips. "Just call out sick. I'm sure it'll work. You *are* engaged to my boss' boss' boss."

The alcohol makes it impossible to stop my wide smile that follows, and Sofia laughs even harder.

"Like he'd allow that."

"Oh, he would. I'm sure you could even convince *him* to call out, too."

I roll my eyes before my phone buzzes against the countertop again, the rim flashing with light as it lies face down.

"You gonna answer that? I think *someone's* writing you a novel. Maybe he's apologizing."

"Damien Bass doesn't apologize."

Irritation flickers against my temple when it buzzes again. Sofia raises her eye to me, and I heave a sigh before I pick it up, half-way convincing myself that he really is apologizing. But the stream of messages and seven missed calls that light up on the screen prove me wrong.

Damien: *Where are you?*

Damien: *Hannah, tell me where you are right now.*

Missed call.

Missed call.

Missed call...

Damien: *You are willingly breaching our contract. Don't think there won't be repercussions.*

Damien: *I'll call the lawyers. Is that what you want?*

My fingers tighten around the phone with each message I read, and a heavy feeling of control winds around my legs like a ball and chain. I break loose before it ensnares me completely, slapping my phone back down without so much as a single reply.

"We're going out, then?" Sofia reads my expression, hitting the base of her drink. Gurgling sounds ring out inside her bowl from the end of her straw.

"Yep, I got some money to spend."

In fifteen minutes flat, Sofia and I are ready for a night out. Both in sparkling cocktail dresses, high heels, false lashes and all. Before we march out the door, our Uber two minutes away, Sofia's arm juts out in front of me.

"There's no way you can go out wearing that ring. You're asking to get robbed."

Holding my hand up to my gaze, I watch the diamond shoot hundreds of sparkles with every tiny movement. Gosh, what is wrong with me? Even in obvious rebellion, my natural instinct is to keep this thing on... I can't imagine how angry Damien would be if I lost something so valuable.

"You're right."

It glides off my finger like butter, and I'm left wondering how Damien figured out my exact ring size when I never wear rings, let alone own any.

Opening the pantry, I hide it underneath a bag of rice, turning around to see Sofia's thin lips. "Hopefully, someone isn't the luckiest burglar on Earth tonight," she says before she locks the door behind us.

I follow her down the tight hallway with fire in my belly and an empty shadow wrapped around my finger.

NEW YORK CITY really lives up to its name.

The city that never sleeps... Even on a Tuesday, this night-club is *packed*. With a name like The Pink Rabbit, I expected suspended cages with dancing women in them like Enigma that's two streets down. But there aren't any. And the energy is totally different.

Techno music blasts from speakers lined across the walls and hypnotic visuals display on a large screen behind a DJ. We've been here for only twenty minutes, and I've already seen two mosh pits break out on the dance floor and more than a handful of drug deals.

"Wow, where'd you hear about this place?" I tap my card —not Damien's—against the bar counter, waiting for our shots to arrive.

Upon our arrival, guilt snuck its way into me. Even if he's a billionaire and I'm technically his fiancée, maybe it was wrong of me to steal his card.

"From Jenna." Sofia leans her back up against the bar, looking to be on the prowl for some lucky gentleman. "She's really into EDM, so she'll regret missing this girls' night to hang with some guy."

A light creeps through the opening of my purse, and I don't need to look to know who it is. I don't know how many more messages there are, but I'm determined to ignore them.

"You could just turn it off," Sofia says, her eyes trailing an older man who walks by. Her shoulders drop when she sees a petite blonde girl following his tracks, their hands interlocked as they barrel through the crowded walkway.

"You'll get the next one." I laugh before she swats at me. "And you're right. I should."

I rummage through my purse, pulling it out. But before I hold the side to turn the phone off, I make the mistake of reading the most recent message.

Damien: *You BOTH work for me, remember?*

Hot, molten rage simmers down my center. *He's threatening me? Threatening Sofia? That's where I draw the line.* I rip the Black Amex from my purse, snapping a picture.

Me: *Each text is another swipe.*

Damien: *You wouldn't fucking dare.*

Me: *Try me.*

Damien: *Tell me which club you're at, so I can lean you over that bar and spank you.*

I bite my lip, not allowing myself to feel anything at the thought of him publicly shaming me, dealing me punishment after punishment. Shaking him from my head, I send another pic, this time using a different angle as I slide the card across the bar.

Damien: *Where's your ring?*

Damien: *Hannah?*

He calls me, and I immediately deny it.

Damien: *My family manufactures that phone you're using. Don't think I'm above tracking you.*

I roll my eyes at his exhausting threat, going into my settings to turn my phone to airplane mode. *What, does he think I'm stupid?* After tossing it back into my purse and zipping it shut, I meet Sofia's gaze.

"That bad, huh?"

"Worse," I grumble as the bartender returns with our shots, salt lining their sides with lime wedges skewered on their rims.

"Anything else?"

He accepts the black card I offer him. "Yes, actually. We'd like to buy another round."

Sofia's head snaps to me.

"Two more, then?" he asks.

"No, another round for every person in this club."

TURNS OUT, when you have an unlimited pile of cash to spend, everyone treats you *real* nice.

Who would've guessed?

With one swipe of a card, I racked up a near thirty-thousand-dollar charge. My eyes nearly bulged from my head when the club owner brought me the bill that I signed soon after. *Thirty thousand?* With how they gauge you with prices for drinks in this club and the insane number of bodies there are in here...

I could see that.

He then questioned me endlessly about who I was and proceeded to explain how I couldn't use the card, especially not one from Damien Bass. But once I told him to look up who his new fiancée is? Then *his* eyes nearly shot from their sockets, and he immediately did the following:

Stopped with the questions.

Brought out an entirely new table with booths and all, setting it up behind the DJ for us.

And assigned us a club promoter who asks if we need anything every ten minutes, it seems.

Matter of fact, here he is now.

"Miss Lockwood," he drawls. "Is there anything else you two ladies might need?"

"What do you think?" I ask Sofia, who sits on the edge of the booth and bangs her head furiously to the beat of the music. Her head pops up, her hair wild in front of her face.

"Hmm..." Her drunken grin widens. "Thirty thousand just doesn't have a good ring to it."

"You're right." I swivel my head to the promoter, his eyes widening when he realizes we mean to spend more. "What's the most expensive bottle of champagne The Pink Rabbit sells?"

"T-that would be our bottles of *Dom Pérignon.* They each run a cost of ten thousand. Shall I bring the owner to show you the—"

"Nonsense," I interrupt him. "We want one—actually, make that two. We'd both like to pop our own bottle, wouldn't we?"

"Oh, yes. *Dom Pérignon."* Sofia lifts her chin, completely butchering the name but still dragging out the syllables like she's tasting a delectable chocolate. "Now *that* has such a lovely ring to it."

I mimic her ridiculous act, pointing my nose higher in the air. "Mmmm. That it does."

The promoter nods slowly, buying into our eccentric behavior, before he turns on his heels and disappears. We both combust with laughter, tears lining our eyelids.

In the matter of minutes, our champagne bottles that couldn't look more fancy return to us. A single person could not possibly drink an entire bottle... But we both grab our own, anyway.

We begin twisting the wires that seal the bottles shut.

"Don't you dare spray me." I narrow my eyes at Sofia, but she doesn't look my way, her laughter still fresh on her lips.

There's no way she's...

She subtly shakes the bottle, angling it towards me.

Oh, hell no.

We lock eyes, and I don't hide the way I shake mine. Her mouth flies open, squeals shooting from her throat in anticipation that's nearly drowned out by the music. Both our corks pop simultaneously, and the promoter watches in horror as twenty-thousand dollars' worth of liquid spews out their glass tips.

Bubbles rain down over our table behind the DJ, and I swear I hear the crowd's roar of excitement. Sofia hits me square in the face, drenching me down to my chin. Whipping my head around, fighting through the pressure, I hose her down in return, painting her dress three shades darker.

When both our bottles run dry, the oddest thing happens... the lights turn on.

All of them.

Sofia and I exchange weird looks before we hear the entire crowd—*the entire club*—moan. They shield their eyes, complaining as the music goes quiet. The DJ's head whirls around everywhere, his face contorting in confusion. He grabs the mic, pressing a finger to his inner ear, presumably listening to someone on the other end.

"Uhh... Sorry, guys. Seems like the club is under new management. Show's over. Refunds will be given within the next few days." And with that, he bounds off the stage, prompting the mass of people to shuffle out of the room.

"Oh my god!" A high-pitched shriek comes from our left, and we discover Jenna with an unknown guy stepping onto the stage. "I thought that was you guys! How on earth did you land a table back here?"

Sofia's jaw sinks. "You bailed on girls' night to come *here?*"

She flattens her lips. "Well, it seems like you two did, too."

They both chuckle, not a flicker of seriousness between them as we all make to leave off the platform. But before I can exit our roped area, I stop in my tracks.

Shit.

"I'll leave you to it. Swing by sometime soon to get your *you know what.* Good luck," Sofia whispers in my ear, and I watch her hop off the stage with the rest of them.

Damien and I lock eyes across the room, him a stark contrast from everyone in the vicinity, with his suit and tie and still dampened hair. We seem to be in a silent battle, waiting to see who will cave first.

And he does.

He bounds across the room, club attendees offering him strange looks as he passes them. As he nears, his anger slowly evaporates into a quizzical brow when he takes in my wet state, until he's right in front of me.

"Uh... This isn't quite how I expected to find you."

"Oh, really?" I fold my arms tightly, still cross with him. "How'd you expect me—grinding up against some guy? I said it was *girls' night.* And, by the way, if you weren't such an ass, we wouldn't even have come here. We would've stayed at my old apartment, watching movies, like we do every Tuesday."

His face falls further, his shoulders following with it. "Hannah... I'm sorry. I should've had more trust."

"You think?" I scoff.

"Well, what'd you think I'd assume you were doing?" He runs his hand through his hair, a worried look painting his features. "You can't run off like that. What're trying to do to me, make me buy every nightclub in New York City?"

I flinch. *"That's* why everyone got kicked out? You—"

"Yes. I guess I'm the new owner of The Pink Rabbit."

I can't stop the laugh that bubbles out my mouth. "Wow, it doesn't seem too fitting for you... How'd you find me, anyway?"

My phone was on airplane mode, I neglect to tell him. He shouldn't have been able to find me.

He rolls his eyes. "I received several alerts regarding mysterious charges to my card, which I'll be taking back here soon."

I bite my lip as his body closes in on mine. "Baby, you'll have to spend a lot more than fifty thousand to get back at me."

He inches me further back until my tailbone hits the guard rail separating us from the drop off the stage. Grabbing my hand, he inspects my bare finger. "Care to explain why you're not wearing your ring?"

"Are you serious?" It's hard to ignore his intense stare that fills over the brim with fire. "It's worth five million. What if I lost it? Or it got stolen?"

The way he rubs the back of my hand with his thumb causes a lump to form in my throat. When he answers, tears prick my eyes.

"Then I'd buy you another one, understand? Never take it off again. That ring tells every man who looks at you that you're mine."

THIRTY-FIVE
HANNAH

TURNS OUT SOFIA WAS RIGHT.

Today, Damien didn't wake me and let me sleep in. But when I awoke to him fresh out of the shower in nothing but a towel, he let me know I could take the day off. I didn't even have to ask. He assumed I'd be nursing a hangover—*which he was right.*

I told him I still plan on coming into the office. After I slept in, of course... *Better late than never.*

Coming out of the bathroom with a white towel twisting my hair into a topknot, I discover a box lying on our bed. Blue ribbon runs along its edges, shining in the afternoon glow through the windows, and crosses into a neat bow containing a white notecard.

I hold back a grin, reminding myself I'm still angry about how Damien overreacted yesterday.

Hannah—it reads in Damien's annoyingly sharp handwriting.

Please accept this gift as my sincere apology and peace-offering.

I made us reservations tonight for dinner. Wear this to the office today, and I'll take it as your acceptance to come.

Intriguing arousal pools in my stomach. He wants me to wear something for him. In public. At his own company with all his employees to see. There's something sexy about the idea, walking around the office with a naughty secret between the two of us. And that he's practically saying he wishes to show me off.

I tug the ribbon before a cold reality washes over me.

He thinks he can buy me some fancy dress and I'll be a good little assistant and forgive him for how he treated me yesterday. He thinks he can buy *me.* I should turn and leave, but curiosity gets the better of me.

Removing the lid, my breath hitches.

Not a dress, then...

Inside are sky-high red stilettos and a black lingerie set. I rub my fingers against the lacy fabric, instantly deciding it's the most delicate material I've ever felt. Tied to a single bra strap is the price tag, face down.

I hesitate.

The price doesn't matter.

But he left it on. He wants me to see. Another, more daring side of me argues. *Besides, whatever it is, it won't change my mind.*

Flipping it, the black ink appears, and I swear my heart must skip a beat.

Nineteen-hundred *fucking* dollars—*for lingerie?*

Eyeing the red stilettos, I notice their bottoms are a lighter shade of red, hinting they're exactly what I suspected them to be. Their tag is nearly double the price of the lingerie.

Calculating my options, I bite my lower lip.

I'll just try them on. It doesn't mean he's buying me. It doesn't even mean I'll wear them to the office.

I snatch the lingerie and race to the bathroom, unable to resist giggling. Hanging the fabric over the edge of the free-standing tub, I free my knotted hair, then slip the bra straps over my shoulders. I clasp the rear hooks before the panties glide along by legs, settling into a perfect fit.

I stare at my reflection.

The silk accentuates my modest breasts, giving them a slight lift. My nipples are faintly visible through the fabric, and the thong has a smooth mesh material in the front that glistens in the room's lighting.

A surge of confidence envelops me.

So, I'm getting bought... So what?

After choosing an outfit that will surely get Damien's attention, I stride out the penthouse door and into the elevator in my new stilettos. The descent is uninterrupted before the doors open to the lobby. My heels clack against the marble flooring, filling the space with my powerful echoes.

I think back to the first time I graced this vast hallway— my confidence miles away from me as I tugged along an embarrassing suitcase... And now? With the way I hold my head, uncaring of who's watching? Although it's Damien who truly does, someone who doesn't know might wonder if *I* own the building.

Once outside, I'm struck by a chilly breeze and the vibrant sounds of the city. I spot John standing beside his car, and I offer him a polite smile.

"Miss Lockwood." He nods, holding the door for me before I settle into the backseat.

Damien said if I wear his gifts, I'm accepting his invitation to go to dinner, not that I completely forgive him. A part of me knows I will, eventually, because it's beginning to become apparent he cares for me.

And that this—whatever *this* is—may be more than what our contract dictates. Is it only an arrangement? No. I can admit that now. Are we truly engaged? Of course not, but there are some feelings between us. So... at some point, I'll need to decide what we are and if I can trust him or not.

But until then...

I smirk.

I'll go today. But no promises I'll behave.

I STRUT towards our shared office. Along the way, I pass a meeting room with rows of tall windows, allowing me to see inside. Men and women wearing blazers and suits sit around a long oval table, their heads turned to the man seated in the center.

With the scenic view of the city as his backdrop, Damien interlocks his fingers and furrows his brow into a frown as he discusses something I can't hear. His eyes flick in my direction for only a moment, and his harsh crease loosens and lips part before he notices the stilettos I wear.

I don't slow under his attention, keeping a steady pace as I smirk back at him. Continuing towards our office with my chin angled upwards, I revel in the feel of having the upper hand between the two of us. I shut the door on the way inside before settling at my desk, responding to emails.

I can't lie. I love sharing an office with him, being in a space with such an important man. It gives me the opportunity few could have, being a fly on the wall as he runs high-stakes meetings. *And the view...* I sigh, watching cars crawl in the traffic below, looking like ants from this height.

My computer chimes with a new email entering my box.

Damien: *Looking forward to tonight, baby. Love having you back as mine.*

I refrain from rolling my eyes at his arrogance. I type up a snarky response, but before I send it off, an idea hits me that causes me to grin wildly, alone in the room.

Leaving the office, I make my way to the bathroom, once again passing by the meeting room that's still full of board members. Once in the bathroom, I instantly lock the door after finding all three stalls unoccupied.

Hopefully no one needs inside. I'll make this quick.

My phone buzzes.

Damien: *Are you ignoring me, Miss Lockwood? If you keep walking by like that, you won't be wearing those heels for much longer.*

I don't respond.

Instead, I lift my black pencil skirt to expose the front of my panties and snap a picture in the mirror before hitting send. I've never sent nude—or semi-nude—pictures to Damien, and I'm unsure how he'll react. With each torturous second that passes, further doubt creeps in.

Maybe this was a stupid idea. He's in a meeting that seems important. He's probably trying to close on a huge business deal, and I'm just some horny girl in a public bathroom sending him nudes... What is wrong with me?

My phone lights up.

Damien: *Get in my office. Now. I'll deal with you soon.*

Deal with me, like I'm some appointment that needs handling. I bite the inside of my lip. Oh, this is going to be fun. My nails clack against the screen as I type my response, the corners of my lips tilting upwards.

Me: *Not so fast, Mr. Bass. Don't you want to see more?*

His responses fly in.

Damien: *Yes.*

Damien: *Where are you?*

I take my precious time adjusting angles, adhering to the surprisingly good lighting.

Damien: *Hello? Answer me.*

Turning around and showing a hint of my ass cheeks, I snap and send the next picture.

Damien: *FUCK. Hannah, your body is incredible.*

Damien: *I'm going to rip that off you later. I don't care how much it costs.*

I send a few more, keeping my skirt hiked around my waistline with my top still on.

Damien: *You're killing me...*

Me: *Do you want to see more?*

Damien: *Yes.*

Damien: *Take off your blouse and skirt, too. I want to see you only in lingerie.*

I wait a minute, contemplating my demands.

Me: *Getting greedy now? That's a big ask... I want something in return.*

Damien: *Anything. I'll buy you anything. What do you want?*

Again with the buying. He thinks he can buy me something and get whatever he wants in return. He bought me this lingerie, so why shouldn't he get any picture he wants?

Me: *Beg.*

Damien: *What?*

Me: *Beg for it. Beg me to send you a picture after I take each and every clothing item off my body.*

Damien: *Jesus, fuck. Do you know who I'm with right now?*

Me: *Don't focus on the board members sitting around you. Don't negotiate the next multi-million-dollar deal for your company. Negotiate with me, that I might give you what you want. Focus on me.*

I can feel the wetness of my sex aching, screaming at me to give in and touch it. The thought of Damien being distracted by me during his meeting is more than enough to get me going.

Gathering my skirt higher to rest below my breasts, I place one bent leg on the countertop, scraping the white tile with my stiletto. Leaving my panties on, I palm my pussy through the fabric with two fingers, rubbing exaggerated circles.

My head tilts back, and I stifle a moan.

God. I didn't mean to get myself so worked up in here. I should stop while I still can.

Ding.

Damien: *I will. I am—every day you're all I can think about. During work, at home, every fucking second.*

I hastily push the fabric to the side, exposing my flesh. Dipping my fingers towards my entrance, I wet them before returning to my most sensitive spot.

Keeping a steady pace, I chase an elusive orgasm as my heel pushes further towards the mirror. When it touches the glass and I gain a steadier footing, I plunge two fingers inside myself.

Damien: *Please.*

My thighs ache with the stance, but I don't relent. Not for a second as I curl my fingers slightly, rubbing against my G-spot. With my other, I work my clit in a vertical motion.

Up. Down. Up. Down.

My inward muscles tighten, gripping my fingers. I want more. I *need* more. My fingers are too small and not enough.

Damien: *Please, Hannah. Show me more.*

Instead of my fingers, I imagine Damien's cock pushing inside me, taking me right here against the counter. A moan escapes from me. And then another. Soon, I can't control them, and I'm pumping fast to the hilt with an additional finger.

Damien: *PLEASE. You got me where you want me, baby. I'll do anything you ask. I swear to fucking God you could ruin this company if you wanted. Ruin me, and I'd gladly let you.*

My climax unleashes from me. I arch over myself, continuing to pump with full force as I struggle to keep my balance and volume in check. Each wave that powers through me is full of bliss that soars pleasure through my insides.

As my breathing slows, I stable myself before staring at my reflection. My hair is in disarray, cheeks are flushed. With two legs back on the ground, I should feel like a bucket of ice water got dumped on my head. But I don't, realizing that's the hardest I've come from touching myself.

Ever.

Damien Bass said I could *ruin him*, only to get more of me. He doesn't grovel for anyone. He is always in full control of every situation, one step ahead of every scenario. Since becoming his assistant, I've learned he's a man who doesn't bend to anyone's will and never utters the words *sorry* or *please.*

And he *begged for me.*

Damien: *Hannah?*

Anticipation and excitement build within me. I'm a woman of my word, and I intend to give him everything I promised and more. I want to see him unhinged, unable to control himself. I loosen the top button of my blouse—

"Hello?" a feminine voice calls as the door handle shakes, followed by a sharp knocking.

I freeze.

Shit. How long have I been in here? I quickly wash my hands and attempt to tame my frazzled hair.

"Sorry!" I open the door, eyeing the woman with aged auburn hair who wears a sophisticated pantsuit. She must be a board member. I smile. "I'm always locking things I shouldn't by accident. Silly me."

With narrowing eyes, her face shrews up like a raisin. My innocent act doesn't seem to have fared well. Did she hear me? I tried to stay quiet, but I failed a few times...

I can't look at her for too long, so I leave and head back to our office, expecting to find Damien waiting for me. But the meeting doesn't seem to be over yet. In fact, more chairs that don't match the others line the table, seating more bodies than before. Whatever session I distracted him from, it must be significant.

When I meet Damien's gaze this time, it's not subtle. His eyes burn into mine, visibly tracking my movements as hunger and determination clouds his sharp features.

Once back in the office, I sink into my chair. My panties feel too tight against my now beyond sensitive clit. I squirm to relieve some pressure, but it only seems to make it worse.

Damien: *You think it's funny blue-balling me, baby? Strip right now and send me what I'm owed.*

I plan to do so—I *did* agree to deliver—but his arrogant message sparks a trickle of annoyance.

Hannah: *Or what?*

His lack of response prompts my knee to bob up and

down, the butt of my heel tapping against the ground. I try to focus on work, only to find my concentration blown.

Another minute passes... No response.

I whip my head to the sound of faint knocking at my door, only to find blond hair and a lengthy male frame smiling at me politely.

"Mr. Bass has requested your attendance in the meeting room."

THIRTY-SIX

HANNAH

"H-HE HAS? Did he say what for?"

"He mentioned needing a note-taker. The meeting is running longer than expected. Some design issues are being discussed."

"Oh, okay." I feel glued to my seat. Damien has never asked me to take notes during a board meeting, and I can't come up with an explanation for why he'd call me in after the last text I sent him.

"I'm sure you'll be brought up to speed." He beckons me with his hand. "Come on."

Grabbing my laptop, I peel myself from my chair and follow him on heavy legs. When the meeting room comes into view, I pale at the number of people sitting around the table. Some who wear more business casual clothing stand with clipboards in hand, as no chairs are available. Except one.

To Damien's right.

My blond escort opens the door for me, and I enter to hear Damien's confident voice fill the room. "—and the latest tests for the Nano-X chip show significant performance bottle-necking."

A man sitting across from Damien lets out an exasperated sigh. "Yes, the board understands that, Mr. Bass. But the throttles were only minor. I've been in this industry long enough to know—"

"*Invested* in this industry," Damien corrects, interrupting him. The man's whole face turns a dark shade of crimson as he folds his arms tightly. "And yes, you have. Long enough to know any slight error could cause catastrophic scenarios for consumers. Why do you think I called five senior engineers in here? Major technology companies will not accept *good enough.*"

A hush descends upon the room, and my legs suddenly feel wobbly. This is the first time I've witnessed Damien control a room with so many people, not to mention the first time being around all the board members at once.

Most of us have yet to be introduced. It's hard to gauge how many of them may or may not know about Damien and I's contract, but I inwardly agree with myself to play it safe.

Act like nobody knows a thing.

Damien's hard eyes meet mine, and he gives me an up-down, followed by a subtle smirk. He clears his throat. "Everyone, I'm sure many of you heard the news, but have not yet gotten the opportunity to meet my personal assistant and new lovely fiancée, Hannah."

I turn to face them and force myself to appear confident as I wave. "Hello. It's nice to meet all of you." I'm met with many unexpectedly warm eyes, several of whom offer their congratulations.

Damien motions to the open chair beside him, and what feels like a mountain of nerves slips off my back as dozens of eyes veer from me. I take my seat, placing my laptop on the table.

"Hannah is here to learn and take notes. There will be an intermission while I inform her of our progress. You're all dismissed."

The members stand up slowly, some stretching their necks or backs. One by one, everyone clears out of the room, chatting.

Silence... painful silence stuffs the air between us. With only us two, the space feels infinitely smaller.

"So..." I drag my nails down my keyboard, looking anywhere but Damien's direction. "What've you discussed so far?"

Damien inches himself closer to me, his knee grazing mine. Placing his hand on my thigh, he grazes against the hem of my skirt. "You think it's fun toying with me?" His voice is deep and sultry as he lifts the hem higher, exposing my skin.

It's been too soon since I came, but I can already feel the thrum between my legs returning. I squish my thighs together, reducing any chance of friction.

"I don't know what you're talking about," I say. He's so near I get a whiff of his intoxicating cologne. Woodsy smells with a hint of citrus.

His thumb rubs the inner part of my thigh in tight, clock-wise motions. "You don't?"

"N-no." I fumble for any ounce of self-respect I have left. "Now, what am I really here to do?"

The room seems to get hotter. My body betrays me, and I part my legs, allowing him better access. I turn and find him staring down at me.

"You're here to apologize."

"What?" My annoyance bursts out, and I snatch my legs together. "I am *not* apologizing. You think you can snap your fingers and get whatever you want from me? That's not how this works."

"Is that what you think this is?" He bites his lower lip in amusement.

The sight of Damien is mouthwatering perfection. He's wearing a navy-blue suit with a black tie, and his Rolex peeks out of his cuffs, gleaming against the room's brightness. His presence screams *in-charge.*

And you're going to contend with him? He just got done chewing out an entire board. Now it's only you.

He leans in close to my ear. "Do you think you can tease me like that and not face the repercussions? I know what you're wearing underneath that little outfit of yours."

I notice some of the board members through the glass, chatting and easing their way back from the breakroom. Swallowing hard, I try to keep my composure.

"Apologize," he coos. "I'll make it easier on you if you do."

"No." My core flames with defiance. "You know what? Whatever you're planning to do—ask me hard questions or make me present something I don't know—go ahead and do it. You won't be hearing me apologize."

His brow ticks upwards, wearing a smug look on his face. He notes the returning members before leaning back in his chair, leaving an appropriate amount of spacing between us.

I smooth out my skirt, a proud calm washing over me. I'm confident he expected me to back down. But I didn't. Whatever he has planned for me, I'm re—

Bzzzz.

I sit up straight, sucking in an audible gasp. A vibrating sensation tickles my clit, and it's deathly quiet. I can barely hear it myself, but there's no denying I *feel* it. My worrying gaze sweeps across the room in confusion until I discover Damien staring right at me.

I glance down. His left hand rests comfortably inside his pocket. Then there's slight movement, followed by an increase in the sensation. I bite my lip hard, prompting a dark chuckle from him.

No, no, no. This can't be happening. It's just lingerie. Nothing was off about the panties. I swear they were completely normal. They felt *normal. Now they feel...*

I stifle a moan. "How did—"

"I *do* own the largest microchip company on the planet, baby." Damien smirks.

A few people enter the room, coffees in hand. Chatter fills the space, and I come to my senses.

I'm attending this meeting with a vibrator on my clit. I'm — fuck, fuck, fuck...

Panic seeps in, solidifying itself into my bones as I watch Damien's smirk morph into a full-on grin. I shouldn't have teased him. I should've given him what he wanted.

I tighten my grip on the table. "I could just leave," I threaten.

"Take your ass off that chair, and I'll turn this up so high you won't be able to hold in your scream when you come."

"You wouldn't."

"I would," he counters, his features lining with a cool, collected calm. "I'll gladly take this opportunity to remind everyone you belong to me."

I don't test him, keeping myself planted in my seat. The vibration intensifies, and I swallow back a reaction.

"Damien," I hiss below my breath. "I'm sorry! I only—"

"It's too late for sorry. Now you'll have to *beg.*"

∼

TEN MINUTES into the meeting feels like a lifetime.

Damien is having each senior engineer present information about how the microchip works. With the window shades down and the lights off, a projector points at the far side of the room.

The members around the table focus on the presentations, so no one catches my silent dilemma. Damien keeps the vibrator on a torturous speed—not fast enough to reach an orgasm, but not slow enough to ignore. The constant rhythm keeps me right on edge.

"—as you see, even though the physical size of the chip has reduced significantly, there is still a possibility to implement multi-core functionality." The engineer points to a portion of the detailed diagram.

I glance down at my laptop. Its brightness is as low as possible, and I haven't taken a single note. The beginning of a bead of sweat forms on my temple, and I take several slow breaths before typing. The notes I write are complete rubbish, but I need the distraction.

"And what of the throttles?" Damien asks, his undertones tightening the reins he has on everyone in the room.

The engineer contemplates his response.

"Ahem," I huff quietly when I feel the vibration intensify, buckling in my chair. I look around nervously, relief pouring over me when I discover no one looking my way.

"What was that, Miss Lockwood?" Damien purrs. "Did you have something to add?"

Heads turn towards me, and it feels like my stomach bottoms out from the butterflies buzzing inside of me. I hold myself still. *Very* still. Because the need to give in, to drop my head back and let my body thrash, is so intense it nearly takes hold of me. Instead, I cross my legs.

"N-no. I'm only taking notes."

I can barely make out his self-satisfied grin in the darkness. "Good." He nods to the engineer, who begins his reply. Turning up the vibrator even higher, he leans in and adds under his breath, "Now keep quiet and rock your hips for me."

My lips part, and I stare at him. The way his eyes thread with a smoldering challenge... *He's serious.*

Scooting closer to the table, I slowly rock my hips back and forth. Every movement is a new sensation against my clit, a new wave threatening to drag me out to sea. Underneath the table, I feel Damien's hand brush up my thigh, and it only proves to heighten my arousal.

"Good girl," he whispers in my ear as he resumes tracing slow circles along my skin with his thumb.

Presentation after presentation begins, and I can't comprehend what any of them are about, finding it impossible to pay attention. All I can focus on is the burning between my legs and the small puddle that forms on my chair.

I stop rocking, desperately fighting the euphoria that's trying to claim me.

He squeezes my thigh.

I remain still.

The speed increases, and he squeezes harder.

Fuckkk.

When I resume my steady rocking, he releases his grip as the vibrations return to an agonizing speed. His mouth brushes against my ear, his voice deep and guttural.

"So perfect."

I DON'T REALIZE Damien called for another intermission until his hand grazes my knee with only us two left in the room. He grabs it possessively, leaning in. "Slow down, baby. We don't want someone seeing what a mess you made of the chair."

I ease up, taking shallow breaths.

"Mmm. Fuck," he groans, and I feel it rumble against my skin. I sway slower, focusing on the friction against the chair as the pressure builds, my muscles tightening to an almost painful level. I sway deeper, harder, inching myself towards the edge of the release I crave.

The vibrations slow suddenly, and his hold on my thigh tightens. "Such a needy pussy. Not yet. Not before I hear what I want."

"I'm sorry," I mumble, refusing to make eye contact. Annoyance blooms across my skin. I'm not at all prepared to be the one who's saying sorry today, after everything he said to me yesterday.

"Speak up, Hannah. I couldn't quite catch that."

But he's made me desperate... "I'm sorry."

"That's nice of you. But I already told you—it's too late for your apology." He turns up the vibrator, higher now than ever.

I lurch forward, straining to keep a straight face. Shocking waves of pleasure power through me and in a matter of seconds, I'm—

Yes, YES. Right there, right there—

He cuts the power, and I soar back down, my pussy throbbing so hard it aches.

"Beg for it." His tone is a challenge, a smooth confidence that I'll cave. "I control when this meeting ends, Hannah. I'll keep us here until fucking sundown. Now *beg.*"

Heat rushes to my cheeks. *He will. I know he will. Dammit. If he wants the upper hand, he can take it.*

"Please, Damien. Let me."

"Let you what?"

"Let me *come.*"

"Mmm." He rubs his chin, appearing like he's in deep thought. "No."

With each flick of his finger on the remote, he turns the pace up slowly, higher and higher, until my breaths are shallow and whimpers sound.

"Please. I'm sorry—*so* sorry." I brace myself against the table as the words fly from my mouth. "I shouldn't have teased you. Really, I shouldn't have. And I was going to give you what you wanted, right then and there. In the bathroom. But then I couldn't help it. I had to touch myself. It felt so good—"

"What?" He perks up, the vibrations ceasing. His jaw clenches, and the knuckles wrapped around his armrest bleach white. "Get in my office. *Now."*

Shock pummels through me, but I don't hesitate, not with his face looking so intense. I don't question his demand, not once, as I beeline it straight to his office on wobbly legs.

When I break through the doors, he's on me in an instant, whirling me around to face him with his mouth a breath away from mine. His hands peruse down my body in an almost examining way, loosening buttons and finishing by sliding off my skirt.

In seconds, I'm left bare for him in nothing but my lingerie and red heels, my exhales coming out of me in choppy waves.

"You think you can orgasm without me?" he growls, his eyes dark and scattering down my body, blatant hunger emerging from them. "Without my permission?"

The need between my legs is a living thing, making me bold, causing me to roll my eyes. "It was one time."

"And that's another thing." Before I know better, he's turning me around and driving me forward until my thighs strike the edge of his desk. He grabs a fistful of my hair, yanking me downward atop the desk littered with paperwork. "It's time you learn what happens when you roll those bratty eyes at me."

Pain scatters across my ass cheek, puffing air from my lungs.

He spanked me…? *He spanked me.*

"Did you just—"

Another *smack* sounds, this time so loud it reverberates across the room. The vibration it produces trickles all the way down between my legs. I stifle a moan while the humiliation burns my cheeks.

"Hey, you can't—"

His fingers fly deep into my mouth, cutting my protest short right as he slides my panties to the side, slamming his cock into me. I shriek from the invasion, not at all ready for the sheer size of him, but all that I hear from me is a muffled whine.

Not waiting for me to compensate for his size, he stretches me to my very limit, retreating all the way out to the tip before crashing back to the hilt. His fingers coat with my saliva, stifling each of my cries when he leans in close to me, his soft lips brushing my ears.

"You make me fucking crazy," he growls, reaching his other hand across my middle before tearing my bra down, freeing my breasts. He pushes his fingers further, grazing the back of my throat and causing tears to pool in my lids. "You want the whole office to know I'm using your pretty cunt, don't you? You want the workers in the other buildings to watch as I fuck every one of your holes?"

He thrusts harder, increasing his pace still, scraping my nipples harshly against the wooden desk. The sensation is brutal, almost as agonizing as the way his balls slap against my clit, barreling me towards a mind-shattering orgasm.

Time seems to slow as we both reduce ourselves to mere animals, with only primal instincts, riding the waves of peak pleasure.

Damien arches into me, conducting a punishing pace and slamming me harder into the desk until he's nearly roaring in my ear as I pulsate against his cock.

When we both subside with heavy breaths and sweat gleaming against our hairlines, I whip around. Feeling energized and bold, I take his mouth against mine. His groan that follows vibrates along my skin and radiates confidence in me as I bury my fingers through his hair.

I pull back, staring into his eyes, hunger racing through my mind. Twisting his head until his ear is to my lips, I lick along his lobe. And my whisper is all it takes for him to shiver underneath my embrace.

"Watch your cum leak out of me."

THIRTY-SEVEN

DAMIEN

HANNAH IS a presence I've grown to need, much like a soothing melody to my ear or oxygen for my soul.

For the past two weeks, her warmth has chipped away the chronic stress from my shoulders like wax dripping from a candle, leaving behind a man I can hardly recognize—with a sense of calm and *joy*.

On several occasions, I've laughed so hard with her at the most mundane of things, that tears lined my eyes in a way they haven't since... *I don't know how long*. It's very clear to me now that she makes me not only a better lover, but a better person, who sees optimism in an unpredictable future, instead of trying to control it.

A week ago, she convinced me to take a day off work to go have tea with my mother. Never would I have done that— obviously, not because of my mother, who I adore. But because the very thought of leaving my company unattended, even though *I know* there are people I specifically hire to handle my affairs when I'm absent, has always been horrid to me. As if one day off could ignite the walls to tumble around me, all that I've worked for taking a major leap backwards.

But, of course, Hannah was right.

The day off cleared my head remarkably. When I went back to work the following day, I had a clear mind and twice the energy as we continued to practice for our Silicon Summit presentation. And the way my mother and Hannah got along so well, sharing stories and looking through my terribly embarrassing baby photos. And seeing her in my childhood estate, butlers and housing staff waiting on her, tending to her every need, and every anxious *thank you* she offered them...

God.

It was beautiful. *She* was beautiful.

It made me realize I *do* want something like that. Maybe not soon. Something of that magnitude needs time to handle with gentle care. But, *yes,* someday. An estate much like the one I grew up in, but with the warmth and kindness my mother offered and without the corruption of my father. One I could nurture and delight in the future I see in it.

In truth, I don't know if I could pull it off myself, if that kind of existence is destined for a man like me...

But with Hannah? I know I could.

Which is why tonight is so nerve-wracking for me. A deadline that zoomed so quickly, I didn't see it coming, and I can hardly think about what it implies.

Tonight is the final social event to network with company owners who are potentially looking to sell, whom my board members or myself are interested in pursuing. One last chance to convince them why Innovex is a good decision.

And then?

At the end of this week on Friday, we present the Nano-X chip at the Silicon Summit, showing the world and the sellers our official, solidified front. Knowing the grandness of that stage very well, I know it carries weight that echoes across all the tech world. Meaning, sellers will be in immediate contact with me soon after, potentially that very night.

And finally...

Our time with one another will finish. Our contract date will have passed. I'll pay off all of Hannah's family's debt, and she will go along on her way. Without me.

Unless I convince her to stay.

"Ah, yes." I hear Hannah's voice beside me. "The chip's market projections are more than satisfactory, Mrs. Carruther. We can schedule you a visit to our headquarters for a demo, if you'd like."

Nerves heat through my middle as I watch Hannah take the lead, seeming to improve on her networking skills with every owner we meet.

I plan to ask her to stay with me, not as my fiancée, of course, but as something else. Something *real,* whatever that may be. My girlfriend, maybe, whatever she wants to call herself to make her stay. But if she wanted the ring, if she wanted this—*me*—forever. Then she can keep it. I don't plan on selling it, anyway, and I definitely don't plan on using it on any other woman other than her.

Because... Look *at her...*

Hannah couldn't be more striking. Her dress is of shimmering gold, conforming to her upper body to reveal her breasts before flaring out at her waist. She tied her hair back in a complicated knot atop her head, with two symmetrical tendrils framing her beautiful features.

"That would be very intriguing, yes. I'd like that." The older business owner smiles at Hannah, grabbing hold of her hands. "Your biddings tonight really impressed my husband and I. You were the star of the night, no doubt."

Tonight's event is another big one, with all people of high society, especially those of the tech sector in New York City. The large venue that normally puts on opera shows in the city holds the Astor family charity auction. Every year, the auction seems to bring in more money than the previous. But none of the regular guests who give so *generously* speak of the real reasons they come—to network and use sneaky tax benefits through charitable donations, landing them a larger profit than they donated.

I'd be lying if I said, in the past, I hadn't used such loopholes. But this year, I won't. Mostly because I wasn't the one dominating the auction tonight, wielding our bidding stick like an eager homeowner handing out piles of candy on Halloween. No, that was Hannah.

I let her have full control, donating to the foundations of her choosing. To my delight and slight horror, she escalated to obscenely high numbers, forwards of millions. Only then did she find out how much she *really* needs to spend to make my hair stand on end.

"Oh, thank you," Hannah says. "It really is all for a great cause."

They both wave their goodbyes, and we depart from Mrs. Carruther, before I manage to land a peck on her cheek.

Hannah molds to my side, her smile wide as she nods to those we pass by. I can't take my eyes off her as we walk all the way to the bar. She's mesmerizing, truly the most beautiful woman in the room.

"Is there anyone else we need to meet with?" she asks.

Running my hand down the length of her arm, I stare at

her hand resting against the countertop. Her engagement ring sparkles with each minute movement of her wrist.

"Not if you don't want to."

"Really?" She smiles at that, the mischief lighting her eyes. "Maybe we can work on making you some friends."

"Woah, now." Curling my arm around her, I tug her shoulders, earning a squeal that warms my insides. "I have many friends."

"Friends *outside of work.*" She squirms in my hold before I release her.

"I'd like that," I admit.

The way her face lifts has my heart twisting into a knot, gnawing at me to have the talk I've thought about for days. I fear the potential of impending doom, yet excite in her reaction I so crave.

My hands wobble as I hold hers, feeling as if I'm about to conduct the most important negotiation of my life. I inhale deeply, calming my nerves. *But this isn't a meeting. This is Hannah—this is us.*

There's only her and me and a wonderful future we could have together. But there's no negotiating that. There's no pressure, no tricks. There's only the opinion she's certainly already formed in her mind about me.

And her answer.

I can only hope I'm enough for her.

"Hannah, I need to ask you something. Something important." I rub my thumbs along the back of her hands.

Her expression softens, the light hitting her in such a way that heightens my nerves further. "Okay... You know you can ask me anything."

I swallow hard, studying her features, imagining the many more memories we could create together. "I know these past few months have been strange, an experience neither of us has ever undergone. But I'd like to ask you to—"

"Mr. Bass." My back straightens at the familiarity of Harrison's voice. "I convinced him to come."

I whip my head to him. "Can this wait?"

"No, sir. I'm sorry. It's the owner of ShutterLux. You know how hard it is to get time with him. He's already had multiple offers from other companies who suspect he's looking to sell. The board is—and has been—most interested in his company. You know this. And we seem to think we'll have a leg up on the competition."

Sighing, I look at Hannah, kindness emerging from behind her eyes. "We can always talk later. This sounds more urgent."

But there's nothing more urgent than you, I want to reply.

Instead, my shoulders slouch as I nod to Harrison. Her arm loops around mine, resting comfortably in my nearness and allowing me to usher ourselves behind him.

"He watched the auction from a box," Harrison informs us as we ascend a flight of stairs. After reaching the top floor, we walk through a curved hallway lined with pairs of curtains that I know separate us from those sitting in private balconies.

Harrison stops in front of an entrance, brushing a curtain aside. The private space reveals itself, with one man seated before a brass railing. Enveloping him on all sides of the box, red velvet marks the wallpaper and his seat facing the stage.

We enter the area, discovering him alone, aside from the two men wearing all black who stand on his either side. They appear to be his bodyguards. I cock my brow, sizing up the man who wears gray, facing the other way as smoke bellows from his fingertips. Soft redness glows at the end of his cigar.

"Mr. Strauss." Harrison's voice prompts the man to turn, revealing his aged yet handsome face.

The arm interlinked with mine turns to lead, an anchor pulling me back. I tug against Hannah, hyper-aware of the importance of this meeting. But she doesn't budge. I glance her way, only to discover her in a state of shock, her face that of stone.

Staring straight ahead.

THIRTY-EIGHT
HANNAH

NOTHING SPARKS *my imagination more than the touch of the wheel beneath my fingertips, even if I'm not tall enough to see through the windshield.*

"Vrr... Vrrr!" I mimic the purr of the engine, feeling vibrations as I pinch my lower lip between my teeth and push air from my lungs.

There's no light inside Daddy's shop, not when it's past midnight, aside from the glow from a small desk lamp on top of his workbench. But that makes the thrill more worth it, sneaking out late without making a sound, letting my mind run rampant.

With one turn of the wheel, I'm roaring down an open road with no destination in sight. A sandy breeze whisks my hair past my shoulders, invading every crevice of the roofless red Mustang I drive beside an endless ocean.

"Brrr." My lips flop with a funny feeling.

With the next turn of the wheel, I'm a champion speed demon on my sure way to win my seventh NASCAR trophy. My legs elongate to their appropriate size, the bottom of my foot pinning the gas pedal to the ground, because I never plan on letting it back up. It's a rush, a high, emanating from the thousands in the crowd, all chanting my name in unison and—

"Don't you turn your back on me, Andre!" Mommy's voice shrieks, loud enough to be heard through the enclosed space.

My hand flies to my mouth, stopping a yelp from escaping my lips. I duck below the windshield, right before I spot Daddy yanking up the garage door. The night sky exposes a loaded pickup truck sitting atop the gravel in front of our house.

My heart thunders in my chest at the thought of being caught awake past my bedtime. Inching myself higher, I peek through the windshield, watching them from the other side of the shop, hoping they don't see me eavesdropping.

"Tell me where it is!" he shouts harshly. The hairs on my arm stand on end as he bounds across the space to his workbench. "I know you took it."

The small lamp shines against his rugged overalls, much different from Mommy's white nightgown she squeezes her arms around. A fury emerges from behind her eyes.

"I don't know what you're talking about."

Drawer after drawer he rips out, shoving his hand into them, rummaging through what sounds like papers. When he finishes with the bottommost one, he whips his head back. Brown locks sprawl across his forehead like a crazed animal. "Don't act so innocent. You know exactly what I mean."

Her silence screams back at him, causing him to strike the drawer shut with the bottom of his work boot. The workbench shakes on its four legs.

"Always the righteous one, Molly. Aren't you?" he spits out on his way to the line of cars, each shinier and more out-of-place than the next, standing beside our own rusted tractors. "Judge me, then turn around and reap all the benefits."

"Fine. But one of us needs to be the righteous one."

Opening the passenger side door, I hear the clicking sound of a glove compartment, and again the rustling of papers. He curses, shoving the chamber closed.

"I'm... They're the only reason we got out of that wretched trailer park and into this precious farm of yours. You understand that, right?" He makes it to the next car in line, my adrenaline hiking as he gets closer to mine. He laughs bitterly. "Of course you do. You always knew. So, why don't you run along and play your end of the deal? Keeping your head in the sand."

Mommy quiets. "That's before I knew what you were really doing... It's dangerous. You're putting us in danger. For heaven's sake, we have children!"

He moves to the next car, blood raging behind his eyes. "Well, maybe you should've thought of that sooner, hmm? It's not really something you stop."

"You're hurting people."

"Fucking hell. Here you go again."

"You are... Maybe not directly, not with your own hands, but you are. You lead them to those people, g-give them a reason t-to..."

Daddy moves again, now only two cars away. My heart lodges into my throat, and I can only watch in fear when he slams the car door. "FUCK! I need to fucking leave, don't you get it?" His strides are long and rushed before he comes face-to-face with Mommy. "Tell me where it is. Now."

But she doesn't back down. She leans into him, until she's a hair from his nose, her neck lifting towards the sky. "Or, what? You going to hit me, Andre?"

Instantly, Daddy jerks away, his tone simmering low. "No—never. Why would you—"

"I don't know? Who knows with you recently?"

"Molly—"

"If you leave, you'll be choosing them over us." A single crack

slips through her voice, before she rips her arms away from herself until they're shoving something I can't see into his chest. It flops in the air on its way down to the ground. "Over this."

Daddy cranes his head down, and whatever he sees makes him speechless for a time. "... I would never. I don't know how long it'll be, but I know it's not forever."

"And who's believing that? Open your eyes and stop acting the fool they hope you are. Because—you listen to me. They'll dig their claws so deeply into your life and into all you hold dear, that if you try to pull them out, it'll be the end of you."

The cries of my baby brother raddle in the distance, and my parents stand there, staring into each other's eyes. He reaches down, his hand lingering for her face, but she twists around before it makes contact, disappearing through the shop door.

Daddy stays still for a while... More than a while, staring into the space lying ahead of him, until he steps over whatever's on the ground and walks to his pickup truck waiting for him outside the shop.

For a reason I can't possibly explain, a lump forms in my throat as a sadness overtakes me. Because that can't be possible. Mommy's making things up. Because why would Daddy leave? He would never do that. He loves us and has everything he could ever want here. He's said so himself.

He'd miss the farm. He'd miss me. He'd miss my new baby brother. And he'd miss Mommy.

But the lump is there, anyway. So I sneak out the driver's side door and scurry over to see what's lying on the ground. But the lump turns to rock-hard cement, a hot tear zipping down my cheek when I see it's a picture. But not just any picture...

Our picture. The one he keeps on his workbench.

Daddy carries me proudly on his shoulder, pigtails poking from either side of my head. We're happy because we finished our biggest project yet—together. The sun hits the red Mustang behind us in the most enchanting way, shining its glossy exterior and newly washed tires. My smile is wide as I display my missing front tooth. Daddy's smile is even brighter. But he's not looking at the car or the camera lens.

He's looking at me.

Panic pumps through my veins, and I drop the photo on the ground, racing towards the old pickup truck. The darkness of the night swallows me whole when I exit the shop, gravitating me towards the bright headlights of the vehicle.

"Daddy!" I scream into the blackness, tears streaming down my face as the tires roll. "Daddy, wait!" I pump my legs harder, my throat as raw as sand. "No, don't go!"

They grind to a halt before the driver's side window inches downwards, revealing his face. An unfamiliar shadow slithers across his features, settling in front of his eyes.

"Don't go!"

And then the shadow lifts, his face softening before he looks me up and down. "What're you doing out here? You'll catch a cold."

"Don't... go..." My breath heaves out on choppy waves, having exacerbated myself from the chase.

His door opens before he hops out, his boots crunching against the gravel. Lifting me up, he sets me on his shoulder like always, walking me back to the house. "I'm not going anywhere."

"But Mommy said—"

He tenses beneath me. "Don't listen to what she says. She doesn't know what she's talking about. I won't be gone long."

I bobble up and down with each of his long strides, grabbing onto the top of his head to stable myself. But worry still swims through me. "How long will you be gone?"

"Not long, pumpkin. Only a few days. I'll be back within the week."

I smile at that, and instantly, the dark feeling inside me vanishes. He sets me down, landing a kiss on my forehead, not saying another word. I sit on the top step, a grin crawling across my lips as he returns to his truck, until the red glow of his taillights creeps all the way off our property.

I knew it—Mommy's talking crazy, *I tell myself,* skipping to the front door. I knew he wouldn't leave forever.

But he did.

Forever...

Until I could scarcely remember what his face looked like. Until the very thought of his name made me cry or combust with rage or feel nothing at all.

But, as it turns out, I can still recognize him.

Even sixteen years later.

THEY SAY you never know if your natural instinct is to fight or flight until you're put into such a situation. Luckily, for me...

Now I know.

I barrel down the hallway, the long nature of my dress and height of my heels proving not a deterrent.

"Hannah!" the two *liars* call after me in unison, my name hot on their tongues as I descend the stairs.

I don't stop, even when the well-dressed and well-mannered people of the evening come into my view. No, I race by them, not caring for their gasps or the flashes of camera lights from their phones. I don't care about making a scene. And I definitely don't care how I may ruin Damien Bass's *reputation.*

He used me.

A knife punctures my heart. In the worst way possible. He really stooped that low—this whole time. He made up some bullshit that he needs me and cares for me... But what he really wanted was a leg up from the competition, using me to get to my father.

Who owns a company I didn't even know about?

And how could I? He vanished from my life sixteen years ago. So, abandoning us wasn't enough? He needed to change his whole life, too? Change his name, probably a whole new family and maybe a new daugh—

I can't even think of it. The very thought makes the food I ate earlier rise in my throat. All I'm certain of is I need to eradicate *both* men from my life, one out of a fresh wound and the other on a wound that should've stayed healed.

I make it out onto the street, nearly tripping down the red-carpeted steps with my dress jumbling between my legs. Reaching the bottom, I barrel through a flock of people, air zipping from my lungs until I'm running down the city pavement with no destination in mind. I only need to get away from the scene and rethink my entire life.

Because, why?

Because I had *plans* with a no-good *liar.* They're both liars, both the same. They really are. They'll do marvelous business together, both spouting bullshit about a future before they rip the carpet clean underneath you, leaving you with black coal for a heart and no air in your lungs.

A strong hand grasps my arm, whipping me back into the encompass of his shoulders, his chest.

"Get off me!" I scream with fury, entirely unhinged and bewildered underneath the night of the city. I don't realize streams of hot, angry tears flood down my face until I see the wet spot on Damien's shirt.

"What's wrong, baby? Tell—"

"DON'T CALL ME THAT." He shies backwards in fear. "You're a liar. And a coward, bringing my father into this."

His eyes bulge from their sockets, but I don't care. I don't care how excellent of an actor he is. He's sure had plenty of time to practice.

I wait to hear his response, a sliver of me wanting him to come up with some magical tale about how he didn't know. Or maybe I could only erase my mind of the past five minutes and go back to the dreamland I was living in.

But he stands there, looking as if I shot him dead.

"Goodbye, Damien."

IT'S BEEN TWO DAYS.

Two days of never leaving my room at my old apartment. Two days of eating next to nothing. Two days of abysmal sleep, replaying the last few months in my head like a movie, wondering where I went wrong and how I could've been so naïve. And two whole days of Sofia and Jenna nagging me through my door, until I finally came out to eat something.

I sit at our kitchen counter, alone with Sofia, twisting my fork in my bowl. The shivering screech of metal against ceramic bounces between our silence as I collect a measly number of noodles between the prongs.

"Aren't you going to hype me up?" I ask bitterly, then press my wineglass to my lips before taking a generous gulp. Even alcohol makes me feel more hollow. "Tell me he's trash and we should go out tonight."

"No."

My heart breaks when I see Sofia so serious, waves of

emotion clouding her eyes. It's the first time in our friendship she's looked at me this way. She comes over, takes a seat next to me and holds my hand between hers. I retaliate against the tears I know are coming from whatever she has to say.

"Hannah... You're *different* with him."

"That doesn't—"

"No." She squeezes my hands, silencing me. "In a good way. You're stronger now. *Braver* than I've ever seen you."

I shake my head, not willing to accept the truth. I'm mentally preparing myself to eradicate him from life, to build up titanium walls around my heart like I did after my father left.

And it's now that I realize I didn't do that with Sterling. I may have moped around for a few days, sure, but there was never a gaping hole the size of a crater dragging down my heart, threatening to make me never care about anything or anyone ever again.

Because I didn't love—

"I can't go back." My eyes burn, unable to accept the truth. "It was all a lie, even more so than I thought."

"And how confident are you?"

Hesitating, my mind races to come up with a valid excuse why Harrison Thornton—who knew of our fake engagement since the beginning—recommended buying out my biological father's company. One I didn't even know he had. He said the board was *most interested* in ShutterLux, the very company I practiced presenting on with the information *they gave me,* conveniently leaving out a picture of the owner.

They knew. And I'd be idiotic to believe Damien didn't.

But... My father. A mechanic…? nothing adds up. Nothing. "Some things are too impossible to be a coincidence."

"Impossible or highly unlikely?"

Rolling my eyes, I rip my hands from her hold. "Sofia—"

"There's a difference." She snatches the wine, irritation lining her brow as she pours the red liquid into my glass, stopping when it reaches the brim.

I'm quiet when I thank her.

Her expression lightens, a serious tone returning to her voice. "Then what's it worth to you? What's *he* worth to you?"

"I don't know what you mean."

"Do you love him?"

My back straightens.

"Hannah." Her eyes bore into mine, a pleading request lying behind them. "I'm your *best friend.* We've been through everything together, and we always will. Which means, if you're going to be honest with anyone, even before yourself, it should be me. It *has* to be me. Don't bear this pain alone."

I look away, blinking furiously.

"Do you love him?"

I can't. *I won't.*

Because if that's true, if I love Damien Bass, then I'm a fool. A silly, stupid, ignorant, little fool, who went along and let one brother damage herself, and then allowed the other to swing the final blow. I don't know how someone recovers from such a colossal mountain of lies.

"Yes," I whisper, and my heart splinters in two as warm tears sweep down my cheeks.

"Then what if you're wrong?" The fight in her tone doesn't quite reach my bones. "I'll admit, it looks bad. *Really* bad. But what if he's the love of your life? If that's true and those are the stakes, then you can't throw it all away without being one-hundred percent sure he knew."

"How would I ever know?" I scrape my face, collecting

tears on my forearm, breathing deep to dampen my emotions. "There's no way to prove that, to know for sure."

"Yes, there is." Her lips form a tight line, dawning an air of pity. My heart sinks before the words leave her mouth, knowing exactly what they're going to be. But I don't know if I'm ready or strong enough...

"You go to the source."

To face him.

THIRTY-NINE
HANNAH

MY BIOLOGICAL FATHER doesn't want to be found.

One quick search of Victor Strauss online gave me all the information I needed, including his company *and* personal phone number. I've called many times—late last night, early this morning and an hour ago—stating who I was and practically begging him to talk to me.

Which felt wrong in and of itself, because why should I have to be the one to beg? Was his reaction at the charity event all an act? He certainly recognized me and tried to chase me down before Damien got to me first.

The only answer I received was as a cryptic envelope slipped underneath our door ten minutes ago. Inside, black ink marked a white slip of paper.

The Crimson Lotus

9:00

Lifting my head to the Vietnamese restaurant glowing neon red against the rainy night sky, I cross the street, studying those inside. But I'm unable to see *anyone.* The windows are quite dark, which wouldn't bother me so much if this wasn't such a sketchy part of the city.

Upon my entrance, a bell above the door frame jingles. Confusion hits me, at the sheer number of people in here, completely different from the empty streets outside.

Diners carry trays to their tables from the ordering counter, wrapped in a see-through glass with a cashier standing at the end. A menu takes up the entire back wall, with an iridescent green glowing up large pictures of dishes, half of them gone black from burnt bulbs.

Sweeping my gaze, I inspect each of the occupied tables, my heart pounding in an unsettling rhythm as I'm starkly aware I may see my father's face for the second time in sixteen years. Disappointment envelops me when my eyes reach the final table. My father's not sitting at any of them.

I check my phone.

9:10

I sigh. Of course, he wouldn't show. Why would he? He decided to not see me for nearly every day of my life. What's one more night apart?

Twisting on my heels, I make to leave, but before I do, I glimpse a table I hadn't seen. Hidden in the back corner, in an alcove near a dark window, lies a single table with two chairs. A man clouded in shadow sits in one, staring right at me. I gulp. My bones know it's him, and I walk across the restaurant until I'm standing next to the table.

His chocolate eyes mirror mine, an unfamiliar hardness shining in them.

He's a ghost. An apparition. A twilight phantom, all mixed in one, brought back to life for a single night, *for a single purpose*. To haunt me until he puffs back into the elusive dust he really is.

"Hello, Hannah."

As if I don't have enough nightmares to deal with.

The sound of his voice hits me with the force of a twelve gauge, and I immediately sit, unable to hold his stare for longer than five seconds. He must barely recognize me from the other night. Knowing the streets I'd be walking down, I put on a pair of rugged jeans, a black zip-up hoodie and knotted my hair into a low bun.

And him? He doesn't wear the denim overalls I remember him donning in my memories, but still keeps a low profile like me. Kind of odd, coming from the supposed *billionaire* he is.

"I know this must be difficult."

"Is it for you?" I ask, devoid of all the emotions buzzing inside me.

There's a pause, followed by the wrinkling of his dry hands as they rub together. The table is empty, with nothing but a teapot and two cups. "Yes," he whispers. "You must have a lot of questions, but I don't have many answers."

"No." I hate the croak in my voice, wanting so desperately to be stronger in this moment. The moment I've spent *years* agonizing over, reciting our dialogue in my mind. I whip my head to him, pinning him in the spot with my furious gaze. "You have all the answers, *Victor.* You're just too much of a coward to say them to my face."

Shame cascades down his features when I speak his new name, plunging him into a lonely darkness. "You don't need to call me that. I'm—"

"I don't know who the fuck you are, so don't pretend that I do."

"I know I wasn't the father you deserved."

I laugh bitterly, staring out the wet window. There have

been so many things I've wished to ask him over the years. Questions much too serious for a young girl. How I longed to tell him about the pain he caused me and not my younger brother.

Me.

I used to hate the thought, *still do,* convincing myself that I'm selfish, that it's not all about me. But... when he left, I was already seven. Jacob was nothing but an infant, ready to accept any father figure into his life. Which he did. And I'm grateful for the amazing parent Marcus has been to us, the love he shows for us and how much Jacob adores him. But the stark truth is, I couldn't replace the ghost in my life with someone real. Because I was...

Abandoned.

Left waiting. Hoping.

Blaming myself.

"Why'd you change your name? So we couldn't find you?"

"Hannah..." His eyes wander past my shoulders, a caution clouding them. "There are things you're not meant to know—*shouldn't* know. It's better that I stay out of your life."

"I don't care. Tell me anyway."

He leans in. *"I can't."*

Rage simmers beneath my skin. "I was very clear on the phone that I'm looking for answers. Why invite me here, then? Did you think we were going to, what... catch up like old times? Share some tea?"

His lack of a response tells me so, and it only proves to anger me further. "Whatever relationship you're hoping to rekindle from this meeting, it's *sixteen years too late."* I burst from my chair, only to delight in being the one to leave him for a change.

But his hand snatches my arm, stopping me in my tracks before he turns me back to him. "Hannah, wait."

I lean into him, burying my hands into my coat pocket before I press the button on my phone I know is for recording. With my face inches from the gray that now speckles his jawline, I feel much like my mother did on that fateful night.

"If you care at all for us, or even have an ounce of respect for me or mom or Jacob, you'll answer one thing." Adrenaline coils in my veins like a deadly wire, shocking me with the bravery I need to ask. To speak the two silent words that've been trapped inside my mind for years.

"What is Project Cache?"

HIS SILENCE BREAKS after what feels like hours, and to my surprise, he doesn't ask how I came to know its name.

"There's a... *society."* He chokes out the word, his voice the sound of sandy grain. "I don't know its name, and I don't know all its members, so don't ask me. But over the many years, I've learned of only a handful of them. Some being of the upper echelons of Silicon Avenue, and some even having connections with the mob."

I don't like where this is going. I pale, but remain in my seat, craving the truth.

"Their eyes seem to be everywhere, *on everyone.* They have a way of knowing things before anyone else... They came to me when I was in need, when *we* were in need. They knew I was desperate, willing to cross boundaries that other mechanics wouldn't dare to get the money we needed to leave that trailer park." A hoarseness sounds in his breath, and his eyes glaze over with a guilty sadness.

"At first, they didn't tell me what they were doing. They told me to keep my mouth shut and not ask questions, and I listened. I knew it looked bad, but I was too desperate for the cash. The deal was... they'd bring a car in the middle of the night, and I'd install a camera or microphone they'd give me, hot-wiring it through the engine so they would always keep a charge. I did it for several years until we had enough to buy the farm and move far away.

"I thought that'd be the last of them, but they found us, showing up on our front doorstep. When I said I wanted an end to our arrangement, they quickly informed me what would happen to our family if I stopped. So, I kept working with them, doing as they told me. They funded the money for the shop, sending more cars than I could barely handle. And they became more expensive too, many of them with makes and models I'd never heard of."

Biting the inside of my cheek, I blink away tears that wish to surface as I recall the rows upon rows of cars in the shop growing up. All of them much too luxurious and out of place for our little farm, for a town like Myrtle Lake.

"And that's how it was... for years." He looks down at his thumbs as they dance in circles. "I tried my best to accept it, act as if it wasn't tearing me from the inside out. Most nights, I couldn't keep down the food I'd eaten, knowing all I was doing in this world was hurting people. But that was the hand I'd dealt myself. And there was no going to the authorities, not without evidence against them... That was the worst part. I didn't even know who *they* were. They always sent different men, clearly workers under the thumbs of bigger players, doing what they were told."

My head spins with the enormous amount of information. A secret society? I couldn't tell if he was making stuff up, but... who would go *that* far? And if he was only their mechanic, then how did he come to own a multi-billion-dollar camera company?

"That still doesn't explain the project."

He pours tea out of an iron pot, filling his round cup. His hands reveal a slight shake when he sets it back down.

"I found out about the project by mere chance, a mess-up on their part. They forgot to wipe one of the cameras they sent me. In its memory card was a single folder named *Project Cache,* and inside contained the photos and the names of those in them. When I started looking up the names... it was truly appalling—wealthy business people, senators, tech CEOs. I knew I had a loaded grenade in my hands then. They couldn't know I saw, so I wiped the camera's memory, but not before I made my own physical copy."

I RECALL MY RECURRING NIGHTMARE, every unknown person captured in those photographs. Their faces are clear yet so unfamiliar, permanently etching into my memory, drowning me under an arsenal of unresolved questions.

"But for what?" I push.

"For blackmail. To control people—*powerful people*—and get them to do the things that they want."

I raise my eyebrows, skeptical. "I thought you said you knew nothing about this secret society."

"I don't know its name, no. But I know it exists. I knew it from the moment one man told me I had been summoned to an estate in New York City. By a man named Oscar..."

A violent doom crashes in my chest, my gut dropping to the floor. "Did you say—"

"Yes, Oscar Bass. It was then that I knew how high up this

thing really went. He was—*is*—one of the most influential people in all the tech world. And I, *Andre Randall from Little Brook Trailer Park,* was to meet and obey tech royalty. So I went, but before I did, I needed protection—*proof.*

I needed those pictures. But your mother took them, assuming I had a choice in the matter of whether or not I worked for them. She didn't know the danger we were under, the threats to our family. I was too scared to tell her... So I left without them, knowing deep within me I might never return." His eyes cloud with sadness, his voice cracking in a way that has tears breaking through my fear.

"But what of ShutterLux?" I pull back, coming to my senses. "You're clearly no pawn of theirs any longer. You chose to be one of them."

"No, Hannah." He grapples for my hand, but I shy away. Darkness shifts in his eyes. "I'm only, and always have been, their pawn. Oscar summoned me, then informed me I had a new task—to be the face of a new camera company. They put everything in my *new* name, made it look legit, and then funded the whole thing. And what almost felt like overnight, I was to play *Victor Strauss* and ShutterLux was booming, proving what kind of power Oscar had on Silicon Avenue.

"I was to never return home, never make ties with my old life, because they needed someone fresh, someone unknown. And it *killed me,* staying away, but I knew if I came back, they'd harm my family to protect their secret... And I don't need an explanation to know what they're doing. It's plain and simple. Project Cache got an upgrade. A major one. Instead of micro cameras in cars, they're now inside any phone they wish manufactured by Bass Mobile—whose cameras are supplied by ShutterLux."

Holy shit.

A sick, violating feeling overtakes me. My phone is from Bass Mobile, and so is Damien's and... "But that could mean they could spy on anyone."

"Not quite anyone. Not yet, anyway."

"What do you mean?"

"Bass Mobile is one of the top phone manufacturers in the world, yes. Even so, more than half the world uses their competitors, which proves to limit their reach for the project. But it's well known in the tech world that the new chip Innovex is unveiling will have no competitor. Everyone, and I do mean *everyone*, wants to get their hands on that chip. Any product that uses it will be leagues above their competitors."

The deal, the contract I watched Damien sign, giving Bass Mobile exclusive rights to the Nano-X chip...

Betrayal hits me hard.

"Damien's one of them?" I avert his gaze, staring out the window as bitter sadness creeps inside me at the horror that—

"No." I jerk back to him, finding his eyes laced with seriousness. *"He's their next fall guy."*

"What?" And then it all makes sense, the puzzle pieces falling into place to form a horrifying picture.

Damien doesn't know.

He doesn't know *anything*.

His board... *Harrison Thornton,* is pushing Damien to buy out ShutterLux, to make him the new owner, the new face of a company that supplies cameras that are being used to spy on people. And if Bass Mobile gets ahold of that chip, there's no stopping them from dominating the mobile phone industry, giving them the power to *truly* know everything.

My chair scrapes against the ground, causing my father to grasp my hand. "No, Hannah. Don't go after him. I know you love him, and you think you can save him by telling him to not buy out ShutterLux, but they'll know you interfered. It's not safe."

Determination sets me ablaze, knowing that Oscar Bass not only ruined Damien's life but ruined *mine,* as well as my family's. But deep down, I know he's right... that interfering is dangerous.

Who am I to go up against a giant?

He must read my pause, because he presses further. "I know I haven't been there for you, Hannah. Not being with you, not having the privilege of watching you grow up into the beautiful and strong woman I know you are, has been the darkest plague of my existence. I've tried it all. Drugs, alcohol, women, money. Nothing has let me forget. I know that. I've *lived* that for sixteen years. But let me protect you, let me be your father this one time. Please, *please,* listen to me. I beg it of you.

"Leave Damien. Leave this city. Leave his entire family behind. Oscar Bass is untouchable. Become nothing to him. Let him have no need of you, so he forgets about you and leaves you and Jacob and Molly alone. And you know Damien—truly know *what* he is. He's the king. He didn't get to where he is today by not doing what's best for him and his business. Leave him, keep him in the dark about this, and he'll let you go. He'll look past that I'm your father, he'll listen to his board and buy out ShutterLux—"

I jerk free from his hold as a war rages inside my mind, both sides crying for my help. My father looks at me in horror. He must regret unveiling the secretive darkness tethering our two families together. But he shouldn't succumb to the fear, not when our chance at a future we never got is on the line.

He should *wake up.*

But I won't entertain the lie that I'm not afraid, because I know what it is he's asking me to do—to allow Damien to fall into disaster in order to save our family. I feel stuck between two tragic pillars whose heights know no bounds, threatening to crush me before they tell me what I already know.

That no matter which side I choose, I doom the ones I love.

FORTY
HANNAH

I WISH I could go back to the girl I was a month ago, who was only trying to save her family from bankruptcy.

Not from their *murder*.

Sitting on the floor of my bedroom, I rest my back against the side of my bed as light streams underneath my closed door. I twist the engagement ring around my finger, embracing the pointless warmth it gives me.

Damien and I can't be. But I still put it on the instant I got back, allowing myself to pretend for a while longer that the world believes we're newly engaged and we're unveiling the most anticipated microchip of the twenty-first century.

But that can never happen. Tomorrow, Damien will be alone on the stage, his father watching with satisfied eyes as he tells the audience it's Bass Mobile who wins the prize for an entire year. Their stocks will skyrocket, their phones soon reigning supreme, and its users will never know the danger they slip into their pockets.

My phone rings on the floor next to me, shining a familiar face I've grown to love on the lock screen.

Fuck! The force of my smack sends it skittering across the hardwood. A wave of sobs follows, kept quiet against my palms in the darkness of my room.

Pounding out near the common room makes me jump, before light footsteps skate past my door. I hear the front door open, cut short by the locking chain.

"Hannah!" Damien's shout only makes me cry more.

"She's not ready to see you," Sofia hisses.

"Please."

His plea sends shivers scattering across my arms. Sofia must recognize the novelty of his tone, because she sighs with a curt *fine*. The lock slipping past its cage sounds before the widening of the front door.

My heart keeps a rhythm of sadness to each of his hurried footfalls towards my door until the streaming light cuts in half. "Hannah, please, let me in..." The knob wiggles. *"Hannah... I didn't know he was... LET ME IN."*

I bite my lip so hard I can taste its metallic blood on my tongue, anything to keep him from hearing my sobs. Slipping off the ring as he continues his protests, I know what I have to do. My vision is so blurry from the tears, I can barely decipher which direction the door is in. And with one definitive sweep, five-million dollars and the possibility of our future slides across the floor then underneath the door.

A hush falls over him, and I hear him drop to the ground. Countless heartbeats pass before he breaks the silence with a voice like thunder. "This isn't yours to give back."

The ring comes skittering back, stopping at the side of my foot. I tighten my hands across my mouth, a sorrowful quake sounding in my throat as I send it back.

"I won't take it. Never will. Sell it, if you must, and take the money. But not before we talk... God-fucking-damnit,

Hannah. Do you want me to break down this door? Because I will."

The tears won't stop, and then I know he needs to hear from me, or he'll never leave. "It's over, Damien," I croak, trying to add as much conviction as I can muster. The sound of his back sliding down the wood sends my heart into overdrive.

"Baby..." he says with a gentle touch. "Let me make this right, please. You can trust me."

I give him nothing, hoping he doesn't grovel in vain.

"You've taught me so much. I've been the luckiest man in the world to have you by my side." His laugh is full of warmth, seeming to tug my body closer to the door. "That's all it took for you to fix me, to make me a better man. You showed me I was living my life so *small,* and only you could teach me the other ways I could live them, if I wanted to. And for the first time in my life, I want *more.* And I really think I could have it, but not on my own... *With you.*"

A piece of my titanium walls loosens, falling to the ground beneath its base. And with it, there's a tug on the string that loops tightly around my common sense. That believes it better to stay silent, to hide in another city and hope Oscar Bass forgets my name and my family forever, to leave my future with Damien behind.

And when I say nothing, his voice only grows, not just in volume but in passion as he recites his love for me. And again, a sharp tug yanks on the string, more of the walls crumbling to the abyss. Until he's practically shouting against my door, the unbridled confidence of his voice strengthening me to resist the enemy that wants to ruin everything I hold dear.

"I love you, Hannah Lockwood. And I choose you over

anything in my life." His shout rings against my door and the entire apartment. "Over expansion. Over money. Over revenge against my father. Over humiliating my brother. Over *everything!*"

The walls topple and the string snaps clean, awakening my dry bones as I stand to my feet, my chest rising in powerful surges of breath.

I brace the knob in a tight grip, whipping it back, exposing my haggard appearance. But I find Damien even worse for wear. His clothes drench with wetness, soaked to his very skin, and his hair sticks flat to his forehead.

When his wild eyes find mine, they soften with anticipation. "Hannah... I know it's so soon, and you must not feel the same. But if you give me time to—"

"Do you really think I don't love you?" I sniffle, whipping my cheek and fighting another wave of tears.

He jerks back, as if I zapped him with a bolt of electricity, before he closes the distance between us.

"You love me?" His voice is a gentle whisper.

Our fingers interlock, his still damp from the rain, before I lean back into the doorframe. Melting beneath his tender gaze, I pull him with me.

"Of course I love you, Damien." I swallow hard, the beautiful concoction of emotions caught in my throat. "You give me the confidence to do things I'd never have dreamed of for myself. There really isn't an hour that goes by that I don't think of you."

The backside of his palm caresses my cheek in silent awe, eyes glistening with passion. What feels like hours but must only be seconds pass, and we both soak in the truth laid bare between us. And the truth feels right.

But it's also dangerous.

"But it's not that simple. It can't be." I break our silence, earning myself a smug look.

"And that's where you're wrong." His minty breath is cool on my lips as he retrieves my engagement ring from his pocket, before slipping it back where I know in my heart it belongs.

Around my finger.

Priscella's and countless articles' words chant a convincing case in my head. "We're from two different worlds," I push.

"That is what they say, isn't it?"

A terrible thought crosses my mind, one that begs me to choose my family over our relationship, to end it right here. Confliction churns my insides, desperately wishing to spare Damien from the doom he doesn't know looms over him.

"What if they're right, and we're not compatible?"

He quirks a brow at my lack of conviction.

"They don't know the first thing about us, do they? They don't know—and maybe you don't know—how much you mean to me. But it's time you understand that I'd take back everything, throw my company and all I've built to the wind, only to have you. I'd even take back the deal I signed. I'd return it all to my brother, nullifying the contract if it were possible. But I don't care that it's too late and that my father will have the chip for nothing. He can have it. I don't care, and I don't need it. But I *do* need you in my world, Hannah —"

My heart races, urging me to save him. I can hardly take anymore, can't bear the thought of a secret—or anything—between us.

He needs to know.

"We can't let Oscar have the Nano-X chip," I spit out, before biting my tongue hard enough to draw blood.

"Forget him." His smile is brash, eyes flickering down to my mouth. "We can start fresh, without any of them."

"No, it's not just…"

I roll my lips between my teeth, my eyes swimming in the ocean depths of his, distinctly aware of the dangerous line I'm about to cross. I've been forewarned of the consequences. But there's one thing my father didn't account for in his final plea to save our family—

Damien is *family.*

He's worth the risk.

"Do you trust me?" I ask, before he learns of the shadowy cataclysm that lies between our two families, threatening to bury him for good.

He's my calling to go to war.

FORTY-ONE
DAMIEN

HANNAH SITS in a simmering silence that would intimidate anyone.

Makeup artists blot fuzzy brushes to her face. A man behind her clamps a strand of her hair between an iron. And another tapes a wire underneath the strap of her blouse. Sitting on a black swivel chair, the bottoms of her flayed pantsuit reach the ends of her thin stilettos.

She hasn't said a single word since entering backstage over an hour ago, and I know she must be planning something, not that she's going to share anything with me. She distinctly left that part out last night when she blew up my entire world to splinters, then informed me to go about our presentation as normal.

Do you trust me? she had asked.

And I didn't hesitate then, and I won't now, even before dozens of live-recording cameras and thousands in the audience.

Mysterious schemes rage behind her eyes like dark tides of the sea, hinting at the rarely seen danger inside the woman before me, making me question who it really is I'm in love with... It's now that I wonder what she would be like, what she could accomplish, if she had the same opportunities as me growing up. The private schools, the tutors, all of it.

The director pokes her head through the cracked door of the changing room, covering the microphone of the headset she wears with her hand. "On in five," she says, and the workers quicken their pace, flecks of stress shining in their eyes. We're the last presentation to go, the one the whole auditorium, *the whole world*, is waiting for.

With our final touches finished, we follow her through the hallway leading to the stage. Hannah is beautiful yet cunning to my side, our fingers interlacing until we're standing beside an enormous, open curtain. It's here we wait for our turn to walk onstage after the current presentation commences.

My gaze falls onto her, tracing the thin wire that matches my own angling down the length of her jawline, and then stops at the puffy ball kissing her lips.

"There's still time to back out, you know." I squeeze her fingers, hoping to lighten her mood.

But when her eyes flick to mine in silence, a seriousness shines behind them like deadly poison.

"Are you nervous?"

She shakes her head, then refocuses her attention to the stage, to the sliver of the crowd we can see at this angle. "I was before. I'm not now."

"Because we practiced so much, right?" My throat bobbles, unsure of the lengths she's willing to go tonight. But I still don't ask about her plans, because I trust her.

With my company and our future.

The group exits in the opposite direction with the clapping from the crowd at their backs. Our fingers fall to our sides before she takes one final look at me.

"There's no reason to be nervous. Not when someone much scarier than the entire crowd will be watching us."

∼

SPOTLIGHTS. Stillness. Anticipation.

A darkened crowd, thousands of eyes holding us at gunpoint.

These are the things that intimidated the Hannah I knew only months ago. But not today. *Not on this stage.*

Her hands rest comfortably at her middle, her chin dawning an air of confidence. "It is with great honor we stand here today on this stage, in front of the entire tech world—enthusiasts, academics, business owners, engineers, bloggers and more. We at Innovex Microchips thank you and extend our sincere gratitude."

She subtly clicks the small remote in her hand, the screen only we can see behind the audience switching to the next slide, queueing my turn to speak. "Today marks a new chapter in the world of technology, one that Innovex is immensely grateful to lead. From the hours of hard work and dedication from our team of engineers, we are proud to unveil the future—the Nano-X microchip."

The enormous screen behind us shines a different color, the crowd murmuring as Hannah steps graciously across the stage. "The Nano-X chip is more than increased speeds and computation. It's a leap in what's possible. Impressively smaller and lighter in weight than all our previous models, and of anything on the market today, it has over *ten times* the computing power of our previous, most advanced model."

We continue our dance, switching off from one another. And with each slide, I watch as Hannah dominates the stage, holding her own in the wake of her fears and everything that happened the night before. Her speech is clear, eyes forward with a confident gleam, and her posture exudes prowess as she explains the technicalities of all she's learned in such a short time at Innovex.

As we near the end of our speech, I'm overcome with anticipation, unsure of what she has planned. She gives me nothing, no head nod, no hint that she's going to take over a section that was previously mine, until I'm already saying the big bomb we're about to drop on the entire world.

I swallow, addressing the crowd with a steady voice. Inwardly, I know the instant *Bass Mobile* flies from my tongue, I'm signing my death sentence and putting the world at risk to deadly listeners. "It is with great optimism but also a heavy heart to announce that Innovex Microchips has given the exclusive rights of the Nano-X chip for one fiscal year to—"

It's Hannah who interrupts me, finishing my sentence in the most dramatic fashion that has my heart somersaulting in my chest.

"To the highest bidder."

FIRST, there is only silence.

Then... *chaos.*

The roar of the crowd erupts in a tangled concoction of gasps and shouts and the hundreds upon hundreds of clicks emanating from camera shutters set loose in a rapid fire. Bright flashes light up the stage, plunging those behind the barrage in absolute darkness.

It's as if the room has forgotten its manners, that we're the speakers and they're the crowd. Because now? Now they're mere savages, chomping at the bits of flesh dangling in front of their noses by a woman, whom only months ago, *was no one to them* —

Hannah Lockwood, my little protégée, no longer.

Observing her in awe, she eats up the madness, a wicked grin tugging her lips. And what does she do next? *She exits the stage,* completely neglecting the rest of our speech. Left dumbfounded, I follow her footsteps, plastering a look of confidence on my face until I'm standing backstage with her.

"Do you know what you just did?" My chest heaves, the rumble of the commotion at our backs still not dying out. *"I signed a contract.* There's no giving that chip away."

Backstage workers hurry over, their eyes wide as they take off our microphones.

"You said you trusted me." She smirks, lifting her arms as wires tug through the holes of her sleeves. "Do you still?"

God, of all the times I've wished I could read Hannah's mind, now would be nice. But there must be a reason she's not telling me something, like she needs me to play the part, pretending that this was really our plan all along.

"I do."

"Good." She grabs my hand, her fingers interlocking with mine, before pressing a soft kiss to my cheek. Her touch is addictive and lingers for much longer as we go through the maze of hallways backstage until we're standing in front of double doors that lead to the auditorium.

I can hear them, can sense the cameras set in perfect position to blast us once we step into their frames.

"Are you ready?" Hannah asks, gripping the handle that will plunge us into insanity.

I nod, finding her shoulders back, head high and an admirable fire in her eyes.

I'll follow her anywhere.

~

THE WORLD MUST BELIEVE her to be a long-lost business titan, or some alluring heiress brought out from the shadows of seclusion, only to bring Silicon Avenue to its knees.

With our backs to each other, with a multitude of microphones held out to us, cameras encircle us like hungry predators as they capture our every answer. Their questions are many, shooting from the lips of reporters in unison.

"This move is strategic, no doubt, Miss Lockwood. Is Innovex planning to expand its business ventures into different fields?" they ask her.

"Is Innovex planning to decrease the volume of chips it manufactures?" they ask me.

And before I begin my answer, the end of Hannah's statement is already out of her mouth. Her response is eloquent, avoiding the whole truth but leaving them wanting more.

"And what about the engagement?" a woman asks behind me. I spot the tip of her microphone outstretching to Hannah in the corner of my vision. "There have been rumors of its business motives. Is that true, or is it really love?"

Smirking, I finish my reply before whirling around to give them a non-verbal answer. I cup her jaw in my palm, savoring the way her eyes seem to flutter up to mine. When I press my lips to hers, bright flashes boom through my closed eyelids.

"You're crazy, Mr. Bass," she mumbles, her teeth tickling my lips.

"Maybe. But only for you." I wrap my hands around her waist, pressing her firm to my side as I extend my hand to the reporters. "That's all for now. Leave my fiancée some room to enjoy the night, would you?"

We part the mass of people like a skittish flock of sheep, and more flashes spark behind our backs. We avoid the crowd entirely, aiming for a side hallway, which proves to be mostly empty.

I push her against the wall, my eyes flickering from her hungry gaze to her lips. *God*, they're irresistible, perfectly plump and *irrevocably made for me.*

Our lips collide, my hands falling between the strands of her silky hair. I growl in response to the moan that leaves her lips. Tightening my grip, I angle her head higher to me. I savor the taste of her on my tongue in front of everyone, uncaring of who might see or snap a picture or tip off some blogger tomorrow.

"We should take this elsewhere, shouldn't we?" The sultriness of her tone is enticing. "Wouldn't want to get you all high and dry before the after party."

She's right.

"Oh, really? Maybe a quiet place backstage? Or I'll kick John out of the car?"

She giggles, taking my hand as we walk further down the hallway, the flocks of people dwindling until we're all alone, turning a corner and—

We stop dead in our tracks.

My father and *Harrison Thornton* wave their hands dramatically, their words hushed and rapid as they leave their lips. I feel Hannah tense against me, and I gulp, coming face-to-face with a scene that confirms everything she told me last night.

They lift their heads, right as I search the fiery depths of Hannah's gaze. I want her to leave, to run as far away as possible from my father, to never experience his poisonous tendrils that corrupt everything they touch. But her hand tightens against mine, silently telling me she's not going anywhere.

"You're really a fool, aren't you?" A voice like a deadly knife punctures itself between us. "You truly think you're the king of this world, *boy.*"

Harrison departs through a side door in a mad dash, much like the errand boy of my father he really is.

Hannah's hand loosens against me, a collective calm falling over her, before she looks at my father as if he's an annoying bug beneath her feet.

"And *you,*" he seethes at her. "There's no erasing his name from that contract. That little stunt you pulled up there will no doubt have consequences."

"Are you threatening my fiancée?" I growl, sizing up his fragile state.

He really is quite frail, with no security to stop me from pummeling him to the ground. But all that frailness morphs into something scary and hideous the moment his twisted laugh sends goosebumps raising down my back. It bounces off the walls in a smug sneer as my grasp of Hannah slackens.

He knows... He knows of our arrangement.

As if my thoughts are nothing but a book to him, he says, "Of course I know. It was of my own doing."

"What do you mean?" Confusion wraps its cord around me, a sinking feeling building inside of me when he smiles.

"Don't you think it a major coincidence your uncle invited you to the club that night, boy? It really wasn't all too hard to convince him to do it, either. And from there, I didn't have to do much. You really can't help yourself from taking every-thing that's your brother's, can you? She was all I needed to push you even further from your brother, to get you to sign your name on the dotted line... Oh, how you truly hate that poor boy—not that I blame you. He's a fucking waste of air, a *disgrace* to my very name."

I jerk back, as if he physically struck me. "H-how would you even know—"

"You think I don't hear the ins and outs of both my sons? What, did you think I saved surveillance for Hannah's family only?" He laughs. "I've had them tapped for decades. All of you. You're all nothing but pawns for me to use when I see fit. The sooner you get that through your thick skull, the better."

A sickness overcomes me, but nothing compares to the horrified look on Hannah's face.

"That's right. That little meeting wasn't a secret. Your father doesn't move, doesn't *breathe,* without me knowing of it. I own him, don't you get that, you stupid brat?" His smug snicker is enough to make my skin boil.

He sighs. "But it was quite sweet, though, the way he tried to rekindle your relationship after the years you've spent apart. Oh, that's just beautiful. I guess the time under my thumb has taught him nothing. Too bad it'll be the last he sees of you. I seem to have run out of a use for him... And, look at you, you really *do* take after him, *trying to record the entire conversation.*"

Oh, fuck... Her gasp rings in my ear, my heart breaking as I watch her fumble for her purse. *That was her plan.*

"Go on and check. You won't be finding anything. *Your phone is from Bass Mobile.*" He *tsks*.

"No," she cries, tears lining her eyes when she looks at her phone, sinking to the ground as she vigorously taps against

the screen. The sounds of her first sob are my breaking point, and I snatch the front of my father's jacket in my fists.

"You're sick." I clench my teeth, bringing him so close I can smell the hint of tobacco on his breath. "I'll fucking kill you. You think I care we share blood?"

Then his eyes reveal an unlimited depth. A well of mysterious knowledge and power that has a shiver making me small. Suddenly, it's as if he's holding his belt over my head all over again, and I'm nothing but a frightened boy beneath his lashings. "Be careful who you threaten, boy. It extends beyond me..." His voice drops low...

"The Oculi see all."

My hold loosens, and he slips back to the balls of his feet, leaving me in a bewildered state. Questions bubble on the tip of my tongue, but I hold them in, thinking better than to voice them. Surrounded by fear, I behold the terrifying man before me as Hannah's sobs fill the hallway.

"It's too bad you always fought me, Damien. You and your petty dreams of ruining me. Well, I created you, did I not? There's no besting the master. We could've ruled this world *together,* but now I'll do it on my own." And with that, he breezes past me and then Hannah, who sits in a fetal position, hands looping around her legs.

When he disappears around the corner, I dash to her and drop to the floor, collecting her in my arms. "We'll run—you, me, your family. We'll disappear and..." The way she shakes against me has hot tears pooling at the corners of my eyes. *"Fuck,* I'll let him use me, only to let you and your family go free. Do you hear me? I'll do everything in my power to—"

She shakes harder, a noise escaping from her lips that sounds surprisingly similar to... *a laugh?* Pulling away from me, her sadness melts off her in a matter of seconds, before she wipes the wetness off her cheeks. "You'll have to meet me at the after-party, babe. I'll be there soon."

"Hannah?" *She must be in shock.* "Did you hear me? Everything's going to be okay. I won't let him hurt you."

Grabbing her waist, I mean to hoist her up and take her away from here, but she stops me, softly cupping my jaw. Both her thumbs swoop down my face in the gentlest of ways, before her lips caress the hollow of my ear.

And then she whispers to me the little secret that changes everything.

FORTY-TWO

DAMIEN

THESE WALLS NEVER BUILT A HOME.

They built a cage.

My steps across my family's estate's hallways are slow, my eyes wandering to key destinations of my childhood that would always spark awful memories.

Because, when I normally pass by the archway that leads to the kitchen, I wouldn't see it as the beautiful architecture that it is. I would see my mother's last act of rebellion, struggling against my father's hold on her, before she received the final blow that turned her into the mindless aristocrat she is now. All the genuine joy expressed through her love of dance—gone.

And when I'd near my father's study, I would hear Sterling's small cries as he banged against the door that always proved to be permanently closed. Often, it was me he'd hear inside, not getting much better treatment, until some maid would sweep him off his feet to carry him back to his room.

But on this day, I don't see the house the same way. Right now, it seems fragile to me. Like glass.

My steps quicken, with one destination burning in my mind. And as I near the ballroom, the guests look quite familiar, and the sounds that emanate from the room mingle with the music and chatter inside.

Their whispers grow when I pass through its double doors, several eyes flicking towards me. And it's to no surprise they do. Because they've come directly from the Summit. My name and Hannah's are no doubt the most popular conversation of the night.

And how opportune for them. We're here to give them one last thing to talk about.

I hear my name called several times, questions bubbling out of their mouths. I hardly look at their faces, don't care to register who's next to pry answers out of me or pitch their claim to the Nano-X chip. Their persuasions go unnoticed, their words bouncing off me like a springboard.

"Would you take two-hundred million?" one asks, before another laughs, stating they grossly undervalued its market share. "A chip like that transcends monetary value. The only thing worthy of a trade is another company in its entirety— and I have *just* the one for you." The man follows me like a hungry beast until he's cut off by a flock of people I burst through.

More barks sound my way. They're drowned out by the blood pumping in my ears, cheering my legs on in glee to keep moving, to reach the destination.

The strings and melodies of the stage fill the darkened room. A composer stands before them, his back to the audience as he vigorously flicks his wrists, commanding the ensemble of fifty-plus chairs. I search their ranks, compelled by the mastery of their fingertips, fueling a fire deep in my being. Then my eyes land on what I came for, what I knew in my heart would still stand there on three thin legs.

For one moment, I'm lost in time with a devastating decision, then the next I'm staring down the eyes of my mother who stands before the stage. Her cheerful, perfect façade breaks for the first time I've seen in public, silent tears shining in her irises before she gives me a tight nod.

Hushed gasps sound behind me when I bound onto the stage in one large step, appearing in madness as I dart by the musicians. Their notes don't falter, but a few of their eyes flicker towards me in confusion. I breeze past them until I'm moving closer to the bench, left enticingly empty in front of the white piano.

It stands in darkness, its beautiful lid propped sideways, begging for a spotlight. The white ivories enchant me, rebuking the fraction of fear trying to stop me, replacing it with molten hot determination before I take my rightful seat.

Breathing what seems to be the last breath of my old life, I slam my fingers down on the keys with a force so great, it shoots a revitalizing, electric shock to *every fucking fiber of my very being.*

Then... it's as if I'm alone on stage, without the competition of the other instruments. For several heartbeats, we battle it out, our melodies in complete contrast. But soon, their sounds die out, even quieter than the crowd, letting my music ring proudly throughout the ballroom.

I feel the weight of dozens—no, *hundreds*—of eyes on my back. I don't need to check to know that the orchestra, the audience, the lenses of every camera in the room, and maybe even the figurines on the ceiling, all drag their curious eyes my way.

And they should. Because I want the sound to invade every crevice, every dark corner of this house, only to strip it raw to its very foundations. I want every guest, butler, doorman and chef to hear the music on my fingertips.

Because it's the sound of Oscar Bass losing control.

My fingers dance along the keys, like I had only played yesterday, and this is just another night, another performance for me in my years of practice. And I laugh... The keys seem to submit under my touch, the sounds growing ever louder after I fiddle my toes on the pedals.

And then he's here, in my face, on this very stage in the black suit he wore tonight. *Him.* The fraud, the *poison* that's always been in this house. His eyes are wild and dangerous, with promises of murder beneath them. But that only makes me laugh louder, tears stinging my eyes.

Words shoot from his lips in a sick percussion, his hands gripping the wood of the piano in front of me.

Oh, I wonder if he thinks I can hear him? If he thinks anything at all that he's saying is entering my brain?

I'd say his words flow from my one ear out the next. But they don't, never having entered. They pass right through my very essence, as if I'm nothing but the wind, caught up in the spirit of an entirely different plane. A beautiful one, where my mother can dance and my brother can grow in peace and I can have a future with Hannah—*one without him.*

Oscar Bass must know the truth.

That his time is ticking.

He fears my lack of fear, revealed by the raising of his voice and the harshness of his movements. He's truly desperate now, because he knows with every stroke of my fingers, my brother is gaining an understanding of the burden that's weighed down on our family. And my mother is getting the jitters, the will to dance and live her life the way it should be.

His gelled hair comes undone in unruly clumps as he leans over the piano, his frame dwarfed underneath the hood of the lid. He screams in my face now, and *still*, he's hardly audible over my booming, skillful sounds.

"YOU'LL BE THE FACE OF SHUTTERLUX, BOY, OR I'LL DELIVER HER FATHER'S HEAD TO HER IN A BOX. IT'LL BE HER FAMILY'S BLOOD ON YOUR HANDS AND—"

It happens so fast.

In one breath, a pair of small hands dart past my shoulders, gripping the edge of the slanted piano lid.

And the next?

The lid comes *crashing down*, toppling over my father on its descent. Blood from his face splatters across the white keys before he tumbles to the ground. My hands shoot from the ivories, my final crescendo echoing across the ballroom as I watch Hannah step into my view. Her dress pokes underneath the trench coat she wears, and it is, too, white and splattered with his blood.

My father cuffs his hands to his nose, blood seeping out the crevices of his fingers. His wrathful eyes shoot upwards at Hannah. *"You little cunt,"* he seethes, the volume of his voice left unchecked. Many of those in the orchestra jump to their feet, craning over each other's shoulders to watch the scene.

"You have nothing." He then has the wits to lower his voice as the flashes of unashamed cameras light up the stage. "All you're doing is marking your entire family for good. There's nothing you can do to stop Bass Mobile from—"

She leans down then, towering over him. He tucks his

chin downward in caution, his back pressing further into the ground, shying away from her.

"You think you're getting that chip?" she mocks him sweetly. *"There won't be a Bass Mobile left to get their hands on it."*

Opening the side of her coat, she retrieves an item I know well but can't quite see. But Oscar does—he contorts on a silent scream, the lines of his face digging into canyons. Horror colors his features so darkly that it infuses satisfaction right into my soul.

Because I know what's inside the manilla folder before she flicks her wrist high in the air—she told me so, after she baited my father into thinking he won, only so she could publicly unveil his secret. Told me how she's kept it hidden with her for over *sixteen years.*

The folder widens, hundreds of papers spewing out before raining down atop his head. Camera shutters clatter across the stage, lighting up the photographs. And I swear I see familiar faces as they fall. Business associates, senators and even ones of our own family.

He really was watching us all.

I laugh again, hoping to savor this moment for eternity, watching the final blow to the glass house. So shiny and alluring and perfect—that is, until its shards splinter all around him, revealing a rotted exterior to everyone in the ballroom.

But then... other flashes fill the room, different from those of the cameras. They trickle through the windows and mix with the wailing of sirens.

Red. White. And blue.

THE ONLY THING better than seeing FBI officers drag my father off stage in handcuffs in front of hundreds of people is that it was all caught on film. Meaning, I can watch it later.

Over, and over, *and over* again.

He writhes against the officer holding his hands behind his back, stopping them in front of the table my cousin and Hannah sit at.

"Lauren," he barks, looking much like a psycho killer, who's undoubtedly going down for murder—but unbeknownst to everyone, it's *so* much worse than that. "Build a team—the best team—of lawyers at your firm."

"Oh, I'll be forming a team, that's for sure." She stands, her hands crossing along her chest. "But not one for you. Because, the way I see it, not even someone *like you* could pull yourself out of this hole."

His face lifts in surprise before his eyes flicker to Hannah, finally noticing she's there. He looks at her with pure disgust as the officer yanks his cuffs, dragging him further from the stage and out of the ballroom. A flock of cameras follows them, their flashes growing weaker as they make their way further down the hallway and out of sight.

Lauren shakes her head, watching the remaining people in the ballroom gather in hushed groups.

"Thank you," Hannah says.

"If everything you said is true, there's no need to worry. There'll be mountains of evidence." Lauren's eyes sparkle with eagerness. "This will no doubt go down as the most notorious trial on Silicon Avenue, maybe in the whole country, so I *have* to be in on it."

Hannah's laugh rings between us, and for a time, it's only the three of us chatting until the room feels nearly empty.

"Oh." I hear Hannah's hushed reaction when her eyes dart past my shoulder. She exchanges a look with Lauren before smiling at me. "We'll be out on the patio."

My brows scrunch when they stand from their seats and walk away. I turn around, finding my brother standing on the balls of his feet before me, not meeting my stare.

"I heard what you did," he mumbles. "Well, more than the piano playing and all—that was cool, too, but giving back my shares."

Rising to my feet, a mountain of nerves bundle in my chest. I gave his shares back the day after our fight in the garden, guilt eating me alive when I realized the pain he's been in. He should sell his shares immediately, before the Bass Mobile trial begins and possibly hurts their value. I plan to advise him through the process, but now's not the time for that.

"Don't thank me, Sterling. Those shares were never mine to take."

His eyes lift and meet mine, a silent defensiveness shielding them. "Do you mean that?"

"Yes," I choke out, trying to keep my emotions in check. "I'm sorry. *For everything.*"

He blinks furiously as that sarcastic and hostile persona I'm so used to crumbles to his feet. "I'm sorry, too."

An awkward stillness plants itself between us.

Should we shake hands or something?

"So..." I bite my lip. "I heard you're a big movie star now."

"Oh, for Christ's sake." He rolls his eyes, a tear shedding down his cheek with a wet laugh and sniffles.

Then I can't contain myself.

I spring forward, my arms tightening around his frame,

my own tears streaming down as he shakes in my embrace. Across the room, I lock eyes with my mother, who stands alone, swiping a hand across her cheek.

And my heart feels fuller than ever before.

FORTY-THREE
HANNAH

"ISN'T it so much better when *I* plan our weekend getaways?"

My lips thin, overlooking the ocean from the balcony of our villa. "You've asked that every day we've been here, *Damien."*

His chuckle is low in my ear as he wraps his arms around me, raising my temperature even higher than the private hot tub we're in. Our view is impeccable, along with the other villas that stand proudly in the water, tracing along the island's coastal line.

Who knew houses come on stilts?

We've been in Bora Bora for over a week, and I've enjoyed every second. At first, he told me we were going for a weekend vacation, just us two, and loaded up the jet with a bag I didn't pack. He then ignored all my questions about where we're headed.

My guesses were Florida and Mexico. But no. I realized I was dead wrong after our flight took over *eighteen hours.* And hen I made the even bigger realization that Damien... *Damien* was taking a real vacation. Not a weekend, but nearly two weeks off.

I smirk.

He's come so far. And so have I.

Before we met, if someone would've told me I'd present at the largest tech summit on the planet—*and nail it*—I would've sadly informed them of their insanity.

My gaze falls on the setting sun along the horizon, tracing the way it paints the sky with long streaks of purple and red. Not a boat or land or *anything* blocks our view, leaving only clear blue water.

"You know I'm right." His lips score a peck on my cheek before his eyes trail down to the skimpy bikini he packed me.

"I'll admit it." I sigh, interlacing my fingers behind his neck, tilting my head up at him. "This beats picking up chicken crap."

"Mhm." He twirls his fingers in my ponytail, giving me a slight tug that has me biting my lip. "And how does it feel to be a billionaire?"

The question has me thinking back to last month, to the memories I've almost achieved in blocking out for our vacation. Not that they're all bad. The way Oscar Bass looked at me as if I was the law finally catching up to him, well... that might've been the greatest accomplishment of my life.

After the showdown, I immediately called Lauren to represent us, thinking we were in some deep shit. But she quickly informed me she'd handle everything, and by the sounds of it, we have nothing to worry about. She even said she'd probably get my father off with minor petty charges, saying everything he did after the trailer park could nullify, given Oscar forced him against his will.

It's no secret ShutterLux will most likely liquidate, leading to government payments and victim settlements, if the trial goes as expected. But it seems my father himself became quite the successful businessman, racking up millions—if not billions—through connections and outside investments.

"I wouldn't call myself a billionaire."

"You're an heiress to billions," he corrects. "It's the same thing."

Lauren informed me of that little tid-bit too. My father never told us he put his fortunes in my and Jacob's names, not wanting to set more malicious eyes on our family than needed, given the stakes of everything. We both now have unlimited access to his accounts, which is more than strange, to say the least.

The first thing I did? Paid off my family's two-million dollars of debt. *Myself.* With an anonymous donation.

Yes, Damien and I had a deal, but... we're so much more than that now. And it makes my father feel that he's helping after all these years, so... win-win?

They'll all know it was from me, anyway, the instant I inform Jacob of his new rich-kid status. I'm thinking of waiting a while—let him have a *real* college experience like I had, cups of ramen and all.

"Enough serious talk." I narrow my eyes at him, a grin prickling at my lips.

"Don't have to tell me twice."

He unhooks my arms, bringing the back of my left hand to his mouth. When he kisses it, his eyes flicker down to the engagement ring I still insist on wearing, even though we're technically not engaged. He said he'd buy me another, when the time is right, of course. But this one will do, for now.

I run my palms down the grooves of his pecs, my eyes following their scorching trail. He lets out a gruff sound, and

I come to find his gaze smoldering, burning brighter than the sunset.

Hands gripping my waist, he twists me, positioning my back to the ocean water as my rear hits the wall of the hot tub. Then his lips are on mine, with a taste of the salty sea and a hint of smoke.

His teeth tickle my lips. "What do you say we extend our visit another week?"

"So you can keep having your way with me?"

"Baby..." He nips at my lip, sparking pleasure between my legs as he lifts me to sit on the edge. "I can have my way with you anywhere in this world." Tilting my chin to the side, his breath brushes the shell of my ear. "Is that what you want?"

"Yes." I shiver, angling my head further.

"Where to, then?" His teeth rake down my neck softly. I grab his biceps, watching as water droplets trickle down from his chest to my cleavage.

He kisses the base of my neck. "Italy?"

Another, higher this time. "Santorini?"

Again. "Mexico?"

An involuntary moan slips past my lips, and I feel my nipples pebble beneath my bathing suit. He spots them, his eyes flashing with hunger before he slips my breast free from its fabric. Jerking down, he suctions the sensitive peak between his lips.

Grinding my hips in response, I tilt my head skyward, leaning further back in pleasure. Teeth scrape, then I'm pushing further off the ledge and—

Feeling weightless.

"Oh!" I gasp, grappling for him.

But he's right there, collecting me in his arms, pulling me

from the ledge. "Easy there. Don't want you taking a plunge from so high up, now would we?"

"No, we wouldn't. Thank you, *good sir,* for saving me," I tease, a laugh bursting from my lips. I'm completely content as he holds me in the air, the backs of my knees resting on his forearm.

The sun has fully set now, and the impossibly bright stars shine above our heads. We stare at each other in near darkness. A seriousness gleams in his eyes for a moment, an intense emotion unfolding behind them.

I could stay in this moment with him, forever, in irrevocable satisfaction. But I know it wouldn't be worth it.

Because there's nothing I want more than a future with Damien in it.

"No, Hannah. It's you who saved me."

EPILOGUE - HANNAH
5 YEARS LATER

"Are you... *crying?"*

Sofia avoids my stare. Her head angles down towards the stage directly below us, to the ballerina twirling in circles on her toes in the hands of her partner. Wearing a white tutu, her brows droop downwards in an expression of pure drama and struggle.

"No." More sniffles.

"Oh my god... You *are."* After shooting me a stern look and retrieving a fresh handkerchief from her purse, she returns to craning over the side of the gold box railing. "And to think, only yesterday, you didn't want to come. Said it'd be too boring."

She ignores me, her eyes widening when fog floats from the corners of the stage, the intense music growing ever louder.

I don't blame her. I was skeptical about attending my first ballet show, too. But now I understand and appreciate its beauty, in a similar way when Damien plays the piano for me when we're alone. I can recognize the same thrill and excitement in his features as the dancers below.

Tonight's performance of Swan Lake, which is nearly three hours long, is directed by Camille Bass. When she announced coming out of retirement, it was a delightful shock to the dancing world. Then, after forming her own ballet school, Aurora Academy, she vowed all show proceeds would go to charity foundations that aid those fallen victim to domestic violence.

And this is undoubtedly their most successful show yet. From our vantage point in the leftmost box to the stage, we have a bird's-eye view of the performers and the rest of the theater. Not a single chair remains open in the entire building.

The male dancer, who dresses in a dark cloak, wrapping him in mystique, spins her again, faster than before. Sofia and the rest of the crowd seem to hold their breaths until she slows her motions. With expert balance, she leans into a stunning pose, one leg sticking straight up in the air as the music stills.

The crowd roars, Sofia shooting to her feet, clapping when the curtains swing shut in front of the performers. The applause seems to go on and on and on as the curtains open again, revealing dozens of ballerinas. With interlocked arms, they all bow in unison, prompting Sofia to holler over the railing.

Containing my laughter, I whirl around in my seat to find Lauren the complete opposite. With one leg crossed over the other, she rests an elbow on the railing, burying her head into her phone.

"Do you ever stop lawyering?" I ask when the applause dies out.

"Come on, Han." She finishes her text, tossing her phone

into her purse. "I think you know the answer to that question by now."

Sofia sighs to our left, her tone of intense wonder. "I'm going to go touch up my makeup... *Not* because I was crying or anything," she adds, before disappearing through the curtains.

Lauren's eyes flicker to mine, a blush staining her cheeks when the lights flicker on.

That's interesting...

And then I know what that's all about. "I see. You can't bear three hours apart from Tristan, can you? Even if he's only one box over?"

Her cheeks redden further, her mouth snapping shut on a retort.

"You're sending dirty texts, aren't you?"

"I was not—"

"Oh, yes, you were," I tease, her jaw dropping low at the accusation. "Do tell. Leave out no details, please."

Wow. When did I turn into Sofia?

She shakes her head, a grin peeking through her innocent expression.

"Keeping secrets now?"

"Hey!" She bats her purse against my shoulder, her eyes narrowing. "Things are... going well with him. And I'm not the one keeping secrets, am I?"

Nerves prick at me, my laughter waning. Lauren must notice, because her tone softens. "You *are* going to tell Damien, right?"

"Of course. I thought tonight would be the perfect night, actually."

"It would. But... why the long face?"

"I don't know... Maybe it's too soon or bad timing." I shrug. "I wonder how he'll react."

"Be serious. You have nothing to worry about, trust me." Her confidence soothes my nerves, earning my smile back. "My cousin couldn't put a real ring on your finger fast enough."

Real. I glance down at the two rings looping around my finger.

I kept my engagement ring. Damien offered to buy me another, but I refused, finding it impossible to let go of the one he first gave me. So, we settled on a compromise. When he re-proposed to me, it was with the same diamond, but in a different band. For real that time, in private. To the world, it seemed we were engaged for quite a long time—three years, to be exact.

And the second ring is my wedding band. With smaller diamonds trailing all the way around the silver loop, Damien slipped it on me almost a year ago today.

Sometimes I forget the circumstances in which we met. It never seems right when I think back on our original arrangement. How could Damien and I ever have been anything but unequivocally real? Because that's what we are to each other now, but even more.

We're perfect.

"Thanks, Lauren." I smile before hugging her and saying my goodbye.

Exiting through the curtains, I head to the box next door. Poking my head in, my heart warms when I spot Sterling laughing at something Damien says. He then looks to Tristan, both of whom turn their backs to watch the hordes of people shuffle into lines out of the room.

Left alone, Damien's eyes catch mine, a sparkle glistening

in them the moment they do. He saunters over, his arms wrapping around my waistline.

"My beautiful wife."

Wife.

I savor the word, heat pooling in my middle like it always does. I'm not quite used to hearing it. That might take another year—or five—to not feel as if I'm bound to wake up from some dream, because...

I'm the director of sales at Innovex Microchips. My family's not in any danger and is worth billions. My biological father never set foot in prison, and we're mending a relationship that was stolen from us. And best of all, I'm married to the love of my life.

Damien.

I stare deep into his eyes, my breath hitching as I wait... and wait... and...

I sigh in relief.

Yep. Still here—not a dream.

"My perfect husband."

Nothing shines brighter than a 1965 Ford Mustang in the sun.

The red convertible barrels down the highway under the mastery of my hands, the road quaking under the roar of its engine. Turning the wheel, I'm pleased to find the endless Atlantic to my right, reflecting the sun off its waves like glass.

We're only a mile out from The Hamptons. Camille gifted us our own beach house as a wedding gift, knowing it's a five-minute ride from her own beach house she stays at during the summer months. We've taken trips here almost every weekend, visiting her A-frame cottage often. And this weekend will be no different.

Damien clutches the door handle, his feet threatening to shoot out through the front of the car. "Baby, I love you. But can you please slow down?"

Not a chance.

I only smile at him, earning myself a mortified expression.

Damien always suggests a quick helicopter ride from New York City, and I don't know if it's because he can't handle my *amazing* driving skills or if he's trying to save some of his precious time. But no matter the case, I never go for it.

Because nothing beats the open road.

I pull through our gate, feeling instantly at peace when I see our house's planked siding and vast windows. "See? We survived."

Damien's shoulders visibly slouch as he melts back into his seat. "Barely. You were calling it pretty close when you passed that semi."

Parking, I hold back my laugh, the sounds of the ocean growing louder when I turn off the engine. I turn to him, running my hand down his arm. "I'll be slower next time. Promise."

"Will you now?" He removes his sunglasses, revealing skeptical eyes. "You're finally having mercy on me?"

"No..."

My heart thunders in my chest, in more excitement than anticipation. Because I know the next words out of my mouth will change the rest of my life. The rest of *our* lives together. But in this moment, there's not one sliver, not one inkling of doubt in my mind about how Damien will react.

"Because there's a baby on board."

"W-what? You're..." He sits up, his expression softening. "Are you saying...?"

I bite my lip, batting the tears that want to show. "Open the glove compartment."

As he does, his hands reveal a slight tremor when he removes a small box. Tugging at the delicate bow tied around it, tears well in his eyes when he sees two pregnancy tests, both showing double pink lines.

"I hope it's not too soon—"

"No." His tears fall as he faces me, leaning over the center console to cup my face with warming tenderness. His thumb catches the tear that slides down my cheek, an incomparable joy overtaking me when he says, "This is the happiest moment of my life."

"Then... you're ready to be a father?" I ask, but with a profound understanding that nothing else could compare thus far in our lives. Because I already know the answer before he speaks.

I know in my soul he is.

"I'm ready to be anything you need me to be."

THANK YOU!

If you enjoyed *Inside Job*, I'd be grateful if you supported me by leaving a review. As an indie author, every review, however short, helps tremendously.

Need more Hannah & Damien?
Read their FREE sexy honeymoon bonus scene:
(Spoiler: it's on a yacht...)

https://BookHip.com/NFJRZTP

THE KNIGHTLY SHOP

Want a signed paperback for your shelf or book plate for the book in your hands?

Go to alexisknightly.com/shop

KEEP IN TOUCH WITH ALEXIS

Readers' Group: facebook.com/groups/knightlyreaders
Newsletter: alexisknightly.com/newsletter
Website: alexisknightly.com
TikTok: tiktok.com/@authoralexisknightly
Instagram: instagram.com/authoralexisknightly
Goodreads: goodreads.com/alexisknightly
BookBub: bookbub.com/profile/alexis-knightly

Join my private Knightly Readers' Facebook Group for writing updates, exclusive giveaways and more by scanning the QR code below!

ABOUT THE AUTHOR

Alexis Knightly is an author who writes romance with angst, family drama and a heavy dose of spice. Heroes in her stories are possessive and obsessive, have filthy mouths and know exactly who they want. Happily-ever-afters are guaranteed, but not before banter ensues and flaws are conquered.

A true lover of rain, she resides in Washington State with her family, two spoiled cats and beloved boyfriend. When she's not writing, she can be found doing yoga, binging Grey's Anatomy, trying her hardest to become a runner, or painting with a glass (or three) of wine.

Printed in Great Britain
by Amazon

42797875R00223